Also by

NANETTE L. AVERY

Orphan in America

A Curious Host

Sixty Jars in A Pioneer Town

The Fortune Teller and Other Short Works

Once Upon A Time Words

My Mother's Tattoo and Other Stories for Kids

First Aid for Readers

OUT OF THE RABBIT HUTCH

Nanette L. Avery

OUT

OF THE

RABBIT
HUTCH

a novel

Out of the Rabbit Hutch

Printed in the United States of America

Print ISBN: 978-1-54396-338-0
eBook ISBN: 978-1-54396-339-7

for

Aaron, Anna, Elizabeth, & Thomas

"*The general experience seems to show that a very large proportion of all the insane are treated more effectively and far more economically among strangers and in well-managed institutions specially provided for their treatment, than at their homes, and surrounded by their families, and by familiar scenes and associations.*

The only mode, then, of taking proper care of this class in a community, it is obvious, as all enlightened experience shows, is to provide in every State just as many special hospitals as may be necessary, to give prompt and proper accommodations for.

The dangers incident to insane persons being at large are much greater than is commonly supposed. Not a week, scarcely a day, indeed, passes without the public press containing the details of some occurrence resulting in loss of life, or serious injuries to individuals, or destruction of property, from a neglect of proper care and supervision on the part of their friends or the public authorities, of those who had become insane and irresponsible for their actions."

Thomas S. Kirkbride, MD – 1854

Chapter 1

dmitted in 1870, Asa Young, a ship's carpenter by trade, was committed to the state lunatic asylum. The medical witness to the probate court affirmed the history of his case as follows, *"He indulges in drawing objects of morbid representation which are in contradiction with his intellectual countenance. Duration has been confirmed by several residents of the community to be for several years. He has never made attempts of violence upon himself or others."*

The woman was seated at the kitchen table and handed the document back to her husband. Her chin stiffly led her head upward, and her dark eyes met his. There was a church like silence in the room, the kind of quiet that ushers in the end of the day with a somber solitude. "How long did you say he was there?" she asked. Her voice colored with sympathy.

"I believe it was four years."

"And you say he hasn't spoken for all that time?" She looked at him with skepticism meant for a child.

The husband leaned back in his chair and set the paper, having folded it neatly in half, on the table. "That's what I was told."

"What makes you think we can help this poor soul if all those so-called doctors can't?" She rose and walked over to the sink and filled the coffee pot with water.

"Kind of late for coffee, isn't it?" he asked.

"Not if we have to settle this, it isn't." There was fierceness in her that he admired.

"He's the soldier I wrote you about; after Petersburg." He had written her every day, and the recollection of another wounded soldier blurred like battle fatigue.

"I remember him. Asa, he has a nice name," she murmured. Colonel nodded. "And you say he is peaceful? With the child, we have to be careful who we let in." The woman struck the match against the flint, and the small flame ignited with a burst of enthusiasm. She placed it against the kindling which caught fire with the same eagerness as the matchstick. She positioned the kettle over the fire. She was proud of her stove, and the fact that she did not have to heat water in the hearth like so many other neighbors gave her a bit of superiority that she liked.

"That's what they tell me." He pulled the cane closer to his chair and let his head rest on the fisted hand that grasped the handle.

"I've got no problem having Asa here. If he's the same man you remember, then it's only charitable that we help him get back his wits. I only hope he's willing." Agnes gathered the crockery from off the shelf and dropped two lumps of sugar into each cup. The water in the kettle was just begging to come to a boil, and she could hear it hiss. She repositioned the kettle so it settled firmly against the iron burner. She turned towards her husband. He could feel her presence but best of all he could smell the sweet scent of rose as she stood beside him, but it wasn't until he felt her hand on his back that he lifted his head.

"It's for the best," he said. And she agreed.

An abyss of vague thoughts filled Asa's brain. Sometimes they were venomous, striking like a cobra and paralyzing all-natural will. With a sudden
tightening of his heart, he would become immovable as a gathering of
faces and voices assembled before him. *"It's only your irrational thoughts,*
all in your head." This mantra was their reality, but he knew what he saw.
He needed to set them free, and the only way was to let them loose on
paper. *"You see, there is no one in the ward except you and the other patients.*
Asa," a stubby finger pressed hard against the prostrate figure, *"do you*
see anyone that looks like this?" His drawings were set down before him,
but hearing this time-and-time-again, he had grown tired of disagreeing.
These morbid pictures defined the dead, not the living. Limbs distorted,
faces disfigured, it was difficult to discern where one body started and the
other ended. The graphite drawings were neither an exaggeration nor an
embellishment. Some had been colorized. Yellow pools of water obscured
the defiled faces and red mounds of clay. A million blades of grass beaten
by thundering hooves and monotonous turning of wheels, gnats and mosquitoes humming, and like the slapping of an oar on the water's surface,
the dragonflies flitted between the cat-o'-nine tails, and then silence. They
consumed him just as spilled blood had occupied all the crevices on all
the battlefields. The rains erupted like a wolf pack charging upon a herd
of bison pummeling the earth. Mud, a pulpy paste impeded all movement and adhered like a calloused layer of skin. It disguised the faces of
the dead and wounded, blackened the tongues lolling in open mouths,
and embroidered the coarse uniforms with its stagnate muck. The doctor
unfurled a drawing and then placed it up to the lantern's yellow light. At
first glance, the paper appeared to be nothing more than a wash of brown,
but a momentary deliverance of images appeared before him; boots, hundreds of meticulously drawn boots held firmly in mud.

Asa's petrified stare petitioned the sights a hundred yards away. Now without paper or pen, he was breathless. He was not permitted to liberate these terrified souls, these soldiers slain in the forests that surrounded the fields like a wall of wrought iron. After a time, he chose not to talk, stepping carefully over the illusionary bodies often mistaken for muddy bundles. Asa was trapped to retrace his way alone; confined in an asylum that did not understand where the origins of his mania had begun. To those who cared for him, he was simply number 191.

Chapter 2

The trees were thick with the persistent chirps of the cicadas and as soon as she thought their song was finished, along came another wave of trills. With a hurried unconscious tap-tap against the bucket with a ladle, she laid it into the cool water and watched the surface break. It shattered as if it were broken glass. A gnat, disturbed by the movement, flitted up and buzzed about as though looking for another place to land until the child swatted it with the dishrag that lay across her shoulder. "Pest," she scowled and dumped the water back into the garden flooding the newly planted mint. The scrawny herb shifted uncomfortably in the muddy earth. The child tossed a glance behind her and seeing no one, sighed with relief at this lucky moment and waited until the water soaked back into the ground.

Ten years had passed since the war, and though she was just an infant when the Confederates surrendered, it seemed that whenever conversations got dull, the Great Rebellion became the topic of discussion. It was either what it had been like before or what it was supposed to be like, but no one ever talked much about the present. There were a lot of things that no one ever spoke of; like what happened to her Aunt. Such a question was answered with only a slight shake of the head.

Flora skipped over to the pump and dropped the ladle and bucket alongside it. She hated when her feet got muddy, but there wasn't much she could do about that. It was either too dry or too wet, and she was glad they were finally going to pave a stony path.

"Flora, what are ya doin'?" a voice called from the open door.

"I'm out here watering the garden."

"Well, get a move on, supper's just about ready!" It was followed with, "and bring Asa in too!"

The little girl turned and walked over to the man who was fingering a small hole in the fence. He picked at a splinter of wood, trying to pinch it free. Flora tapped him lightly on the elbow and as he turned around his blank expression slowly transformed into a satisfied look of recognition, and he smiled. "Come on inside, Asa," she said and stretched her hand out for him to take. She looked over at the small hole in the fence. "You know you can't leave," she explained in a voice more like the adult than the child. "Besides, where ya going to go?"

Pulling his fingers away from the hole, he accepted the small hand and permitted her to lead him back to the house. "Now, I won't tell what you were doin', but you've got to promise not to try and leave anymore," she whispered as they headed towards the house. A chill had risen in the morning air, and she let go of his hand to tighten her scarf. "Cross yer heart?" There was an understanding between this simple man and the child, and though he appeared as if he had as much spirit in him as a colt, he owned the alacrity of a forgotten soul. With a gesture of agreement, he took his finger and ran an X over his chest. "That's fine, Asa. Real fine," she commended. "Now come on in and don't forget to wipe your feet on the mat before going in."

The man obeyed her, not because his shoes wore a coat of mud, but rather because he didn't want to relinquish his only pair of boots to the woman inside.

——— • ———

There was a dampness attached to the room, and no matter how hard the wood stove tried, it could not seem to get ahead of the chill. The cast iron kettle fumed angrily at the woman ignoring it as she paid heed to the refueling of the stove. A cord of firewood was stacked against the side of the house, while concealed under an oilcloth a rick of kindling was stored in the corner by the stove. "You did a fine job, Asa," Agnes said. She pointed to the wood. "A real fine job," she repeated, but her accolades did not afford any pleasure to the boarder. "Come and sit down and we can talk while I fix you and Flora something to eat. You're hungry, aren't you?" The man looked through the woman and fixed his eyes on the doorway behind her. He remained quietly content, staring into the dark hallway. A slight pursing of his lips was the only sign of animation he exhibited. Again, she spoke. "Something got you spooked, Asa?" She twisted around and walked towards the door. "Come and look, there is nothing here," she explained and crooked her finger for him to follow. But the tormenting lines in his face silently answered her with a resolute no.

Flora took up the request and followed her mother, just stopping short of the dark passageway. She put her hands against the portal and peered in as her mother stepped across the threshold. Though the child knew there was nothing to fear, she was not going to take any chances. There was something very different about him, a second sense that he shared with animals. "Some men came back from the war without their limbs, and some came back without their minds," was her mother's explanation. Asa belonged in the latter category.

The man pulled the chair away from the table and sat down. He yanked the cloth napkin from off the table and tucked it into his shirt, letting it hang down like a bib. He tapped his feet together impatiently. Clods of dried mud scattered around his feet. His boots were worn thin at the big toe even though they were made of a better grade of leather than many in his regiment. His footprints divulged signs of the soles having been patched; leaving behind imperfections in the tracks when he walked, and when they got wet, water always seemed to find his feet by way of these repairs. But these were his shoes, and like snowflakes, each man's shoes gave him his distinction. So it was with Asa, he would rather give up all his clothes in a winter storm then get a new pair of boots.

———— • ————

When lunch was over, and Agnes had finished talking, and Flora had helped clear the table, Asa was instructed to bring in the cottontail. The rose-handled cleaver was set aside next to the skillet on the stove top. "Bring it round the back door," she directed. Flora took the man's hand as she led him down the planked steps.

"Come on, Asa," she complained. "I know you can walk faster than this!" She pulled his arm as her impatience guided him toward the rabbit hutch. A small wooden structure on rickety legs nestled along the back-garden fence. A rock-lined dirt path led the way up to a very plain wooden hutch, making for a rather grand entrance. Flora let go of the limp hand and ran with delight as if greeting a friend! "We're comin' for you!" she called in an almost devious voice. However, when she opened the tiny door and peered inside, she was disappointed, for unlike the usual attendance of a small furry head with long tapered ears, it was empty. She stuck her hand into the cavernous hole, patted the straw bedding, and reached around. "It's gone!" she exclaimed. Peering inside again, now with greater interest, she strained to see what was not. "Maybe it escaped! You know it is pretty clever!" she cried. Taking it upon herself to find the small animal, she bowed beneath the hutch, crouching between the opening and then coming back up on the other side.

Asa, stony-faced, walked back round to the rear of the hutch while the child scurried about weaving in and out of the tomatoes and eggplants.

"Oh, it better not had gotten loose; you know what this rabbit would do to all these vegetables if it gets a chance." But if the man heard her or not, he was not the least bit concerned for he followed the child about as if it were a game. "Careful of the cabbage, Asa!" she called as he clumsily drifted here and there. However, after several laps about it was soon quite apparent that none of the vegetables were ravaged. "I better go on in and tell Agnes the rabbit has run off; you keep lookin'!"

He watched as the child ran back down the path and then around the building to the front of the house. The wind had picked up, and he brushed the hair from his eyes and looked up into the sky. The clouds shielded the sunlight, and he greedily accepted the cool fresh air. He closed his eyes and listened, slipping away in the quiet and solitude of the afternoon. And then, he smiled.

Chapter 3

Asa removed the carrots from his back pocket and then hid them beneath the pillow; but not before taking a bite for himself. The hint of soil remained in his mouth even after he had swallowed. It was a taste that was all too familiar; one that he could never seem to rid himself of. He wiped his mouth on his sleeve and then sat down on the bed. He was not particularly fond of the coverlet, a floral quilt. It was a constant reminder that he was a guest. But he liked the room; it had a window, a window that stretched out well beyond its wooden frame yielding one the ability to see for many miles. A man at this window could keep a good eye on things, and when the moonlight availed itself, there was no telling what he would see. "Having a window is good," he had decided.

He could hear the unpleasant goings-on downstairs. The slamming of doors and the rattling of dishes and cookware created more of a commotion than he deemed necessary. He listened as voices raised and lowered between tones of annoyance and the tenor of bewilderment. But when finally all had been said there remained only the humming of Agnes's voice and the cackle of a chicken.

A hush ascended the stairs, and he knew he was alone. The last chords of dissonance had been played as his thoughts of the others in the house faded away. He bent down and slowly pulled open the bottom dresser drawer. He looked in and smiled. He blinked, and the rabbit blinked back. He could almost hear the little heart beating, so fast and so nervous. He placed his hand over his heart and thumped his fingers over his chest. He got up and retrieved the carrots and laid all but one on top of the dresser. He fed it to the small creature. This time he was not the rabbit but rather the agent between life and death. He pet the small head and then placed his ear next to it while listening as it ate noisily. It did not take long for the hungry animal to devour the carrot. Asa fed him another, and when finished, he fed it the last one and then closed the drawer.

**LONG AGO THERE WAS A SIMPLE TALE
MADE FROM SILKY CATERPILLARS.
I CAPTURED SOME IN AN APRON,
AND WHEN I SHOOK THE CLOTH
THEY FLUTTERED AWAY
AS CARE-FREE BUTTERFLIES.
IGNORING MY CALLS, I BID THEM RETURN,
ONLY TO SWIRL HIGHER
UNTIL THEY WERE AS LIGHT AS SNOWFLAKES
DRIFTING BETWEEN ME AND THE HEAVENS.**

Colonel Jameson let the muck slide across his palm as he meticulously ran his fingers across the earth. Years of sifting had rewarded him with pieces of broken pottery and arrowheads; artifacts most folks believed were worthless junk. He dipped his hands back into the cold water and washed them clean. Then he started again, digging his fingers into the soft creek bed. The mouth of the river was rumored to have been an ancestral homeplace, but all the Indians were gone now, and only the silence of their inhabitance remained. He scooped up another mound, and as it dripped over the sides of his hands, it carelessly plopped back into the water. The water resonated with unnatural thuds spiraling outward on rings wavering across the surface until they were broken by the heavier flow of the water. The squatting man waited until it quieted down before he started to sift through the remaining handful of mud. It was one of two bodies of water that converged several miles downstream to a once known hunters' paradise, a salt lick where deer and elk and bison drank from the salty pools in the rock. Now as it heals from the war, it offers difficult entrance for the briars entangle the trace where it was ravaged for its salt. An ironic reminder of the past, this thorny scrub claws and tears those who wish to enter. There wasn't much around that didn't bare a scar or disfigurement. Some healed, and some didn't, but those that had may still be wearing their scars on the inside.

He fed his hands back into the water and for several more attempts let them retrieve and release handfuls of muck. He rolled his palms together and slid them around until he felt a small imperfection wedged between the two. With attendance to care, he made a fist and allowed only the slightest bit of water to wash over the object lest it falls back into the mud where it was unearthed. But as he turned it about in his palm, he no longer needed any visible confirmation to recognize its identity.

Colonel raised his hat and looked out over the creek. "Angel's gold," he whispered. This is what he said each morning as the sunlight unfurled over the land like the ocean rolling onto the shore. The sunlight, gold and shimmering, leaped across the wet rocks and rode the current whereupon it began to thin itself out as it reached the shadow's edge at the tree-line. He raised himself up with the assistance of the cane, and though he was not the whole man he once was, his upper-strength rivaled men a generation his younger. He didn't examine the object with any particular care seeing that it didn't matter from which side of the war the bullet had originated. With a mighty heave, he flung it back into the creek and delivered it to the water with all its anonymity.

The secluded creek winds through the wood that has slowly grown up around it. Only in the winter does the running water take time to lie still, waiting for the warmth of the sun's breath to seek a path between the canopies and fell trees to loosen its icy cap. In all other seasons, the stream runs freely, widening and deepening and depositing new silt. And though the unwhole man's cane was whittled from a sturdy hickory branch, the journey to and fro is cumbersome for the uneven ground is pitted with holes and littered with broken branches and twigs. Weariness has been relieved in this remote embankment for over a decade, and during this time he has found and thrown back the past.

As a young man, he learned that a name yields the power to invoke fear among the weak and respect among the wealthy. When he was born his mother wanted to name him Calvin, but his father, a man with a natural sense of wit and humor, decided that his boy would have distinction, even if it were only inferred. The name Colonel offered him a military title regardless of the true rank he might earn in the future. It was a big name for such a small baby, but he grew into it with time. When his father died, he left him his debts, a small broken farm, and a saying, "Poor does not mean stupid."

———— · ————

"There is a wild beast sleeping inside you, Flora," the woman explained. "It's in all the Robinsen women, just that your beast is tamed. Let it out, and you let out trouble." The child had heard this explanation of her wild spirit whenever she had misbehaved. Her father had told her the story of her mother's family. It was the season of sailing ships, and those of Scottish ancestry were a fearless people who traveled across the ocean, adopting their new country with a willingness and acceptance of duty. His was a heartfelt tale, one that Colonel expressed with sincerity, using a voice expected as if offering a homily.

But it was her mother that told her the unabridged version, the narrative of the first Robinsen's arrival in 1651, not as a willful passenger but as a prisoner of war. Captured in the defeat of the Battle of Worchester during the English Civil War, he was taken prisoner and deported from England to the colonies. Chained aboard the ship the "John and Mary" he and the other 'undesirables' set sail for Massachusetts. Indentured into hard labor for the next seven years, they were sold into servitude and disposed of; some sentenced to the sawmills and some to the iron works. "The Robinsen men are strong; brave too. The enemy may have broken up the brothers, but they could not break the bond." The child seized upon this idea, and though she may be young, there was a maturity attached to her aptitude which was far more expected of an adult. "Is this why Asa lives with us now?" Her head cocked to the side like a baby bird waiting to be fed.

"Asa is like my brother," the woman said, parceling her words with care to her hungry fledging.

"And my uncle," the child announced. The woman nodded in agreement. "So then, he could have been sent to the iron works too, if he had been on the ship."

The mother smiled. She was pleased that her daughter was so attentive. "Very possibly. But that was a long time ago," Agnes said.

However, time was not important to the small listener; her innocent belief of right and wrong framed her understanding of the past and present. "But instead he was sent to the war, like Colonel."

"Like your father," corrected Agnes.

"Like Papa." By now the child was tired of listening and asked if she could go outside to look for the cottontail. "It's got to be around somewhere," she explained with a sigh too big for her small physique. She untied the sash and removed her pinafore, handing it to the woman. "Here, Mama, would you please keep it clean for me?" she asked comforting herself that it would not be in harm's way. She placed her hand on the latch and watched as the pinafore was hung on a peg up beside the kitchen aprons. Then with a two-handed push, for the latch had a terrible habit of sticking, she pulled open the heavy door and scurried out.

So it was that Colonel and Agnes did not see eye-to-eye in regards to the raising of Flora. He was a gentle man who wished to raise his daughter in a gentleman's world. The child was a crocus in the spring, the earliest flower after the long winter. So was her birth like the first buds, arriving after the dirty business of war; a small gift of happiness among a country embroiled in rebirth. How Agnes wished she could be more like her husband. He was goodness; a patient soul that the war couldn't reshape. But she could not emulate all his ways. After the surrender, they were left with both the gleanings of life before the war and the inescapable yearning to gather time back. But like a jigsaw puzzle that had been shattered, trying to rejoin the pieces seemed futile; for what was once whole was now scattered, stolen, broken, maimed, or lost. Only a few of the center pieces remained intact, but trying to wedge the ones together that did not fit made for a very unbalanced puzzle. Colonel thought he was succeeding, forcing smiles and half-truths; these were the pieces he contributed to the puzzle. But there were spaces between the malformed shapes that Agnes felt she had to fill in.

In the center of the garden was the tattie-bogle whose job it was to scare, as Colonel called them, the "devilish crows." It was a lonesome fellow that dangled from a stake like an old drunk. And when the wind blew, its scraggly arms that were far too long for its hay stuffed body and legs would pitch back and forth, not like a windmill but more like a pendulum on a grandfather clock. It was dressed in a mismatch of tattered clothes that were far too worn-out to mend. Its trousers weathered as is the muslin shirt, but when you got up close it was easy to see a gingham patch stitched over a hole in the very spot a heart would beat if it had one. From a distance, one would have thought it a carpetbagger come to raid the vegetables rather than a wheat colored scarecrow.

"Hello there Wooley, have ya seen a rabbit come by today?" With a slight shuffle of her feet, she moved closer to the raggedy man and tapped the post. The tattie-bogle shuddered as she rattled it several more times. "No, ya say?" Her voice raised a pitch with the question. She pushed the dangly arm and let it swing. A handful of dry hay dropped, and with a bit of remorse for her playfulness, she gathered up the straw and began to thread it back into the stiff sleeve.

"Looks like Wooley has lost some of his dignity," exclaimed Colonel. He had been watching his daughter from the garden fence, a pastime he enjoyed more than anything else.

"I was just asking him if he'd seen the brown bunny, but now I don't think he knows since he can't see too well." Her thoughts trailed her voice as she stared up at the muslin head. "See, there, he's missing an eye!" Her finger pointed to the empty socket where only loose threads hinted of a missing button. "Maybe we ought to give him a patch, like Mr. Wheatly."

The father made his way into the garden, but his once cheerful expression had dissolved. With each step, the cane produced a small hole in the soft ground, and he stepped across each depression as if he were deliberately erasing the markings of a disabled man. The little girl quickly interpreted his demeanor and reached for his hand. "I didn't mean any disrespect towards Mr. Wheatly, Colonel. Just thought that we could get Wooley a patch like his." But her words began to become quite twisted in her innocent mind and the more she tried to explain the more tongue-tied she became.

"You didn't mean to say anything wrong, Flora. Mr. Wheatly would be happy to know that you thought of him." However, it was not what the child said but more the sobering reminder of the casualty of war. Each man, if they came home, brought back or left behind on the battlefield a part of themselves. He returned with a cane, Wheatly lost an eye. "But I bet we could find a button for Wooley," he said. "Your Mama has plenty that she would spare."

His answer seemed to satisfy the child for she released his hand and waved for him to follow. "Colonel, come over and look at the latch on the rabbit hutch, maybe you need to fix it?" But before she could run off, he bent down to her level and leaned into the cane so their eyes met. "What's wrong, Colonel, you look so serious?" she said. However, even the twinkle in her eyes could not get him to turn a smile.

"The fact that you used to call me Papa but have taken up calling me Colonel has got your mother and me wondering, why."

The deliverance of such a question may have been serious to her elders, but to Flora, it was rather rudimentary. "Don't you like your name?"

"Oh, it is a fine name, have been using it since I was born. But it's just unnatural for a child to call their parents by their first name."

As he slowly raised himself up, this declaration was maturing in Flora's mind. "It's not that I don't want to call you Papa, it's just that," but for a brief instant she hesitated and began to shuffle her feet as she always did when she was hiding something.

"Go on Flora, speak your mind," he said.

"It's just, just that, well you see," she stammered.

"Just what?" he asked.

"Just that you were Colonel before anyone else and now there are others that want to be called Colonel. But you were the first, long before that silly war started to give out names. But if I call you Papa, you're just like all the other Papas."

The man dared not laugh aloud, lest the child thinks he was not sincere. "Those other fellows earned the title of Colonel. I earned the military title of Lieutenant. But I suppose you have a good point, I was

Colonel fair and square, so I reckon if you feel that you need to, then call me what you wish as long as you keep me in your heart as Papa. That's the title I like most of all. Now," he said, "let's take a look at the rabbit hutch. I can't imagine the cottontail could have gotten free."

Chapter 4

Asa saw the man and the child from the open window. He tipped his chair forward and breathed in the newly warmed air. The soft folds of the curtains brushed against his neck before engaging with the breeze. He watched the interaction between father and daughter, the fumbling over a rusty latch; sliding it back and forth until Colonel was satisfied to let it be. "I guess it was time for the cottontail to leave the rabbit hutch," the father said.

"How can you tell?" the little girl asked with a bit of remorse. "It's got a nice bed of straw and lots of food."

"I guess this coop's usefulness was all used up. That ol' rabbit must have known it was time for it to get out, more so than we needed to eat it."

Flora paid little mind to his response and called for the rabbit as she skipped between shapes made from a garden of shadows. Colonel leaned against the fence and watched; he really didn't care either way if the rabbit was found. Only Agnes had her plans altered.

Asa abandoned his position, eliminating the figures of the man and child. They were reduced to objects in the foreground. He crouched down so only the crown of his head tipped up over the window sill. But now it was difficult to see anything that was not straight out in front of the window, only the parallel landscape of craggy mountaintops were aligned. Now kneeling, he slowly edged upward, his body rising steadily in order to get a better view. *The path heading away from the garden wrangled round and round leading to the forbidden boundaries and a long steady walk. No, a march, a long, arduous march in boots, wet boots, and wet trousers, and a wet shirt, and a wet cap, wet knapsack, wet rifle, and mud. He marched shoulder to shoulder, but still, all attempts of hearing were made impossible for the beating of the heart deafened any and all sounds. Even the bugle's cry was muted by the tremendous thumping which escalated with the anticipation set before him. Then, as if an impassable trench had been dug the entire brigade halted. All became still, all ten thousand eyes turned to watch the silent hand that had raised, a gloved hand more prominent and more foreboding than any he had ever witnessed. The wind fell upon all five thousand souls. The trees whispered, the heart trumpeted, and the silence was exhausting. All life seemed to be stripped away except for the ever-present reminder of fear. Out from a thicket, a terrified hare raced away from beneath its hiding place. And though it was mute its race to survival broke every branch and twig beneath its feet. All five thousand men heard it flee and without regard to the source, five thousand rifles sounded. A gloved hand, raised flat and stiff, commanded the signal to stop, but the fury unleashed in the aftermath of the escaping rabbit was more potent than the greatest tempest storm. The power to survive could not be recorded until the last body was counted.*

The image of the man and child came back into view. Asa slid forward in the broken-backed chair. The breeze continued to come and go, easing in and out as if it were his breath. He stood up and crossed over to the opposite side of the room. He slid the bureau drawer open and poked around. The cottontail was asleep in the folds of his muslin shirt. The tip of its ears flickered, and he knew it was now awake. He bent down and stroked its fur, so pure and soft. He slid the drawer closed again. He liked the rabbit; he liked it a lot but was also troubled. Always having to listen, always having to be so silent, how tiring that state of being is.

The man and the child were no longer by the garden. He would have liked to sit by the window all day to watch the light falling into shadow and the hills green turning violet, but he expected that he would be called downstairs by one of the three. He smiled at the thought of Flora, such a small child. It was kind of her to give up her bedroom. Most children would have made a fuss when relegated to under the stairwell. But the small nook fits her quite well, for being not much bigger than a sprite she was finding it as entertaining as a secret hiding place. "Come on inside, Asa. Just bend your head, see you can do it!" The eagerness in her voice led him to believe he could as he reluctantly obeyed. "See, it's big enough for the two of us, and Eloise too!" Her delight was almost convincing yet, the moment she shut the door doubts surrounded him like a field of fears. *"There now, you've done it, but, he's dead; shot in the right breast."* The oil lantern fixed over the bed filled the cubby with a glow of iridescent light that offered enough brightness to read by. "Come and sit down, I can tell you and Eloise a story if you like," she suggested and propped the baby doll up against the pillow. But for Asa, the child and the doll held little meaning; they were as transparent as if they were figments of his mind, only the compulsion to flee had taken over the order of his thinking. He reached for the door, but the child thought this a game. "You can't go, Asa!" she laughed and held her hand over the latch. All color had drained from his face, and he pulled away from the hand of the unsuspecting child. "What's wrong Asa, don't you want to stay?" she asked innocently. But as his eyes darted about this tiny prison, the uncontrollable desire to escape was overtaken by his inability to breathe. Impeded by deep gasps, he found it almost impossible to catch his breath and he was startled by his desire for air. "Here, Asa!' she cried and releasing her hand from the door latch she allowed the liberation of the terrified man. Flora watched as he rolled upon the floor, restrained only by his own inhibitions when within a few moments he found his breath and was calm again. "Poor Asa," whispered Flora to the doll, "he's just not too right in his head."

———•———

"Colonel, I know you don't like eavesdropping, but what if someone heard something that they weren't supposed, what would you say?" the child asked. She was sitting quite diligently waiting for her father at the foot of the stairs.

"You say that you heard something but weren't supposed to?" he declared in a more authoritative voice than usual, especially so early in the morning. He was a cheerful man and wished to start the day without any discord.

"It wasn't that I was eavesdropping, it's just, well, just that I think I heard Asa, and so I went up the stairs and listened at the door." She shuffled her feet back and forth in the manner that she did when she had done something wrong.

"Flora, might it be that you were dreaming, you know that Asa can't talk," he reminded her and made his way down the stairs.

With the child in tow, he hobbled down the hallway towards the kitchen. "No, honest, it was Asa. Well, maybe he wasn't talking. It's more clear, no, it wasn't talking, more like singing."

"Singing, Asa?" the man looked incredulous. "Poor Asa, I don't think he has any song left in his head."

"I'm sure it was him. At first, I heard talking, and then I heard a little ditty, but I couldn't make out the tune," she explained.

Colonel folded his hands across the handle of his cane. "Well then, how come no one else heard him?" he asked testing her story. But without an answer, she merely shrugged her shoulders.

"What's all this about Asa?" Agnes questioned, privy to the conversation between her husband and child. She stood before the sink with a dish rag tossed across her shoulder as she washed the dishes. The suds rolled up her forearm as if she were bathing a doll and not dirty crockery.

"Seems that Asa was doing some singing last night, but no one heard it except Flora." The man winked at his wife.

"Singing? Well, that's news to me," she said. "I didn't know he'd taken to singing." But without any more need for an explanation, she twisted round and as she gestured to the child to sit down several small bubbles ascended into the air and then dropped down into the sink again.

"Do that again!" exclaimed Flora as she hoped the bubbles would jump up again. But the woman was in no mood to play and only flattened them with her rag. "Come and have your breakfast. Your father and Asa already ate. As soon as you finish your egg, you can go out and see what Asa is up to. I sent him out to fetch some greens, but no telling what he's doing." The impatience in her voice echoed her sentiment for the day. The child knew when and when not to be heard, and right now she was betting on the latter. She looked down at the egg, and it looked back at her. She poked her finger into the yolk and then pushed a little harder. It split apart, running across the plate making a gooey yellow film. She smiled and without delay lapped it up with her bread as she had seen Asa do so many times before. This was his way of eating eggs, far more satisfying than using a spoon. To Flora, Asa was the cleverest person she had ever known.

Agnes turned toward the child and then to her husband. He was an educated man with a unique interest for antiquity. Curiosities that were uninteresting to most folks were relics to him. So when the war broke out, he spent many weeks digging holes; burying beneath the earth sealed boxes containing treasures. Not the treasures of the pirates but treasures of ordinary people. She liked Colonel's oddities, and though she did not share in his interests, she believed in him. Colonel seemed to enjoy all life had to offer, content in the field, in the hills, in the small town. He was content just watching Flora, and from the start of the day with the ritualistic rise of the sun to the exchange of the moon at night, he rarely made any mention of his displeasures. But she knew this easy disposition had been cultivated, orchestrated, evenly measured out in hourly increments in the form of pure contentment. However painful the collection of memories he harbored, he would not leave behind his dead comrades, he could not let them go. The war had been over, and why he did not unearth the small boxes, she never inquired of him. When he was ready, he would.

The child had inherited blue eyes, auburn hair, his guiltless smile, and his inquisitive nature. They shared a spirit that moved through the day finding goodness in things that others traipsed over. When slate clouds swelled and threatened the land, Flora and Colonel saw this not an omen of impending storms but rather as a day devoted to irrigating the gardens and fields. Such virtuous qualities did Colonel bestow, and in the course of Agnes's life, what had she contributed? It was not difficult to answer though she brooded for a moment, watching the child spoon her milk as if it were hot tea. Flora had acquired her pragmatism, and she wondered if this was good.

Patience was not the virtue that Agnes controlled by the end of the war. Towns occupied, houses deserted, and those villages that were not in enemy hands turned into secondary bases or garrisons. Dwellings were commissioned as hospitals, and all available provisions stocked the war efforts. Nothing was immune, and no one escaped the ravages and ruins, the curse put upon by the enemy. Wives of the farmers and wives of the shopkeepers, wives of the blacksmiths and wives of the bankers, all women pooled their resources together. The youngest and the eldest, those married and those widowed, women provided the workforce behind the scenes, and when it was over, they were there to pick up the pieces. Thoughts of the old life had died while contempt for its loss had survived. All her patience had been exhausted, all hopes were shackled, and now years later Agnes had earned the right to be irritable.

Flora wiped her mouth with the napkin and waited patiently for her mother to hand her the pinafore that was hanging on the peg. "Thank you, Mother. Now," she said and slipped down from her chair, "will you please tie my sash?" She placed her arms through the holes and fitted the tie around her waist. Agnes drew the child towards her and placed a kiss on her head.

"Flora, you are quite a lass," she said. "There, a bow fit for a princess!" she exclaimed. "Now, run along and see what Asa is doing."

"I will, but don't be too cross with him," Flora sighed. But before she could skip out the door, she was snapped up by a warm embrace.

"Where's my kiss, young lady!" exclaimed Colonel and with a bear hug grabbed her playfully while she dutifully bestowed upon his tawny cheek several small pecks. "That's much better!" he said releasing her from his grip. "Now I can start my chores!"

There was a certain air of contentment that now consumed both Flora and Colonel. But if Agnes felt this simple sensation, she did not reveal it, for she was too busy clearing the table and wondering what had happened to Asa.

———— • ————

Beyond the shelter of the trees, the green hills rose majestically, slowly, elevating so gradually that those who walked the hidden paths could only tell the increase by the exhilaration of their breathing. The cottontail trembled. He held it close against his body, supporting its legs and underbelly with his arm. It was still dark when he had taken it from the drawer and sat by the open window for a time waiting for the sun. The rabbit lay on his lap, and he stroked its ears, its head, and its back. He followed the path out from the garden and to the fence line. Through the hole and down across the golden field, over the ditches, and then into the black forest. He felt the heart, and it thumped. He pet the head and caressed it until it seemed to relax. The veil of night was breaking. The morning would show what night had hidden. Beyond the fence, graves, open graves? The field of the forgotten, no not forgotten. He leaned forward and with his free hand, moved the curtain further apart. He squinted into the gray day. A mist was rising like the fog off the ocean, and he listened. Crickets called, and the rabbit's ears perked. Asa leaned back and unbuttoned his shirt placing the rabbit beneath his undergarment. It was too fat, so he could only button every other button. He stood up and held the hostage securely and slipped noiselessly down the stairs and out the door.

He stood before the fence and placed the rabbit by the hole folding its ears down and then nudged the head through. It resisted, so he pushed it again. It slipped from his fingers and with trepidation moved in the only direction it could, forward. The cottontail sat on the other side of the fence and waited, trembling, while Asa felt the consequence of its choices. The light of day unfolded with the sunlight sliding up between the hills. A crow circled overhead and landed on the top of the fence. Within an instant the cottontail fled towards the fields, racing between the sage grass and disappearing.

Only winter and her blanket of white snow could hide the crimson battle scars, but when it melted all memories, too, thawed with spring. Youth is the time for valor, and so they were swept up in the glory of the moment, in the splendor of being young; sometimes victorious, sometimes defeated, and sometimes silenced forever. The golden field was dolefully impressive. Asa waited by the fence with sidelong eyes and a sentry's trance; he looked to the hills.

The sun was shining overhead when Flora found him. She peered down at his feet, noticing the hole in the fence. But it wasn't the breach in the plank that had her interest. "What's ya doing out here without your boots?" she asked. His dead feeling suddenly reversed as the man became aware of his naked feet. As if he had been stepping on glass he frantically leaned over to examine his toes, lifting each foot consecutively and then running his fingers over the soles. "You got on your summertime feet," the child laughed. But noticing the man was not pleased with his situation she began to console him. "Come on Asa, let's go in and get your shoes.

It's okay; your feet won't mind. See," she said bending down and tapping the top of his big toe with her doll. Asa wiggled his toes, but his legs did not want to move. "Follow me and Eloise, Asa, one foot at a time." He looked curiously at the child as she made exaggerated strides towards the garden path.

"You don't want to die here!" Alarmed by the commanding voice, he cupped his hands over his ears.

"You don't want to stay here!" insisted Flora. "Just march through the little gate, and then we're almost home."

"You'll be marching right through the enemy's gate if you don't hurry! It's barely passable." The brassy voice loomed in his head. *They marched amidst a field of spring mud, and like adhesive, it was claiming boots with the ferocity of quicksand. "Keep moving, keep moving!"*

"Get moving, Asa, you want your boots, don't you?" The child waited for him just yards ahead and tapped her foot impatiently.

A few steps in front of him a small black object had rolled into a mud puddle. Asa glanced up and saw the doll she cradled was missing a shoe and without hesitation, he waded in to retrieve it.

"Oh, I didn't even see she lost a shoe! Thank you, Asa!' she exclaimed. "Look, we're almost back home." She wriggled the doll's stiff foot and popped the shoe into place. The man watched as the little hands effortlessly placed the muddy article back on the doll's foot. It wasn't very easy putting shoes on in the mud. But the child did it with such ease. His mind flitted from the past to the present until he found himself standing in the doorway of the kitchen.

"Don't be mad at him, Mother," explained Flora as she pointed to the mud-stained feet. "Asa did like you asked," she added and lifted a handful of greens that were sticking out of the crumpled man's back pocket. However, with her unsolicited revelation came a rather immature carrot along with the bunch. "Oh, I wonder how this got here," the child said picking it apart from the rest. But such a sad sight was he that no one took notice of the intentions surrounding the vegetable imposter, for what would be the use of accusing him of any wrongdoings.

"Go on upstairs, Asa," sighed the woman. "Go on and get your boots." Asa followed the trail of sunlight around the corner and up the stairs.

The little girl's eyes clouded with compassion as she spoke. "See, this is a happy way to start the day. I returned Asa, you got your greens, and he found Eloise's shoe." Flora hoped to quell any of her mother's disappointments.

"If it was all so easy," mumbled the woman and with a half-smile agreed with the child.

———— •————

The Jameson farm was protected, cloaked by the green hills stretching upward towards the heavens and outward into the countryside. In all seasons they reaped the benefits that Mother Nature provided. Unlike some acreage that was subject to runoff during winter's thaw, a natural creek, wide and deep, provided a haven for the down-flow of water to seek its natural course. And unlike what was assumed to be where the seasons for flooding might have been a problem, Colonel had acquired the skills to engineer a series of irrigation canals and vector the water away from his homestead. But despite his ingenuity, Colonel was not a natural farmer, and like his father, he did not inherit the agrarian talent of most men of his time, but instead he was wealthy in books. Nor was he a blacksmith or builder, but rather a dabbler with an innate ability to reason out most problems to satisfaction.

Agnes did not mind his inadequacies and supplemented what her husband did not know; for she was a farmer's daughter. Brought up with the smells of cow manure and paraffin, she knew the tales the lark told and where the squirrels hid their acorns before the frost. Her fingers were nimble and her mind clever, and she was happy to leave her father's house.

Theirs was a short courtship; there was little time for romance. Fort Sumter had been attacked not more than a month earlier. Any plans extinguished, all dreams put on hold; one did not have to be a soothsayer but need only to read the papers to predict the future of all able men. It promised to be a short war, and like those who wished to believe such rhetoric held faithful to this notion that those on both sides would not lose.

Her father, Lori Richardsen, was a stubborn man, and his wife, Ella, was equally as stubborn; never having changed the spelling of their last name by keeping it in the manner designed by their country of origin. He was a large man, portly and red-faced, a decent man but not gentle. His temper often got the best of him on account of his drinking, more so than his lack of discipline. Many nights he would leave the ale house on legs too wobbly to ride a horse and many nights did he sleep in the cow barn, for Ella, like her husband could be short-tempered, and on such occasions, like these, he found her considerably intolerant. But with all their shortcomings, they liked Colonel, despite him being younger than Agnes and not a Scott. He was of good faith and well-educated, both traits that defined a man's character and offered the makings of a good husband.

Where one finds happiness is not contingent on searching far from home nor journeying across the oceans, sometimes all it takes is to look in one's backyard and to take notice of your surroundings. So it was regarding the attraction between Agnes and Colonel; a desire to go forward, to start anew, to find their place in a country that was on a collision course with itself. And had they been able to predict their future, that the daily presence of terminal degradation would rob them of any form of tranquility, then perhaps they would have cherished this juncture a little bit longer. But neither youth nor old age has the foresight to linger when in the presence of delight, rather it is time passed that reminds us we have squandered the moment.

Agnes was raised on the assumption that man served best when not under the rule of tyranny. Such a belief had been commissioned during their family's participation during the War of Independence. Scottish born Lachlan McIntosh was Agnes's great-great uncle with a colorful beginning. The McIntosh family emigrated from Scotland in the early 1700s to forge out the colony of Georgia with Governor Oglethorpe. "Uncle Lachlan was a free thinker and a free spirit," explained Agnes. "Here was a man who lived by his convictions, who defended his country and family by whatever means." When asked how; she explained that he killed his political oppressor in a dual. As for his bravery, after seeing his brother eaten by an alligator when first arriving in Florida, she simply said, "I can understand why a few redcoats, in all their pomp and presumption, couldn't scare him." But Agnes was forever humble, and though she could laud her heroic Uncle with accolades and praises as a patriotic General in the Continental Army, she kept this information to herself acknowledging, "Honor is what you earn, not what you inherit."

Colonel liked to watch Agnes as she spoke. Her gray eyes would sparkle, her lips would move quickly, and when she related stories about her family, there was a slight lilt in her voice. When she tilted her head, her hair would tumble to her shoulders, and she would brush the strands aside and readjust her bandana with a slight tug. Her skirt was full and gathered, and when she walked her stride would break the pleats with each confident step. In the early mornings before the sun had time to rise, he would stand by the barn door as she milked the cow. She would not lift her head until she was finished, and even though she was quite capable of doing her chores, he would carry the full pail over to the vat and empty it. One morning, Colonel arrived at the barn, but Agnes was not sitting at her usual place by the piebald heifer. He looked in the other stalls but did not discover her whereabouts until he heard a soft voice coming from the hayloft. It would have been unjust to impose on these gentle whispers, so he waited by the foot of the ladder. Through the drop, he could see Agnes

clutching something between her palms. Her arms were stretched forward, and her neck craned back. Within the second it takes one to exhale a
breath, she opened her hands and released a small black bird. It appeared
to falter for just a moment, but as if it knew it was free, it persisted and
flew out the narrow wooden vent. Such a sight to behold, for without help
the poor little fledgling surely would have perished. The barn resumed its
place of reverence while Agnes peered through the wind eye. She watched
her bird fly away until it became just a spot in the sky. Colonel hastily
retreated outside before Agnes could notice him. The morning was settling on the land, and he knew this was the woman he wanted to marry.

It was chilly the evening Colonel proposed. Agnes sat close to him,
half-hidden by her woolen cloak, and if prying eyes were watching they
would have thought she was shy. But bashful was not an emotion Agnes
was in possession of, and when Colonel asked for her hand in marriage,
she accepted his intent readily. This was the month of daffodils, hyacinth,
and lilac blooms, the first souvenirs of spring. But even with the hint of
fragrance, no flower could pervade the first evidence of war. And with all
its might even the pale moon rising in the darkening sky was blurred by
the amber fires in the distance. The superstitious would interpret this to
be a bad omen, but if this was a warning the couple was either too young
or too naïve to notice.

Chapter 5

No literal description can parallel the conditions of those fighting in battle, and while words grant the reader a sense of its horror, it dwarfs in comparison to the actual events. Before the end of the battle, the wide-eyed soldier's grit is tested. Prophetic, mortal, frayed, and muddy, they prayed for water, for food, for warmth; for guns, for mothers, for lovers, for mercy, and splendor; but regardless of what side they were on, no two prayers were identical. Atheists and sinners, saints and ordinary folks, each looked to their own solitude. The war had consumed all mental and moral powers belonging to soldiers and civilians, and it continued to contaminate years after.

Opposing parties enter into combat with the same unabated lust for victory. And while both armies' officers bear likeness to each other and both commanding officers lead their troops like ecclesiastical synods escorting their followers, no prize of victory is free. Dawn had arrived in a veil of fog, and like a thief, the Commander stole all free moments. There was no time; the thickened morning would conceal the brigade, and while they moved in unison like a cloud Asa clutched his rifle against his chest and hoped that the chattering of his teeth could not be heard.

He crouched low behind a barricade of rotten oak, and when the bugle sounded, he charged forward leading with his bayonet to pursue the flag.

To count the fallen Asa would have needed a thousand tongues. Was it evening or the morning? The sky had turned charcoal gray; all sense of time and space displaced. He was like a drowning man falling deeper into leagues of turbulent water, plunging downward, somersaulting around and around, unable to discern the direction of the surface. Hours earlier he was a soldier, not this trespasser navigating across a farmer's field. He wandered about confused while his eyes took charge scouring for some semblance of life. There was no one source but many crimson tributaries springing from limbs, severed and punctured. Long after the fires of battle were extinguished the pitiful cries and mournful sounds of wounded horses continued to injure Asa more than if he himself was stabbed. With his life spared he had inherited the duty to defend once again, and when he looked around, he did not understand. His definition of what was righteous had been severely altered.

"You better sit down Private, and let me take a look at that wound." A compassionate voice grasped his attention, and for the first time, Asa realized that he was standing in his own blood. "Go on, over there," pointed the medic, hinting to a small clearing beneath the hawthorn tree. It was a tree of expansive reach extending its branches outward and upward to award a canopy of shade to those who remained beneath its leafy awning. The wounded were laid side-by-side on the blood-washed earth having been carried away from the fields of dead and dying. Asa leaned against the trunk and closed his eyes. His whole being sighed as his thoughts crumbled with despair. He tried to stand but his legs buckled beneath him and as if he had been sawed away from the tree, he slipped to the ground. His soles blistered, the skin chafed from the thick woolen stockings, though it was the loss of blood that made him light-headed. The medic returned with a haversack of provisions and water and knelt beside him. The youthful soldier, having just added the eighteenth summer to his age, methodically dressed and bandaged the injured shoulder. When he was done, he spoke with perfect military precision and reminded Asa that his good arm could still manage a rifle.

Bayonets, cartridge boxes, fragments of shells, pieces of clothes, caps, and musketry; the field claimed all mementos of battle. A scurry of activity had erupted and in the peripheral men foraged the ground as if they were squirrels in the winter. A clean-shaven soldier like himself was meticulously inventorying the personal possessions of the deceased and placing them into a canvas which he wore slung over his shoulder. Unlike the other men, his lapels shouldered the stripes of an officer, and his face wore the disposition of intellect. The wounded man watched as the Lieutenant took his time, sifting individual items from the dead bodies and then attaching it to a name on a list. For over half-an-hour this rummaging went on until the man ventured over to rest in the shade. "Mind if I sit down?"

Asa tried to salute but realizing his arm would not cooperate he began to raise his uninjured one. "At-Ease, Private, I can see your intentions are honorable," the officer instructed and tossed the haversack he was shouldering to the ground. "I'm Lieutenant Colonel Jameson," he remarked, settling himself against the wide root. Then without pause, he asked, "First battle?" Asa shook his head no and then put up four fingers. "Four." Colonel nodded and turned away. His eyes canvassed the field. "I guess you know then that this is hell," he said. Asa watched the man's expression as the firm jaw tensed and a tincture of remorse coated his throat.

The two men sat for a spell. Theirs was a ghastly end to the day, and the enemy had delivered a blow that would be difficult to recover from. Asa struggled for a moment as he reached into his jacket. He fumbled for the small patch of material strategically sewn into the inside lining; a sort of secret pocket designed to keep predators, as he had just witnessed, from stealing his possession if he was deemed unconscious or dead. "Keep this," he said and placed before Colonel a leather-bound book. It could have been misconstrued for the Bible, but upon further investigation, it was instead a small pocketbook.

Colonel raised his palm up in refusal, but Asa placed the book in his hand. "Take it," he said. "I might not make it next time."

"This is highly irregular," continued the officer. "Besides, what do you mean you won't make it? Your wounds aren't life-threatening, are they?" He tried to make light of the situation, and though he was correct, for the bayonet puncture would heal, there was more to the solicitor's suffering.

"Please, just put it with the other things," he urged.

There was something in the Private's rawness that had strangely called forth the Lieutenant's sympathy. The soldier carried his pain silently, but it was a suffering as real as those convulsing and writhing. If Lieutenant Jameson's interpretation of character was correct, he wished not to be the one to have refused such a small request. But having been exposed to accounts of exaggerations, the Officer thought more readily before submitting to his gut feelings. "I hope you're not concocting a plan to run because you know they'll hang you," he warned.

A possessed glare suddenly exposed a side of Asa that had remained dormant for the past hour. "Runaway! I'd rather be shot dead on this spot then run away. I have no intention of desertion."

"Very well, then, as a Gentleman and fellow soldier, I will take your word." Colonel reached over and opened the pouch whereupon the small book was deposited. "Let's hope we meet again, under better circumstances," said Colonel. "Perhaps over whiskey."

Asa grinned. "Whiskey, I would like that, Sir."

There was nothing one could surmise or say that would unburden the load of doubt and misery. Lives had been lost as well as the dignity attached to the losing side. Suffering and sorrow were consuming the countryside, the towns, and all who assumed the pattern of the familiar and disrupted. This exchange of civility between Asa and Colonel was a brief but courteous interlude in a day when adversaries were triumphant. But on this day their paths would abruptly part as brigades were reassigned and dispersed to different assignments.

The handing over of the property he had taken off the dead soldier was just one of numerous items Asa wished to relinquish. It was of no use to him and just in case he was captured he didn't want to be found with it on his person. Asa pondered the list of counterfeiters remembering one that was underlined, Samuel Upham. He calculated this must have been someone of interest or importance. The Lieutenant would know what to do with the information it contained.

Colonel thumbed through the leaves of the small book before slipping it back into his haversack. He wondered if Asa knew what he had been in possession of and if he had, why the Private hadn't tried to sell it? Colonel sat in considerate silence thinking hard. For a moment the implied expression of confusion expelled guilt. "Fatigue does something erroneous to a man's brain," he decided. "There are two kinds of people, those who take advantage of an opportunity such as what he now possessed and those who let others decide. Even the possum knows when to come alive." Colonel stomped the mud off his boots and faced straight ahead. He couldn't stop the disease and despair from spreading. The army was forever burying someone. When grandma died, she left a note with instructions about what kind of casket she wanted. But in war, there are no wishes to oblige the dead, just deep green hollows.

———— • ————

"If Asa isn't real family, why do I call him by his first name?" the child asked. The gray drizzle was as constant as the tide. It was a somber morning; Agnes peered over her knitting needles at the only bright spot of the day. It was a good question, one however that she believed she had answered before.

"On account that Asa is part of the family," the mother said.

"Then why don't you call him your brother?" the child questioned, knowing that she was now testing her mother's patience.

However, Agnes did not give in to her daughter's mischievous nature. "Sometimes children call folks that aren't blood relations by their first name instead of Mr. or Mrs. It makes that person feel special." She stopped knitting and with the needles crossed rested the scarf on her lap. The child had slipped off the stool and was reaching for a bun from the counter. Her shoulders reached just above the countertop, and she was tipping up on her toes as if she were being pulled upward by a cord. "You are a ballerina, aren't you!" laughed the mother.

Flora pirouetted around and then made a full curtsey, pulling her skirt wider at the hemline while bending at the knee. "Oh, it would be such fun to be a dancer!" she exclaimed happily. Her attention then turned to the intent of her hunger. "May I have this?" she asked, extending the cinnamon twist to her mother.

The woman nodded agreeably, and then went back to her knitting.

"So, I will keep calling him plain old Asa," Flora continued between bites. "I imagine it might make him happy when I do. What do you think, Mother, does he get happy?" the child requested with doe-like eyes. Asa was the recipient of much of her affection, and she felt emotionally responsible for his happiness.

Flora's sensitive nature was cultivated by her father, while her pragmatism was of her mother's nurturing. She was a combination of the two and the response to her question was one based on truth and a little bit of "sugar" considering the child's young age. "Asa was sad when Colonel found him again. But you knew that, didn't you Flora?" The child nodded yes. "I certainly hope he is happy living with us. He certainly deserves some peace," said the mother hopefully

"Was he lost for a long time before Colonel found him?"

"Well, yes and no. Asa went through some very difficult years right after the war. He just needs a little bit of kindness," Agnes replied with maternal compassion; but the nagging voice in her head made the woman wonder if that was all he needed.

"I guess I will just have to help him remember what he lost," declared the little girl. The rain that had drowned the morning with dreariness had turned into a sun shower. Through the gaps in the hill once joined by slate clouds now showed blue sky. Agnes raised her knitting from her lap, and as the needles clattered one against the other, the skein of yarn grew smaller. Flora reached down and placed the ball in her hand. She rolled it over her flattened palm and then put it back on the floor where it would move intermittently with the flutter of the knitting needles.

"Mother, I think Asa is like this ball of yarn. Right now it is very dull, but soon it will become something very beautiful."

Agnes glanced at the child who was playfully rolling the yarn back along the floor. "Sometimes her wisdom frightens me," thought the mother and continued to work even more feverishly than before.

———•———

Asa was the same age as Colonel when he was conscripted into the army; but unlike Colonel who become a Lieutenant, Asa did not rise through the ranks and achieve the same prestige. Although he could read and write, he never took to schooling and so when opportunities arrived for him to better himself; he did so with his hands and not with books. His father, Neville Young, was a good-natured man, but Neville's father was devoid of any adventure. Your Grandfather Niles was a rather "unimaginative fellow," quoted Neville to Asa, "but it was my Uncle Callum that proved

life was filled with untapped opportunities if you just dared take a risk."
The Uncle, several years younger than his older brother, established himself a successful privateer. During the War of 1812, he was hired by the
new government to attack and confiscate British ships. In the start of
the Revolution, there was no American navy; instead, privateersmen were
hired and authorized to retrofit their own ships and prey on British com-
merce vessels. Mostly coming from families of wealth and prestige, these
independent seamen earned considerable sums of money by attacking the
enemy. And though Uncle Callum partook in only two rather successful
raids in the Caribbean, he earned a reputation as being fearless as well
as profiting a substantial amount of silver. By the end of the war of 1812,
the ambitious uncle retired from the sea a wealthy man with more than
enough money to employ Neville's father in his ship's carpentry business.

The tale of his Uncle ignited the youthful Neville's desires to stray
from the ordinary. It did not take long for seaman's fables of gaff-rigged
sails to capture his enterprising spirit, yet unlike many entrepreneurs that
were turning back to the land; Neville did not yearn for his own plot of
American soil, but rather felt more at home onboard a ship. With inspiration from Uncle Callum and the blessing of his father, he took to the
sea. He was quick to see many opportunities for an experienced sailor and
those with the skills and energy of a romantic could earn a sizable wage.
Ambitious and frugal, he did not squander his money on rum. Unbridled
from family ties and free of financial burdens, he explored his prospects
and joined the crew of a packet ship delivering mail and cargo from
America to Europe. However, as the crew was preparing the ship, there
arrived word that pirates plundered a packet vessel sailing southward off
the Bahama Banks. According to the story, chaos ensued as the ship's crew
was overtaken; those that did not submit to the seizure were executed,
while the ship emerged with little damage. As for the Captain, a gentleman of Spanish descent, his life was spared and ordered to change course
for Cuba. Upon their arrival, the obliging man was released penniless,

barefoot, (for his boots made of fine leather were confiscated by a tooth-less drunkard), and with only the clothes on his back.

The narrative of the pirated ship had extinguished all "blue moons" and deposited in its place the affirmation of mortality. "What if I had been aboard that ship and murdered? Who would light a candle for me, who?" The morose sailor grew melancholy. An unfamiliar feeling of disquiet was overpowering Neville like a winter blizzard. He reflected on his choices and decided that what was in order was a wife. Where to find one would not be difficult since the only criteria she had to subscribe to was his nautical lifestyle. With all his belongings packed, which faired few items of clothes, a firearm, and several maritime books, he boarded a ship heading northward for the whaling village of Sag Harbor.

So it was that he courted Asa's mother, the daughter of a retired seaman and schoolmarm. Lucie Beth Reed, a round cheerful woman, owned a lively laugh and had a fondness for cats. She cared for her aging parents in a small but comfortable clapboard cottage, and at the age of twenty, her parents were quite willing to have her married off. The old sailor's pension had been scarcely enough to feed two stomachs without the burden of the daughter.

For two years Neville and Lucie lived in the extra room with her parents. Sag Harbor could boast of a Main Street and stage route between New York and the burgeoning town, but this lifestyle soon began to grow quite mundane for the adventurous man. With a baby now on the way he wanted to assume a more lucrative enterprise than fishing. The elder Reeds had been kind but rather useless, and as they aged so did their dwelling. Like rheumatism that swelled their old joints, the damp salt-air swelled the joiners of the old house. The red shingles leaked, and the single-bay porch creaked. Time is often not generous, and as Neville surveyed his situation, he felt it closing in. Though grateful to his in-laws for what they had provided Lucie, the up-keep of the house and his own growing family was a financial responsibility he needed to reconcile.

———— • ————

"At birth, the newborn's head is remarkably large as compared to the rest of the body. The infant should be kept warm and comfortable by sleeping in a well-ventilated room to prevent the air from becoming foul. A foolish mother will try to harden the baby in wintertime by dipping him in cold water or allowing him to sleep in a room with no direct heat. Rather, the temperature in the bedroom during winter should be at least 60 degrees F. When the baby begins to teethe; it is best not to give him anything too hard, preference is given to a piece of bridle-leather or an Indian-rubber ring that will better stimulate the gums. When he is older, a horsehair mattress and a horse-hair pillow are best in lieu of a feather pillow that will make his head perspire. But, if he is at all crooked or weak in his neck, then no pillow is recommended. Bathe the baby in lukewarm rainwater; wear an ankle-length bathing apron stitched from of thick, soft flannel, a material that will dry quickly. Maintain bedtime to a regular schedule, summertime at 7 and in the winter at 6. Before offering young children fruits such as plums and peaches, examine them for wasps since they may be hiding in the sweet flesh."

Management Advise for the New Mother

In the early morning of a weary season, autumn, Asa entered the world in the same untimely hour Mika the calico, gave birth to her litter of kittens. The sound of meows dwarfed the small cries of the newborn until both the mother cat and the new mother nursed their new arrivals. Within a few days after the births, Mika paraded her kittens to-and-fro, carrying them by the scruffs of the neck until finally settling upon a well-concealed niche beneath the oak dresser. All-the-night-long, while the whole house slept, restless kittens complained, each taking turns as though they were purposely provoking the mother cat. And all the while Asa remained awake, listening to Mika tending to her kittens.

As husband and wife, Neville and Lucie lived in the spare room with very little distinction. Lucie, devoted to her husband and parents, came and went like an ant preparing for winter. There was very little difference in her temperaments, where cheery indifference seemed to rule her continence. Neville did not mind his wife's subdued disposition; she provided him with all the needs a man desired as well as the space he demanded. Lucie went about motherhood in the same diligent manner she would go about any other womanly requirement, but the birth of the boy breathed new life into Neville's days, which had otherwise had become quite stale.

Neville doted over his new son, but as much as he enjoyed fatherhood, it was not enough to keep his adventurous spirits bridled. What he wished to do was a mystery even to himself, while his future was derailed with each rational decision he made. It wasn't until he read the weekly edition of *The Corrector*, Sag Harbor's newspaper, where he came across an article describing the historic capture of a whale of unknown species in the Piscataqua River. The hunters boasted of its length in the measurement of 50 feet and a horse-shaped head, 16 feet broad. This bit of trivia, for the voyage dated back to the 1820s, escalated into defining the reason for rehashing the past in the local newspaper. To whet the appetite of readers, the reporter transcribed his interview with Captain Thomas Roys, who was commissioned to set sail on his second whaling expedition. Having been injured while hunting bowhead whales in the waters between Petropavlovsk and the Commander Islands during his first exploration, the Captain had spent several months recuperating in Petropavlovsk. Now back in Sag Harbor, he was preparing the next hunt and needed experienced seamen to join him aboard the *Superior*.

Neville reflected on the contents of the article. An enterprise of such grand scale grew with his imagination giving him reason to pause. For five years he had narrowed his world, and though Sag Harbor's waters were laced with fine sailing vessels and greedy sailors, a combination that would grant him the method and means to prosperity, he had pledged to remain near home until the boy was old enough to be of help. Well, the boy was now more than a help. The old couple had since died and left

Lucie with a small inheritance. Wasn't this the perfect time? 1847, the future could not be brighter.

The elated man raised his lids as his eyes fell over the page and he continued to read. *"Whaling voyages typically lasted two years. By setting sail in the fall, we will round the tip of South America, and hunt whales in the southern Pacific until early spring. Oil and baleen will be offloaded in the Hawaiian Islands in tandem to the restocking of water and provisions."* The description shared by Captain Roys was more than a geography lesson; it was an invitation to become part of the future.

Neville perused the rest of the article, noting the name and whereabouts of the Dockmaster to inquire. The passage navigated either around the Cape of Good Hope at the tip of Africa or by way of Cape Horn at the tip of South America; both proved exceedingly long and dangerous. He folded the paper in half and placed it on the bench. He tapped it for good measure and heaved a great sigh of both satisfaction and contentment. Lucie was a good woman, and as long as there were fishing and the salt works, there would be a steady income, even while he was away. For as long as his wife could remember, the salt works were located on the peninsula, northwest of the village. Here on the eastern shore was Shelter Island Sound, an anchorage fit for whaling ships waiting to be outfitted with cured meats and barrels of salt.

The contemplative man leaned forward, took his briar pipe from the table, and opened the leather pouch. Before slicing several wafers off the plug, he placed it under his nose and inhaled slowly. The aroma of rum flavored tobacco settled in his nostrils. The ritual of packing the pipe was part of the mystic of smoking, this he did with the utmost sincerity, breaking it up with his fingers and then sprinkling the tobacco into the bowl. As if shaking Asa's hand, he gently tamped down until the bowl partially filled. Then he drizzled and tamped with the lightness of shaking Lucie's hand until finally the filling and tamping took on a man's firm handshake. With a single strike against the flint-stone, the match-stick ignited releasing a hint of sulfur. He cupped the bowl and puffed until the tobacco came alive. Each man's pipe was unique to his individuality. Neville drew on the mouthpiece and puffed. He could feel the ragged marking from his teeth. He let the pipe hang from his lip keeping it firm with his strong jaw. He leaned back in the chair, gazing, suspended in time, just he with his pipe and his thoughts.

———·———

Asa stood alone on the shore. His lanky arms dangled by his side, and his hand felt strangely unfamiliar, free from his father's large and calloused grip. The clouds were devouring the sky, blocking any attempts of sunlight to escape. Two years would be a long time. He already longed to hear his father's husky voice, but for now, he would have to settle for the chant of untamed sailors. He would reserve his emptiness for something truly regrettable. It was not a sad time, just one marbled with absence. His heart struggled with this contradiction of feelings, and as he stood listening to the roll of the surf, he watched the great ship sail away with his father.

Chapter 6

They were a pair of dog-hungry drifters. The Timpson brothers huddled over the pathetic fire, each sheltered by the army-issued blankets they never gave back; discolored and thread worn, dirty reminders of the years lost. Dennet wrapped a rag around the pot's handle and poured the boiling water into his tin cup and set it back in the firepit. He stirred the sugar and coffee grounds with a stick.

"Where's yer spoon?" complained the elder of the two.

Dennet didn't bother to look over at his brother who was stirring his own concoction of barley and water. "Over there," he said and raised his chin in the direction of the haversack. It too, like most everything in their possession, had been army-issue. But ten years later, it no longer seemed relevant. "You cold?" he asked and lifted the hot coffee to his mouth and blew across the top. The steam might have burned his lips had he held it any closer to his face.

"Course, I'm cold," Lucas remarked indifferently. "But what good would it do to complain?"

The younger shrugged and then asked. "What do you think we ought to do when we see him?"

"When we see him?" the question appeared irrelevant and rather insipid. "We'll invite him to join us in a glass of Grant's whiskey!" He glared round, and with his harsh look, the anemic man seemed to wither under the blanket. The irritated brother shook his head, exaggerating his disgust with mutterings of, "when we see him!"

"I just meant that we should have a plan, you know, what we're gonna do when we get there." The voice trembled under the weight of the elder's caustic and anticipated reply. But there was no reply, only the loud slurping of the watery broth followed by a clanging of tins. Lucas wrapped his utensils neatly back into his pack, strapped it shut, and then placed it on the ground so it would support his head like a pillow. "Be sure you put more wood on the fire after you clean up this mess," the irritated man charged. He maintained his orderly practice of neatness and regulation; a habit he had learned while commanding his brigade and continued to follow long after both sides had exhausted all the soldiers they were willing to lose. He spread the blanket out on the ground and lay down, rolling himself up like a stuffed cabbage. And within a few minutes, he was asleep.

The younger man envied his brother's ability to fall so quickly to sleep. He tossed the grounds into the fire and watched them shrivel up and disintegrate with the rest of the residue. He squatted before the flames and leaned into the fire savoring its warmth. It would not be long before it would dwindle out. He was resigned to the reluctant conclusion of the evening; he tossed the blanket over his shoulders and walked out into the night following the moonlit path in search of kindling. He kept the snoring man in earshot knowing that as long as he was able to hear the grunts and snorts, he could find his way back to the small campsite without a torch. Lucas had trained himself to sleep in the most undesirable situations, even the enemies' antagonistic shots behind the lines did not disturb his rest; while Dennet never seemed to completely consign himself to sleep. His nights were divided into small dog-like naps with one ear always on guard.

It was not the dawning light that woke the older brother, but the rumbling of his stomach. He turned over on his back and opened his eyes. The gray clouds swelled as if purposely trying to smother the faint outline of the moon. He sat up and pulled his knees towards his chest. The air was still and damp, and he wished he had more than the frayed blanket to pull over his shoulders. His brother lay a few yards away, still asleep. Dennet was his younger brother but seemed more like a son. They had lost a cousin at Hoover's Gap and Chickamauga. A twenty-three-pound shell rolled through the underbrush where he and his company were waiting. Its explosion scattered the youth's brains. When night fell, and the firing had died, the company's soldiers dug a shallow grave and buried him. Lucas often wondered if perhaps the death had been a punishment for past indiscretions. He wanted to go back to find the grave, to give his kin a righteous headstone, but after the war things got too complicated.

"Dennet!" A quail that had taken up temporary residence in a neighboring shrub flew out from the brush startling the man. "Shit! Dennet, get up!" He reached down, scooped up a handful of pebbles, and pelted them at his brother. "Get up!" he shouted.

"Damn! What'd ya do that for?" cried the target shielding his face with his hands.

"Time to git goin'!"

"You didn't have to hit me!" But knowing better than to retaliate, he slowly lowered his hands away from his face.

"Get up and let's go!" Lucas demanded and adhering to his prescribed routine, he rolled his blanket into a tight, neat coil. Dennet followed his brother, but his attempts delivered only a rumpled bundle that he quickly crammed into his haversack.

By now the clouds had turned to ribbons and lay upon the whitening sky like striated pieces of white silk. The sun exposed itself warning the travelers that they would soon be at its mercy. Lucas shoved his hand into the leather bag and retrieved a shabby deck of cards. He shimmied them out of their case and held them up for his brother to see. It was the reminder of why they were desolate, homeless, and determined.

"I haven't forgotten, trust me!"

"Good," said Lucas and forced the cards back to the bottom of the bag with the blanket on top. "Haven't heard the eight-o-clock yet." He looked down the hill towards the rail tracks and cupped his hand to his ear. "Too early," he said and then without waiting for his brother, who was busy stamping out the embers, he started away.

An outbreak of dandelions and clover had invaded the knoll. Not intimidated by the rocky soil, they overtook the grass with an explosion of yellow and white. Dennet rambled behind, stopping to watch a brown rabbit that too had stopped to nibble; only it didn't know it was being observed. The wind was not working in favor of the animal; if it weren't careful, it would be taken prey. Dennet clapped his hands. The tall pair of ears stood erect; the entire body remained motionless, and then like a bullet discharging it sped down the hill. Lucas caught sight of the wrinkle in the underbrush as the panicked rabbit darted beneath the briar patch. He pointed in its direction, turned up toward his brother and laughed. "Damn rabbit, he thinks he's free!" And then, with a shake of his head, he hiked ahead.

Dennet followed Lucas's path, but his mind was not on their mission but rather on the rabbit, hoping that his brother was wrong. But Lucas was seldom wrong, and sometimes that was not a good thing.

The two men hid behind the line of trees until they heard the long complaining hiss of a train whistle. A stream of black smoke was unsnarling from the chimney like a sooty meteor tail. Lucas and Dennet watched from behind the thickets, and when the engine followed the curve along the tracks it slackened its speed, and the two men ran towards the slowly approaching train. Out of an open car an arm reached as far forward as it could in anticipation of assisting the freeloaders. The dangling hand waved frantically as if its movement were going to hurry the legs of the soon to be passengers. "Hurry up! Hurry up!" But the loud screeching whistle overpowered any audible sound coming from the scamp as his mouth gestured with exaggerated movement. "There you go, leg up, leg up!" He pulled Dennet into the car, but by the time he had turned to help the other, Lucas had already managed to climb aboard. "There!" smiled the toothless tramp. "Welcome, welcome!" he cried, apparently quite pleased that there was company, although, he was not alone. Obscured in the shadow of the train car sat a pair of unsavory looking travelers.

"So," exclaimed the helper, "who do we have here today?" He cocked his head to the side and inspected the brothers. But neither man gave the tramp the satisfaction of a response and settled themselves on the opposite side of the car. "Suit yourself," said the speaker sliding back towards the others. However, they too rejected him like rotting meat, and the sorry man scooted away. Dreary would be a generous word for the railcar, for it stank from cattle and waste. Had it not been for the partially-open door, it would have left them in impenetrable darkness. The wooden planks had recently been sealed with tar, admitting not a single beam of light nor a hint of fresh air. But no one seemed to care, and not a word was spoken for over an hour.

The train rattled along the rough tracks and every now and again it would pitch the car, toppling the men over. Finally, the tramp broke the silence. "So," he exclaimed and slid over to where Dennet and Lucas were sitting, "where ya headed?" It was the first time that they got a good look at his appearance. Though not much older than Lucas, he had the weighty troubles and continence of an old man. The poor wretch had neither a left foot nor a right leg, the latter having been amputated below the knee. A rickety pair of crutches lay on the floor in the corner of the train beside a bed of straw. "You fellahs graybacks?" he asked raising his eyebrows. "Not that I care, it's just that if you are, well I sure would like you to find the rest of my limbs!" He laughed, and with it, a foul smell emanated from his open jaw.

The train rumbled painfully, and the long mournful whistle carried with it the only sound of remorse for the man. Lucas squinted at the face but said nothing. Grave-like silence lay heavy in the car. "Well," said the outcast possessed with a reservoir of stories to rehash, "when Mr. Lincoln's army was short on meat I was on picket duty a half-a-mile from camp when what did I see 'bout 25 rods from where I was patrolling, a heifer and 'er fat calf. I was soakin' wet since it had rained all day and my feet were cold, and all I wanted was supper and a coffee. But that calf sure was getting my stomach goin'. When I got back to camp, I told the cook, and sure as shit, he fell into action. He asked me where it was and then waited till it was pitch dark. He got a bundle of sweet hay and a short rope and in no time was leading our next meal back to camp. All night I was dreaming of eating that calf. Trouble was, next morning our brigade was movin' out. Never did get to eat any of my find. All I got was orders to scale the bluff and hardtack for my empty belly. In a few hours the contest was over, and the lucky sons of bitches back at camp were pickin' the meat off the bones."

The bulk of the story had been told, but as he took a breath before finishing his tale one of the other shiftless travelers crept over to examine his belongings sticking out from beneath the hay bed. Like a cobra, the limbless man lunged forward and toppled all his weight upon the ignorant thief. "It's mine!" screamed the attacker. "It's mine!" and in an instant was brandishing a knife. "This is my home!" threatened the wretch, "and I will put your lights out!"

No sooner did the warning leave his lips when the brute at the far side of the car, dressed from head to toe in black, stood up. His massive girth was impressive, and his voice filled the entire car with it tenor of disgust. "If anyone's gonna kill 'em, it'll be me!" stormed the Confederate. The train swerved, and the man held his balance as he pitched back and forth moving with a determined gait. Then, like a cat takes a kitten, he pushed aside the deformed man and lifted his comrade by the back of his neck. Pulling the left arm behind the thief's back, he started for the open door. The whistle blew long and hard the very instant the man squealed, "No, Bodie, no, don't!" He kicked and pleaded, but his relentless efforts were no match for the beast-of-a-man who tossed him out of the car with the same indifference used to dump a sack of potatoes.

"Piece of Yankee shit!" the disposer grimaced and hanging on to the sides of the door, he swayed back and forth as he watched the hillside rush by.

The toothless vagabond slipped his knife into its sheath where it was concealed by the gloom of the boxcar and his filthy shirttails. He rolled over on his side and pulled himself up with his arms, scooting along on his behind towards the makeshift bed. Then as if nothing had occurred, he retrieved a leather satchel, snuck something from its contents, and turned to continue with his chatter. "I've got something in my possession which I think you'll like. Ain't a man I've met that didn't want one of these," he whispered. With his crooked finger, he beckoned. However, neither Lucas nor Dennet took his bait for they had their eyes on the brute who now lumbered back to his corner. "Come on, don't be shy," and tucking the folded parchment under his arm, he slid over to the two travelers. Again, he bent his finger for them to follow, but this time the refusal was emphatically proclaimed.

"Not interested in what you've got," retorted Lucas and shoved his hand towards the solicitor.

But the eager man was not deterred and leering at the two, opened the folded paper and withdrew a photograph. He cowered before the men, looking about as if someone was watching them from the shadows, and then handed it to the younger brother. Dennet held it up to his eyes since the photograph was small, and the light did not offer much luminosity. In his palm he held the image of a woman posed against a veil of drapery. Her hair, black as a raven, pulled to one side, and her smile, suggestively seductive; this dark-haired woman was not only voluptuous but clearly bare-breasted. Dennet smiled and then handed the photograph to Lucas. "She's a lot of woman, isn't she? For only seventy-five cents you can look at her every night!" the seller exclaimed.

"Not interested," Lucas said and began to hand the picture back to the limbless man when Dennet snatched it away.

"I think she's got a lot of personality!" he announced and fingered the image. "Seventy-five, ya say?"

The seller nodded, sweating a bit at the idea of a sale.

"Give you fifty cents," Dennet countered.

The man stroked his chin. "I don't have too many more of these beauties," he said. "Sixty cents!" he yelped.

The murderous brute had settled himself, stretching out on the other side of the car. He laughed crudely after the offer was announced. Evidently, he too had been solicited. Whether he had bought a picture or not, he did reveal, however, he was eager to share his opinion. "Ask him to show you the blonde!" he cried out and then laughed again.

"No, I like her," smiled Dennet. "Okay, sixty cents." And he reached into his pocket and sorted out his coins. One by one he dropped them into the grimy hand and like the beggar that he was the man grasped the money and stuffed it into his pocket.

"You say you got more?" Lucas asked with a modicum of curiosity.

"Why, you want to see more? Told you, ain't a man worth his weight that wouldn't want one." Then with a moment of hesitation, he looked away and scooted back towards his stash.

Lucas watched as the suspicious man placed himself in front of his goods. "Just wanted to know if you had any more, 'cause seems to me a man could make a good living with what you're selling," he remarked.

"Well, I still have my connections; been in business since the war," he boasted. "Guess you could say I'm an entrepreneur. Not as easy as it was before, but I make do. Matter of fact, General Hooker himself was one of my customers." He stretched out and tucked his satchel under his head and rested his hand on the sheath.

Lucas gave Dennet a nod and pulled his hat over his eyes. The day had turned more interesting, and as he was left with his thoughts, he felt his spirits lift. Dennet glanced around and shyly pulled the photograph from his shirt pocket, and he smiled at the woman. She was older than he was and he imagined that she could teach him a thing or two. He rested his head against the wall; he was pleased with his purchase. The train rumbled and snorted with the temperament of a bull. Dennet eyed the woman again, and he felt himself blush. Hastily, he slipped her back into his pocket and closed his eyes. However, only a few minutes had passed when a rush of curiosity consumed him, a sudden urge to catch a glimpse of the "blonde."

Like a baby that awakens when the cradle no longer swings, the men were awakened by the premature stopping of the train. Voices from the outside made their way into the boxcar, but they were muffled by the distance between the speaker and the listeners making the exchange difficult to discern. Each man held his breath while listening for a reason to the train's untimely interruption.

"Maybe we ought to get out right now," suggested Dennet in a whisper. "We can walk the rest of the way." His brother turned and put his finger to his lips. The younger man shrugged his shoulders, slumped over, and rested his head on his crossed arms.

"Scared, fellah?" asked the limbless man. The darkness of the car made his question all the more macabre. "Trains stop all the time on the track; cow hit, broken rail, hold-up."

"Shut up, you fool," hushed the brute. Footsteps rustled around the cars, and a voice of authority began to speak. "I don't think we need to delay anymore. We already searched the front cars, and we're behind schedule as it is."

There was a long pause between the speakers; enough to interpret the listener doubted the wisdom of what he had heard. "I suppose so. But the last thing we need is trouble," the engineer warned.

"It's dark already!" the irritated voice summoned. "I say we let it go and get started. If Pinkerton wants to send their Pinkies around to snoop, let them. I'm sure they'll be waiting at the next depot anyway."

Again, there was a tepid response. "Okay," the reluctant man agreed. "Okay."

A scuffling of feet along clay and dirt marked their departure towards the engineer's car. "See," said the toothless fellow when they were gone, "they're probably looking for our friend, Bodie. No need for you two to be concerned." He lay his head down and waited for the locomotive to move. An exaggerated hump and hiss were expelled, and a slow churning of the enormous wheels set the train in motion.

However ignorant the limbless man played, he was no fool and having planted the seeds of doubt in the murder's mind, as the train began to pick up momentum, the culprit gathered his meager belongings and lumbered over to the door. He teetered for a moment, grasping the bar with his right hand until, like an ape reaching for a nearby limb, he swung his arms back and leaped from the moving car to freedom. Whether the daredevil landed safely or not would remain an enigma since none of the travelers, no matter how keen their hearing, could possibly have heard anything over the rumble of the iron wheels.

"Just who was that?" asked Dennet. His tone was more of confusion than concern for the audacious performance he had witnessed.

"You mean, Bodie?" he trifled, knowing full well what the question proposed. "Why he's one of my contacts." The words floated about the boxcar like bait waiting to be snatched.

Little more was said and as the train jostled its way down the tracks darkness fell over the world like a sable coverlet. Only the stars and a sliver of moon shined above them, wrapping the sky in a ring of fire. There was much to think about, especially when one has been living a desolate and bleak existence. Had an unexpected parcel of opportunity arrived? Was it possible the two brothers were placed alongside this wretch for a reason? Lucas and Dennet, independent of the other, cast a glance in the direction of the sleeping man. And while locked in their own fantasies, each believed that fate may have just turned the corner for the Timpson brothers.

Chapter 7

D r. Richard Bushnell stood by the open window collecting his thoughts. He hoped that working in the asylum had not weakened him having overheard his name associated with being "soft" or "more like a woman" in his approach to the patients. He fingered his mustache; a handlebar that often-generated compliments before most conversations had begun. This triggered a reminder to have his wife order some of the fine wax from the pharmacy. It was Major Conrad that had recommended the product; a sweet-scented pomade that elongated and stiffened each well-groomed hair. As far as he was concerned, there weren't many positive acquaintances that had come out of the war, but the Major proved one that was worth the trouble.

Bushnell's appointment to the State Asylum could not have come at a more inconvenient time. He and Sydney had planned on taking some time away, a trip overseas to Europe. She was a well-bred woman, who became a lover of the arts after a chance viewing of Samuel Morse's painting, *Gallery of the Louvre*, in New York City. The large six by nine-foot painting, though depicting masterpieces by Leonardo da Vinci, Caravaggio, Rubens, and other prominent European artists, fell short of being accepted by the American public. Sharing these popular sentiments, the Doctor felt the work was a boorish attempt at trying to influence the country with European snobbery and arrogance. "It's a good thing Morse came to his senses with the telegraph," he would add, giving the man his merit as a scientist. But Sydney did not abandon her ideals and the fact that most had found the work to be pretentious only gave her more reason to defend it. Although she was just a young girl when first introduced to the painting, her habit of name-dropping those persons deemed to have fine artistic taste had been well honed through the years and provided her an edge over most of the other wives.

So, when the trip to Europe was derailed, she was more than disappointed. Her tolerance for the mundane had been exceeded. Early in her war efforts, she accompanied Mrs. Col. Ellwood T. Reilly in raising funds intended for provisions and medicine to aid wounded and sick soldiers. But the cry for help was far-reaching, and the need was greater than they had at first imagined. Appeals came from hospitals, prisons, widows, and orphans. The call for charity was as rampant as the diseases incurred by war. Soldiers' Aid Societies, Sewing Circles, and Societies for Relief filled the shortages as women's participation was organized in every village, town, and city. The war had given Sydney a purpose and an opportunity to feel self-worth. But as soon as the war had ended, she resumed her role as the society lady she wished to be and was ready for a trip across the Atlantic.

Her husband, although not a young man, believed it was his patriotic duty to enlist and had joined up with a unit of field surgeons. Unprepared for what lay ahead; his skills and resourcefulness were quickly tested. On one occasion, amid heavy skirmishes, the medical supplies had not arrived. Enemy reinforcements had prevented the wagons from getting through the lines. There was no sleep that night as artillery and shelling were as thick as locust. The wounded lay amongst the groans of the dying, and in the darkness, the battle raged. Those injured soldiers that could be carried off to the field hospital were cared for by the impressionable Dr. Bushnell who felt as impotent as the dwindling oil in his lantern.

Stopping the hemorrhages, cauterizing the tissue, but without bandages? His mind whirled as more wounded and dying filled the tent. The smell of burned flesh and ether was potent. He was losing himself to the childish musings of "I wish we had..." and wiping the wounded soldier's blood off his hands, the disgusted doctor muttered angrily over feeling helpless. A middle-aged orderly wearing horned-rimmed glasses spoke to him, but all he could hear was the tying back of the tent's flaps.

Darkness had faded and in its place was a hazy gray mist. Where had the night retreated to? When did it surrender to the day? Death may have withdrawn for the moment but would appear again with the advent of more soldiers, more wounded, more limbs to remove, more skulls to bandage. Bushnell stepped outside and walked around to the washing bucket. The mist was parting with the warmth of the morning, a small but favorable endorsement for the day. But it was what he saw behind the tent that mustered his enthusiasm. "Corporal!" he commanded, pointing across the ditch. "That cornfield, get your men and start husking!"

"Sir?" was the reply, with a clear sense of misunderstanding. In the midst of this disaster such an order seemed more than just odd but rather irresponsible.

Ignoring the soldier's tone, he gave the order again. "Quickly now, bring back only the husks, they'll make fine bandages until our supplies can get through."

The doctor moralized the war. He identified with having served his country, but now a decade later, just how much good was he doing in this lunatic asylum?

———•———

Sydney was bored and disillusioned. Her place in society was little more than a footnote, and the receptions and parties she hosted made her all the unhappier. Letters from overseas just fueled her jealousy; it should have been her flitting from country to country; she should be the subject of society pages or the very least living in New York City. However, she made do with the cramped living quarters and the ill-trained help. By virtue of their housing being part of Richard's contract, she could not really complain. But it was oh, so hard not to.

"Darling," she said and pressed the teacup to her lips. Sydney used that term of endearment when she wanted something, and her husband knew it. "Darling, what would you think about me coming to help at the hospital?"

Dr. Bushnell was buttering his morning toast, but hearing her suggestion, his fingers slipped, and the knife fell onto the neatly pressed table linen. "Don't worry 'bout that," cried the housekeeper. And using the hem of her apron, she dappled the butter stain as if she were cleaning a wound.

"Lucretia, please. Dr. Bushnell doesn't need all that fussing. Go into the kitchen and get him a fresh plate of toast," compelled his wife. But the doctor simply waved his hand at the doughty woman not to bother and picked up where he had been, buttering the perfectly intact piece of toast. His wife had a bad habit of being wasteful, even during the lean years of the war. "Well, what do you think?"

He knew better than to ignore her ridiculous request and gave it a perfunctory pondering. "What did you have in mind?" he asked putting the question back at her. He did not wish to say aloud, but the idea of having to work with the lunatics and his wife, it was all too much to think about.

"I thought maybe I could help you." She smiled and turned to Lucretia, her cup raised in anticipation of having the portly woman serve her a bit more tea. Sadly, the woman did not take the cue whereupon Sydney made a most annoying sound by clearing of her throat, the prompt she had told the household staff to mean, "Look at me." After a few guttural throat clearings, Lucretia stepped livelier and filled the teacup, and Dr. Bushnell's too, despite the fact he was quite satiated.

"Help me do what, Dear?" Now it was his turn to return the fictitious endearment. His was calling Sydney, "Dear."

"You know, with the papers. I could file your papers."

"That would be good," he said, "but we have Mr. Vole to do that sort of thing."

"Vole? I don't recall a Mr. Vole on your staff? Is he new?" Like unraveling a knit sweater, Sydney tried to fasten herself into the thick of all things.

"He has been with us for several years; a veteran."

"Who isn't," the annoyed wife smirked.

"Well there is Josiah, I'm pretty sure he was too old to fight," the Doctor was venturing into dangerous territory.

"Richard! Are trying to make me mad?" she asked and wagged her finger at the man.

"No, Dear, I would never do that. I am sure that if you come down, say around noontime, I could find something for you to do." He knew he would regret this and hoped that perhaps she might forget.

"Noon, you heard that, Lucretia, noon!"

"Yes, Ma'am, I heard noon." A moment of contemplation fell over the woman, and she rang out, "the same as twelve o'clock!"

However, neither of the two diners reacted to the maid's revelation for each was steeped in their own thoughts; Sydney, on what she should wear, and Richard Bushnell, on how to survive his noon appointment. All the while Lucretia was quite pleased with herself for making the association of noon and twelve o'clock as she busied herself sweeping up the crumbs that had settled around the doctor's chair.

Sydney arrived a few minutes after noon giving the hopeful doctor enough wait time to believe she had changed her plans, however, as luck never seemed to be on his side, several tepid raps on the door alerted him to her arrival. "Come in," he said forcing some enthusiasm into a reluctant reply.

"It's Mrs. Bushnell, Sir," announced Vole. "Are you free?" But before he could answer the brassy woman slid between the thin assistant and the half-open door.

"He's expecting me!" she announced and with a smile, she kissed her husband on the cheek and settled herself comfortably on the champagne colored settee.

"Should I hold your 12:30, Sir?" the frail man asked, looking at the woman like a spider eyes a fly.

"I'll let you know Vole, thank you."

It was uncomfortably warm, and despite the stuffiness, the windows were tightly shut, and the drapes were drawn as if it were a funeral parlor. Mrs. Bushnell fanned herself with her gloves and then wiped her brow with a silk handkerchief she pulled from her sleeve.

Dr. Bushnell was not a harsh man, just busy. He looked at his wife and tried to be sympathetic towards her. Sentimentality bubbled to the forefront. The war had stolen her youth, but it did not steal her spirit or her beauty. She was the same women that shared long walks along the edge of the river with him. It was their special place once lined by oak with streamers of ornamental moss shading the path that led to a white-washed chapel. That was a while ago. It was no longer a place one would stroll. All the trees had been razed and cut up for firewood. The chapel walls were torn down and split for timber. In war, the winters are colder.

"So, you are here," the Doctor commenced gathering his composure. "As you can see," he said gliding his hand around the room as if he were a maître d', "things are quite in order."

She nodded. "Quite." She leaned back casually and then erupted as if having been tickled. "There was a man when I came in, a sorry looking fellow standing by the gate."

"We have an entire population of sorry looking fellows," replied the Doctor.

"Yes, I suppose you do," she said regrettably. However, her sympathy was soon overshadowed by her interest in her immediate mission. Getting up from her comfortable position, she sallied towards the over-burdened desk and with both hands resting on the edge leaned over. "Darling, have you thought about my idea."

"Nothing more has entered my mind since breakfast," he assured her. His mustache twitched like a rabbit's whiskers when confronted by noise.

"And?" she said.

"And frankly, I believe," he hesitated a moment and stood up from his grand chair and walked around to the front; an obvious ploy to stall for he had not any plan nor any intention of concocting a job for the eager but medically unskilled woman. He cleared his throat and slid his finger across his mustache. "I believe you would be wasting your time here. Your talents are far better suited in, perhaps, the arena of..." he was not sure what would come out of his mouth.

"Woman's suffrage?" she smiled and batted her eyes.

"Woman's suffrage!" he exclaimed. Suddenly everything began to fall into place. Why she didn't have any intention of wanting a job. By being turned down at the asylum, he would have no recourse but to agree to her, her... her shameful scheme!

"Now, Richard, hear me out before you get upset!" But that ship had sailed for the idea of his wife parading around with signs, bullhorns and the like; it was too much. Too much. Had he not paid his dues? Had the war taken from him not only his time, his livelihood; but now in the aftermath, it had impregnated the opposite sex with ideas of equality! It was too much to think about.

"Darling, you look positively flushed! Here, let me open a window!" And with a slip of her hand, she pulled open the shades and allowed the light to fall upon them as if they were now standing in the moonlight.

"Sydney," he protested, "I cannot have you lobbying against what is simply good common sense. Aren't you happy?" he stammered.

The dull room could not have been a more perfect setting had she put herself on a soapbox in the middle of the street. "This is precisely why I have decided to make my voice heard," she proclaimed. "Why the very fact that the government has left out women again! You would think that with all the lobbying something would have changed, but oh no! Congress still failed to include women in the provisions of the 14th and 15th Amendments. No, no, we have been patient far too long!" Tapping her foot like a disappointed mother, she summoned for an immediate response.

But the poor man had nothing on his plate, and like a beaten dog he flopped down on the chair. He knew that her will was stronger than his. He could fight with her or just let it take its course. His instinct went with the latter. "Well, Dear, I suppose if this is important to you," he said. "Who am I to stand before progress. But let me be put on record that I am not in favor, not the least bit."

"Oh Richard, you are a darling!" she squealed. "Don't fret; I promise not to have your name ever appear in the paper!" And with a quick peck on the cheek, she grabbed her gloves and dashed out calling for Vole to get her a carriage.

"Name in the paper?" he repeated his thoughts aloud. A sudden feeling of deep regret overpowered his already sour disposition as he drew the drapes closed, returning him to his cocoon of familiarity.

————•————

There were three short raps on the door. "Sir, I have your afternoon schedule." The door was pushed open far enough for Doctor Bushnell to see Vole waiting with a leather satchel.

He nodded, and dutifully the gangly secretary entered the room and lay the agenda on the desk. "You are scheduled to make rounds at 2 p.m.," he said reinforcing its importance by placing his finger on the line. We have had some problems with one of our attendants playing rough with a few of the male patients." "Rough" was a code generally to mean abusive. The doctor nodded that he understood. "And then there is this." Vole again pressed his finger on the line which read 4:00.

"I thought we took care of this matter," replied Bushnell. He opened his desk and pulled out his private calendar. Flipping back several months, he scanned his sketchy notes. "There, yes, we already had a unanimous opinion about restraints. I don't see why we need another discussion." But his words were only met with the deadpan eyes of Vole whose opinion amounted to little more than if a dormouse had been present.

"What would you like me to do?" questioned the frail man.

"Leave me to my work, will you Vole," he was irritated, but there was no reason to take it out on the deliverer.

"Very well, Sir?" Vole said snapping up the satchel. He then looked at the Doctor and then up at the wall clock. Time was of the utmost importance to the secretary and any deviation from punctuality caused him a great deal of discomfort. He hoped he would not have to return with a reminder of the 2:00 appointment.

Chapter 8

Flora pulled the door open and placed the carrot before the new brown rabbit. "There you are Mr. Wiggles," she exclaimed and laughed at its name. The frightened animal twitched its nose and waited until the hatch was shut tight before starting to eat. "See him in there, Asa? Our new bunny." Flora stepped aside to let the man peer in. He poked his finger through the grates and wiggled it, but the rabbit backed cautiously away from the protruding object. "Call his name, Asa!" the child laughed. "It's Mr. Wiggles!" But the curious man did not have any desire to call the animal's name; rather he pulled his finger out of the hole and began to unbolt the latch. "No, Asa! No!" Flora squealed. "Mr. Wiggles just got here!" Pushing his hands away, the child stepped between him and the hutch with the desire of keeping the rabbit in. "No, Asa!" she said coldly. "He needs to stay in here. Now," she noted firmly. "Let's go back to the garden and pull another carrot for Mr. Wiggles." This time she did not laugh when she announced its name.

Asa drew away from the hutch and followed the child towards the garden. On this occasion, her words became transfixed in his mind displacing him to another time. *"He needs to stay in here!" A bowl of gray liquid: soup, gruel? He wasn't sure what it was. It had been set before him, but before*

he could lift it to his lips, several pairs of greedy hands shoved it away, tipping
it over. He sat dumbfounded as the gruel flooded the table and spilled onto the
floor. A fight over the toppled broth had broken out, and as the liquid spread, the
fools grappled and spat at one another until they tired themselves out and began
to lick the floor. No one in authority seemed to care; no one tried to maintain any
order. It was only when he attempted to exit through the door did an authority
interpose. "You need to say in here!" The gentle man did not understand why he
could not leave. He had done no harm, no malice, no injustice to anyone. The
room was a chaotic mixture of the dejected, all were without sound mind, and all
were just the shell of a human form. The dead on the battlefield, as maimed and
as dismembered and scorched as he remembered were still men with the spirit of
the living, but these pathetic creatures were lost.

Asa did not follow the little girl to the garden but took the path to
the shed. "Come on, Asa!" cried Flora. She was kneeling before a row of
carrots eagerly waiting to let him pull one for Mr. Wiggles. "Where are
you going, now?" an exasperated Flora moaned, and with a pouty frown
scrambled to her feet to go after him. Among the sundry items in the
shed, he picked through several kinds of vessels until reaching around on
the highest wooden shelf; he came across a small tin cup. It was relegated
to the refuse items, usable for gardening but not kitchenware. Satisfied
with its ability to balance without tipping, he brought it over to the pump,
filled it half-way up with water, and then carefully carried it out towards
the hutch. Flora scampered ahead, delighted with Asa's ingenuity. "Oh,
Asa, what a great idea! Here, Mr. Wiggles!" she announced and laughed,
saying "wiggles" again for good measure. This time she did not hesitate
to allow the latch to be opened and watched with an eye on the man as
he placed the cup of water alongside the carrot. Then, without delay, she
locked the hatch again and turned. "That was very nice, Asa. Very nice,
indeed." The man did not reciprocate although she suspected that she saw
a measure of satisfaction in his eyes. "He is safe in here, Asa."

"You are safe in here, Asa," said the echo. He blinked, and so did the rabbit.

Flora meandered about the garden talking to anything and everything. She was delighted with nature and with each blade of grass and each flower that bloomed she accompanied its arrival with affection. Asa trailed slowly behind but made no mind to his surroundings except for an occasional interruption as he swatted a gnat or stopped to ponder what was beyond the wooden fence.

Boundaries had come between him and his freedom in all parts of his life. Some boundaries had been established by a threat and others had been obstructed by a wall, and then there were those natural ones that came with man's limitations. He was accustomed to being on one side or another, and as he placed his hands on the fence rail, he silently sighed. Flora tip-toed past the rabbit hutch, sure that the small creature was napping after having ingested such a grand carrot. "Shhhh, don't make a sound, it's asleep." Then she waved her hand for him to follow her back to the house.

Asa nodded "yes," but not before peering into the hutch would he continue to the house. The rabbit was not asleep but instead stared back with its red eyes and twitched nervously. The carrot had been eaten, a few black droppings were scattered on its hay-bed, and the water cup remained upright. He leaned his forehead against the wooden planks. The brown rabbit appeared to tremble. Asa moved his head slowly away and placed his flat palm up against the open grid. His heart beat hard and fast, and his mouth grew dry. He bent down again and strained into the dark hutch to see the rabbit. Its crimson eyes glowed, its nose flickered, and its filament-like-whiskers twitched. Asa opened his lips but could not find his voice. He hit his hand against the grate, and the rabbit flinched, backing up as far as it could go for there was no exit, no way out, except for the latched door. Asa kneeled and put his face up to the opening just as a light breeze blew, carrying away with it a promise.

The moving train belched smoke as it bored through the third hour of the night and all signs of life were smeared black. But looking from the outside in, the lantern-light cast a ghoulish shadow of three men playing cards. The night was ticking by leaving nothing in its wake but the expectation of day; while in-between the shuffling of the deck the wind reminded them that they were not alone. They had set the stakes at a penny, but as the night grew longer boredom dictated that they establish a more fitting set of winnings. But none had much to offer the other on account of their lack of money and property. So they talked more than they bet knowing idle chatter can distract a concentrating man.

"I never did find the son-of-a-bitch that shot off my legs."

"I don't imagine you would seeing as you lost them in battle," laughed Dennet.

"Well, I was determined. After the war, I tried, traveled to different towns asking folks if they knew any fellah that might have been braggin' that he'd shot off a leg and a foot. But after a year or so, folks were tired of me hanging around." He pulled a card from the deck and mulled over his new hand.

"What happened?" Dennet asked. He had already folded and was losing interest in the game; with not much to win it was a waste of time although time was all he owned right now.

"I was sentenced to prison for loitering. But before they took me away, I hid in a railcar and never been caught since. I ain't got nothin'," he exclaimed and slapped his cards down in disgust.

"So, you're kind of a traveling man," remarked Lucas with sarcasm and pulled the meager winnings to his side of the floor.

"I like to think of myself as an adventurer. I seen lots of men come and go; like my connection." He grinned like a cat.

Dennet split the cards into two piles and shuffled the deck. He slipped the top card to the bottom and then began to distribute five to each player. He leaned against his knee and let his eyes fall upon his hand. He had two of a kind. "Here, in this boxcar?" He repeated the words under his breath.

"You're full of shit!" cried Lucas.

"Don't matter if you believe me or not," said the wretch and picked through his fanned cards repositioning them as if they were a floral arrangement. "But I've been making a living right here. Hell, met some fine men, fine men. Okay, maybe a little loco but not more than anyone else out there!" He crowed and pointed to the open door.

"Connection, there was that word again," Dennet thought. "You've been braggin' a whole lot about your connections. Tell you what, why don't we play for some big stakes." There was a gleam in his eyes that in the dimly lit car appeared almost demonic.

"Well, what did you have in mind seeing as I have the only thing of value," the wretch said coolly. One could tell that he had been propositioned before.

Lucas glared at his brother, however, decided not to interfere with the younger man's game plan. "We'll cut the cards, high card wins. If you lose, I get the name of your connection. If I lose, you can have my pinkie."

Lucas's eyes widened in horror. He turned to Dennet with a start, shuddering beneath the thought of such a grotesque wager; however, the determined look and calm demeanor of his brother made him realize that there was no point in interfering.

The cripple grinned exposing his toothless jaw, "Both pinkies!" he screamed. "I want them both!"

A warm gust of wind swallowed all the air and casually blew it outside as if it were exhaling smoke from a cigarette. The wheels rumbled and squeaked moving steadily along the tracks, and a hint of green made an outline behind the veil of darkness. Night began to make room for the day.

Lucas could no longer contain himself, "Damn stupid bet!" he said. "Damn stupid!"

"It's too late," squealed the cripple. "He can't back down now!"

"I have no reason to back down," agreed Dennet. He looked at his hands and wiggled his fingers. "The pinkies for your connection. But first, you have to write it down."

"Fine, fine!" the cantankerous man agreed and slid himself across the floor where he retrieved his satchel. He leaned further forward, unbuckled the strap, and rooted inside the pouch until he extricated a piece of graphite and paper. He lay the paper on the ground and tried to smooth out the wrinkles. Then with square, artless letters, he began to write. When he was finished, he folded the paper in half.

"And the blonde!" exclaimed Dennet. "I want the blonde."

The wretched man looked up and grimaced, but the look on Dennet's face read more firmly than his reluctance. "The blonde and my connection to your two pinkies." He nodded and sliding towards the two travelers set the folded paper in the wager pile and slid the Bowie knife out of its sheath and placed it on top. "We'll use that," he said. "It'll make a clean cut."

"Pretty sure of yourself, aren't you?" Lucas announced. The limbless man smiled, delighted at the prospect of his win.

The landscape, a green and brown cutout against the slate sky whisked by with undetermined urgency. Dennet stood up and looked outside. He held on to the doorframe and watched as the morning released runners of light "Ready?" the words were harsh and guttural.

He turned and steadied himself before walking back over to the limbless man.

Lucas held the deck in his hands. He tried to hold them steady, but his fingers did not wish to obey. He split the deck in half and shuffled them half-dozen time. "Enough!" whined the wretch and put his hand up for him to stop.

"Seems to me," said Lucas, eyeing the broken man, "we don't even know your name."

"It's Jeremiah, Jeremiah Johnson."

"Okay then, Jeremiah," he announced handing over the deck. "Cut them!"

There was a moment of euphoric anticipation he wished to savor; the same feeling one gets before tossing a pair of dice or spinning the roulette wheel. Taking the cards, he closed his eyes and with his left hand split the deck in half, turned the top half over, and then opened his eyes. Immediately they widened as the elation of having picked such a high card swept through his body. A one-eyed Jack! The knave's smug profile stared at them with its black outlined-eye, like that of a fish. "Ohhhh! Look!" he cried holding the card up above his head and waving it as if it were a banner. Surely had the man had legs, he would have paraded around. "Your turn!" he snapped and handed the full deck back to Lucas.

The elder looked at the younger and then back to the cards. Hastily he set them into two piles, crossed himself as if he were before the Virgin Mary, and then began to shuffle. The cards slipped through his fingers with ease, too easily he thought. Lucas glanced at the broken man's appearance; a strained expression now dominated all the facial muscles accentuating the furrow between his brows and a line of perspiration beading above them. As for Dennet, he was composed, almost too reserved for a man that was in the throes of losing his appendages. The knife's blade was almost nine inches long with a chipped tip and most likely had been taken from a dead soldier for the initials on the wooden handle read L.D.

"Whose, L.D.?" asked Lucas. His eyes ran from the knife handle to the tense man.

Jerimiah's head snapped towards the speaker as if it had been mechanically yanked. "L.D.?" He repeated the question.

"On the handle." Lucas picked up the knife and showed it up.

The man shrugged and laughed. "Don't know," he said. Lucas ran his fingers over the crudely carved initials. He knew that in less than a second, he could plunge the blade into the throat of this contemptuous creature, the same amount of time it may have taken for him to have picked it off the dead soldier before slipping it into his sheath. He hated this cretin even more now. "Let's get on with the wager!" Jeremiah demanded. "It's almost daybreak!" So it was that no one had noticed the fledgling candle had snuffed itself out and the boxcar, once as obscure as night, was a morbid gray. The train rolled up and around the wooly hillside like a clumsy caterpillar unconcerned with the freeloaders onboard.

Lucas released the knife and placed it reluctantly back. The cards lay on the floor, ready to be cut. Dennet reached across and picked them up. He did not look away but kept his stare on the deck. His heart pounded, but he was determined not to show any fear. He glanced around the floor, first at the polished blade, then to the stubs of what was once a leg and foot stretched-out on the floor, and then over to his brother's sole-worn boots. Remarkably his hands did not tremble but instead firmly planted around the cards like a pair of roots holding the earth. With his fingers pinched against the top half of the deck, he slowly pulled upward like he was removing a weed. He leaned into the cards and turned it slowly over so only he could see.

"What is it?" screamed the wretch. The anticipation was stifling. Suddenly his ability to breathe had been interrupted. Expectation consumed all the air as if filling a balloon.

Dennet raised his head; his face was the same pallid color it had turned during the first battle he fought in. "Well," said his brother and grabbing his hand, he pried the cards away and turned them over for all to see.

"What the devil is that!" squealed the wretched man.

"Why it's the joker!" cried Lucas.

"The what?" repeated Jeremiah

"It's a joker, all card decks have a joker in them!" explained Dennet confidently. "See," he said and flipped over the card to show that it wore the same design on the back like all the other suits in the deck. It was undeniably a match.

"Well, I'll be damned!" The limbless man examined the cards with much bewilderment. "What's it mean?"

"It means we got this deck off a pair of Germans!" grinned Dennet. He saw the man was dumbfounded. "Obviously you never played Euchre before or ever met up with any Germans. Let's just say it's the trump card! Let's just say," he smiled deviously, "I win!"

The loser was uncommonly quiet while the idea of him being duped set in. "Not so fast, not so fast!" exclaimed the man.

But before he could protest anymore, the train made an abrupt twist and veered as it rounded the corner. All three men toppled over, the knife and cards slid across the floor while the papers, now freed from beneath the weight of the weapon, went helter-skelter too. Dennet scrambled to retrieve the folded note while the limbless man tried to get his bearings, and Lucas confiscated Jerimiah's pack.

"The blonde," Lucas demanded and tossed the satchel over. By now the limbless man knew he was beaten. He looked through his portfolio and found a small envelope. He opened it up, lifted it to his lips and kissed the photograph. "This means we're business partners!" he exclaimed. For without me you got nothin'!"

Dennet opened the slip of paper and read the name to himself. Looking over at his brother, he then read the name aloud. "Bushnell."

The wretched man wiped his face with his filthy sleeve and shifted positions like a tired dog before lying down.

Chapter 9

"**I**f hell were cold, this would be hell!" complained the first mate. All those around him nodded in agreement; to lift away the wool from their lips would be inviting frostbite. Never had the crew seen or felt the sea to be more wretched, never had they encountered more misery than what they were enduring on this voyage. The roar of thunder had proceeded the siege, and like a cork in boiling water, the ship bobbled and rolled. Black waves lifted the vessel and then plunged her back down. There was little mercy for the crew as they labored vigorously, each man on deck kept his eyes on another, lest a mate slipped overboard. The water had found its way below deck as the ocean found its way in through the cracks and crevices, leaking down upon the berths and bedding.

"We're passing through the sailors' graveyard." mumbled the sailor. His hands wrapped in shredded cloth wore the first stages of the inevitable marking of frostbite, the skin raw and stiff.

"Graveyard?" questioned the youth.

"Shut up with yer talk of death and drink your rum!" commanded the tipsy sailor. He leaned his head against the planked table and as the ship rocked from port to starboard he skillfully slid his mug to the opposite side preventing him from losing even a drop. This was a talent he had acquired by way of many previous voyages, earning him his sea legs.

But no one agreed with the drunk, and as the boy sought some confirmation, he could find none, for all had turned their eyes away.

"The sea, she likes to chew things up, a regular cur!" the mate laughed. "I bet you'd like to see an acre of wooded pine right now, wouldn't ya boy!" wheedled the sailor. "I bet you'd like that real fine!" The boy flashed a frightened appeal around the room, but no one stirred.

"Shut up!" shouted the drunk and as he lifted his capped head only a pair of bloodshot pupils were revealed for his face was bound in a tartan's scarf of tattered wool. The boy trembled again for such a stare could only affirm his greatest fear.

"All ships have a few aboard that are cursed." The sailor beckoned for the youngest mate to come towards him. Reluctantly the boy rose from his spot and weeded his way around the decrepit table. The cabin was small, stinking from man and beast. Swinging from a hook was a lantern, offering its meager contribution of light. "Why it's more than being cursed," the stinking man hissed, "it's damnation!" His declaration fell upon the men like the strong breath of a storm. Only the drunk laughed in defiance, but none of the superstitious men dared. It was true, there were a few among them deserving of such an ill-fated journey. "Show the slightest fear, and it will be your death," he exclaimed. "We're hedged in by the sea, a mountain of water so high and so vast; there is nowhere else to go but ride this one out!" And as he spoke the vessel was overpowered, devoured by a wave that wished to swallow her whole, and only the sturdiness of her hull proved itself to defy Poseidon's wishes.

Darkness consumed the cabin as the tumultuous cries from above sent the men scrambling up the ladder. All was awash, a storm so ferocious had erupted over the pitiless men. "Shorten the sails," commanded the Captain, "shorten the damn sails!" and as the trembling boy braced himself, he wondered who had relieved the Captain at the helm. Assaulted by hail and wind, the bitter cold tore at the sailors, each too frantic and too busy to shiver. Hands and faces once hidden behind scarves and cloth were exposed. The wind howled as the sails slapped those who desperately tried to bring them down. There had been no warning, no rising or falling of distant moans of the sea, only a wall of slate clouds that fell from the heavens down to the horizon. The sound of the sea was more frightening than the swells, and she roared like a jungle animal one cannot spot but induces a panic more fearful than if one could see it.

The ship tipped upward, tilting back on its stern as a great wave thrust over them in a colossal shower. Those not tied-in were thrust forward, arms flaying, grasping for anything to hold on to. The ship propelled downward, striking the crest. The wind unforgiving, the sides of the ship boiled over with seawater, the only compassion was its short-lived fury. And when it was over even the drunkard knew the inevitable, damnation had not been reserved for a few, but for many.

Had the owners of the *Superior* been aware of the Captain's true plans, the audacious voyage would have never been authorized. As far as they understood this was to be only a ten-month voyage to South America. But two years prior, in 1845, while recuperating from an injury in a remote town in Siberia, several Russian naval officers took Roys into their confidence; the waters in the Bering Strait were populated with more whales than he could ever imagine. Purchasing charts from the Russians, the intrigued captain returned to Sag Harbor with new ambitions. And now, in the throes of a storm of such great magnitude, the *Superior's* destination into forbidden waters seemed inconceivable. No whaling ship had ever traveled so far north. Yet the inevitable passage was presently unbeknownst to the crew, and for all intents and purposes, illegal. Like the others, when Neville Young decided to join the illustrious Captain, he too did not know that the restocking of provisions in the Hawaiian Islands was not to prepare homeward, but for the Alaskan summer. Missing in

the equation was that the actual course was charted through the Bering
Straits and upward into the Arctic Ocean to continue the hunt until the
fall storms and ice forces the crew to abandon southward.

The ship rocked blandly, and the once reefed sails were now raised
giving themselves entirely to the wind. The gale forces that had tri-
umphed over all the water had withered away. The temperament of the
day changed from vengeful, giving a pardon to the vessel that dared to
wander into the dominion of a tempest. The boy, now having been initiated by his first storm, leaned against the railing with a new-found respect
for his surroundings. The day still wore its gray coating, but it was a softer
shade having dispersed all the water from the black clouds. A squadron
of gulls flew overhead, some now feeling restless and slicing the ocean
with their sharp beaks looking for crustaceans that had been churned and
whipped up to the surface. "Where did they go?" asked the boy to the
sailor smoking his pipe. He pointed at the fleet of birds.

Neville raised his eyes to the clearing sky and took several long
puffs. "Some say they are carrying souls," he said. He puffed more vigorously but the pipe had given up on him, and it hung limply against his
lip. "So I suppose they are flying back from a shipwreck." The young mate
shivered with the man's words when his attention was interrupted by a
determined tapping. The first mate was hammering something above the
cabin-door.

"Too little too late," remarked Neville and led the boy's interest
pointing with his pipe to the horseshoe. It was met with a meek smile of
approval. "What's ya name, son?" asked Neville.

An unexpected look of distrust overcame the boy. What was once
a feeling of calm was exchanged by overwhelming uncertainty. He dared
not look directly at the man and spoke in a low voice so that only the man
could hear his response, "It's Jo."

"Well Jo, when you speak to a man you need to look up," he directed and lifted the chin of the young boy. Not more than thirteen, he was a tow-headed child who cowered at the mere challenge of showing his face. But the grip on his chin was stronger than the child's will, and he was forced to turn his eyes upward. Fearing reprisal, he had no choice but to show the sailor his secret and being as he was not of quick of mind or wit, adding to the gruffness of Neville's question, all refusals resonated with a promise of a lashing if he did not reply.

But Neville acted with clemency towards the boy. After all, he had a son of his own and hoped that someone would offer the same understanding to his boy if a similar misfortune were to befall him. Having been born with one eye blue and the other violet, Jo was destined for a voyage of ill-treatment and suspicion. Simply put, having these eyes was purely bad luck.

"Jo is a fine name," Neville said and patted the boy on his head with a tinge of fatherly comfort. The young mate was pleased, however, still a bit reticent and hoped this man could be trusted.

———•———

A moment-in-time is a constant measurement like the twenty-four hours it takes the Earth to rotate on its axis. It is always the same yet the impact felt at a given moment can be small or big, tiny or enormous. It can leave one feeling light in thought or heavy with burden, so little like a whisper yet so strong like a hurricane. Jo slept soundly having relinquished his secret while upon Neville it was resting heavily. The man was not convinced that he was truly devoid of harboring suspicions. Just perhaps this hapless 'Jonah' might bring to pass a parcel of bad luck. On-the-other-hand, he had made a promise, which outweighed any superstitious thoughts. It was necessary for him to think of his newfound knowledge in the same way a slice of bread falls buttered side down in the soot, an unfortunate set of circumstances. Like testimony given and pronounced circumstantial, so is it that the boy cannot be convicted as the cause of the great storm.

Neville wondered if he had been too hasty in taking up a friendship based solely on his sympathy towards the youth. He knew very little about the lad and thus decided in the morning to challenge his instincts and find out more. Neville pulled the blanket up over his shoulders and closed his eyes. The ship rocked, and his hammock rocked, and it swayed to and fro. He was pleased that he was not on watch, although after a storm there is an immeasurable pleasure to be found. The stars, the moon, the light tipping off the wave caps; no, perhaps it would not be a bad night to be on watch," he thought. Finally, with the slow grandeur we call sleep, he fell into a slumber, and within a matter of moments, he wandered into a dream. *A confused path of water was plunging over the side of a mountain, and on the edge of this rushing chaos, Neville saw himself stepping from the banks impetuously forward. He started to turn back but felt himself being pushed. He twisted around, slipping off the ledge, rushing down-stream madly, and all-the-while the deadpan stare of the boy with two different colored eyes was fixed upon him.*

The old seaman in the adjoining hammock coughed. Neville winced, slid the blanket over his mouth, and exhaled short static breaths. His heart was beating against his chest. "Jo," he heard himself call back. "Jo, look away, look away!" But no one was there to help him as he was pulled under by the great weight of the falling water.

———·———

Full against the rose-tinted sky the white canvas shook with lethargy as if not wishing to awaken. The vessel glided across the cloud's shadows, rolling in and out, from dark to light. The captain, a leathery-skinned man with hardened features, had earned his rest and now stood on the poop deck, revived and confident. He was conversing with the first mate, a giant of a man who wore an air of superiority that had been secured by his ranking above the other sailors. And though they were in the service of keeping all aspects of the ship in order, neither man was aware of the goings-on deep below in the belly of the ship. But seldom is there a time where peace reigns over the sea, and being that they were seasoned seamen, the mere idea that things were tranquil should have been in itself an omen of devilry. For below deck a cluster of men huddled together, some just having gone off watch and inquiring as to the meaning of this informal gathering.

"I'll tell you what's the matter," groaned the German seaman. "I heard a voice in the dead of night confirming my expectations." Then with a wink of his good eye, for one of the pair had been injured and its lid lay swollen shut started up again. "It's the young mate who calls himself Jo."

The breeze was more energetic now and carried with it the rattle of the great sails above. A copper-faced man with a thin aquiline nose moved in to hear what was going on. His manner, more brutal than curious gave the others reason to heed and allowed him to take his position in the group next to the speaker. "Where did this voice come from?" he asked with skepticism.

"Well, we were all asleep when out of the blackness a cry wakes me. I opened my eyes, but it was too dark to see. But I know what I heard. 'Jo, look away!' Yep, that's exactly what I heard! 'Look away.'"

"Are you sure?" asked the cook; his doubts had been raised to a higher level as the man was becoming even more inebriated.

The drunken German brought his sour face downward meeting it with that of the sailor. "I was visited by the Klabautermann last night. It had been hiding behind the wooden planks since the day the *Superior* was built, and finally, when we crossed over the equator, he came out from hiding. But it was not until last night that he appeared." The drunk paused for a moment and then turned with sunken eyes toward the other man and shook his head. "He spoke to me confirming my suspicions about der Junge, the boy."

"You're a drunken fool, Clas!" and with a hearty slap on the back offered his friend some grog. But the German did not take the drink nor was there any change in his solemn appearance. "Tis not a foolish man's drunken talk," he warned. His voice was low but calmly deliberate. Then he gestured for the other to bow his head again and whispered. "The Klabautermann, it's a trickster, but his truth comes in the disguise of a small, gray-bearded man as tiny as an elf. Though some claim to see him as a horseman, he's on this very ship in the form I have described. Mark my words or throw me overboard. Look for yourselves; look at the boy's eyes. One blue, the other violet! He will cast an evil eye on you and every-one on this ship!" His voice shuddered with fear and terror contrary to his stalwart appearance. The tale of the Klabautermann sounded like the ramblings of a drunk, but the warning delivered could not be taken lightly. Where the omen came from was not of importance, and in the little time it took to deliver, the flame for the suspicious was fueled.

"I knew it!" crowed the cook. He nodded approvingly and like the others a sudden urge for retribution needled his spirit. His tone now took on a more reserved note in fear that even within the confinement of the cuddy his plan might be overheard. "We must exterminate the boy," he whispered, and with brooding eyes, he challenged any man to defy him.

All wagged their heads in agreement, however, how to execute such a contemptuous act was one that needed more brains than time, an attri-bute the group seemed to lack; all that is except for the cook. For although he was never considered daring, his ability to measure and count, together with his skills as a butcher, the others agreed he was the best candidate to design a scheme. But time was of the essence and seeing as he was expected to prepare the captain's noon meal, he abruptly abdicated his position in the group and threaded his way to the galley set amidships.

The men continued to mumble a few suggestions, but it was finally agreed upon that the only course of action was to rid the ship of the unlucky boy before more trouble could ensue. How the crime would be committed came unanimously when the boatswain's charging voice echoed a cry to "give more sail" for the promise of wind was evident to even a layman's eye. The clouds had gathered once again and were flitting across the sky like an anxious butterfly. "Then it is settled," the hooked-nosed man cawed. He doused the sailors with his brand of terror, brandishing his dagger in a low swooping motion that slit a cut across the billowy blouse of the nearest seaman; a subtle but effective reminder of their sworn secrecy.

————— · —————

The quartermaster teetered on the edge of the crate bare-chested as he mended the rip in his blouse. The tawny man held the needle to his eye and tried to insert the thread back into the narrow slot, holding it firmly between his two nimble fingers. He was muttering to himself with a smattering of protests; grumbles that could be interpreted as complaints more than idle chatter. He was in a hurry and wished not to be disturbed; however, the rocking of the ship made the task at hand more difficult for with each roll of a wave the needle yawed from the stitching. Meanwhile, at the very same time, the cook, who had become privy to the plan, stirred the broth with the same gusto owed to soup served to royalty. How he enjoyed a bit of treachery and the kind he was about to embark upon was the "pièce de résistance"! He laughed as he thought about his choice of terms, gloating to himself that he was a clever man indeed. After all, the true definition of pièce de résistance was "the principal dish of a meal." Regrettably, there was no one aboard that could share in such oblique nuances of the language; except perhaps the Captain. "Another bit of irony," he thought and stirred the gruel with more vigor.

To lay a course demands the energy of the entire crew. From the supreme ruler, the Captain, down to the lowliest swabber its success is as great as their toil. Workers on shore, though obscured by nautical miles, are proportionately essential to the voyage making the livelihood of the seaman and the landlubbers entangled. From the candle-makers to the blacksmith who forged the harpoons, to the rope makers that produced thousands of miles of twisted whale lines, each relied upon the ship's timely return. The practice of using casks of whale oil as currency to pay the wages of some workers, such as teachers and ministers, was not uncommon. Undoubtedly the whaling industry was a profitable and essential business, offering profits three times the initial investment. Wealthy ship owners, as rich as they were, understood this to be a risky enterprise. A sunken ship could account for the loss of more than just seaman; it would also mean the loss of revenue and vessel.

So, with all this in mind, just perhaps the treacherous sailors, the designers of the murderous scheme, were able to justify their actions. But whatever malevolence was running through their minds, without intervention, the boy with the evil eyes would meet his maker.

Neville was standing watch, his cap lowered just above his brow, puffing vigorously on his pipe. His thoughts concentrated on his work, wandering up and over the combing sea. Sighting a whale could relegate him more than favor; it could be lucrative. Rewards for such a find were often quite handsome, which kept every man alert at all times. He pinched his lids and then stared out to where the ocean and the sky melted and thinned, blurring any distinction between upper and lower realms.

The wind lay docile across the sails reviving the smell of salt and brine. Despite the light wind, frequent tacking required the attention of many. A sailor of youthful vigor was sent aloft to free a block trapped between the canvas folds. He was lanky, stronger than he appeared, and as he placed one foot above the other, his arched foot and curled toes seemed to grasp the taut rope like an animal. It was a task he was accustomed to so when he extended his leg up and stepped down with the same motion one does while climbing a ladder; he must have been startled when the fairlead he was stepping onto suddenly broke free. It had not taken him very long to reach the mizzen-topmast for he was as agile as a gray squirrel, yet the unexpected compromise to the rope set his fears in motion. Accompanied by a free-falling cry that struck the deck as abruptly as if he had dropped to Neville's feet, the dangling climber was grasping the halyard with his foot outstretched as far as it could go in anticipation of reaching another sturdy hold. Each sailor's neck was twisted back with chins thrust upward in the direction of the boy, but no one moved. All eyes watched, some mouths agape. Neville turned quickly, and as he started to climb the ropes, he felt a strong clasp of resistance upon his shoulder. "Let him be," sneered the crooked-nosed man. "Your fatherly instinct to help could result in more harm lest you frighten the boy. The lad knows best what to do, don't you think?" Neville quickly digested the suggestion, and though not convinced decided that perhaps the advice was prudent, and he stepped back.

It was a harrowing few moments, each time the barefoot lad attempted to secure a strong brace; he was stymied by too-long-a-reach. He held his breath as the thought of a "lifeline" became all too real. His palms calloused and hardened amassed not enough strength to hold him firmly and with each lapsing moment, they slipped just a bit more inching down the line. Below him, huddled beneath the canvas awning, several men were laying wagers; however, it was evident that those who were betting on a fall had the advantage of time.

"To your right!" cried the cook, who now had come up from the belly of the ship.

"No, the left, the left!" shouted the pock-marked sailor. His eyes gleamed in delight as the boy swayed with indecision.

"I agree, swing to the left, secure your footing!" laughed the man with the swollen eye. "Reach left, reach left!"

The boy's determination to obey was noticeable and with each call of 'go left' or 'reach right' the weight of his body and the tiring of his arms were working against his will. But then, as if a gift from Mother Nature herself was pronounced, a full gust of wind pushed both the rope and boy towards a sturdy line. Feeling himself move, the grateful young mate stretched out his leg and with all the flexibility he could muster, pointed his toes and reached as far as a human leg was able until he felt the top of his foot rest on the free line. Without taking a breath, he leaned forward anticipating his safe approach when the wind, which had carried him to safety, also carried with it the words from below, "Don't look down, don't look down!" The horrified sailor did exactly as he was told not to do and although too far aloft to see the deck clearly, he could feel their menacing stares, and without any warning his grip on the rope suddenly released, plummeting the frightened boy downward. Too frightened to even scream, his silent fall was deafening, landing him face-down on the deck. Several astounded seamen rushed to the spot where he lay motionless; blood trickling out from around his skull, his neck twisted and broken.

An immediate rush of curiosity ensued, and like a hive of bees the swarm of men broke free from their rituals and ran towards the fallen victim. A stout Yankee sailor kneeled beside the boy, and as he started to turn him over he was pushed away, "Don't touch him!" squealed the cook. "You don't want the evil eye on you, do ya?" he warned. Such a statement was more powerful than any moral obligation, and as soon as it was uttered the ring of men began to break apart.

But this much commotion could not be unnoticed and the Captain, a man that rarely meddled in the seaman's affairs, was obliged to investigate the scene. "What's this I hear about evil eyes?" he demanded. Yet when he approached the fallen victim, he could not dispute the remark, acknowledging that the accident was indeed more than unlucky but "a damned unfortunate accident!"

"Yes it was," agreed the crooked-nosed man, hovering over the body as if he were the angel of death himself. A chorus of heads nodded in agreement.

"I think he's dead, Sir," remarked the cook as he tapped the body with the tip of his shoe.

The captain turned his eyes towards the first mate, ignoring the insipid remarks of a crew. "Turn him over, Blake; let's have a look at him." Like hungry peasants waiting for bread, the crew had reassembled, each hoping for a chance to see the unlucky boy's face. Neville had wedged a place in the human ring and leaned his head forward, but his interest was not so much for the dead but rather on the living.

"Finally rid of our bad luck," whispered the cook and elbowed the aquiline-nosed man. The latter grinned and discreetly tapped the sailor to his left. As this signal passed down the line, each seaman felt as if a great burden had been lifted by the demise of the ill-fated crewmember. Without any regard for the victim, Blake rolled the body over. The pool of blood that had been delivered by the broken nose and cracked teeth was growing in size and drenched the scant clothing worn by the fallen youth. The crew's faces were now contorted with confused expressions as the identification of the stricken mate became obvious. Neville watched as the cook's eyes widened with surprise. "It's Rodney," cawed the Yankee. "It's Rodney!" And as the full disclosure became clear, it was apparent that the dead lad was not the intended prey, but a brown-eyed youth.

The Captain ordered the men to disperse as he contemplated the removal of the deceased. One by one they walked away from the prone body to tend to their business until finally, all that remained was the dead mate, a host of noisy seagulls above, and a restless dusting of disappointment.

———•———

"His mother trusted me with him," the Captain remarked. He drummed his fingers with great rapidity against the railing as if keeping time with his thinking. The first mate could see that the Captain was strangely affected by this young sailor's death and was ready to offer his advice when he was interrupted by the man's out-loud thoughts. "His father was a drunkard; she believed the lad would have more of a chance with us than at home," he added looking at the shrouded corpse. Burial at sea was not uncommon, but the accidental death of a shipman always seemed like such a waste. "Well, we can't go on being remorseful, what's done is done," he said shrugging off his responsibility with ease. "Blake," he said to the sailor, "let's get on with it." And with little more than a glance in the dead man's direction, the Captain gestured for the two sailors to throw the body overboard.

Down below in the ship's galley, the cook was flattening dough. He furiously stamped the dough-balls into pancake-like-wafers and lined them up single-file. "You see," he smirked at the aquiline-nosed man, "easy does it. You did a fine job, my friend, a fine job indeed, but it was the wrong boy!"

The murderer grinned unappreciatively, not taking a liking to the sarcastic tone of the cook. His prowess to have shimmied up the lines in the black of night and weaken the rope took more than courage, it took skill. The cook had no right to take offense at him, but he decided he would take that matter up later. Without any mention, both men were wondering the same thing, as were many of the other conspiring seamen. If the body dropped overboard was not Jo, then where could he be? And, if he were hiding, then bad luck was still looming over the ill-fated ship.

———— • ————

Gross negligence was formally entered into the logbook as the weary day stumbled upon several more disastrous episodes. After examination of the vessel, the young mate, Jo, was reported nowhere to be found. However, it was the discovery of a missing row boat which enraged the Captain more than both the missing and dead mates. It was far easier to gain two new crew members than to obtain another boat. "Line them up!" demanded the Captain; his tongue charged with the venom of an Asp. "Line their mangy asses on deck! One of those thieving sailors knows the whereabouts of my boat!" The ship upheld the same tack, and with the light wind, all reefs were turned out, and those men close to the Captain maintained the uninterrupted momentum.

The severity of the crime ordinarily would be met with no leniency. However, the Captain wishing to keep his crew from any mutinous ideas, decided in a most unorthodox measure, a bribe. "As you know by now," he started out, his voice loud and firm, "it appears that we have misplaced two important items." He reviewed the crew as he slowly strode up and back along the deck. "We have confirmed that a young sailor and a small rowboat have gone astray." He hoped that taking a humorous approach might appeal to the men's good nature if they had any. "Naturally, anyone acknowledging whereabouts of either item or the knowledge of any misconduct must surrender this information, and in return, a reward of two gold decocts will be yours." He then lifted from his pocket two gold coins and displayed them above his head for all to see. Silence prevailed, and though the Captain had hoped for an immediate resolution, there was none.

Like a brush fire burning out of control, rumors spread about the ship. For although the crew may come from all walks of life, they had one thing in common, the cunning to put random facts together. And so it became evident that as much as Neville had tried to keep his deed a secret, several "trustworthy" allies breached their allegiance over several grogs of rum.

"We can't have any more accidents," complained the aquiline-nosed man. "Pretty damn smart, him puttin' the kid out to sea. But maybe he did us a favor. We're rid of him, ain't we?"

The cook scowled, "But Neville can't be trusted. He must 'av known of our plan. If he gets to the Captain, we'll hang." Though few in number, the words of the cook lay heavy on the mate. It was obvious that the ship's bad luck was not as easily annulled as they would have liked.

———————•———————

Neville rested in the swaying hammock. The sea air, thick and salty, lay heavily like a moist blanket. The trunks and crates shifted when the ship rolled, making scratching noises that could be confused with rodents foraging for food. The prospect of a storm reshaped his thoughts as he imagined the boy in the dinghy, and he wondered if the choice had been wise. If Jo had remained on board he would have been murdered; his chances of being picked up by another whaler were likely. Neville tried to find a more comfortable position, but the knots in the ropes were digging into his back. He stretched his arms over his head and pushed his feet against the woven hemp trying to redistribute some of his weight off his lower back. He usually had little trouble getting to sleep, but tonight his mind and body could not find peace. Something was unsettling, something that he could not pinpoint, but he knew that he must be on his guard.

———————•———————

The *Superior* darted between the chain of islands until reaching Van Diemen's Land by the path of early light and a good compass. A few hundred miles out before anchoring off this Pacific island, Captain Roys had disclosed to his crew that this port was merely a place to fit out the ship. That their voyage to the Bering Straits would not only supply them with great wealth but indeed their courage would ensure them a place in history. Under the grumblings of a few, the promise of money was far more of an incentive than fear of the unknown was a deterrent. As they made their way toward land, enormous seafaring birds, giant pelicans, flew above the sea and into a line of low hanging clouds that masked the lofty hills and mountains. However beautiful it appeared, the country was scarred.

The discovery of Van Diemen's Land in 1642 is credited to the Dutch commander Abel Jans Tasman, on the authority of General Anthony Van Diemen, Governor of the Dutch Settlements in the Indian Archipelago, and the mighty mercantile enterprise The Dutch East India Company. Upon the approach of the rising mountains in the distance, Tasman anchored his flagship Heemskerck and an armed transport ship Zeehaen. There he set his sights on the new territory and named the island Van Diemen's Land after his comrade and sponsor. However, those who claimed this spectacular land had no regard for the evolution of its native people, inhabitants who had lived in isolation at least 6,000 years before the first Europeans arrived. And though Tasman left no written records of meeting these people, those who followed did.

In 1777, Australia was claimed by Captain Cook for the British with the inclusion of Van Diemen's Land in 1788. Abundant in fish and ample in oysters wedged along its rocky shoreline, its coves hug the coast making a naturally protective port for anchoring ships. In spite of the island's inviting tranquility, its temperament can be misleading. With snow covering the highest peaks most of the year, its mountain ranges create intense winds with turbulence as violent as a hurricane.

The British had decided to establish its colony, Hobart Town, on Van Diemen's Land with two main purposes: (1) to discourage and end any French expansionism that started in the late 1790s, and (2) to relieve Port Jackson's (Sydney Harbor) penal colony of its overflow of criminals, establishing a new place of exile for the most dangerous convicts. In 1788, Britain began transporting its criminals from England to New South Wales. The six-month voyage often claimed the lives of ten percent or more of the human cargo. There was barely six feet of headroom below deck, and the only ventilation was vectored through the hatchway that was often padlocked shut. Infractions were met with lashes, irons, or cramping boxes. Distant and remote, Van Diemen's Land was deemed a perfect location for a prison. As such, convicts, both men and women, some for petty crimes and others for heinous offenses, arrived in mass in contrast to the Aboriginal inhabitants numbering between five and seven thousand. The European invasion augmented the influx of outsiders by land grants issued to law-abiding adventurers. Those that were settled voluntarily or exiled relied on rations shipped from New South Wales.

But by 1806, few ships were stopping with provisions; the region was devastated by rain and floods, and dire conditions had befallen the colonists. Additionally, a military regiment from New South Wales was permitted to take charge of the commissary and greedily hiked the prices of goods up 500 percent. The convicts and settlers had little recourse, whereby many were now starving. Ultimately the majority took matters into their own hands by hunting the indigenous people's staple animal, the kangaroo. The defenseless marsupial was no match for dogs and guns, and the kangaroo population declined with devastating consequences. Lands that were hunting grounds for the Aborigines were cleared, and in very little time the settlers acted out in violence against the native people. Lawlessness and evil plagued the island, and in this seemingly remote region of the world, atrocious crimes were routinely committed. During these early years, European settlers were inflicting cruelty on the Aboriginals. As time went on hostilities grew, and European colonists secured their place by confiscating the land primarily for sheep herding. The infiltration of sheep farms encroaching on the natural kangaroo hunting grounds of the natives had escalated in addition to the already growing conflicts. As the tensions rose and fighting ensued, Governor George Arthur declared the native men were fair game and could be eliminated by whatever force was needed. By 1832 a collective atrocity was enforced; the Europeans governing Van Diemen's Land forced the remaining Aboriginal people out of their country, sending them to relocate to Flinders Island.

Preceded by a series of sharp squalls, the winds had finally died away, and the sea was as calm as a sleeping giant. Water slapped against the ship breaking the silence of a gray morning. The hull pitched lightly, receiving her motion from the rise and fall of the waves. He thought of his wife and his son, his home, and pleasures of family life awaiting him. "They would like this," Neville decided as he looked out at the blue mountains. But his thoughts quickly turned to his task when a muscular fellow with copper skin and bright blue tattooing that reached from his neck to his wrists walked out of the shadows. The sailor unfolded his arms and made himself present. Neville addressed the man with a "good morning," and received a favorable nod. His watch was over, and with a yawn, they exchanged positions. The man never spoke a word, and Neville remembered this was the Mali they called Swan, nicknamed for the rare mute bird.

"How 'bout some crowdie?" asked the cook as Neville navigated through the cramped galley. "I suppose you'll be one of the first goin' ashore." His question was answered with an affirmative nod to both the porridge and the imminent departure. He scooped up a generous helping and plopped it into a bowl. "Looks like a fine day," the cook said, his conversation uncommonly jovial for such a hardened man. And though he may have appeared to be kindly, he was hiding behind a charade which could change expressions as fast as the wind could change directions. He was wearing the remnants of the yesterday's disappointment, clothed in revenge but crowned in false empathy. "Eat up, eat up," he exclaimed and filled the half-eaten bowl with another spoonful from the large pot cradled above the burning embers. A hideous squeal slipped in from the adjacent cabin and drew an instant cringe of disgust. "The sow will make a grand dinner for the Captain, don't you think?" he asked acknowledging the cry. Neville never looked up from spooning his breakfast but nodded. He salivated with the idea of meat and licked the sides of his bowl like a dog until there was not a trace of porridge left. He pushed the dish away and then stood up, wiping his mouth with his sleeve. "Thanks."

"Sure ya don't want a little more?" the cook asked, and ran his index finger over his molar, rolling it around until he removed a wedged piece of barley. Pleased with the find, he licked his finger, swallowed, and grinned. For an instant it seemed as if he was going to speak, but instead, there was a gleam in the cook's eyes that caused Neville to be suspicious. The generosity of the cook and his good humor was out of character with the man's usual abusive personality.

"No, had enough," Neville said. "Goin' up for a smoke," and dug his pipe out of his pocket and backed away as one would with an unfriendly dog. A series of coarse laughs followed Neville up the narrow companion-way, and when he raised the hatch, he wondered if he had been ratted-out as Jo's savior.

On the heels of first light, three jolly boats set out for shore. A waddle of web-footed penguins was loitering along the rocks like short men and women dressed in their best tailor-made suits and pinafores. Walking upright on their little legs, they eyed the sailors with curious side-glances. There was a uniformed degree of contentment as the men rowed. Most were weathered seamen, but even for these Jack Tars, legends of the lengthy journey to the Arctic were unfamiliar to their ears. The voyage to the Bering Strait was to be dangerous, sailing to a region of the earth where night and day ripples into one, where the vast darkness of the ocean is like an endless vault. There days become months and keeping count will only redeem freedom from the past. Neville turned inward with this sublime revelation; it was daunting. Yet, his companions did not appear to be under the same influence of awe, and they rowed with no more enthusiasm than needed for the task at hand. Theirs was to acquire provisions ahead of the long journey before the season of the ice, not to question.

The island welcomed them ashore with its snug harbor sheltering the coast. It wore a fringe of mountains while sitting at the feet of Mount Wellington. Unaccustomed to being greeted by men of their same race and language, the crewmen were at first surprised and then disappointed. Most had previous experiences by way of the Hawaiian Islands or westward in Tahiti. But here the indigenous people did not hold a presence. The sailors were crestfallen, having their sites set upon native women scantily dressed, dark-eyed, and perfumed hair. To their dismay, the European inhabitants were not unlike those men at home, all business, who directed them to Georgian style warehouses cut from sandstone. Hobart Town was one of the great whaling ports. Its dockside warehouses had been recently rebuilt by hundreds of convicts that cut stones from quarry cliffs. With the ability to store fruit, grains, wool, and goods from around the world, the sailors understood why Captain Roys had sailed to this location for supplies. In such a well-equipped port, there was little they could not find. "Except Fräuleins," protested the German.

The aquiline-nosed man agreed, but his mind was preoccupied with a more rewarding job. He tapped the Jack-knife hidden in his pocket but knew that he must be patient. Neville lifted the crate of vegetables up onto his shoulder and under the heavy load lumbered along the road towards the shore and back to the dinghies. Laden with goods, each sailor heaved and groaned as he lifted and hauled the provisions into the waiting boats.

"We'll stay behind," said the German pointing to Neville. "They'll take these casks to the ship; there's no more room for us. We can wait for their return."

The sun overhead was beastly hot as they helped launch the small boats. The seawater lapped against their legs as the shadows of the two sailors crisscrossed one over the other. They waded knee-deep watching the quarreling scullers complain back and forth. But soon the banter began to take on a more hostile tone when it appeared that the trailing dingy was headed directly for the lead boat's bow. A threat was made followed by a compliment of swear words until slowly their voices dropped off as the rolling waves breaking against the shore became more prominent.

Like a pair of old comrades, they stared out into the water, each lost in thought; Neville, thinking about his wife and son, and the German wondering when the poison was going to work. "Let's go up and sit in the shade," suggested the cagey sailor. "I saw a lean-to on our way back from the warehouse." The sand under his feet made him walk as if he had drunk a pint of rum. Neville followed a few paces behind. A seagull made a harmless splash in the water, gaining the attention of both men when it flew off with a silver fish. But in the midst of the bird's thievery, a blood-curdling howl that was more animal-like than human was released. The German spun around and as if he needed reminding demanded, "What's wrong!" But Neville could not answer and pressed his hands against his abdomen, stooping under the weight of his misery. There was a burst of laughter and applause from Clas when the victim turned his head revealing fiercely dilated pupils and a ghostly complexion. An overwhelming feeling of nausea and pain forced him to hang his head below his knees. He was dripping with sweat as the cramps in his stomach were paralyzing. The anguished sailor swooned and shivered; all his extremities were cold; he was losing to the demon inside him. Neville put his hand over his mouth with a violent urge to vomit, but all that he purged was bitter tasting bile. His heart thumped with the panic of gasping for breath and reached his arm forward to gather the attention of the gawking sailor that stood before him. But no sooner did a piteous cry for help finally leave his lips, did the German run away towards the shore with every intention of leaving the helpless victim behind, dead.

———— .————

The German and his murderous party of sailors were in the small boat when they scripted their final tale; Neville had fallen ill and was too sick to return to the ship. Deciding to leave him behind to convalesce with a kindly government official who had taken mercy upon the man, it was the only compassionate and plausible resolution. Not altogether untrue, merely an omission of the infirmity's cause, they knew it would be months before the acknowledgment of his death could reach home. And so, the odious men felt no remorse, their sinister plan was complete, and they boarded the *Superior* with their rancid story intact.

Chapter 10

A coal-fire produced an exotic smell of roasting meat but kindled no familiar aroma to the stricken man's senses. Roasting over a smoldering fire was a pan of entrails coiled in a ball and a wooden skewer piercing the belly of a skinless animal. A single thread of smoke was directed upward and found its way outside through a narrow channel in the roof. If it were night or day, he didn't know which; a panel of muslin had been drawn closed with either the intention of keeping the darkness in or intruders out. A weatherboard table had been moved from under the window to accommodate the makeshift bed of animal skins. Neville slid his hand across his blanket made of kangaroo pelts. The action of the morning fell short of remembering how he had come to be at this location. He had no clear recollection of anything after his collapse. The caw of the seagulls branded the day as good for fishing, and whether the fisherman was returning with his morning catch or if he had been stalking foreigners rowing dinghies, it constituted little significance. Rather, it was his benevolent decision to help the poisoned sailor that renders his usual mundane activity most paramount to the story.

Neville felt the presence of the man even before he accosted the room with his heavy stride. The crude shelf next to a narrow cot had

curious carvings probably made of bone, while the top shelf housed utensils and a rather large jug of what one can only presume was rum. Leaning
into the corner of the room was a weapon resembling those guns which
dated back to an earlier era. Though a relic, it had all the makings of
proving itself deadly. The door fell open, and as the bedridden man tried
to lift his head and raised himself up, he fell back on his bent arms as the
shadowy image entered through the portal. Neville stared up at the dark
figure wondering if this large and sinewy man could be the resident of
the hut or an unwelcome stranger. The room, dark and smoky, added to
the already supernatural atmosphere, whereupon the illumination of an
oil-burning lamp stoked the unearthly mood.

He was an ebony man with cropped black hair and sable eyes. Neither
smile nor a grimace fell over his countenance, and Neville watched as the
large hand came forward and then fell heavily upon the ill man's forehead.
After a few moments, the palm lifted away, and the austere image walked
over to a pitcher of water, soaked a strip of linen, and then wrung it out
before placing it across Neville's feverish forehead. He brought a cup to
the sailor's quivering lips, a blend of brewed leaves that had been steeping
over the open pit. Then, he pointed with all intentions that the sick man
lay his head down. "Thank you," Neville said, wondering if his caretaker
could speak English. But it would be several days until he would find out
for the tall man dipped beneath the portal, locking the door behind him.

The only reference of time was measured by a ribbon of light that
found its way between the two snug pieces of fabric that had fluttered
apart with the breeze. The ill man lay still as the sliver of sunlight crept
over him like a curious insect. Sleep took over and as he napped he floated
into a vision where time had no boundaries and miseries were only words,
where days were not sealed in hours or minutes. *He reached out to the
ghostly shape of his young wife. They were sharing the same space, yet she floated
just beyond his fingertips. He tried again, but she flitted too quickly. "Time is passing us by," he called, but she did not hear or did not care to stop for she vanished.*

The delirium of his dream mingled with consciousness, fusing reality with deceit and dreams into nightmares. He struggled to rouse himself but could not, and the more he tossed and turned the more he felt that there was an opposition fighting him, pulling him in a direction all mortals would interpret as death.

But it was not death, and when he awoke, he was met by a muscular figure who stood before him angling a plate of unfamiliar victuals. Neville assumed him to be the owner of the small hut, but when he asked for his name, the fellow's only reply was to hand him a plate of food and a tin of bush tea before leaving. At first, the infirmed sailor could manage only a morsel, barely tolerating the herbal decoctions that made him dream. But as days passed, he had finally regained most of his vigor and developed a heartier appetite.

By the earliest light, the dweller left, and by dusk, he returned with provisions of meat and bundles of leafy stalked plants. Sometimes the hunt provided kangaroo or wallaby and other times it was fish. The unfamiliar smells of cooking flesh and boiling leaves filled the small sanctuary with an acrid smell, and though it was miserably unpleasant, it was returning his frail body to health. This went on for a week, and still the provider did not speak. Finally, on what may have been the ninth day of Neville's recuperation, an unexpected declaration greeted the sick man. "Where did you get those?" It came from a voice that could have belonged to a Professor. Neville, who had graduated from the cot to a stool, turned to the speaker who was leaning against the doorframe. And though the sailor was familiar with the man's appearance, it was during this encounter that he first became aware of his composure. Slung over his shoulder was a boka, a loose-fitting kangaroo skin cloak. His muslin shirt clung to his chest like the skin of an onion, and the pantaloons of woven cloth fit snuggly around his taut waist and cinched with a braided rope. Barefoot and hatless, he was an in fine physical shape, and now as a speaker of the English tongue, there was a curiosity that Neville had overlooked.

Astonished by such a pronouncement, the sailor lifted his feet. "These?" he said pointing to the boots he was wearing.

"Of course, those!" replied the exotic fellow, "I have never seen such fine leather on a lowly sailor. Those," he emphasized while pointing to the boots, "were made for an Officer."

Such a response gave Neville reason to stammer even though it was not he who was speaking. He surveyed his situation trolling his mind for something insightful to say. However, all he could do was demonstrate his delight that this unnatural bond was met with a mutual understanding, the English language. As such, he offered back a smile. But this gesture of new found camaraderie was not returned by the speaker, and only silence prevailed. If this was a game of giving and take it was quite evident that it was Neville's turn to reciprocate some truth about himself. It was time to explain the origins of how he unintentionally found himself on Van Damien's Island.

Several vagabond birds stirred noisily outside in the scrub brush; a welcome sound in this room overcrowded with unanswered questions. The native man pulled a chair away from the corner and sat down. His grand size dwarfed Neville who was perched on the stool like a schoolboy. The sailor leaned forward, placing his weight upon his knees and willingly began to relinquish the burden within him. And as he narrated the story he tried to interpret the listener's opinion of what was being relayed, however, no facial or body language was revealed, rather before him was an uncommitted listener, unmoved and unaltered. For all that, the man was polite as well as hospitable, following Neville's journey from New England, the crossing of two oceans, and the callous abandonment by his shipmates. When the tale was finished, a long gloom hovered over the small room. Like the lifting of fog, the large man stood up and brought over two mugs from off the shelf. He approached with an air of having much to say, but for this storyteller, revealing his name, Mallabal, was just the beginning of his story; one that was best related over rum.

His life was at first simple, a descendant of indigenous people who inhab-
ited the Pacific islands as one of the oldest civilizations on Earth. They
were the first to migrate out of Africa 50,000 years ago. "Thousands of
the Aboriginal people once lived on this island, but now there are but only
a few of us remaining." Mallabal's sincerity was accentuated by his slow
and deliberate explanation. "How can the disappearance of people become
as easy to accomplish as the felling of trees that depletes a forest? The
British tolerated cruelty by the settlers; families torn apart, men hunted
like animals, and women victimized for indiscriminate pleasures. Did we
retaliate, yes, but did we win? The lawlessness and brutality committed
can only be cataloged by its genocide." He spoke not with lilting sorrow,
but with hardened repugnance; for loss is not always tangible; its calam-
itous effects are greater than a mountain range, an ocean, and even the
boundless stars in the heavens. Such was Mallabal's plight, one that he
shared with an exiled nation. "The British made our island a penal colony,
home to convicts of all calibers, a purging of their undesirables. Those that
served out their time and released to remain on the island mingled with
officials of the colonial government. The land was divided into parcels
and confiscated; the settlers wanted more for grazing sheep and farming.
When we did not readily agree to the British terms, when we retaliated,
there was war. We were fighting to protect our women, our children, our
hunting grounds, our way of life; they were fighting to conquer and exterminate. Our weapons were ineffective against their guns." He pointed to
the Brown Bess leaning into the corner of the room. "My souvenir musket," he smiled wily. "At the end of the war, it was arranged that the few
Aborigines still left would be exiled to an island in the Straits." He paused
and then added. "Less than 200." If the latter was added for sympathetic
appeal it worked, for Neville chewed the number over like it had been a
radish; a bitter charge.

Mallabal poked the remaining hot coals with a twig. Bending forward, he blew lightly until they glowed red while disturbed specks of ash scattered like gnats. He pitched the stick into the smoldering ring and sat back into his chair. "Rianna was my wife; she was a woman of many talents. One was stringing shell necklaces. She made each one with patience, piercing the shells with a sharpened kangaroo tooth. Sometimes she would use a wallaby tooth for the smallest shells, so tiny they could slip under her fingernail." Neville looked at his fingers; such an image gave him reason to open his eyes wide with astonishment. "To bring out the pearly surface of the larger shells, they were smoked over the fire and then rubbed with grass to remove their dull coating. Each was then threaded on the sinews of kangaroo tail and polished with muttonbird oil. We used these necklaces and pearly shells to trade with other fishermen. She was a tireless woman, she helped me harvest oysters from the shallow waters, and I would dive for them. It wasn't until the colonists came did our pearls give us bad luck." The voice of the storyteller grew low as though someone had begged him to stop. Silence fastened itself to his lips.

"Bad luck?" Neville questioned. "I don't know much about pearling, except it will bring in quite a lot of money."

Mallabal stood up, walked over to the shelf, and presently returned with three pearls, all of which were splendid specimens and placed them on the ground and pushed them over to Neville to examine. He picked them up and rolled them in his palm. "In Hawaii, a local buyer would offer you a hundred pounds each for gray pearls like these," said Neville before setting them safely back in the owner's palm. Mallabal carelessly dropped each into a sack which was placed between himself and the other.

"The richness of a full bag such as this," he said, dangling it before the sailor, "may bring sleepless nights to some. Or, it may bring eternal sleep. Dreams are paved with the shells and the stink of rotting oysters.

Men and women were kidnapped, some taken to ships and forced to work as pearl divers."

Neville pondered this despicable practice "Black-birding," he muttered with disgust. The Aborigine linked eyes with Neville's. "Black-birding," Neville repeated. "First heard about it from a mate aboard ship. South Pacific Islanders were being kidnapped and taken to Queensland as forced labors to work on the sugar and cotton plantations. Called it black-birding."

Mallabal defined the word in his mind. These were the forces in the world he could not explain, yet its shadows were spreading out like limbs of a tree and taking root in places it had no business growing in. "Rianna was stolen from our home," he said matter-of-factly. "When I returned and discovered she was taken I set out to kill. But it was of no use; I was too late. She had jumped over the cliff rather than to live as another's property." Neither man looked at the other for such a sobering statement left both the speaker and listener reflective. The bottle of rum was now empty as the liquor began to fill each man's void, even if it were just for a few hours.

The wild rose, it sits upon a thorny stem with its face to the sun emitting a fragrance uniquely distinct to its name. But when this lovely flower is plucked from the plant, it will soon wither and die. First, its color will fade, then the bloom will wilt and curl until its velvet petals finally drop off one by one. Those indigenous survivors exiled to Flinders Island lived in a settlement they called Wybalenna. Forced from their land, they were expected to be transformed into the British interpretation of civilized Christian tillers of the land. This campaign of cultural destruction forbade the practice of their old ways. So, like the rose cut from its plant, the Aborigines were dying from respiratory disease, poor nourishment, and despair. Unwilling to assimilate, like an invasive species takes over the natural habitat, they too were overrun.

Neville considered the events recounted, but there were two questions he needed answered; how the unschooled native learned to speak such literate English, and why was the man still alive? Mallabal smirked at the questions, he may have been subjugated, but he was not without guile. "Survival," he remarked. "I listened. I listened with both my ears and my mind and then I learned how to peddle my knowledge. Even the conquerors will need the conquered someday. And so, I waited." The spirit of the Aborigine had not worn away, but rather, despite his tumultuous life, he had remained strangely stoic. The prejudices of those governing his world imbued all that represented ignorance and evil.

From where he sat Neville could see the day had drifted into evening. The sun that fell between the split in the curtain was replaced with a hazy gray streak. A basket of eggs and another of corn were stored on the bottom shelf. An iron pan, kettle, and pot were stacked on the floor. Noting he had been unaware of their placement before this moment, Neville wondered, "Was this strange man more domesticated than he believed?" Into his mind, he retraced a repertoire of friends and acquaintances. He could find no one to compare with Mallabal. Nevertheless, the American sailor remained leery. If confronted he was unsure whether he would take the side of this formerly savage man, yet on the other hand, the Aborigine had brought him back to health. On the assumption that the information narrated was forthright, then it would exonerate any wrongdoing Mallabal may have carried out. Naturally, if the story was untrue, he had only himself to blame seeing that he was taken in by the wits and rum of this exotic con-artist.

But had Neville been present in Van Diemen's Land only a few years prior, he may have read an account from the 1836 April edition of the *Hobert Town* which would have arrested any of his doubts. *"They have been murdered in cold blood. They have been shot in the woods and hunted down as beasts of prey. Their women have been contaminated, and then had their throats cut, or been shot, by the British residents, who would fain call themselves civilized people. The Government too, by the common hangman, sacrificed the lives of such of the Aborigines in retaliation, and the Government, to its shame be it recorded, in no one instance, on no single occasion, ever punished, or threatened to punish, the acknowledged murderers of the Aboriginal inhabitants."*

But Neville did not read this statement or any other newspaper articles slanted for or against the native population. He would have to use his intuition to weed out the truth and form his own opinion. But regardless of what the stranded sailor wished to believe, the only relevant truth pointed to the fact that he owed his life to this man.

———•———

Hindsight is the jury and verdict of a crime while collecting the evidence during the committing of a transgression takes foresight.

———•———

They were small, docile creatures, the likes of which the American had never seen. "You say they are muttonbirds," whispered Neville. The dark plumaged birds with silver lined wings and webbed feet skimmed over the water like a dark cloud. "It's larger than our pigeon," he proclaimed as a few landed on shore. "More like a mallard!"

"Pidgon?" asked Mallabal.

"Yes, pigeons. They're pretty common where I'm from, but not water birds. They like the land. Grey in color, actually somewhat dull, with pink legs and feet." The listener was not impressed with the description as he tried to assemble in his head what the bird looked like.

Time was all inclusive to Neville; he measured a day by dark and light, not by hours or minutes. He was not sure how many weeks he had been on this island but knew it must be at least three for the growth of his beard was longer than he liked. His days were spent in the company of Mallabal, learning how he speared fish. He observed the use of a wangno to hunt the kangaroo and wallaroo and helped pluck the feathers of the muttonbird, yet the Aborigine always kept to the shadows, avoiding the settlers, remaining invisible. Neville wished he had a quill-pen and paper to record all the new animals and plants. But as much as his host was hospitable; these were among the essentials he lacked, as such, Neville would have to remember all that he saw and learned. The father thought about his son, especially when encountering a baby opossum or a clutch of gull chicks. He envisioned what Asa would do, what he might say if he was there to see a marsupial hopping through the bushland as freely as a horse gallops across the fields. Then he laughed as he conjured up his wife, her face horrified at the sight of wallaby meat cooking over an open coal fire.

"Mallabal, are you happy?" Neville asked. The two men were sitting outside the hut and as the sun set it exposed a million stars. Like a bank of diamonds that had shattered, they scattered across the heavens with extraordinary brilliance. Neville waited as the other seemed to be deeply engaged in thought.

"I am not sure of the word," he said.

"Happy, you know, feeling pleased, content."

Again, there was a long pause between the speakers. "I have what I need. Is that happy?" he asked. Neville realized to ask this man such an insipid question was perhaps like asking a starving man if he were hungry. How could he be happy, everything that he knew as home and family and kin was extinguished by no fault of his. "If happy means full, then yes, I am happy. I have a place to sleep and keep out of the rain. I have enough to eat."

"I suppose," said the sailor.

Chapter 11

ow that Neville had recovered there was no reason to remain on Van Damien's and no reason to stay hidden from the officials. He had not committed a crime nor was he a subject of the Crown; he was eager to return home. Such movements of impatience rattled around in his head as he contemplated a solution. Once his unfortunate situation was explained to the authorities, they would have no reason not to help him procure passage back to New England. Van Damien's harbor anchored a trove of sailing vessels, and certainly there was a ship that could use another experienced seaman. Standing before the rain-barrel, he peered down at his gaunt reflection. He had lost a considerable amount of weight, and though the island's diet may have agreed with his sustenance, it was by no means a substitute for his cravings. He dipped the dried-gourd into the barrel and brought fresh rainwater to his lips. There was a part of him that would miss this modest lifestyle. The bond he discovered with the land had proved to be different than his connection with the ocean. With the ocean, he never felt in total control. Instead, he was under its intoxicating spell, subservient to its erratic behavior. On this island he was a curious dweller that reveled in the beauty of this island's vast forests from afar, aware that among its foliage lurked danger. Beyond the western coast of

the barren Sandy Cape is the infamous entrance to Macquarie Harbor and within its bass-like mouth lies a landmass with a lovely name, Sarah Island. She sounds like a most congenial place of refuge, but to those confined behind her prison walls, even her air is noxious. The inhabitants of the penal colony are relegated to the life of beasts with little hope. So it was, that colonial discipline distinguished itself to those banished from the "motherland, England" for "rehabilitation" by means of corporal punishment.

With Mallabal by his side, he was invited to wander. The wind, the rain, the animals, the birds; the island was talkative like an old scamp, mischievous and audacious. A feeling of gratitude put Neville in a better mood, and as the native man's silhouette emerged out of the dusty path ahead, a most extraordinary idea was being formulated by the thirsty man. He had come to trust this Aborigine, finding his simple and honest ways far richer than the wealthiest of New Englanders. He wished to pay Mallabal back, to offer him a life that he well-deserved. It was evident that success could not be achieved on this island; here he could only remain safe in the shadows. The enthusiasm around his idea grew like an orchestral overture, and the more Neville mulled it over it took on the intensity of the crescendo. The decision to take Mallabal back with him was as brilliant as a perfectly played coda; one that he hoped would have similar merit in the mind of the Aborigine.

Neville's persuasive efforts were a mere splinter in comparison to the Mallabal's reason to leave; he was anything but naïve to his circumstance. "There is no future when oppressed." Neville hoped to find passage home by finding them work aboard a whaler, not because of the handsome wages, but because these ships took crew both black and white. A few years back an ex-slave, Captain Absolom Boston of Nantucket, commanded *The Industry* sailing with an all-black crew. But that was an anomaly. The most prudent arrangement would be to sail on a Colonial vessel. Theirs were checkerboard crews and didn't care about the race of the man if they were good seamen. As for Mallabal, he was a fine navigator of small catamarans, had a natural disposition for the ocean, and willingly placed his luck in the hands of the American.

Those that are born with luck are not always the same individuals that are born with intelligence. And those that are born with intelligence often make their luck. As for those that have neither luck nor wit, they are either trusting or beyond reproach, while the rest waffle like the tide.

Sullivan's Cove is the first layer when approaching Hobart Town. Its appearance, much like the skin of an onion, seems harmless enough. Upon sailing into the inlet, all eyes are fixed on a host of low ragged cliffs reaching down into a narrow band of beach. Vessels of all sizes and character have found a reason to be anchored, some to deliver goods, others to obtain provisions. Mizzen-masts are scarfed in colors that are tossed and snapped by the wind.

Neville followed the dusty road into Hobart Town. He was a sorry sight, and though he was well-fed and clean, his ranking as an educated man was disguised by his rumpled clothes and unkempt hair. His sallow skin and sunken jaw revealed traces of his illness despite the weeks spent accompanying the Aborigine across the hinterlands. He walked with his hands in his pockets and mentally counted his money. The sailor had not been robbed by his shipmate when left for dead. By some miracle in the haste by which the culprit committed his atrocity, he had not stripped Neville of his money or his boots. The German's covert escape from the island may have been the reason for his failure as a thief.

The approach into Town peeled away the next layer; once lush with trees and brushwood, its green margins had been felled, presenting to the newcomer a controlled and cultivated land. In place of the natural environment was the workings of progress. Here stood the government stockyards, slaughterhouse, and sale-yard. Such transparency of layers revealed the stunning consequence of Hobart Rivulet, once vital to the establishment of this colony; it was now heavily polluted functioning as a repository for the slaughterhouse waste. Finely dressed Garrison officers and ladies were a sharp contrast to the poorly dressed settlers and depraved convicts clothed in gray or blue, while the most irredeemable wore yellow. One had to keep alert to avoid prisoners pushing handcarts and the zigzagging sailors sauntering in and out of the breweries. The hand-me-down culture of the colonists has dispensed with the native customs and origins of the islanders and imposed their own imported belief system. More than three-fourths of the population were now convicts.

However, the early years of Hobart were unfamiliar and equally not of any interest to the displaced sailor; what he saw he paid little attention to. He couldn't feel any remorse for what he didn't know, and so he entered the stony government building with the same high hopes as a man entering a church on his wedding day. "What can I do you for?" inquired a small and wiry fellow. He looked up from his overburdened desk with an obligatory glance. He appeared to be about the same age as Neville but had half as much hair which he crossed over a balding spot and flattened down with a perfumed pomade. An equally pale cat sat on the desk, and at first glance it appeared as though it was stuffed. The sailor envied the well-groomed officer in his starched white uniform and imagined the leather shoes hidden under the desk polished to a fault. The cat stirred when the man spoke, opening one eye and then stretching its paw in a perfunctory manner.

"I hope you can help me," Neville said. He glanced down at the tarnished nameplate wedged between the cat and a pile of leather-bound ledgers. "You see, Mr. Walker, I'm a stranded American in need of help. I want to return to the United States." The thin fellow sat forward and stroked the cat as if getting inspiration from it before he spoke. The feline purred with content as the man patted its head. It was uncomfortably warm in the building's great hall making Neville feel even more the subordinate. "Perhaps I should first explain my circumstance," the fatigued sailor continued. "May I sit down?" His eyes petitioned one of a pair of high backed chairs in front of the desk like a thirsty dog looking down from a bridge.

"Please," smiled Walker and nodded his head with approval. "Passage back to the United States." His brow furrowed as he cogitated the request aloud when another visitor appeared at the edge of the desk, handed the officer a few papers, and as if waiting for scraps by the kitchen door tarried impatiently, swaying from side to side. He was a strange little figure with a screwed-up nose and a pale, emaciated face who scrutinized the new acquaintance like a leery cur. "Say hello to the gentleman, Bo." The boy, a barefooted lad not much older than twelve, muttered the sentiment and quickly turned and slipped away into the shadows before Neville could get a chance to reply.

Neville's misery returned with his impatient desire to find passage home to his own family. But if the strange boy's sudden leave seemed odd, it was displaced by the officer's attention to the cat that had jumped from one side of the desk to the other with the impunity of ownership. It circled the only orderly stack of documents, disrupting several papers and the blotter, whereupon the writer lifted the animal off and placed it on the floor. Possibly embarrassed by its removal, it slinked over towards Neville, arched its back, and acting like a cat, began to rub itself against the chair leg. Edging closer to the sitter, it wished to be pet, however, to its surprise, not everyone was pleased with its presence and did not receive the intention it desired. Unbeknownst to the man across the large desk, Neville discretely hastened the feline's departure with a quick shove of his foot.

Noticeably startled, the cat sprang up, detouring across the desk, and then jumped down the opposing side where it dashed away; once again scattering the man's work with its impetuous retreat. "Wonder what got into him?" the official asked with a half-interested notion and began to restack the misaligned papers

"Cats? They are an independent lot," Neville answered with a perfunctory shrug. "Never figured them out."

"Suppose not." The officer drummed his fingers against the desk as if trying to recollect his train of thought.

"The boy, Bo? Is he your son?"

"Bo? Mine? That waif, my boy? Oh no!" he reiterated. A great gasp of disbelief was expelled. "Good heavens man, what would make you think that? He's here in a work program. A scamp, a good for nothing! We've got over one hundred such sprats, but I don't think there is much help for their kind." Neville's expression of bewilderment was met with intolerance. "I suppose you have a right to know what I'm talking about. We have a great many young convicts transported from England, a few as young as seven years old. Our island is a natural penitentiary, and their destination, Point Puer, has been more than generous in trying to rehabilitate them."

But as he contemplated his next sentence, Neville sat forward. "You mean that they were sent here by the courts?"

"The First Fleet's original eleven ships sailed to Botany Bay, New South Wales in the late 1780s, a few decades before we got our first group. Men and boys alike, prisoners of the Crown." At the mere mention of boys being transported, Neville winced. Such a malignancy considered as rehabilitation deserved his own mental interpretation of the English penal system. "Seven years to life is what these luckless boys get. You've probably seen a transport vessel in the harbor but didn't know it as such. It can appear quite ordinary but get aboard, and you'll find that it has been drastically altered to accommodate its cargo. There is a quartered area on deck like a cattle-pen, only stationed with armed sentries. Within its confines the prisoners pick out their place to sit, to stand, crouch, or pace, and pick the lice; all permitted to come up from below to breathe the salty air." The simpering man pulled a clean handkerchief from his pocket and wiped his forehead. "I remember when I was young, maybe six or seven years old, I was at the train station with my grandmother. On the platform was a line of cages each containing a wild animal. It was the most breathtaking sight for me; all kinds of exotic beasts, some with claws, some with razor-sharp teeth, some growling, and a few were almost timid. But what struck me the most was the look in all these animal's eyes, a look of both dread and evil as if each knew its fate. It wasn't until I came to here that I saw those eyes again." There was nothing malicious about the way he spoke, rather, it was as if he had waited to find a willing listener. Perhaps he finally had. "But during most of the six-month voyage, these delinquents are penned below in the ship's prison, between the decks and the main hatchway. They sleep side-by-side of pickpockets, murderers, forgers, thieves, house-breakers.... It's quite an education these nibs receive. By the time they arrive, they will have acquired the skills and habits of a seasoned criminal. The youngest are taken to Point Puer, located in the vicinity of what is known as the Island of the Dead; where they bury the prisoners. I would imagine it might be a good deterrent for our impressionable youth, don't you think?" With a crooked smile, he slithered out the next bit of information. "Yes, indeed, Point Puer, the place the government's magistrate set aside to confine offenders. Boys seven to twenty sent alone without friend or family to a life of labor; infractions of the law are not tolerated." The lightness in his attitude had now all but dissolved, and as though trying to console his conscience he cleared his throat and continued. "Now I didn't say it's a good idea; I'm just telling you like it is. Van Diemen's Land, it is what it is."

Neville's thoughts turned inward. From where he was sitting he was on the edge of a roof with his legs dangling down; if he were to speak his mind, he would never find passage home. "My problem, do you think you could help me?" Those who hold power should not be served gruel. Neville needed to feed this fellow as much praise as he could muster. "I understand that you're a very busy and important man, but I would be so grateful for any help at all."

"My good man," the surly official replied and lowered his voice so only the listener was privy to their conversation. "What you are asking for will first have to be secured with more than just your good word. And by the looks of you, I would say your word is all you have to offer." It was equally evident to Neville that Officer Walker did not have much reason to care about the motives or reasons for his being on the island; nor was he concerned why the American wished to return home. These were personal matters that Neville need not burden the man in charge with. Neville stood up, and as he untied his small leather pouch, he could feel Walker in the thick of the untangling like an impatient boy anticipating a piece of candy. Everything was riding on the gold eagle he now placed on the desk. The silent watcher turned it over, placed it between his teeth, and bit down. Even within the veiled light, the coin shimmered. Convinced of its value, he dropped it into his top desk drawer along with several other foreign coins.

"I aim to work my way home," added Neville.

"Naturally," the man contrived. "Now, had you said you wanted to get to the Kangaroo Islands or Australia, you could leave within the hour. But you have presented more of a challenge." He pulled a ledger from the stack and opened it. Particles of dust scattered and followed a trail of sunlight. Several columns were audited and a few pages were turned and while the man bent over the book he was interrupted by, "I will also need passage for a companion."

"A woman?" he grinned.

"No, no," Neville stumbled on his own words. "It's someone I consider my savior."

"Savior? A clergyman, then?"

"Hell, no!" exclaimed Neville and laughed at the misinterpretation. "I was near death when he found me and nursed me back to health. Had it not been for him, why I would have surely have died. No, I owe my life to this man."

The officer nodded in agreement but with little empathy for the tale. Those who lived on Van Damien's Land had heard far worse a story than this sentimental dribble. "Passage for two then. A convict will be harder to secure a place for."

"He's nothing of the kind! No, not a convict. On the contrary, he's a most honorable man; he's an Aborigine." He paused while an anxious moment ensued.

The official fixed his eyes on Neville certain that what he had heard was perhaps a joke. "A native-born Aborigine." he clarified.

"Yes, quite so."

Such an admission brought the wiry fellow to his feet. There was a clearing of his throat and a few ahems, after which he produced a clean handkerchief and blew his nose. Then he came around to the front of the desk and slid the adjacent chair next to Neville. Unexpectedly, the officer who navigated without any moral compass was now wearing an expression of unlikely concern. "I believe that I may have been too hasty," he whispered. "If what you say is true, then you may be putting this fellow into grave danger. As circumstances have changed, I think you had better start at the beginning."

Chapter 12

gnes slid the curtains apart and raised the window. A strong scent of honeysuckle wafted into the kitchen with the true language of spring. She breathed and sighed with a feeling of contentment but was pulled back to the present as she tugged on the end of the dishcloth slung over her shoulder. The crockery could have been left drying on the rack, but she needed the counter space. She dried the earthenware plate, the same one that had been her mother's platter, the very dish that her grandmother had used in her home. She glanced at the ancestral reminder deciding to handle it with a bit more care. There wasn't a chip on it, and she attributed its flawless condition to the fact that it was only brought down off the shelf whenever meat was served. It was a long time since they had a good cut of beef, and she hoped tonight's dinner was just the beginning of many uses of this platter.

Her cloth ran around and around, and as Agnes wiped the oblong platter, she was called back in time with the same magnitude with which one is transfixed while looking at an old photograph. The Robinsen women were preparing Father's favorite meal, haggis. Colonel, a guest for Sunday dinner, silently turned his nose up when served, but he was a good sport and ate his entire helping, asking for seconds of the mashed neeps (turnips) and tatties (potatoes) that got him through supper. "No waste in this house," her father reminded all, for this was a recipe that combined the sheep's liver, lungs, stomach, and heart. Indeed, it is a dish that's not to the satisfaction of everyone's taste buds, but her mother had learned the art of its preparation, and in celebration of both the meal and their heritage, they concluded with a verse of *Address to a Haggis*. But as the whole family sang the original Scottish rendition of Robert Burns' poem, Agnes recalled the look on poor Colonel's face; he was at a loss. So as not to make him feel like an outsider, her father recited the first verse in what he dubbed 'the foreigners' translation.

"FAIR AND FULL IS YOUR HONEST, JOLLY FACE, GREAT CHIEFTAIN OF THE SAUSAGE RACE! ABOVE THEM ALL, YOU TAKE YOUR PLACE, STOMACH, TRIPE, OR INTESTINES: WELL ARE YOU WORTHY OF A GRACE AS LONG AS MY ARM..."

Colonel was a good man, and she was very thankful that he did not take to haggis like her father. To this day, she cannot rid her nostrils of the putrid stink of boiling sheep offal. Only once did she complain, at which her father gave her a lecture about Scottish pride; that to dislike haggis was an offense as unpatriotic as disliking Scotland herself. The Scottish guilt was far more powerful than the stench, and so she decided that it was not worth the trouble of being disagreeable.

Agnes set the platter on the table and turned her eyes outside the window. Flora was leading Asa about the garden, and he followed her with the same allegiance as a dutiful guard dog. She smiled as she watched this unusual bond and wondered if perhaps she had been too selfish. Perhaps a sibling would have given her daughter a playmate; but again, another child may have stunted the child's innate ability to relate to adults. Yet, as she turned her attention to Asa, Agnes could hardly think of him as a grown man. Maybe before the war, but now, he was barely a whole being.

The garden delighted the child, and the child must have agreed with the garden for its hedged-in space seemed to flourish by her youthful presence. Such a garden was created for a child; contrary to being under the dominion of an adult who would pick and prod, cut and prune, and restrain any natural freedom for it to cultivate at will. The butterflies flitted from flower to flower, the berries clustered defining their purples and reds, while the greens were more verdant and the stalks thick and hearty; even the bumblebees appeared to be domesticated, keeping their distance when she bent down to sniff the squash blossoms lest one might accidentally sting her. And there was Asa, all the while lingering behind like a distracted puppy until Flora would turn and call him, and like a dog wagging its tail, he would smile when he heard his name and took heed of her request. Most often she would remind him not to walk in the vegetable beds or step outside the rock-lined path. But largely it was to coax him away from the rabbit hutch, a location in the fenced compound that he was drawn to. "Come along, Asa, come along. Let the cottontail alone." Did he hear her voice, or did he just ignore her demand? His stubbornness often required more prodding, and like an old mule that needed a nudge, she'd grab his hand and pull until he submitted.

"Perhaps that's why the other children never come around to play," Agnes half-heartedly lamented, "she can be awfully bossy. On the other hand, she won't have to worry that any man will get the better of her." Such recognition of the child's character revived the mother's spirit, which she attributed to her Scottish heritage, and she sighed. It was a sigh consumed with both relief and uncertainty.

The garden wind was light, and with a few gentle breaths, Wooley came alive. "See that?" she asked Asa, "that old tattie-bogle will keep them away!" Flora pointed to a pair of ravens that had positioned themselves on the fence. The passive fellow looked up at the birds and then back to the scarecrow. Its scrawny arms wavered as the spring breeze fetched the hay appendages up and then let them go, gently rocking the arms. As if never having seen the stuffed man before, he wandered over to the center of the garden to get a better look. The vacant eye socket had been repaired, and now it wore two buttons but of mismatched size and color; one gray and the other black, the larger being black. "He can't really see you, Asa," explained the child when she noticed the grimace of concern for the ragged scarecrow. "See, Agnes sewed on a new eye." Flora grinned and gave the pole a smart kick with her foot making the tattie-bogle shake. The crows cawed and flew up and away. "See what a good job he did. Those crows would have tried to eat our vegetables if Wooley wasn't here. He always does a good job." She scampered around the stake a few times and then stopped. "Imagine, not even a brain in his head, and he still works," Flora exclaimed. Then she pushed the gingham stuffed arm and let it swing.

"Imagine, not even a brain in his head," the words were followed by a sadistic pinch on the scaly arm. "See, he can't feel anything, not a thing." The pair of orderlies laughed as Asa watched the goings on from his hospital bed. Black pupils filled the cavernous sockets with eyes that only blinked, only stared up at the ceiling. Perhaps they were right; maybe this soldier had no more brains. Some skulls were blown off, and others just lost their wits without even a puncture wound.

"Come on, Asa, let's fetch the water for the plants," Flora said as she tapped his arm.

Asa crooked his head back and glanced up at the stuffed head. His attention drew away from the hospital where the conversation was going on and back into the garden, where the prairie colored face with button eyes looked out but could see nothing. Westward lay a line of unbroken clouds. He was eaten up with a swarm of confused feelings, shuttering at the thought of all the living tattie-bogles that had come home from the war.

The warning came not during the dark of night when most bad news finds its way into a resting home nor was it sent by way of a letter neatly scrolled after the salutation. Rather, the warning arrived during the cheeriest part of the day; the hour when the sparrows were stealing seeds away from the chickens and shielded in the shadow of the porch as the last of the morning dew was feeding the June bugs. It is well known that a warning may be designed to intimidate in lieu of counsel, setting the entire household on edge or it may have the opposite effect by instigating revenge by the receivers. This day's warning arrived by way of a knock on the door, too loud to be friendly and too impetuous to be a person of authority; so it seemed to Agnes before setting herself to answer it. And as one often does before answering a door, she unscrambled a number of conjectures. Perhaps it was the neighbor boy looking for some flour to borrow, but no, his knock would have been accompanied by, "Mrs. Jameson, are you in?" And then there was the pesky Widower Carlson who, bless his soul, could never seem to be able to darn his own socks. There again, he would have knocked with the cadence of his impecunious and timid character, offering several hesitant taps.

Agnes glanced out the window into the garden, but neither Flora nor Asa was in her sights, meaning they were fetching water for the plants. "Such a good child," she thought. The door rattled with a few more vigorous raps, and she decided that the deliverer most likely owned a set of very hard knuckles. "Coming, I'm coming," she called in her sunniest voice and as she smoothed her palm over her hair, she re-pinned the stray curls that had come loose. It was strange to be receiving company so early in the day, but then she reminded herself this might not be company. No, maybe it's Julio Tamayo, the farmer down the road that has come to tell her something terrible. An accident, a tragic accident; how many times had she warned Colonel to be careful! She gasped with such an idea as her hands trembled while she fumbled with the latch. It was never stubborn, and today it was playing games with hers. The disconcerted woman felt herself becoming more agitated. "Just a moment, just a moment," she cried and pulling on the stiff handle, she slid it across at which the door fell open, and she stumbled over the threshold and into the warning.

It was a box, a small snakeskin box with brass hinges and shut tight with a strap that looked more like a belt. Agnes picked it up and shook it. It had a distinct smell of animal, reptile to be exact. She stepped out onto the porch and down the steps, looking about for the voices but only undistinguishable footprints marked the ground. Not even an army scout would be able to make out who they belonged to for as quickly as they walked upon on the dusty earth; the wind erased the prints as if they had been broom swept.

"Damn," she thought with both disappointment and a bit of disgust for those individuals lacking the patience to wait for her to open the door. She stood under the shade of the porch and put the box to her ear. It was light but not so light that it couldn't house something more than paper. Agnes assumed that it was meant for Colonel and wished he would get home to open it. But that would be this afternoon, and her curiosity was baited by this mystery. Not much ever happened and this was indeed something to stir a little adventure into the day. However, had she known the true nature of the fiends that delivered it, she may not have been so eager to open what, in retrospect, could be interpreted as another Pandora's Box.

As the sun rose so did Agnes's curiosity. The reptilian smelling box was placed on the small round table in the living room in anticipation of Colonel's return. The peas had been shelled and were soaking in a pot of water while the freshly slaughtered meat had been heavily salted and peppered. She had roasted beef many times before, however, just to be sure she pulled from her library of cookbooks her new favorite, *Domestic Cookery*. Grease stained fingerprints impregnated the pages, a reminder of the last time she used the "hastener." She reread the recipe, and before she got to the end, she closed the book. *Place skewered meat in the tin kitchen affixed to the spit, add a pint of water in the bottom; baste and turn it frequently so that every part may have the fire.* She flipped the meat over and salted it again. "A piece of beef like this will take at least three hours to roast," she thought and added a pinch more salt. Flies generally will keep away if salted enough. The half-cylindrical oven was an ingenious device, having been fabricated in the last century, but Agnes never took advantage of its cooking benefits. There was a door on the back that opened so the cook could baste at will, a hand crank on the side to rotate the skewered meat, and a curved pan at the bottom to collect the cooking juices. Most relevant was the reflective property inside the roaster to speed up the cooking time. Agnes stared at the slab of pink flesh and then at the 3-foot-long tin-oven and stuck her tongue out at it. It just seemed like so much work for the same outcome that would be if she just boiled dinner in the iron kettle-pot as usual. Certainly, there would be less cleanup, less time fussing, less time in the kitchen. But no matter how she tried to convince herself that it would be easier not to use it, she knew that this tin obstruction needed to be employed every now and again. "Damn," she said and then winced; this was the second time today she cursed her situation.

So, taking her dissatisfaction out on the meat, she held it down with one hand and inserted the skewer with vengeful retaliation for her overly domesticated day. But if revenge was indeed the object of her intentions, the beef had already paid the ultimate sacrifice; for not more than several days ago, it was grazing in Julio Tamayo's pasture without a care in the world.

The wall clock ticked away. Agnes stood outside on the porch and watched as Flora watered the vegetables with the same care as a mother bird feeds her fledglings. "Here you are, Mrs. Cucumber," she said, and with the help of Asa who steadied the rather heavy watering can, they showered the plants. "See, Asa, see how they love it!" she exclaimed. And indeed, it appeared that the thirsty vegetables were most grateful for the dry earth sucked up the water and the drooping leaves perked up as if they were reaching forward to offer thanks to their givers. Agnes watched for several minutes, but unlike most days when she would relish the moment just to enjoy her daughter's youthful antics, something was pressing on her mind, the box.

"What could it hurt to just open it," she decided and shrugged her shoulders as if talking to another. "Colonel doesn't care. Why if the situation were reversed I certainly wouldn't mind. It wasn't as if it was addressed to him." Agnes walked back into the house and into the living room where she sat down in the overstuffed armchair next to the parlor table and picked up the box. "Perhaps it's for the both of us. Yes, that makes much more sense," she surmised. "It's for the both of us." Yet this bit of compromise was a half-truth that she knew was designed to satisfy her insatiable curiosity. "Well, it matters not. It's not like Colonel and I keep secrets from each other!" And with those words, she placed the box on her lap and began to unbuckle the strap. However, just as her fingers loosened the secured clasp, she hesitated. "It would be dreadful if Flora came in and saw me!" she shuttered as a parcel of guilt began to fill her head. Although she was not doing anything wrong, the fact that she was acting sneaky made her feel less of a positive role model for her daughter. This fact gave her reason to exercise her self-reproach and just before uttering another condemnation she stopped herself and said, "Darn!" Its tone was not nearly as effective but was all the same much more genteel. The ill-smelling box had barely been compromised, and with a hint of larceny in her step, she headed for the stairs and up to the privacy of her bedroom.

Chapter 13

Like a pair of hound dogs, the Timpson brothers found their way through the thickets and brush until they came upon dusk. And unlike the closing of another day filling the sky with stars and mist, they brought upon the twilight the foul stench of yesterday's ill will. Though once youths filled with hope and promise, their souls were now tarnished with battlefield stains and betrayal. And so, with the full intention of revenge, they came within viewing distance of the Jameson home. As a pair of vipers would slither along the ground until coming upon a suitable resting place, so did the brothers find a secluded place to sleep, behind the thickets.

"What do you suppose that is?" whispered Dennet with his eyes staring out over the garden wall. In the shadows of dusk, the tattie-bogle was devilish.

Lucas lifted his head. Within the fading light, the stuffed man hung limply over the steak as if having been impaled. Its hat had fallen below the brow, and the chin rested on a deflated chest. The rest of the body was a mere silhouette of a lifeless figure. "Looks like a dead guy," muttered the elder.

"Yeah, but it ain't." Dennet's voice dropped off as if he was not convinced. The tattie-bogle swayed lightly in the cooling air and as the night fell upon it so did the moon withdraw its shadow and cast its glow upon the scraggly legs. The beam inched up the body until it found its way to the top of the scarecrow where all its energy was placed upon the soulless man. "Who does it look like?" Dennet asked. But in the moments that were unresponsive, the inquisitive man spoke again. "Who does it look like?" This time the question was more emphatic.

"Shut the hell up!" groaned the elder rolling over onto his back. He pulled his blanket up to his chin, but now he was awake and annoyed.

"Like that Private, you know the one we brought back." Dennet stared hard into the night at the tattie-bogle. It seemed to be lit up with all the moon's glory.

"Shit!' exclaimed Lucas. He flipped on to his stomach and looked at the propped man dangling from the pole. He hated to admit it, but the figure brought back to the forefront a reminder he had buried away, and like a dog that remembers the location of each bone it hides, Lucas recalled the heinous incident.

"He shouldn't have tried to run, nothin' would have happened if he just didn't try to run!" Dennet explained. The words stirred the emotions already embroiled in his brother's thoughts. The tormented man buried his head in his arms.

"Cut the crap!" Lucas threatened. "It's only a damned scarecrow!" His protest was as intimidating as his voice, yet all the while he too was tormented by this ghoulish reminder. "Besides," he whispered, "we were just obeying orders. Don't ferget, obeying orders." But his contemplations trailed behind his voice, and the image of the writhing body, a soldier not much older than eighteen, was caught up in his brain like a fish in a net that flounders to get out. "Orders, we obeyed military orders. Now go to sleep," he said with a trickle of compassion. But that was all the under-standing he was going to dole out. Ten years had passed, and as close as they were to their target, this was no time to get soft. He looked over at his resting brother and wanted to say something, but nothing came to mind. The man was under his blanket and perhaps almost asleep.

However, the younger was not sleeping and had stealthily retrieved the picture of the blonde from out of his pocket. He held it up close to his face but no matter how hard he tried to make out the picture, the blackness of the night permitted her image to be revealed only from his memory. "I'll find you when this is all over!" he thought and then kissed her and placed the picture back in his pocket.

The stirrings of night arrived from all directions. The insects, the birds, the small creatures that delighted in leaving home after dark were emancipated, free to mingle; only the two men remained silent, quiet, amidst the grip of slumber. Night smothered the heavens and the earth, a formidable blanket of the unknown.

———— •̶ ————

What is the first to awaken; the rooster, the warbler, the gray squirrel? Is it the morning-glory, the crocus, or the crimson poppy? Perhaps the fish drifting in the darkness, idling with the tide until day breaks? Like the refrain in a chorus, the sun is predictably early, always returning to lighten the world. But first, it feigns sleep slipping upward in silence until it pounces upon us in perfect brilliance. However, in that upside-down time of the day, neither morning nor night, when quiet prevails and the sky is mute from colors, it was the devious pair that awoke ahead of even the lark.

The dusty brothers lay side-by-side, heads resting on all the possessions they owned and when they stretched each was conscious of the discomfort relegated from sleeping on the ground. Trickery had got the best of them and all teachings of "turn the other cheek" could not ease their festering need for vengeance.

Dennet yawned and opened his eyes. "Think anyone saw us last night?" It was a curious first thought for the day, especially when he knew there was no possibility.

"Couldn't have." But the foremost thought on his mind was keeping the plan together. Patience was their only deterrent, and like a child waiting until Christmas morning to open the gifts, he too was feeling restless. At the time when the first scheme of revenge was put into motion neither knew about the little girl, yesterday was their first encounter with this crumb of good fortune. As for the outcome of their design, the casualties of war were too numerous to burden one's self with individuals. Useless as trying to segregate each grain of sand from an hourglass, Dennet and Lucas could not be burdened with sentimentality. There had been no immunity for any man, woman, or child. Some fared better than others. However, the majority were maimed in some way or another; physically, psychologically, financially, morally. Before, during, and after, the effects spread like manure over the land germinating seeds of misery and despair. And when the war was over, despondency and sadness flourished for families on both sides of the battlefields; a grieving period that never seemed to end for so many dead souls.

They gathered their meager belongings and crouched behind the rotting oak's trunk. Dennet picked a blade of grass and wiggled it in front of a line of ants. They appeared to be marching over the burly tree without a specific destination. The leader of the troop traipsed over the leafy stalk, and the others followed until one foolish ant scampered along the blade breaking the momentum of the others. "Too bad," Dennet said, and with a light brush of the reed, the rest tumbled off onto the ground.

"Quit yer foolin' around," grumbled Lucas as he yanked the grass blade out of his brother's hand and flicked it away. "Get yer shit together!"

The younger paid little attention and with his finger proceeded to antagonize the ants until he became bored and leaned his back against the gnarled bark. "Nature sure doesn't want us to be comfortable," he complained as he shifted to reposition himself. But no matter how he fidgeted he could not get settled.

"What the hell's the matter with you?" The explosion in Lucas's temperament was barely contained, and though he blamed it on his younger brother, in reality, it was his wild and untamed character that fueled his anger. Dennet turned and shrugged his shoulders with a gesture of an adolescent. It was difficult for the elder to remain angry for long and he often wondered if perhaps his younger brother had lost some of his smartness in the war. There was a slowness about him that had developed over the years, and as tough and bravado as Dennet was, he now exhibited a sort of innocence that needed guarding; it was the kind of innocence that could get a man into trouble.

As if having been separated from a pack of jackals, the Timpson brothers were not an uncommon breed among those that roamed the countryside. They were opportunists and clever men, both resourceful and dangerous. A massive shadow fell over the garden and the house as clouds were swept up by the morning breeze and attached one to the other like sticky pieces of white cotton candy. Hunger had crept into the mouths of both men during the night, and they peeked over the bulwark with a single sensation, to find something to eat. It was just a matter of a few hours until these fiends would scavenge, reclaim, and eliminate. But by the light of the tapering stars, they would satisfy the most primal need, a charge that could be relieved by way of the garden.

———•———

A gray film lifted into the sky. It was lighter than air, so it easily ascended. Dusty gray, the vapor was not more than a billow of smoke, and after a time its edgeless shape dissipated, leaving in its wake a faint aroma of cooked meat.

"Oh, no!" exclaimed Flora. Her eyes burned with disbelief. "Asa, did you let the cottontail out?" The accusation was as stunning as the revelation of the missing rabbit; however, the look of denial in the man's eyes only softened her blame. "Well, how did it get out?" she asked in wonderment. Both the man and child walked around the hutch where a set of footprints was quickly revealed. "Those aren't yours!" she said pointing to the criss-crossed prints of boots. Asa bent down and with an eye to discovery poked his finger into the imprint of the sole. With raw-edged curiosity, he stood up and followed the trail that traveled helter-skelter around the garden, meandering along the back fence. He leaned forward between the timbers and then stood back upright. Flora, who had been busy scurrying about the vegetables, scampered to his side with excited enthusiasm. "You suppose someone came in and took our bunny?" She knew that Asa would not reply yet she wished for at least a wordless acknowledgment to her question. She tugged on his shirtsleeve. "You think it's stolen?" she whispered. The notion was both intriguing and frightening. She tugged again at his sleeve, but all the while he stared about with quickened glances as if he were searching for an overboard seaman. Moments passed, and then without warning, Asa lifted his foot onto the first rung and with a quick spring, hoisted himself over the fence. Sheer panic followed as Flora squealed. "Asa!" But his ears did not hear. The child's cry of concern had now turned away from the missing rabbit. She clenched the wooden rails with both hands and with her head between the slats tipped forward. "Asa, it's just an old cottontail!" But he did not heed her despondent call, and as if being led by a rope he did not turn but proceeded into the stony field ahead.

Flora's mind squandered valuable time as she debated whether to go back home to get her mother or to fetch Asa herself. She watched the man as he took long deliberate steps, stopping every now and again, dropping below the horizon line as he scanned the ground for human tracks.

However, the field was burly and filled with thickets, not revealing its trespassers. "Why is he leaving?" Flora's thoughts skipped from one idea to another. Asa was her responsibility, what would Agnes and Colonel think if she lost him? Her heart raced as her indecisions made her all the more confused until finally she made up her mind and slid between a pair of fenced timbers. "Wait, Asa, wait up!" she shouted, and if the wind bothered to carry her demand, she did not know for she could hear nothing but the beating of an anxious heart.

———•———

"I'm back!" Colonel climbed the stairs listening for some heartfelt reply. "Agnes, I'm home," he called.

"In here, Colonel." Agnes's voice drifted through the keyhole and out into the hallway.

"What are you doing locked away in here?" asked the man as he opened the door. But as soon as he entered his usual ruddy complexion grew anemic. "Where did that come from?" he asked. His eyes met the box as if he had just reunited with an old enemy.

She lifted the box from off her lap and extended it to him. "Found it out front, kind of unusual. I was cleaning up, and there was a rapping on the door. When I finally got to it, no one was there; just this out on the porch." He took the box and sat down on the bed next to her with his cane resting against his knee. It was a four-poster bed, far too expensive for their taste, but when the Widow Conrad gave it to them as a wedding gift, it was much too nice to turn down. At first, Agnes thought it was unlucky to take a bed from a widow, but when Colonel came home with a new horsehair mattress, it stifled all superstition. Such a comfortable bed she had never slept in.

"You say no one was there?" he resumed placidly.

"Well, must have been somebody or somebodies to deliver it, but I guess they were in a hurry. I thought it was kind of strange."

Colonel nodded while still holding the reptilian container. He set it aside without offering any intention of investigating its contents.

"You're gonna open it, aren't you?" Agnes asked and crossed over his lap to retrieve what she believed to be a call to action. "Cause if you're not curious I sure am. This is the most excitement we've had in ages." She smiled and kissed him on his cheek.

A long sigh fell over the man as he smiled with approval for the sentiment bestowed by his wife. She shook the box next to her ear and then handed it back. "Where's Flora?" he asked as his thought descended upon the child.

"Watering the vegetables with Asa." But by now the woman's patience was at its breaking point. "Come on, let's see!" she whispered. "It might be something magical, you never know!"

"That's the Scottish blood in you talking," he laughed. "Magic usually doesn't come disguised in snakeskin. I'm afraid if you want magic then you had better wait for a brass lamp!" But before slipping the buckle open, he fingered the casing. "Looks to me like it might not be snake at all. Here feel it," he said.

Agnes placed her finger against the box and then pulled back with revulsion. "What is it then?"

"It just might be a lizard. These scales feel more pebble-like, and if it were skin off a snake, they would be flatter." He rubbed his hand along the lid with a self-assurance that his diagnosis was correct. "If I were a betting man, I'd put my money on Gila monster."

"Good lord!" she exclaimed and what was once a rather curious box had turned instantly ghastly.

"Poisonous critters," Colonel added. "But you don't have to worry about Gila monsters. Unless we go west, we won't run into one of those." He turned to get her reaction but could see that she was not smiling. Rather, her thoughts were rushing ahead of his fingers, and as he began to unfasten the lid, she placed her hand over his.

"Colonel, this doesn't feel right," she warned and pressed down to prevent him from lifting the lid. "Maybe we should throw it away. Take it to the river and sink it!"

"Now you're talking nonsense. What could fit into a box that could hurt us?" his voice, so sincere, did make her fears seem suddenly childish. After all, it was only a box, no bigger than a jewelry box or even a music box.

"I guess I am being silly," she said and slowly placed her hand on her lap. "Go ahead then, open it."

A silence fell over the room; the same kind of silence one feels when lowering a casket into a grave. The sun had found the open window and crept inside and across the bed. It fell over the two pillows that lay tucked under the quilted spread; only it made a detour down the side to the floor as if deliberately avoiding the seated man and woman.

Colonel handed the lid to Agnes and placed the box on his lap. As if a gavel had been dropped to pronounce a verdict his chin lowered, and he picked up the bundle within its confines. Wide-eyed, he stared at the papers.

"What is it? What's got you so spooked?" She placed her hand on his shoulder as he sifted through the pile disclosing a worthless fortune in Confederate bonds. But it wasn't until he came to the bottom of the stack did the adjudication of the contents become evident. He turned the lone playing card over and then handed it to his wife.

"What is this?" she asked. It was at first unfamiliar, but then in only a moment she too recognized the all too familiar face. "It's the joker," she muttered, her words barely audible as her breathing was drawing from shallow pools of air. "It's the joker!" she repeated with noticeable misgivings.

As though rooted in the spot, Colonel reached for his cane and pried himself up. He seemed taller now, and as if the contents of the box had re-energized the man, Agnes no longer felt afraid. But as he unfolded himself, a satin ribbon that was dislodged during the investigation of the papers had fallen to the floor and was now made aware of by the gathering up of the cane. Reaching down, he picked up the pink sash and extended it before him. A light gust entered the room, and like the menacing swing of a noose, it rocked the back and forth. "Flora!" Agnes gasped and pulled the ribbon away from her husband's hand grasping it tightly in her fist. The unforeseen actions ushered forth a torrent of fear, a fear so great that every part of her body seemed to shake.

Colonel hobbled across the bedroom and leaned out the open window. The bond between parent and child ignited; every atom, every breath, every sound, and sight; he was blind to anything else. "Flora," he bellowed. "Flora get inside!"

Consternation was trying to swallow her up as Agnes retreated from the bed and pushed the father aside. "Flora come inside!" Her voice raged with motherly persuasion. But as hard as she tried, she did not see nor hear the little girl. Both listened for the child's reply, but the only response they received was the wind whistling through the leaves and the mimic of a mockingbird toying with their emotions. The crumpled ribbon unraveled as Agnes opened her clenched fist and then clasping it to her cheek she shook her head in dismay, "What have we done!" she bemoaned, "Dear Lord, what have we done!"

Beyond the fence line was familiar territory that had been traversed only with a chaperone; a mud-bed creek; a lovely place Flora had journeyed many times with Colonel. It was a summertime favorite of blooming jewelweed and marsh marigolds where she would wade in the cold water that rifled over her feet as if it were always late for an appointment. She liked to skim her hand across the stream and let it slip through her fingers, all the while lifting her petticoat so as to keep the hem dry. But beyond the creek, it was foreboding. The trees isolated the land from the sky with a canopy that allows only a fraction of the sun to penetrate its leafy awning. This was unchartered territory, and she only meant to stay away long enough to persuade the man home. But intentions do not always coincide with well-intended plans for their journey into the wood had been met by a most unexpected storm, and as the rain fell heavily, it created a blinding sheet of wind and rain. Flora followed Asa as he maneuvered his way, aligning himself with a wall of rock until he came to a hollow alcove recessed into the barrier. The child followed the man as he dipped his head beneath the rocky jaw and hunched over where he sat down just a few feet from the opening. The only source of light was ushered in by the oval entrance, and she made no protests though it was as dingy and dank a place she had ever ventured. But being it was barely deep enough to hold the title of cave, she felt little fear. It took a few moments for her eyes to adjust to the dim surroundings. Any bats that made this a home would have lined the ceiling with their upside-down way of sleeping and Flora sighed with relief that the only sign of life was a trail of ants. Asa sat rigid, his knees up and his head bowed between his resting arms. "Don't worry, Asa," she said. "It should stop raining soon." Flora felt strangely cozy, and she tapped his arm with reassurance for she knew he didn't like to be confined. Flora leaned her head against the man's shoulder. "I think we better rest here, Asa," she said. "I don't think Agnes or Colonel would mind if we stayed here til' it's over." He reached into his pocket and retrieved a piece of bread and handed it to the child and she accepted it. But before she put it to her lips, she broke it into two pieces and opening his fist, placed half back into his hand.

He looked down at his boots and tapped them together. *The mud had fused onto the soles. When he walked, they made a squeaking sound, and when ten thousand men walked in the mud, it resonated through the forest like one tremendous squeal. He raised the bread to his mouth but refused the food. There were too many hungrier mouths.* Such an insignificant amount of food would do little for him. He placed the piece back into the small palm. "What wrong Asa, aren't you hungry?" the inquisitive voice asked.

"What's wrong Private, aren't you hungry?" The squatting soldier stabbed the end of a bayonet through three slices of sowbelly and heating them over the coals let the fat drip onto the hardtack. He turned into the eyes of the voice and shook a reply "no." A canon explosion drew closer, and he rested his head in his hands and winced. It stopped and then grew bolder, louder, the noise approaching with merely a minute between each new blast. He peered up at his feet, glad that he still had his boots. He leaned forward and turned his head to the opening. "Keep yer head down! Keep yer head down!" The holler of thunder was loud and violent, but like a locomotive roaring along the tracks, it soon could only be heard grumbling in the near distance reminding the listener of its presence.

Flora held the bread in her hand and waited for a few minutes before speaking. "Maybe when you get home, you could make a picture of the cottontail." Asa stomped his boots on the bare earth, and a clump of mud fell from the heel as Flora surrendered to her hunger and ate the remaining piece. The rain pitched its anger, the wind howled, and the drabness of the day continued to creep into the hollow refuge, and they patiently waited for it to stop. Flora's passing hours were measured by the storm and the beating of the raindrops against the earth, while the marching in mud had taken up permanent residence in Asa's head.

———— • ————

Time dripped like a leaky faucet with the reminder that no matter what indiscretions or malice had been performed all regrets were set aside for the moment. Like a hornet circling a hive, the warning had been initiated, and Agnes and Colonel needed to take action. War had brought out both the worst and the best in humankind; some maintained their integrity while others sought to take advantage. It was a time of valor, a time of dishonor, a time of jubilation, and a time of retribution. The sense of remorse that Agnes and Colonel should have felt had been hijacked by the quick dispensing of doom. Such a calculated reaction the Timpson brothers hoped to evoke had been successfully marshaled.

It had been a dry, rainless few weeks and when evil unleashed its revenge, there was no mercy. At first, the flames coiled around the house, scorching the grass and sedge and scratching the walls. But like a dog that wants to gain entry, the blaze raised itself up and effortlessly lifted onto the porch. The fire was a wild thing, roaring, crackling, growing more ravenous with each plank it fed upon. With an insatiable appetite, it consumed everything in its way. It had become the master and mistress of the house, gaining entrance with intolerance towards whatever lay in its path. The wild beast ran blindly throughout the home while the chairs and tables, the rugs and crockery, even the books on the shelves sat stiffly with the subservient complacency of a Sunday school class receiving a fire and brimstone sermon.

Mayhem fueled by the roar of the blazing mass rendering the cries of the trapped parents akin to a trickle of water in a flood; muting all human sounds to indistinguishable muffles of misery. And then as if it were delivered by the supplication of the child, the day that had begun so filled with the sunshine was suddenly deluged by a wall of gray clouds that split apart and releasing a sheet of gray water pouring forth from the heavens retribution. It rained with a vengeance soaking the unquenchable earth, and the torrent never stopped until it tamed the flames into smoldering ash.

Julio Tamayo ran across the waterlogged field as fast as his stubby legs would allow. The rain had subsided, leaving behind a scent of wet grasses and charred lumber. Flora stood tip-toed, trying to raise herself to get a better sighting of the clumsy man. "What's he saying?" she asked aloud. "Something has him very excited." But the indistinct phrases of the harried man and the distance between him and the two made it nearly impossible to understand. "I think he's speaking Spanish," she whispered, turning to Asa. "Agnes said he talks Spanish whenever he gets upset." He approached with worry. His straw hat clutched in his hand as the wind tousled his black hair, and every few steps he would mop his sweaty forehead with a knotted handkerchief.

"Mantente alejado, stay, stay!" he cried and held up his hands with the intention of preventing the child from coming any closer.

Asa eyed the farmer and then wistfully fixed upon Flora. "Why does he want us to stay here?" she asked, her tone laced with confusion. But as she unraveled the warning, her mind exposed the fears he hoarded. Suddenly the proximity of her house mixed with the noxious smell of burned wood made a clear portrait. Flora stepped forward and began to scurry across the sunlit field. She quickened her pace, darting like a startled rabbit, and then she began to run. Asa paused in the clearing, looking beyond the child and the man. A bloodhound on the scent, he rushed up behind Flora and caught her, pulling her to his side. "I want to go home, Asa!" she squealed. "I want to see my mother! Take me to my mother and father!" How audacious of the sun to settle its rays over the distraught child. Has nature no feelings, no sense of humility. Such a moment as this has no place for sunbeams; rather such a time ought to be relegated to somber or lugubrious shade offered by gray clouds or fog-laden skies.

Julio Tamayo huffed and panted as he rambled alongside. He leaned forward, trying to catch his breath.

"Why are you here?" Flora cried. "Go away, go away! I want to go home!" The overwrought child wiggled and struggled, but Asa held her fast in his arms.

The portly farmer shook his head with misery. "There is nothing to see, Flora. Nothing, nothing, nada, nada!" His words burned savagely and the more he said "nothing," the more they resurrected images of Agnes and Colonel. The good-hearted man trembled with pity, and all he could mumble was "nada, nada" as he blamelessly nodded his head back and forth wishing to find some reasonable explanation not just for the little girl, but also for himself.

Asa restrained the child, and while she struggled to be set free, he shielded her from seeing any of the destructive furies from afar. Her wails filled the air, exposing her pain and he listened with brooding silence. Torment such as this is inextinguishable, destined to remain a flickering part of the soul for pain has no distinction between young or old.

———•———

Flora had finally fallen off to sleep. Señora Tamayo tucked the blanket around the child and then stood over the bed for several minutes. The middle-aged woman was shaped like a ripe pear, but in contrast to her rotund figure, she had a comely face graced with dark eyes and full pink lips. Her head was round like a harvest moon, and when she smiled, she exposed a set of straight pearly teeth, unique for a woman of her age. She and her husband were fine, generous people and though they had been prosperous farmers their luck had not outwitted the war having lost a son in the battle of Gettysburg. A small American flag and a photograph of Abraham Lincoln were positioned over the bed, and anywhere you stood Lincoln's sad eyes seemed to follow. "Julio," the woman's whisper hinted she had an idea. "Julio, can we keep her? The child, she has no one."

The farmer settled in the easy chair, and when he opened his eyes, he sighed.

"Julio, what do you say? Can we keep her?"

He allowed a few moments to settle and like waiting for debris to rinse through a sieve, he let the idea cogitate. "You mean like a stray kitten? A feral cat would be easier to tame don't you think?"

The Señora looked at the sleeping child as one looks over a new purchase. She leaned over and then stroked the pink ribbon tied at the end of one pigtail. "She is missing one," said the middle-aged woman. "She is such a meticulous child, strange that she would not have both ribbons." Her voice lingered in her throat, and she swallowed as if intending to relieve herself of the pity that was beginning to accumulate. She dimmed the lantern that had been placed on the mahogany table beside the cot and turned toward the man sitting in the cane chair.

"Julio," whispered the Señora, "what about Asa?" She shifted over to her husband and tapped him on his forearm. The tired farmer seemed quite content, half-asleep in the comfortable chair he had titled, "the chair." His legs were propped up on the ottoman, and he was wearing a pair of freshly darned woolen socks and having unbuttoned his vest and rolled up his sleeves, he portrayed a man that was not moving for quite a while. Stirring like an annoyed cat, he opened one eye as the woman spoke again. "What about him, what are we to do?"

If Asa heard her question, he did not give away any gestures of such for he sat quite still, facing both the man and now the woman, who had pulled over a spindly wooden chair that appeared not to have the strength to hold a lady of her grand physique.

Again, Julio sighed, but this time with a bit more uncertainty. "No se, no se," he muttered. Then he closed his eyes with all intentions of blocking out the world.

Señora Tamayo sat quietly, her large posterior filled the seat and although she looked rather uncomfortable, she maintained the posture of a woman seated in a confessional. She reached into her generous apron pocket, pulled out a garland of beads, made a sign of the cross, and smiled at Asa. His eyes met the kindly woman, and he watched as she lowered her lids and nimbly began to run her fingers along the glassy rosary. Her lips moved elegantly with the movement of her fingers transfixed in a personal moment of peace. It was a curious thing; each had retreated into their own space. Only Asa was restless.

He stared at the woman sitting across the room and then at the man. He watched the rise and fall of the farmer's stomach as the sleeping man snored in a stuttering fashion, his mouth agape and his fat fingers pinched together over his belly. The moon-faced woman's lips were moving without uttering a sound while Flora stirred softly every now and again. The quiet of room was stifling, and he felt as if he would suffocate. *"You know you won't be able to leave so you might as well stop your pacing."* He laced his fingers through his hairline and tugged down to the nape of his neck. He could feel that it had all grown back. Asa stood up, but Señora Tamayo did not hear him, only her fingers remained moving, the lips that had been so quick were now still. He turned to Flora and walked over to the end of the cot. He lifted the blanket and then pulled it up to her ankles. His eyes widened as the stocking feet were revealed. He bent down on his knees and reached beneath the bed. He groped wildly, sliding his hand along the dusty floorboards until he felt the pair of small leather boots that had shifted out of reach. *"Looking for these?" the attendant gloated. He wanted to pull them away, but the more he tugged, the more the restraints burned his wrist. Such articles commanded a premium, and Asa was willing to crack a skull for these. He twisted and pulled, shouting profanities, but his feet and hands were bound, all attempts to raise himself up were futile. "Too bad you're tied to your bed, but don't worry I'll keep them for you til' morning."* Asa stretched his arm along the side and reclaimed the child's boots, setting them on the table beside the lantern. Then he leaned over the sleeping child and listened. Flora's breathing was light as a hummingbird. He moved away and as quiet as a rabbit slipped out the front door.

The shadows of the hills fell over the land shaping headstones upon the earth. The past hours unnerved the eldest brother like the respite at the gallows, and even the simple act of drinking water caught up in his throat nauseating him with the same unpleasant feeling of being seasick. He was a brutal man, coarse, ruthless, and at times pitiless, but a murderer? The events of the day had gotten out of hand. What started as a threat was reduced to cold-blooded murder. After setting the torch to the house, the younger had absconded with what food he had lifted off the countertop, and now he was eating it as if invited to a picnic.

Lucas sat with the full weight of his torso and head against the tree as his brother leaned over the bread and greedily pulled apart the soft dough. "Must have just been taken out of the oven," he said, offering up a generous piece. But Lucas closed his eyes and ignored the other who ravaged the loaf with the same veracity of a coyote tearing at the flesh of its last kill.

"If I hadn't fallen asleep…," his mind shot to the earlier part of the day while he ignored the obvious answer to his question, what if. But he had fallen asleep and when he awoke it was too late. "Shit!" His exclamation evoked anger, disgust, and now dread was churning in his stomach. "How can you eat? How can you eat?" he hollered.

"Guess yesterday's rabbit didn't fill me up." He smiled slyly and wiped his mouth on his shirtsleeve soiled with the sooty ash. He brushed his hands lightly along his pant leg and then stood up to stretch. "Think I'll go for a walk. Want to come?"

The elder opened his eyes and glared at the standing man. "Where you goin'?" he asked. No longer did he trust the younger brother; all confidence in him to make any rational judgment had been eradicated by his impetuous act.

"Just trampin' down the hill." His eyes searched in the direction of his intentions.

Lucas snorted with disgust. Dennet was still his brother, but he couldn't help but feel that his transgressions were a noose around his neck.

He pulled his legs up and leaned his head back to get a better look at the man standing above him. However, when he tilted his chin up all he saw was the back of the fair-head walking in the opposite direction. The day had been eaten up with a grotesque example of revenge. On the battle-field, he had been a party to countless ruthless attacks, yet this deliberate setting of a fire hinted at something even more savage. He hated Dennet not for what he had done or for whom he had become, but rather hated the idea that he might be responsible for his younger brother's calculated and treacherous deed. Dennet's indifference to the arson made him even more dangerous than he thought imaginable and though they had both agreed, both wanted to even the score, he couldn't help but wonder if perhaps he had been too successful in his molding of the youth.

Dennet plodded through the scrubby brush. Yesterday's fire had consumed all his energy, but now that he was refortified with bread and water, the eerie stillness of the wood and oncoming dusk hurried him towards the site. He was sure nothing had been accidentally left behind that would point to his wrongdoing, however, not wanting to leave any-thing to chance, the decision to survey the property seemed necessary. "Ain't nobody around there for at least half-a-mile," he told himself as he struggled against the fantasy attached to his thoughts. He was experienc-ing what some would call a guilty conscience, a noble gesture he was not accustomed to. Dennet grappled with a host of concerns, yet being an unscrupulous man, his defective morality supplanted his uneasiness by glorifying his actions as having righted a wrong. And so, he bounded down towards the house as if he were on his way to a musical affair whistling a war tune, *Tramp, Tramp, Tramp*. *"In the battlefront, we stood, when their fiercest charge they made, and they swept us off, a hundred men or more."* His first encounter with the song was during the march towards Petersburg, and though it lit up the brigade like fireflies in the summer, its lyrics had been sprouted in the prison camp of Andersonville. *"Tramp, tramp, tramp. The boys are marching. Cheer up, comrades, they will come."* Dennet didn't see the irony in his selection of songs as he traipsed through the deepening grass, and most likely he never gave any thought to the lyrics which had been sung by imprisoned soldiers to displace despair with the hope of liberation from out of their man-made hell.

Sunshine tumbled over the land as it dried the dewy field. A brooding heat was dispensed, and he slid the sweat-soaked rim of his hat to the back of his head exposing his forehead and eyes to the elements. For a moment he cursed the heat, but when his sights fell upon the distant image of the ruinous structure, he left behind his temporary discomfort. He squatted behind a thinning thicket of scrubs and lowered the brim back over his brow. Regret was a feeling he had squandered at the gambling tables and whore houses; he wasn't quite sure what he was feeling now, but he knew it wasn't regret. To even a score was as natural as accepting a free drink of whiskey; some things can't be disputed or accepted as more than good luck. He ran his fingers along the yellowing spikelets until one of the heads crumbled into a powder of dried dust and dropped onto the earth. Dennet mashed his foot down and crushed the sole into the damp soil. Being at the right place at the right time was the Timpson Brother's catalyst to execute the law of retaliation, "an eye for an eye." Dennet peered through the rows of spiny shoots, one behind the other they grew in mass until the eye was tricked into seeing one greenish brown mound in the near distance, appearing too thick to get around. He pushed the weeds apart and still the columns before him were tall and strong. Slowly, raising up with a soldier's guile, he twisted left and right as if looking for an enemy rifle-pit before attending to a full stance. A timid gust of wind blew, and he relished the moment. Then, without delay, he began to walk.

———— •————

Despite its shabby clothes and a stuffed head sprinkled with ash and despair, the tattie-bogle dominated the garden as its protector and the only witness to the fiery destruction. Asa stood beside Wooley and swung the limp foot as if the action would resurrect the scarecrow. Remarkable as it was, the garden remained unintimidated, inviting the birds to peck its ripening vegetables and the worms to aerate the soil. So, if there was such a thing as magic, it could certainly be ascertained that the stuffed man had indeed saved the small plot of land from destruction. Perhaps the forces that create the winds to blow had evoked an edict, relegating the fire to only the structure of the house and keeping Mother Nature's work intact.

The wooden house that had once consisted of two stories and a wraparound porch sheltering the dwellers from the morning sun was now little more than a roof and blackened timbers. Like the last soldier standing on the battlefield, it was considerably wounded with scorched planks and charred joists, though refused to surrender. Supported only by the will of its fine construction, the Jameson home had ultimately met its match. However, the chimney of red and orange brick appeared unaltered, while the kitchen's hearth too had not been destroyed. Silent and merciless, the smoke-choked whatever took a breath, and the absence of birds and insects was a reminder of the hideous crime. There had been no compassion for the house, its inhabitants, or the surrounding property. All of humanity seemed to have turned its back.

The man who was responsible approached the property by the garden fence. A tomato plant, too heavy to stand up on its own, had found refuge resting along the bottom rail where the greedy man pulled off a red but immature fruit from the vine. However, the bitterness of the tomato was not to his liking, and he tossed it over the fence back into the garden, striking the tattie-bogle squarely on its back. Dennet stepped lively as he rounded the garden and as if entering the walkway as a guest, he was undaunted by the ruinous structure that stood before him. He stopped for a moment to consider his alternatives. But as a fox eyes the chicken coop, it does not always know the farmer is behind him. Such was the situation now for at the moment Dennet was approaching, he was grabbed from behind causing him to lose his footing. Without a moment's loss, the fallen man jumped to his feet, but not before retrieving the knife sheathed on his belt. The razor-like edge cut the air as Dennet flaunted the blade; his stance positioned with arms and body wavering like a cobra ready to strike.

Asa stood motionless, his eyes fixed upon the murder's, and though they did not flicker nor offer any recognition of remembrance, Dennet's deadly glare softened. "Hey, I know you!" he exclaimed. "Five Forks, right?" Asa's head moved slowly, acknowledging the man's recognition. Dennet lowered the blade and returned to a more relaxed stance. "Shit, why didn't you say something instead of kidding around just now?" Dennet lifted his shirt and slipped the knife back in the holder and then with a sudden burst of energy wagged his finger. "Asa, you're, Asa! Wow, how long has it been? Ten years, right? No, maybe more like twelve!" But Asa did not move; he only stared blankly at the man who was pouring out his war-time sentimentality of comradeship. "Wait till I tell Lucas. He won't believe it. Ten years, damn!"

Dennet spoke with a moody nervousness in his voice. With no regard to the listener's possible condemnation, he freely released a torrent of accusations. Dennet was comforted by the quiet nature of the day and the man before him, but as the sun smothered them with its blistering rays, Asa drifted towards the shade of the lean-to, while Dennet followed like a sinner to a confessional. Open on three sides; the makeshift struc-ture housed the Jameson tools and several empty crates. Asa sat down on one of the smaller wooden boxes taking up a considerable amount of room with his outstretched legs. Dennet picked out a smaller crate, faced it towards the other and sat down, distinctly pleased to be resting his legs. It has been said that those who commit a crime often find solace in talking. So, as if the evil man were before a priest, he spoke freely and without interruption, for who better a listener to find than Asa. "That bastard Colonel had it comin' to him," he snarled. "He was a liar and a cheat! All through the war me and Lucas trusted him, but then, come time to cash in, we find out everything we won was nothing but worthless shit. Everything! We lost everything!" He shifted uneasily on the small box when his venomous accusations turned to laughter, and his eyes appeared tigerish yellow. "Now look who got the last word!" The delight in his situation only magnified the cruel man's vengeance.

Asa bent over and ran his fingers along the ground, drawing a few lines in the dirt as he listened to the ravings. "Confederate bonds, he said they were good and would be worth twice as much as the printed value. We believed the son-of-a-bitch. Well, we showed him, and that wife. You can't go around cheating without gettin' what's comin' to you!" The voice that had been pent up for a decade shook with anger and as he spoke he trembled, spewing out his torment like an animal that has been caged and finally freed. "We were damn stupid. He told us that even the French were buyin' them up. Said bonds would be better than any money, and the way the war was going, we could sell them for twice their worth. Twice the worth!" Dennet shook his head and spat in disgust. "Damn French, damn all of them, liars!" Asa ran his boot heel across the picture, wiping it away and sat back up in a pose that suggested he was listening with his attention upon the speaker.

"You hungry?" Dennet asked, now aware of his stomach grumbling. "We could go forage the garden. There's a hutch out by the back fence, but me and Lucas already killed the rabbit. Skinned and ate it. Damn fools didn't even hear us the night before. Why we just came in, opened the cage and with one good squeeze broke its neck." With the litheness of a cat, he stood up and stretched his arms over his head. A dwindling stream of sunlight had entered the shelter and now trickled inside, spilling over his boots. "Well, looky here, must be from that doe." He lifted his leg to display the blood-stained boot and then wiped the tip on the back of his pant leg.

More permanent than a memory which can be temporarily distracted, the smell of death can never be washed away. No matter how much mud and rain, there was never enough to coat the earth or cover the stench. Asa loathed the smell, and its presence was ever more prominent right now. Dominating all senses, he heard the silent cry of the rabbit, saw its pink eyes blinking, felt its body trembling, terrified, helpless, and for the second before life is exterminated there was only the sensation of sheer terror. Asa now stood close enough to Dennet to shake hands although such a sentiment was pure fiction. But Dennet found the company of Asa, though strange in its one-sided conversation, refreshing. "Come on, let's find something to eat!" he urged, however, if he heard the death bells tolling, he was deaf to their meaning.

Retribution crushed Dennet in deadly silence as the mute man clasped his hand around the muscular neck and with fatal precision slowly applied Herculean strength. He heard the gasping for breath by the stunned man, saw his gray eyes blinking. Like the first quiver of an avalanche he felt the body tremble, and for the second before life is exterminated there was the sensation of sheer terror. The chin fell upon the chest, the muscles in the neck too weak to hold up the head as the windpipe was crushed. Asa stepped back and let the man fall forward on his face. He gave Dennet a kick, and without delay stripped the torso free from its shirt. He slid the knife from the exposed sheath and sliced into the back of the head and neck, slashing an X as if marking a spot. Blood filled the incision forming a red tattoo and quickly trickled down the back of the ears and dripped to the ground. Asa bent down and pulled the right arm out from under the body and stretched the hand flat against the earth. Several flies had already begun to hover, buzzing feverishly over the head wound. Asa straddled the body and stretched the other arm outward.

The vindicator stared down at the slain man while he listened to the wind, a restless visitor, stir in and out of the lean-to. The thirsty ground soaked up the blood as fast as it was escaping. Asa walked around the prone body, sized up the dead man's boots and pulled them free, but before exiting back into the garden, he reached into the pants pocket and retrieved a fist full of greenbacks and a gold piece. He wrestled his fist into the other pocket finding a pair of sultry photographs and a folded parcel of paper.

Asa unfolded the paper and read the single entry. He folded it back again and placed it into his pocket. *"You're not supposed to be in this part of the hospital, Mrs. Bushnell. Are you lost?"* Asa walked to the opening of the lean-to and lifted the photograph of the blonde into the sunlight. Only his lids flickered as he stared motionless at the woman. *"Mrs. Bushnell, where are you going?"* Asa shoved the photographs into his pocket with the paper and stood in the sun. *"Are these your drawings? Are these your drawings? Are they?"* The sympathetic voice resonated in his head. *"Are they? Are they yours?"* He shifted back inside and picked up the hat, the boots, and the shirt. He balled them up, and without giving any more attention to the dead body, he meandered back outside and down along the well-groomed path towards the garden gate.

———•———

Luck is something acquired; sometimes it is a matter of location, sometimes it is a matter of acquaintance. But for Dennet, though he had happened upon both, neither worked in his favor since the same circumstances are also the connecting links for those who acquire bad luck.

———•———

The day did not hear the suffering, but rather it doled out its misery as carefree as the chore of tossing feed to the poultry. However, make no mistake, the inhabitants who had been fed such wretchedness were as unaware of their approaching demise as the chicken eating its grain right before Sunday dinner.

When Flora awoke, Señora Tamayo was waiting for the child with a cup of fresh milk, ladled from the full bucket that was sitting on the kitchen floor. The elder woman, having encountered quite enough excitement for one day, did not notice the two cunning cats eyeing the creamy contents with all intentions of helping themselves. That is until the sleeping Sheltie came to life and chased the two away, though a bit too slow to capture the pair of culprits that were too spry and quick for even this athletic dog. The generally agile cats, however, were not so nimble and toppled over the stack of books on their mad dash to get away! "Perro malo, malo!" agonized the ill-tempered woman, whacking the dog across its behind with a long-handled soup spoon as it trotted back inside.

"He was only helping," Flora explained and excused the dog for its poor manners, though heroic in her mind, she petted the top of its soft head as it lay down by the foot of the cot. But the Sheltie did not even pretend to fall asleep and kept one eye on its mistress as she neared the bed.

The woman found her motherly side and handed the child the milk, which Flora drank heartily. Yet, the sweet taste could not erase the bitterness that had accumulated in the short unthinkable hours of the day. "I want to go home now," she announced and reaching for her shoes, she began to put them back on. By this time Señora had awoken her husband, who would have been quite content to remain sleeping in his chair and leave the child to his wife instead of the curt chastising he was receiving by his well-meaning but annoying wife.

"Thank you, but it is time for me to go, now!" Flora announced and slid off the bed. Running her hands along the front of her smock, she straightened out the creases and then looked up. "Please tell Asa that I am going back to the house, and he can meet me at the end of the road," the little girl added, and raising her hand on the door latch she turned to speak once again. "Thank you for the nap and the milk. It was very kind of you." Both adults stood aghast and wide-eyed at the departing child. "Please don't be too mad at the dog, he is a very nice fellow." Flora smiled at the dog who appeared to smile back, for his head was not resting on the floor as before, but rather sitting like an ancient sphinx.

But before she could have a chance to pull open the heavy wooden door, Señora tootled over and pulled her hand gently away from the latch. "No, no, Flora. You must stay with us for just a little while," she petitioned as the woman beckoned with her eyes for her husband to respond. But the man, too astounded by the little girl's gallantry could not be discreetly prompted by his wife and continued to stare as if he were in the presence of Joan of Arc herself. "Jorge! Habla!" she shouted, awakening the man from his stupor.

"Si, si," he fumbled with his words. "Señora is right, Flora. You need to stay with us. Your house is no longer what it was. It met an accident. A very bad accident."

"Fire," the child retorted. "There was a fire, I know. That's why I have to go home, to help Colonel and Agnes clean-up the mess."

In the minds of the good-hearted neighbors, the interpretation of the catastrophe conveyed a more sinister ending which smothered any of their well-intended explanations. How could they tell Flora that her parents were dead? They were not equipped to shoulder such a responsibility. "Perhaps," whispered the elder man, "we could get Asa to explain."

"Asa?" the woman replied with an incredulous air. "The fool never speaks."

Julio Tamayo nodded his head and in his usual manner sighed deeply, giving way for his wife to add her own sigh of disgust, but not for the situation, rather towards her husband.

"Come, Flora. Let us wait until later. There are chores you can help me with." The dog that seemed to be listening for a cue tottered over to the door and nudged its head against Flora's leg. It looked up with sad eyes, and as if saying, "stay with me" must have appealed to her sweet sentiments. "What's its name?" she asked.

"This is Toro," introduced the jolly farmer with a chuckle. "Do you know what the name means," he laughed again as the dog wagged its tail upon hearing its name. Flora shrugged "no." "Bull! It means bull!"

Flora wriggled her nose at this disagreeable name for such a soft and innocent dog saddled with a brute of a name seemed unjust. "Toro!" she called, "I will stay with you tonight. Then I will go home tomorrow." The child nodded in agreement, and the dog sealed it with several licks on her hand.

"He likes you!" cried Señora. "Yes, you stay with us tonight," she said, "but first, go outside and fetch some water to wash with. You will like it here." Then with little else to do, Flora did as she was told.

Flora was not in the habit of telling a fib, but she was presently under the influence of the most extraordinary set of circumstances, so her actions, or misdeeds if you like, should not be found offensive. She had visited the Tamayo farm on several occasions, having been sent by Agnes to retrieve fresh eggs or bacon as an exchange for interpreting legal documents or bank papers. Those trips across the field and up the knoll were traversed during daylight with either Asa or Agnes. This would be the first time she was venturing back in the dusky evening, the time when some creatures go to sleep, and others are just awakening. Flora headed out into the gray evening and followed the lively Sheltie as if she had not a care in the world and no intentions of returning to the farmer's house.

———•———

The house would have presented itself in a most grand manner had the eye not been distracted by the charred walls and smoldering wooden porch. But to the child, it was home, and she extended her vision beyond what was provided by the arsonist. She wished to return, and nothing would keep her away.

Toro nosed about, disturbing what seemed to be every leaf and every twig, and although Flora was pleased for the company, the curious animal would soon prove to be a nuisance. "Go home, Toro," she insisted in her most commanding voice, but he ignored her plea since her tone was comparatively youthful and sweet in contrast to the gruffness he was accustomed to and continued on his way. Wearily she traipsed on and the further she ventured away from the farmhouse the lonelier and grayer it grew. Twilight was falling quickly and had the dog not been splattered with touches of white fur, he would be camouflaged between the folds of evening. There were no stars or moon to guide; there were no house lanterns in the distance or torches in the garden. Only the revival of her memory would set her on the correct path, but sometimes no matter how one tries the evening plays tricks. As if having been tossed about by a great wave in the sea, what is the bottom or top can be mistaken one for the other. So it was with the shadowy path, the greens and browns, the rocky terrain, all were blending into a confusion of earthly colors. Her only hope of reaching the ruinous home before dark was to follow the little dog that was applying all its senses towards her house. "Toro, how do you know your way to my house?" she called. But the dog cared not for the child's questioning voice; it was drawn only towards the smoldering smells omitted by the burned-out structure.

Dusk was buried in darkness and worry. Flora shuffled her feet kicking up stones and fallen leaves. With the loneliness came night sounds that had never troubled her before, and she shivered as the brisk winds whipped and tugged on her pinafore. "Toro!" she called and reached along the ground for a stick, picking up what felt like a long smooth branch. The dog's yips and yelps made her hurry with his impatience. She crossed the stick along the ground in front as she walked; her thoughts flitted feverously with unanswered questions. As hard as she tried, she could not hold back the choking fear of the unknown. But it was her trust in the small dog that was leading her and perhaps this false sense of security was just the element of surprise that the viper needed when he crawled out of his hole to take an airing. The snake was slithering silently along the ground when it was suddenly disturbed by the very stick that was intended to keep the child safe. A grotesque hissing seethed from the viper's mouth, and it licked the air with its black tongue winding up the stick. Darkness was more than a black veil over Flora, cloaking all visible senses. Only the immediate sensation of cold, clammy scales on the child's hand gave Flora reason to scream while at the very moment of this hideous terror, she released her hold on the stick and tossed it away. The snake too released its hold. Like a spring that had lost its coil, it sailed through the blackness landing only a few feet from the unsuspecting dog. Seconds passed, and within those moments the serpent lunged at the dog, propelling its fangs into the canine's soft flesh and inflicting a wound before slithering away beneath the brush.

The frightened dog's yelp pierced the night like a slash made from a knife's blade. "Toro, Toro!" Flora shouted its name; she held her arms out before her, practically sightless. She called again, pleading more frantically in hopes of retrieving the dog, but it must have scurried away, too frightened to make its presence known. Flora sensed she was alone. Too afraid to proceed much further, she stumbled about until she came to a single oak tree offering her shelter beneath the low branches. Shaken and troubled, the exhausted child rested her head on her knees, and there she remained huddled until morning.

Asa did not sleep this night; he was too busy digging holes. It was dark, but it didn't matter to him that night had fallen for he was accustomed to the darkness. He knew the land by its smell and its features; the direction of the wind by the movement of the waves and could detect his whereabouts even if the midnight sky held no stars or moonlight. Darkness was neither friend nor foe; rather it was candlelight that reminded him of what he didn't or couldn't have. In the asylum, there were only two colors, black and gray, and while those who were afraid of the dark always ended up in it. He adapted.

He lined up the tin boxes, four in all and when he was done he emptied the contents into an old sugar sack that had been laid aside. Then, he repositioned the empty tins, put them back in the holes, and replaced the dirt. It was easy work; easier than the first time he had seen Colonel bury them. From his window, he saw just about the whole world. There were more hidden about, but this would do for now. He carried the sack over his shoulder and brought the shovel back into the corner. The dead man was a ghostly white for his blood had been slowly draining out through the gashes in his head. Asa stepped over the trail of blood, making a concerted effort not to create any footprints. He didn't want to mark up his boots with the stain of this murderer. Anyone who happened to find this cadaver would most likely link it to the starting of the fire.

The house would no longer comfort; even the dirt it once stood on was blowing away. In this gruesome hour, Asa stood to witness this slow, sentimental tragedy. His thoughts strayed to an earlier time drinking cider on the front porch, and while he resurrected the moments, it was as if he were watching a play. *Colonel poured two glasses of cider and handed one to him. The thirsty man considered his glass and then in several gulps swallowed the sweet beverage and set the glass back on the table. "More?" Colonel offered up the pitcher. Asa nodded "no" and hunched over, tipping forward on his stool. His hair was shaggy, and he pushed the strands back with his fingers. "Agnes can give you a haircut if you want. She does a good job." The younger man turned his head and smiled. His observant eyes drew downward again. He rested with his hands wrapped around his knees. He was a sturdy man in contrast to Colonel who was shorter and looked stiff as he sat with one leg straight out in front. The cane leaned against his side, a necessary impediment that was his constant reminder of the war. The man beside him carried a modest disposition, not tainted with reproach or self-pity. Though voiceless, what he did not say was made up for with devoted interest. As such, he could be trusted and taken into confidence.*

"You and me, Asa, aren't so different. We each have "a cross-to-bear." There isn't a man or woman who hasn't been touched by the war. Some more than others. It didn't matter what side of the battlefield or homestead you were on; misery found its way to every survivor." He took a long drink of the cider and set it back down hard as if it were whiskey. "But ya know, not all bad came out of it. No, every now and again out of the hell an angel appears." He twisted his neck and tossed his head in the direction of the garden. Asa raised his eyes and reviewed the words. He looked back blankly. "Don't play innocent with me, boy. I bet you got your little secrets too. Just you can't spill yours. But I'm going to tell you mine. A man has to have someone he can confide in since secrets have a way of growing too big." He shifted uncomfortably in his seat, readjusting his outstretched leg that resisted his movements. "I'm not a religious man but know my way around the Bible."

Asa's mind strayed to his mother's family Bible. Rarely opened except when pulled off the shelf during times of strife, it was a book she was particularly careful with. Inscribed by the scrawling handwriting of past readers it documented the deceased dates of family members and what ailments they had died from. His small fingers ran up the pages. "What's yellow fever, what's diphtheria, what's smallpox?" She searched through her sewing box, unraveling the spool of thread or fumbling with the thimbles; it seemed to Asa that it always took her a long time to answer. Then she would wander back to his question, but by then he didn't care. He carried with him to war these questions, and one-by-one the answers were made known.

"Do not forget to show hospitality to strangers, for by so doing some people have shown hospitality to angels without knowing it, Hebrews 13.2." Colonel bent his leg back and shifted forward. "My angel, Flora, is my flesh and blood, but not as father and daughter. She was my sister's child and was brought to Agnes and me to raise as our own. My sister was a complicated woman, but now aren't they all?" Asa looked up, his eyes falling on Colonel. "But then maybe you already

knew that? When one of the senses gets dull, the others get stronger. I have a feeling you have more good sense than most. I got a feeling you got an angel some-where. But that's okay; you can keep it to yourself." The confessing man grinned and then poured himself the last of the cider. After taking a drink, he smacked his lips and slipped his watch-case out of his pocket. A charm in the shape of half-a-heart dangled off the fob. He opened the case displaying side-by-side the clock face and an image of a woman who was neither Agnes nor little Flora. He snapped the case shut and with a strained voice muttered, *"A most complicated woman, indeed."*

Asa reckoned that he might discover the watch and fob in the sack, but there wasn't time to pilfer through the contents. The courting of the katydid that he often ignored was breaking into his silent thoughts, and now like a mill-saw, it gnawed at him with its splintering noise. But the insect's annoyances were short-lived for after gathering all the day's despair; it flew off leaving behind silence once again. He thought nothing of his revengeful act and set out with only the weight of his sack over his shoulder.

Chapter 14

Lucas didn't have to see it to know that his brother had run into trouble. "Shit," he grumbled. His first impulse was to leave Dennet behind, but that lasted only for as long as he remained angry. He pulled together the few articles they both owned and hid them in the brush. He had made a solemn promise never to let anything happen to his kid brother, no matter how foolhardy an act he may commit. There were a few things that couldn't be broken and loyalty to kin was one of them. He tossed some twigs and leaves over the haversacks and brushed his foot along the ground. His thoughts meandered to the house and the fire. "Damn it!" he exclaimed and spit. He was sure that Dennet had gone back to pilfer what may have survived the blaze, some jewelry, silver, coins. A spark of greed filtered out his feelings of gloom and now he began to think that this might not have been such a bad idea after all. The prospects of getting some monetary retribution gave him reason to hasten his steps and the idea that his brother was in trouble disappeared with the light of daybreak.

The war had taught him to be vigilant, and as he made his way through the brush, he kept his eyes and ears alert, listening and watching. The only unnatural feature was the smell; and though the rains had doused the embers, there was a distinct odor of charred wood. The path narrowed as he approached the top of the hill, but before he trundled down, he took notice of a series of low flying vultures over the property concluding that these buzzards had already discovered the remains of the deceased couple. Lucas navigated his way, finding a well-worn path that led to the scorched ruin. The flattened grass gave way to easy access and as Lucas hastened his steps the breaking of newly fallen twigs beneath his weight muffled the steps of a stealth pair of feet several meters behind him. He was an easy game for the stealth follower, being as the discreet pursuer was familiar with the trail now that it was daylight.

The garden's morning blossoms and unfurled leaves glistened in the sunlight. The raindrops still freshly sprinkled upon the vegetation was a bright comparison to its adjacent neighbor, a blackened and smoky rubble of a house; life and death, the product of man's good and man's evil, they were side-by-side. And then there was Wooley, the sightless tattie-bogle that saw everything. Lucas slipped between the gate's partial opening and entered paradise. He was famished and scrounged the first bed of carrots, pulling the immature plants free from the earth. Not much more than stubs, the fistful dangled like orange minnows on a green lure. He shook them before stuffing several into his mouth, spitting out the dirt.

He pawed the earth for more vegetables unpacking the soil with his fingers, when a hollow thud sounded dispatching a claim that he might not be alone. The noise startled the hungry man, and he jumped up, scouting his surroundings before noting that it was only the wind sweeping slowly through the garden. The tattie-bogle's foot rapped against the pole each time the breeze pushed it. "Damn scarecrow," he muttered. At first, he only sneered at the creature, but as he drew nearer, he discovered that its covering was strangely too familiar. He tossed the greens aside and yanked the dangling arm. He reached up and rubbed the fabric between his fingers. It was wearing his brother's shirt. The hat and head had flopped over, resting on the overstuffed torso as if its straw neck was broken; resembling too much of a hanging. A gruesome reminder of his hideous past was resurrected and hunger pangs turned to nausea. "Where the hell is Dennet?" Lucas exclaimed, and as if he were standing at the gallows, he tore out of the garden and followed the fence-line. In the rear of the property behind where the house once grandly stood, Lucas saw the lean-to. A flurry of activity was taking place, not a kind of human activity, but the hectic flurry of flies entering and exiting, attending to something under the crooked roof. A chronic drone, more like one large coordinated buzz reverberated; a sound signaling that the insects had discovered something of great interest, while the erratic caws of a half-dozen ravens united their unruly squawks. The smell of charred wet wood mingled with another putrid odor; a battlefield stench that got stuck in the nostrils and never seemed to clear itself out. Maybe it wasn't supposed to; maybe it was intended to be a reminder of war, a sensory deterrent to end the madness. Lucas sniffed and then exhaled, expelling its rancid fetor. He kicked aside a log; it rolled into the lean-to and then stopped with a thud. A stain of crimson like a long red carpet had tinted the earth. He stepped inside and then ran out, leaned over, and vomited.

His mournful wail scared away the birds pecking at the bare torso. The dead man's flesh was savagely pocked, and the holes delivered by the sharp beaks were crusting over with dried blood. The flying devils fluttered every which way, fleeing just high enough to keep out of Lucas's reach, alighting and ready to re-enter. But not the flies, they continued to feast upon the shirtless body, nourishing themselves in the open wounds. Lucas stared dumbstruck at his dead brother and wondered who could have left him here to rot. He was unsure what to do. To stay would mean putting himself at risk yet to leave meant not giving his brother a righteous burial. He looked about for something to cover the dead man with, but there was nothing. He stepped closer and tried to shoo away the vermin that were flying up and about. He covered his nose with his left hand hoping not to puke, while he reached his other hand on the back of the head and slowly turned the face toward him. Lucas shrank back in horror when he saw the mark slashed in his brother's skull. A raven flew in and dared to approach. "Bastard!" Lucas screamed. "I'll kill you, you bastard!" Eyeing a shovel in the corner, the furious man lunged forward, raised it above his head, and commenced to fling it downward. The bird, too smart and too fast, cawed in defiance and with its ebony wings spread, it flapped overhead and flew away. The shovel hit the dirt, scattering the flies and dust. A powder keg of dirt fell over both men. Lucas sobbed with anger, his heart racing with a vengeance. Sweat was pouring off his brow, running down his face and into the creases of his neck. He removed his hat and kneeled before his brother. "I'll find whoever done this to you, mark my word, little brother. The killin' of Colonel is just the beginning. I promise you that!" His coarse voice, intense and tender at the same time, was accompanied by the buzzing of flies.

The gruesome discovery of his mutilated brother muddied Lucas's thinking. What to do with the remains, he couldn't leave Dennet to rot. Surely someone would come along looking for the residents, and the discovery of the dead man would lead them to the conclusion that he had been the murderer. Any half-witted lawman would find it easy to establish identity, inviting inquiry to open an investigation. Army records alone would point in the direction of both Timpson brothers. "No," Lucas concluded. He had no choice but to dispose of the body as quickly as possible. Afterward, he would continue their plan on his own.

Lucas reached over and reluctantly searched his brother's pockets only to discover each had already been pilfered. A sensation of anger and panic struck as he tried to piece together what evidence might have been exposed by the few personal items. "Shit!" He stood up and bowed his head. His only course of action was to drag the body outside and bury it. Even a shallow grave would be better than none. The flies continued to assail the cadaver, and as he swatted them away with his hat, the fleeing swarm was quickly reinforced by another squadron. He tried to rid the flies of their claim, but they demonstrated more persistence than his ability to scare them off.

Lucas rounded the body towards the feet when he discovered Dennet was barefooted. He was still a tall man, even in death. "Go all the way through the war and end up like this," Lucas rebuked and began to lift the stiffening legs by the ankles. He was provoked by irony and disgust. Well-crafted boots were difficult to come by; a man would have to be a fool to leave behind ones as fine as those missing. They cost a month's army wage but worth the price since the value isn't placed on quality, but rather their ability to turn the eye of many a young lady. The stolen pair had pegged soles, welt seams, and identical eagles stitched on each toe-box. They were too fine a pair to have traipsed through the muddy slop, but Dennet never took them off. A punctuated spasm of envy swelled as Lucas silently lamented that it wasn't he that had them on.

He toiled with his soul and his heart as he dragged the dead load, leaving behind a track of blood-stained dirt. The head lolled back but miraculously remained attached to the neck as the ghoulish corpse made its way across the yard and into the field. Lucas cursed as he pulled and tugged his brother in the direction of an irrigation ditch. Damning the person who had committed this desecration, he set the legs down, rolled his brother into the trench, and commenced to cover the body with dirt. On his hands and knees, he worked the surrounding soil, tossing dirt and rocks, and small branches until finally there was no evidence that anything lay beneath the top layer of black soil and foliage. It was a pitiful grave, but a grave none-the-less. Lucas removed his hat and returned to a stance that he had done too many times after a battle. He clutched his hat in front of him, looked to the heavens and then downward. His eyes roamed over his feet and then the resting place. He fumbled for words, but they got caught in his throat before he tried again. "Shit, Dennet," he began. "This is not what was supposed to happen. I know we've done a lot of bad things, but not everything has been bad. You were a good brother and a good son. Now you tell Ma and Pa not to worry 'bout ole' Lucas. I love you. I'll finish what we started for the both of us. Whoever did this is wearin' your boots. I'll find him, and after he's dead I'll bring you back your boots!" Lucas stood in a soldiery manner and then put his hat back on. He looked about knowing he had taken far too much time and without any more regard for the dead brother, hurried towards the garden.

Quiet had now overtaken the morning's tumultuous activity. A restless quiet stirred the air. It wasn't the wind or the frequent caw of birds, or the rustle of an animal in the scrubs. It was an unsettling of time; it was the departure of souls.

The bushes were thick and leafy enough to conceal a small squatting child such as young Flora. And though she was close by, she did not see the gory state of the dead man. She remained well-hidden, crouching so low that only a very wily individual would discover her whereabouts, and as she peered between the close-knit branches, she witnessed the dragging of the body pulled away from the lean-to and into the field. But the mere fact that she could identify the culprit put her in a grave situation indeed; if revealed, her life would be in danger.

Flora crept backward on all fours, keeping her head low and her eyes to the ground when she suddenly felt the tight grip of a pair of hands around her waist. "Got you!" sounded an enthusiastic cry "So, you thought you could get away!" Flora shrieked as Julio Tamayo pulled the child up and to her feet. "Señora has been worried sick!" he scolded. The kindly man tried to look stern, but his tender heart could not become angry with the little girl. Flora brushed her dirty hands over her pinafore and watched the round-faced man as he shook his head disagreeably. Not offering her a chance to explain he continued with his prattle. "Do you know what she made me do? She had me searching the woods all night. I was too afraid to go home without you. She would not have let me back into the house if I dared appear empty-handed. So, I have been out all night, except for a few hours this morning when I fell asleep in the barn.

The hay is not as comfortable as you may think. But all is good, very very good now that I found you." He signed with a great deal of comfort, not for the child but rather for himself, and patted her head as if she were a calf that had strayed away.

The farmer's words splashed over the child with the startled sensation of a cold shower. She was awakened to her grim reality, frightened and feeling quite alone her upper lip began to tremble. "Mother?" she murmured. She turned an about-face and then twisted back to the stout man. Her eyes welled up with tears, and the speaker now appeared as a watery mirage through the teardrops. She wiped her eyes on the hem of her pinafore and tried very hard to remain brave. "I want to show you something in the field," she said. "I saw something you need to see!"

She pulled his hand as she took a step forward, but the stout man was planted firmly in his place. "No," shook his head. A pair of cooing doves was challenging the dark mood that was smothering them both. The charred smell of the house nagged at the farmer to take the child away. "Come along, Flora. We must hurry back. It is time for breakfast."

Her thoughts reclaimed her emotions as the dragging away of what she believed was a half-clothed man quickly withdrew from her mind. "I want to see Mother, let me look for my parents," she petitioned, but the request was ignored, and the sad farmer urged her to follow with a gentle but firm tug of the hand.

Tearfully, Flora submitted. Exhausted and tired she walked in front of Señor Tamayo, feeling as desolate as a prisoner headed to the gallows. All life that she understood was altered. It was a solemn journey to the farmhouse, one that gave the child a private moment to reflect. She was confronted by a secret, one that she wished to share but now too afraid to reveal. The only other soul that it could be told to was Asa, but not just because he was her friend, but because it would never be divulged by the mute man. Flora smiled at the prospect; "Yes, Asa," she touted to her secret-self. "Now everything will get better."

Chapter 15

Sydney Bushnell's marriage had not been instigated by love or lust, but rather by a timely convenience to become betrothed. At her age most eligible women were already engaged, and when the newly graduated surgeon, Dr. Richard Bushnell asked for her hand, she decided it was time to settle down; or at least offer the impression of such.

Having been brought up in a world that few can even dream of, she had access to all the privileges allotted to those who have influence, money, and power. Her father, Benjamin P. Thorle, presided over a prestigious and reputable law firm, which for a matter of knowledge had not been passed down, but rather created solely by his progressive thinking. Those who knew him well called him Dobbins and casual acquaintances called him Mr. Thorle. Sydney called him Papa, and his wife, having earned him the seal of masculinity, called him Dob. No one could disagree that he was anything but intelligent, sociable, and wealthy; with the latter being the most favored adjective. It was his wife's favorite beverage, tea, which catapulted his income from comfortable to rich in just a few short years. Having arranged for a shipment of teas from China, he was introduced by one of his clients to Russell Sturgis, a Massachusetts lawyer and gentleman, who traveled to Canton on behalf of the Boston mogul, John

Perkings Cushing, importing desirable commodities such as tea, silk, and porcelain. It was shortly after several business encounters that Thorle distinguished himself as a risk taker. A ship was being dispatched to China which offered him an opportunity to invest in a most unlikely commodity, opium.

Martha Thorle marveled at her husband, and though she may have appeared to embody the essence of her time, she did not let her position as a woman weigh her down. Declaring an outward appearance as sympathetic and genteel, private conversations between her and Dob were more than idle chatter about the weather or how good the cook's dinner was on a particular evening. Mrs. Thorle enjoyed her home, her servants, and her life. Whatever entanglement her husband might involve himself in would always be sorted out. There was little that could not be manipulated with the right amount of money. Opium crops were grown during the winter and processed in the spring and summer. As such, the transport to China from western India was also dependent upon the weather. Brokering such a deal was considered a coup; Turkish opium smuggled by American ships was not as favored by Chinese customers and considered lower grade product. Thorle's opportunity to invest meant he would share in the closed British market of Indian opium. In defense of his decision, he listed several prominent businessmen, all civic-minded church-goers, among his fellow investors.

He had been seated adjacent to the head of the long table, and he felt as if this was a historic occasion. Bottles of champagne were being popped behind the chairs of the guests, as white-gloved stewards filled the glasses. The polished financier, Mr. Cushing, rose to his feet, his glass held out before him, when at the same time the entire table mirrored his actions and raised their glasses. "It had been a most gallant reception," Benjamin told his wife. Gender divisions prevented his wife's participation in this business event, though it certainly would have been more festive if she had secured a seat.

"Ambitions squandered are the same as idleness. And you, my Dear, will never let grass grow under your feet," she pointed out. "I don't remember the last time you brought home an empty game bag. Your aim is always high, and you rarely miss your target." A comfortable silence settled into the room. "You look tired, Dob," his wife replied drifting back into the conversation. She stood up and began to tidy the chrysanthemum arrangements. "There," she exclaimed. "That's better."

"We stand to make a great deal of money, Martha." They both understood the power of wealth; she knew that this was not an impulsive decision, rather one that her husband had spent the last few sleepless nights ruminating on.

"In my view, I believe it would be foolish to toss and turn over a matter that seems simply one that is decided." Her eyes smiled as she placed a kiss on his head and gently tapped his shoulder. He reached up and stroked her soft hand silently chastising the stupidity that a woman of her intelligence did not have the right to vote.

Mr. Thorle's success brought Sydney all the pleasures money could buy, and while he was the protector of dominion and improprieties, it was Mother who presided over decorum. From her, Sydney received appreciation for the arts, her social graces, the ability to manipulate her female charms, and ultimately the acquisition of a husband. However, unlike the other heads-of-households, Benjamin was a progressive thinker, believing his daughter should be prepared in business principals and responsibilities; and when engaged in such matters, she should press forward with persistence and aggressiveness as energetic as would a son. During all seasons, their parlor was frequented by reformers committed to discussions that deliberated the ideals of individualism, abolition, and the legal rights of women. And as years rolled away, Sydney's mind flourished.

Despite all the advantages, Sydney remained restless; desirous to cross the line drawn for young debutantes. It was an invisible thread that she yearned to snap. And so, it came to her one lazy spring day, after bribing her Nanny with chocolate to remain behind at the hotel, Sydney was left unchaperoned to explore the streets of Manhattan. Their trip was only to have lasted for a few weeks. However, she convinced Mother, a most pliable woman when it came to Sydney, that if she could not go to Paris, then New York City was next best. And it was just off Broadway where Sydney discovered a most intriguing salon, a portrait gallery nestled in the upper floors of a corner building. The fashionable young lady climbed the three flights of stairs and entered the lavish foyer of the *Saint and Dickie Portrait Studio*. She was greeted by a well-manicured gentleman, who offered her his card with embossed gold lettering, *Proprietor-Mr. Dickie*. She immediately became conscious of the strong odor of rose water and wondered if he was aware of his over-indulgence. She accepted the card and couldn't help but appraise his pale skin. "Thank you," she said and slipped the card into her bag.

"Your first time here?"

She stared past him as if he were an inanimate object in her way. "No, if you mean New York, and yes, if you mean here, the gallery."

"Well then, let me show you around," he proposed and waited momentarily for her to follow. She mingled with the portraits, sparked by recognition of an untamed intimacy defined in each. She diverted her desire to comment respecting the integrity of the sitter. "Mr. Saint, our photographer, is remarkable, don't you think?" said Mr. Dickie. "The hair, the eyes, the expression, he fills the space with more than an image. Age makes no difference, seventeen or ninety, the sitter knows who she is." The proprietor lifted his eyes and smiled. "I see you like this one," he remarked.

"She has her dog with her."

"Yes, Madame takes Butch everywhere. As I recall, the dog was better behaved. Oh, what a wild one she is. It must have taken two days

for her to decide what to wear, but finally decided on playing Joséphine."
Sydney's look of misunderstanding suggested clarification. "Napoleon's,
Joséphine."

"Oh, yes, the Empress."

"Madame didn't want to wear a crown, so we tried to put it on
the spaniel, but he wouldn't wear it either. Then she insisted on a velvet
recamier to lie on; so, she brought one in from her estate. I hope you're not
planning on using one?" he remarked. "It was quite an ordeal to get the
dog hair off!" His idea of a joke appeared to go unnoticed by the young
woman, who only seemed mildly amused. "Are you interested in having
a portrait taken?" he asked. "You would make a most striking model."
Sydney blushed. It was evident that he had struck a nerve with the young
woman. "Perhaps for your sweetheart?" Again, Sydney's interest appeared
to peak as she felt her face go flush. She pulled out her fan and lightly
cooled her cheeks. Mr. Dickie was accustomed to women wavering about
their decisions. They only needed a bit of flattery to be convinced that
they were more than worthy of the camera. "We have private studio
space that can accommodate any kind of scene. Some of society's most
prominent ladies are our clients. The camera allows a woman to become
someone quite different than her usual self." Sydney turned, and her eyes
sparkled although she dared not show that she was of the same lot as these
women. "I only meant," interrupted the slick-tongued man interpreting
her expression, "that one does not have to come from the wrong side of
the tracks to have some fun. Our services are priced very fairly." Sydney's
fan fluttered feverishly as she contemplated his words. "Totally private
and such a vast array of wardrobes to select. Have you ever wanted to
become Cleopatra, Guinevere, or even Lady Godiva?" He chuckled, however, there was nothing but sincerity in his question.

"Totally private." She reinforced his promise in her mind. Sydney
imagined handing Richard a risqué portrait and laughed at the thought of

her prudish fiancé. But why not, no one would have to know. The thought of it was irresistibly stimulating.

"Are you nervous, Miss…"

"Miss Bella, you can call me Bella," Sydney blurted out. The lie flowed so easily that it scared even her.

"Don't be nervous, Miss Bella, we have something that will relax you if you like." He took her gloved hand and tapped it gently. "Nothing harmful, just a touch of our imported opium mixture, and you will be as happy as a Chinese nightingale."

"Laudanum?" she asked.

"So, you've heard of it then." The man winked, and as he sauntered away, she followed him into a hallway. Sydney fumbled with her lace handkerchief as he reached for the doorknob. "Come now; you aren't losing your nerve, are you? After all, you certainly shouldn't deprive yourself of a few feminine indulgences. A woman with your beauty should not hide behind brocade. You should flaunt yourself; yes, you were born to wear gossamer and silk."

"You are quite persuasive, Mr. Dickie. I suppose it would be fun to be just a tiny bit mischievous," she agreed. "And how could there be any harm. I am the only one who will see the photograph; that is so, isn't it?" she asked with a suspicious intonation.

"Miss Bella," the indignant man professed, "this is a legitimate portrait studio. Why the mere idea that something scandalous goes on behind these doors is nothing but insulting. You are the one who came to us. If you wish to have your portrait taken, so be it. But I will not stand here and be insulted. Perhaps you should take your business elsewhere. *The Sarony Gallery* is not far from here, however, let me prepare you, I don't think he would be interested in you as a client. His are all famous and aspiring thespians; he rarely works with undiscovered subjects."

Sydney was beginning to feel a bit guilty, and while her misgivings did not mean any harm, she had ignored her manners. Finding her courage, she drew closer to the door. "Is Mr. Saint going to be the one to take my photograph?" She smiled as if nothing had happened.

"Yes, my dear; if you so choose."

"Then it might do very well if we get started," she replied. With her answer taking on the spirit of élan; she stepped aside and allowed Mr. Dickie to open the door where a pair of legs and half a torso was sticking out from beneath a black cloth. The camera, a strange contraption balanced on spindly legs, was aimed at a staged set. A pair of crimson draperies made a winding path behind a round oak table set with a gold candelabra holding three unlit tapers. Beside the table was a straight-back chair draped with several layers of midnight-blue taffeta. The sheets of cloth stretched out along the floor; it was a scene that smothered the room with lusty ambiance. The photographer was motioning to his assistant, a young man barely old enough to sport a mustache let alone a beard, to move the lantern towards the staged area.

"Forward, slowly forward, more, more," he commanded beneath the drape. "Good, Albert," and he held his palm up signaling for the lantern to remain stationary. Albert smiled, not always exactly following what the finicky artist wanted, and sighed with relief. The beam offered a minimal amount of yellow light, producing a milieu of suggestive secrecy. It was an intimate cove waiting for just the right model to fill the scene with sensuality and seduction.

"Mario, we have a young lady I would like you to meet," said Mr. Dickie, adding a pinch of a Spanish accent like sprinkling oregano in his spaghetti sauce when he annunciated the man's name. "We don't mean to interrupt; however, Mademoiselle Bella has a limited amount of time and wishes to engage our services." He turned to Sydney and grinned like a cat. She smiled back, like a kitten. Both waited for a moment while there resumed a lot of posturing and mumbling from beneath the black cloth. When the photographer finally revealed himself, Sydney immediately scrutinized his appearance. He was an older gentleman, a bit disheveled, but in an artistic sort of way. That suited her just fine. His hair hung loose, tipping the top of his shoulders, and his white shirt rumpled, as were his trousers. Dark eyes, a graying mustache, fine features, and a small scar across his cheek gave him a touch of mystery, but she didn't know why.

"I can do this," she thought. But her heart was telling her differently, and within several minutes of some rudimentary introductions and side conversations between the two men about staging and costuming, Sydney was suddenly growing faint. She steered herself towards the nearest chair, held fast to the armrest, and sat down. "I think we got a scared one, Mr. Dickie," called the young assistant as he watched her collapse into the cushion.

Both pairs of eyes turned toward Sydney, who had become fearfully pale. "Don't be a dolt, Albert, get her some water!" Dickie shouted. "And a compress!"

"A compress?" the boy asked, as his mind rummaged frantically for an answer to that order.

"Never mind, just the water," called Saint and taking his handkerchief from his pocket he stood over the anxious woman and mopped her brow. "Here now, don't be afraid." His voice was both commanding and soothing. "Let Dickie give you a bit of laudanum; it will calm your nerves. Then when you're ready, we can get started. You are a perfect model, yes, you remind me of the goddess Aphrodite."

Sydney listened and began to fan herself with her glove. She had studied Greek and Roman art and was charmed that she reminded him of a Classical beauty. Even though she knew flattery was not a metaphor for a compliment, such a notion filled her ego with just the right amount of nerve. "I don't know what came over me; perhaps it was the heat. I am quite level-headed," she protested. "Quite level-headed," she emphatically repeated.

Albert stood awkwardly behind the two men who were fawning over the woman. "I got the water," he announced, shifting uneasily from one foot to the next.

Mr. Dickie scowled at the boy and took the glass out of his hand. "Well, just don't stand there, Albert, get the wardrobe trunk marked "special" and put it behind the dressing screen." Albert looked at the man wide-eyed and snickered while he hurried towards the storage area.

"Here," said Dickie gesturing for her to take the water. Sydney sipped it and handed him back the glass, exchanging it for another smaller cup. "Take this; it's bitter so drink it up quickly."

Without question, she reached for the cup and in one gulp swallowed its potent contents, wrinkling her nose in defiance at the taste. She handed the cup back, finding that her hands were trembling. Mr. Saint lifted her palms to his and squeezed them gently. "Don't fear, Bella. Relax, you have nothing to worry about." Sydney leaned back into the coziness of the large chair. She felt her cheeks flush, her lids grew limp, and before she closed her eyes, she saw the face of Mr. Saint bent over her and could feel the unbuttoning of her collar buttons. Her head felt light, and the voices around her were giving directions which she easily abided. She rounded behind the screen and kneeling over the open trunk, tossed the costumes to the floor until she found what she liked. She slipped the pink décolleté chemise over her head, and it unfurled to the top of her feet. It fit loosely like an ancient tunic, only gauzy and light with a plunging neckline that she tried to pull up. But it would not oblige, and as the eager voice of "Are you ready, Bella?" called from outside of the screen, she let her hands fall to her sides. Then, without hesitation, she transformed herself into a new persona which the camera and Mr. Saint found ever so rewarding.

Sydney walked briskly back towards Aster House having declined Mr.
Dickie's offer of hiring a cab. "The sunshine will do me good," she had
explained. She experienced no ill effects from the sedative and felt more
relaxed than she could remember in quite a while. She came away from
the gallery with new perspectives of herself both physically and mentally.
She clutched the carte-de-visite in her gloved hand, and every now and
again would open it up to admire. The small albumen print was mounted
on a stiff card. Mario Saint had matted and inserted the portrait in a
velvet-lined case. He had explained that the photographic process was
rather new to the United States, invented by a Frenchman, André Disdéri.
"These little portrait cards are becoming very popular; many who sit for
us use them as calling cards." Sydney blushed when she thought of her
pose, this "calling card" was for her eyes only. "You are an elegant lady, a
shame to hide such loveliness." Those were his words, and she devoured
them like a hungry peasant. She eased the framed-cover open and held it
close to her face so-as-to conceal its contents; she gazed privately at herself. It hadn't taken much persuasion and when Mario continued to say, "A
trifle more cleavage Bella, more skin, a little more, good, very good," she
could not help but listen to his command and surrender. She played with
his suggestions, using her eyes, her body language, her expressions and
poses; she was a natural flirt. "Make them enjoy what they aren't supposed
to," he directed. And so, she did.

The whole of Broadway was in an intoxicating fever of tempta-
tions. The new Sydney was roused by the hustle and bustle of the street,
by the stable smells of the horse-drawn carriages, and the pearl-topped
omnibuses drawn by pairs of drafts all vying for a position on the city
street. Ragamuffin newsboys and girls shouting the headlines skirted
between Bulletin wagons soliciting theater shows. It was a hodge-podge
of people of all shades, all sizes, and all walks of life. When only this
morning it seemed overcrowded and dirty, now she didn't flinch at the
construction workers' sordid gawks or cower from their catcalls. Instead

of being offended and appalled, as the old Sydney would have been, the new Sydney felt sorry for them. These lower-class workers were not in her league. If they were lucky, their wanton glances could only be satisfied with a chance look as she strolled by, but if they wanted more, they would be sadly disappointed. "Mr. Saint had summed it up," she smiled. "I am like a fine piece of crystal in a museum, meant to look at and admire. But not to touch." She pulled at the drawstrings and dropped the case into her purse thinking, "No one else can see."

For the rest of the week Sydney sulked, and no matter how much Nanny tried to cheer her up with strolls in the park, shopping at Stewart's grandiose store, and the taking of mid-day tea at the best establishments, all efforts to revive her spirits were thwarted by her glum mood. The carte-de-visite was Sydney's only source of pleasure, a secret reminder that there was more for a woman than the doldrums of provincial servitude. New York City baited her wild side, and she yearned for another adventure. The new Sydney was taken in by the sights, sounds, and smells. Plans to be married were now more than in the preliminary stages. By summer's end she was going home, and with that simple fact, she would have to take care not to squander the unrestricted time she had left.

The whole of New York City proved to be quite impersonal as the inhabitants tended to themselves, engaging little interaction with one another. Vagrants, like pesky gnats in the summertime, are resident imposters, showing up on doorsteps of homes and businesses. Although begging is not permitted on streetcars, ferry-boats, or places of amusement, there is no law against its practice on the streets. And since Broadway was a favored promenade of the fashionable, so too did it become a favorite target for the disreputable. A mosaic of female palliards preyed on the sympathetic. They give opium to their children to make them sleep and prick them with pins to make them cry. Self-inflicted sores often prompted an extra coin in an outstretched hand. When the sun sets, and the beggars find shelter in the shadows, they are replaced by streetwalkers that pass up and down Broadway in their finest clothes.

It is a city of paradoxes. Private carriages and high-fashion window shoppers promenade by day while the night transforms Broadway into a magical light show. Gas lamps make halos, and lanterns atop of omnibuses leave a wake of illumination behind them. Yet, the ordinary tempo exists only blocks away. Here cartmen, butchers, laborers, shipbuilders, domestics, draymen, women and men, the lame, sick, pocked, and healthy work and live. New York houses them all and cares little for any.

Not taken aback by the rudeness or brashness of the city's inhabitants, their lack of morality enticed the young woman, and Sydney recognized this not as a weakness in character but as an opportunity to learn from. The slang expressions, their coarse mannerisms, the audacious selling of everything and anything out of the back of a wagon or slung over a peddler's cart gave her reason to contemplate. This city provided an ideal backdrop for a business opportunity and how she could use it to satisfy her ambition was virtually at her fingertips. She knew that women were at a societal disadvantage. However, she was shrewd enough to recognize that her gender's femininity had the potential to be more profitable than all the political benefits designed for men. Sydney looked into the mirror, ran her tongue over her lips, and pinched her cheeks. A sudden pink glow emerged as she cocked her hat to the side of her head. "But what to do?" she wondered. This, she was not sure of.

Nanny was a fierce-eyed woman whose only undertaking was to chaperone Sydney while preserving proper etiquette and protocol required and expected of an upper-society single woman. But to her charge, the matron was proving to be an impediment, and despite the housemaid's good-nature and protective manner, it was smothering the younger woman's lifestyle. The new Sydney had discovered freedom, and since this liberation had only a summertime shelf-life, it confirmed the urgency of getting Nanny out of the picture.

So, when the bellboy delivered the fictitious letter, the crestfallen woman could do nothing more than to pack her bags. The parchment lay open on the desk, a simple hand-written note dismissing the woman for her service and two months' severance pay. "I don't understand," cried the elder, blowing her pug nose into the lace handkerchief. Her sobs were so deep that the Sydney almost felt sorry that she had designed such a scheme.

"I can't understand it either," bemoaned the deceitful girl and she stroked the troubled woman's shoulder. "But you know how Mother can be; one never can tell what she is thinking."

The old woman peered up from her sorrow, red-faced and tear-stained, her dark eyes sunken with disappointment. "What will you do?" she inquired with a great deal of concern. "You must go home now that I have been dismissed." Her mouth turned downward at the thought of heading to her sister's; the image of the two spinsters sharing the small provincial house made her whimper again.

"Oh, don't worry, Nanny. After you are safe and sound on the next coach, I'll pack my bags and get along home right behind you." She smiled and patted the dear lady as if she too had felt betrayed.

Sydney stood on the sidewalk watching as the coach pulled away, and though the deceived did not occupy the seat next to the window, the distraught woman cared not for her fellow passengers. With all intentions of waving goodbye, she leaned across the seated man who appeared to struggle beneath the heavy girth of the large woman and fluttered her hand feverishly until they drove out of sight. "

The next morning Sydney emerged from beneath the covers and sighed. From behind drowsy eyes, she called out for Nanny to ring for coffee and a scone, however, when she raised her head from the pillow and wiped the sleepers from her eyes, the incident of the day before was quickly resurrected. "Well, that is that," smiled Sydney and turned over again to bask in the delight of her solitude.

Chapter 16

Pitiful, haggard-eyed, and dirty, the portrait of misery; where the wretched meet the wretched. The old hag sits on a curbstone, a sentinel of her street, while in the cellar a tattered old man is curled up on a bed of straw. She speaks not of her dying mate and simply puts out a withered hand. "Bless you, missy," she says even before the coins drop. The hand snaps shut like a trap as soon as the charity is received. The drayman, the author, the tailor, the dandy and fop, the milkman, the adulterer, even the Minister, the Rabbi, and policeman have dropped a coin from time to time. So, it would only be right for Sydney to do the same. Across the street is a man and woman feeding doves. They toss the crumbs and delight in watching the birds zigzag about pecking the filthy street. A St. Bernard taking its master for a walk saunters past. Sydney wriggles her nose at an odiferous smell. "It's the oysterman you smell," says the droopy-mustached dog owner as he stops to let the animal relieve itself. "Ever eat a raw oyster?" But he doesn't wait for her answer as his head is spasmodically jerked forward when the satisfied dog begins to trot down the street.

"Stupid man," says the hag, her voice much stronger than her decrepit appearance would suggest.

"Why is that?" asks Sydney.

"Well, he looks down his nose down at me every day, but look who's at the other end of a shitting dog?"

———— • ————

The spirit of the entrepreneur can be heard on every street corner. The prattling and bartering between buyers and sellers provoked a constant din which might rattle the nerves of anyone that was not accustomed to their methods. These are a curious lot of patterers, the city's street vendors, who hawk their goods. They are not a handsome group of people, just ordinary men and women; middle-aged, old, and young. Some get pity, and others get contempt, and most all live hand to mouth. "Ripe peach, lady?" petitioned the merchant, responding readily to what seemed to be a potential buyer. "Fresh, very fresh," she says, and with an abrupt strike of her knife she split the fruit in two and let the juice run down her wrist as she offered half to Sydney.

"No thank you," Sydney responded. "I've had my breakfast already," and as if it were poison, she turned her hand in front of the fruit while passing by.

"Bitch," mumbled the woman, and with a toothless grin the merchant took the peach between her lips and sucked the juice until all that was left was a knurled pit. "Did ya hear what I said, uppity bitch?" cawed the fruit-seller.

"What's she done?" pried a hard-faced young woman who had been keeping her ear to the conversation as she pawed over the plums.

"Thinks she's better than us!" snapped the vendor.

"Ya don't say!" The younger winked, and with her eye towards the middle of the block, she picked up a green apple and heaved it! Both women squealed in delight as the small projectile sailed through the air and landed squarely, knocking the hat to the ground. "Bullseye!" shouted the meddlesome woman. "Did you see it go? I ought to pitch for the Knickerbockers!"

"Not so fast," grinned the vendor, "yer aim was off!" And sure enough, rather than striking the target, it went left, flinging the derby off a coachman that had unfortunately been standing in the direct line of the fruit. Without hesitation, he bent over, placed his hat back on his head and offered the apple to his nag that relished it happily. Then tipping his brim, he acknowledged the two women who waved back and went about his business of currycombing the poor old horse.

"Oh my," exclaimed Sydney, taking refuge under the shade of an overhang. She stepped back and with a slight bow of her waist, peered around the corner at the fruit stand. But if the two women cared or not, they seemed to have forgotten about her and were now in the midst of bartering with the dry goods peddler, a ragged fellow that was as tattered as his wares. Sydney sighed with relief, feeling that this was not the kind of adventure she wished to repeat.

"Something for your nerves?" asked a man. A cart with several wooden shelves neatly arranged were set up under duck cloth. Beside him stood a tall, muscular, and exotic looking dark skinned man. "Something for your nerves," the question was repeated.

"Am I that transparent?" she asked.

"No, but I imagine that you might be a little shaken after your run-in with those two," he said motioning down the street with a tilt of his chin. "We're the only ones selling ancestral remedies from the South Seas. Ordinary folk medicines are not nearly as effective. I'm a living example of the healing powers of Mallabal's medicines." With an expression of gratitude, he dispatched an even nod of approval. "Yep, I'd be dead if it weren't for him."

Sydney eyed the dark man and wondered if he were standing there as a prop since the only sign of life was a slight inhale and exhale of his chest. He had made no voluntary movement nor was there a sound uttered. "Surely you can't be serious," she replied and turned away from his deadpan stare. Her eyes roamed over the items in the cart until she picked up a small cloth bag tied shut with a piece of twine. She lifted it to her nose and then set it down. "What is it?" she asked. A look of distrust fell over the countenance of the seller, and as he started for the bag, the woman placed her hand over his. "If it is in the cart then it is for sale, correct?" He pulled his hand away and nodded, 'yes.' "Good, then perhaps you might tell me what this little bit of cloth contains."

"It's pituri, that's what the Aboriginal natives call it."

"Pituri," she clarified the name. "And what is this pituri used for?"

"It takes on the same form as tobacco; it can be chewed or smoked. When prepared correctly it's a stimulant. Not unlike the coca leaves grown in Peru."

She listened and then pointed to another pouch of similar size. "What's inside this one?"

"This," he said and repositioned the new pouch in front of the pituri, is from the same plant, however, prepared differently. Just a small amount can be extremely intoxicating. Some claim it possesses the same effects as smoking opium. But I don't believe a woman of your position would find this narcotic inviting." He hoped that he had struck a nerve and this impressionable woman would come to her senses. Some things were not for the weaker gender. "Perhaps you would be interested in this," and slid forward a corked vial. "It's citratum oil, guaranteed to keep your hair healthy and smell as sweet as lemongrass." But the potential buyer showed no interest in the bottle's contents and pushed it aside.

Sydney looked up at Mallabal, and though he did not express any outward emotions, she interpreted his solemn personality to be judging her, a feeling that she did not like. She tossed her head away from the man and turned again to the vendor. "What do you have to calm the nerves?" she asked remembering her positive experience with laudanum.

A coarse burlap pouch was brought forward. "This," he said and handed it the customer, "is a preparation made from seeds of the white sapote plant. Burned into a fine powder, it will help the user relax. All ours remedies, unlike opiates," he added pointing to the array of small packets, "have not been exploited or tinctured."

She poked her finger against the pouch with suggestive indecision and then put it down. A moment passed as the woman fingered the assortment of packets as if they were ripe produce. But it soon became apparent that the buyer needed some persuasive assistance when a large muscular hand reached over and plucked from the pile of cloth pouches a well-stuffed muslin sack and tossed it lightly in front of Sydney. "Manuka," said the dark man and nodded affirmatively. Sydney returned a frosty glare and picked it up.

"Of course, manuka tea, an excellent sedative!" cried Neville. He unraveled the twine, loosening the cord from around the throat of the pouch. He dipped his hand into the opening and brought up a handful of broken pieces of bark. "Steep these in a cup of boiling water until it turns color." Sydney wrinkled her nose at the prospect of bits of wood floating around her delicate porcelain cup. "You'll have a most inviting sleep," he promised and dropped the contents back into the bag, pulled the strings taut, and wiped his hands together. A sprinkle of residue fell from his palms.

"Alright, I'll take it, and the other one over there," she claimed pointing to the sapote. "How much do I owe you?".

"Sixty cents for both," the vendor said.

Retrieving a small change purse from her bag, she placed a few coins down on the cart. "Fifty," she said sliding the money forward. "Make it fifty. Take it or leave it," Sydney challenged and coolly quashed his offer.

Neville glanced at his friend and waited until the solemn man nodded 'yes.' "You drive a hard bargain," remarked the reluctant vendor. He slid the money into a square box, where the buyer noticed a full container of coins from earlier sales, exchanging her less than enthusiastic interest with a bit more attention.

"If I like your products then I will be back for more." She gathered up her two purchases and crammed them into her bag. "Are you always here on this corner?" she asked.

Neville nodded and like a man who had endured many disappointments arrived at an agreeable answer. "Yes, that is until we make enough money to travel north. I was on my way home, but our ship made port here instead of going further up the coast. So, this is where destiny landed us." He shrugged his shoulders with a noncommittal degree of great concern.

"Well, your misfortune is my good luck," she quipped. "And your man here, is he going with you?" Sydney wasn't exactly sure why she asked, but there was something rather different about this foreigner that made her dislike him. However, if she was feeling disdain towards Mallabal, his feelings towards her were mutual. She had poured tension into the air, and his instincts were warning him that this woman could be trouble. Neville sensed the hostility, and though his companion's face may have appeared expressionless, the vendor felt compelled to squelch any misconceptions about him on the part of the purchaser. "Mallabal, why he's free to come and go as he pleases. But he has a standing invitation to my home, which I hope he continues to accept. The man saved my life, and for that, I am eternally grateful."

"Yes, you said that before," Sydney scoffed. She was now bored with these two and had spent far too much time mulling over her purchases. She fumbled with her hat and tipped it slightly to the side, and when she was finished tidying herself, as women of her social position like to do, she said, "Thank you," and without giving Mallabal a glance, she hastened away.

Sydney's white dress grayed as she weaved between the other pedestrians on the sidewalk, sliding further out of view until she became transparent and vanished. Neville opened the tin box and fingered the coins. "A few more weeks and we'll have plenty enough to get us north," he exclaimed and shook the contents.

Mallabal listened to the rattling of coins: earned coins, lucky coins, coins with finger grime, should've bought bread coins, and stolen coins; they had all made their way out from dark pockets and silk purses into the box. For most sellers, this was a good sound, it meant prosperity, but to the Aborigine, it had been an imported sound signaling greed; voracious greed that had consumed Van Damien's Island and annihilated the native inhabitants. But what he had quickly learned since their arrival about this new country was that it made him feel quite alone. It was an unnatural place devoid of scrubs and vegetation; and though Hobart had been dramatically transformed by the British, in this city, there was no place to escape from the smoky chimneys or horse-drawn carriages. New York was populated as he never would have imagined; the locals were filled with distrust that clung to their character like ivy. Each emigrant arrived with a traveling bag of clothes, and culture, and memories; and while their shirts and pants freely crisscrossed over clotheslines, their differences did not like to mingle. "People are the same everywhere," Mallabal observed, and his concern for his present condition made him ever warier of his surroundings. In the daytime, he could see the faces, and at night he could feel their presence. He was never alone, an experience that was new to the native man. There were those that gambled, drank stale beer, and entertained themselves in "scrappin'." Others would congregate, sit on the benches and rest their chins on their chest, and with bloodshot eyes glower at those who passed by. Between gulps of ale, they argued and reminisced about the old days. Loud and opinionated their talk turned to politics and always ended with a crude joke about a wife or a girlfriend or both. The women used their talents and their voices slyly. Dressed in the fashion of a lady, they were all but genial, but instead a rough and sassy counterfeit.

The two men rented a first-floor flat in a rooming house managed by an Irish widow, Janie Magill. Her two dirty and dull boys play on the stoop and stay amused by tossing pebbles at the feet of the pedestrians. Like a pair of mangy dogs, she keeps them in line with several good smacks a day, if they needed it or not. Mrs. Magill was at first not keen on having the dark man as a boarder. However, she was quickly persuaded of his usefulness when during their introductions her colicky toddler wouldn't stop crying. The child's complaints were quickly extinguished by a soothing tonic the Aborigine had prepared, and with a dose of two sweetened tablespoons, the imp became contently quiet. "He's an odd one, might scare off the other tenants!" the landlady protested eyeing Mallabal with contempt. "But he did good for Kyle," she added, cradling the happy child that was as pink and plump as a piglet, "so the dark fellow can stay. But I'm keeping my eye on the two of you."

The room was stuffy and small, consisting of a single horse-hair mattress disproportionally long for the cot, a wobbly oak dresser with one leg too short for its intended height, and a mahogany wash-stand yielding a yellowing porcelain pitcher. For a dollar-a-week more, she offered coffee and scones for breakfast and stew or soup for dinner, which the men happily accepted. It wasn't until several days into their stay that Neville discovered their rent was inflated on account of Mallabal, but he held his tongue instead of having to find another place to rent.

"Mrs. Magill's rough around the edges alright," exclaimed the portly man sitting beside the fire. "But you're better off here than a Sailor's Boarding House. Theirs's is a shifty business, alright. Crimps meet the ships, and before the anchor's lowered, they lay in wait like wolves stalking sheep. Armed with whiskey, the naive Jacks go off with 'em to the boarding house where they're seduced with food, more liquor, and women. When the sea-crab runs out of money, the boarding house master gives 'em an advance; the dupes get in debt, and when they've been plied with so much rum that they can't even see, they sign over their articles. They're clean- done."

He paused and grinned with the satisfaction that he had a captive audience. "No good comes to them water rats, no good at all." There was a mournful tone in his voice as if he had once been a victim. "After the tricked sailor's been scoured like a barnacle, he's at their mercy." John Rex puffed vigorously on his pipe and then swore when he couldn't get it to light. His already ruddy cheeks reddened even more as he clenched his teeth and struck the match against the flint stone. The end of the stick ignited, and he placed it up to the bowl. After several more attempts to catch the edge, he blew the match out and puffed. A dense, sweet odor was followed by a twizzle of smoke, it lifted upward and around his greasy mustache. "Like I said," he started again, growing melodramatic as he acknowledged himself as the orator, "Janie Magill's a tough one, but then you gotta be to keep a family fed. Take this rooming house, do ya know how she came to be the landlady?" The smoker leaned forward in the rocker and as if about to divulge a great secret beckoned Neville towards him with a tilt of his grizzled chin. "It was given to her as compensation for her man's murder." John sat back and continued to enjoy his pipe.

Neville glanced up at the boarder. "Murder?" he exclaimed. "Why the poor woman."

The pipe-smoker laughed and then slid forward again. "Don't ever let 'er hear ya call her a poor woman," he warned, "and she's not one to take charity neither." Neville sat quietly wondering if he should continue to indulge the speaker or bid him good night but decided it wouldn't hurt to know more about the Widow Magill. He nodded his head that he under-stood which started the story up again. "It was a few summers ago, not too far from here. She sez that she knew he was dead, on account that he always came back home to sleep in his own bed. But in the morn-ing when he wasn't there, she just kissed his good luck goodbye. There's always fights between gangs; that ain't nothin'. This time it was between the Blackbirds and Bowery Boys. I'd be tellin you a lie if I said I remember what the hell it was about, but it doesn't take much to start a fight... red hair, a pink ribbon, and too much whiskey." John winked at the suggestion. "Magill was a hardheaded Paddy, but no match for the likes of a wrench. Some son-of-a-bitch cracked it across his skull, but his brains must have been made of rocks 'cause it took a second blow to get him off his feet." The boarder rocked a bit, and he clenched the pipe in his teeth, talking out of the side of his mouth. "He was a good fellow, that Brian Magill. A good man. A collection was taken up for Janie along with givin'er the job of taking charge of the rooming house. It don't earn her much, but at least there's a roof and bed for the boys. Damn shame, damn shame." John Rex removed the stem piece from his mouth and set the pipe in the stand. "Janie may not have a husband, but she's got plenty of landsmen watchin' out for her. We're family, not blood relation, but when one loses a bread-winner, then we take care of his wife and children." It was perfectly clear what the dockworker meant, and Neville noted the words as a warning.

The parlor was the largest and warmest room where the evening's boarders traded stories and passed the time playing cards. Mrs. Magill prohibited drinking, which relegated those who wished to cavort to the neighborhood saloons. Neville enjoyed the warmth of the parlor's hearth, while Mallabal stayed in their room away from the others, away from those who did not take kindly to the dark stranger. There were no earthly voices, no night birds or running streams to lull him to sleep. Instead, Mallabal would steep the flowers of the Banksia plant into a fermented tea he called "Bool." The sweet taste on his tongue, the joy of tranquility, he rested until he became drunk with sleep. Guided by a dream, he takes the unconscious journey home. Sleep, a gift, an instrument of goodness that would temporarily erase the memory of loss and misery; sleep, where he could hold an entire country in his head with its animals, people, green mountains, and salt water. But the skin of night is thin, and at the break of daylight, he opens his eyes and remembers.

In Van Damien's Land, he had become less than a person in the eyes of the colonists, and here in America, he was learning of the plight of the African. All persons of color were mingled into one culture, one race, all looked upon with disdain and mistrust. The city streets invited a mass of confusion, a rushing of humanity, crowded and almost paralyzing. At first, he dared not look into the windows of the horse-drawn omnibuses lest he offended the cold eyes staring out. Such a strange and unfamiliar mode of travel for those who could afford the two bits. Seven windows long and a narrow entrance door made it almost impossible for the hoop-skirted lady to board. The omnibuses rolled freely and dominated the streets providing a mode of service that was well-received despite the rude drivers who thought nothing of raising bedlam with the passengers and the teams of horses, where each animal added over twenty pounds of manure a day to the already filthy streets. Mallabal found the smells of the new city putrid, the open baskets of fish, oysters, shrimp, meat, and chicken parts. Flies hovered and flitted from crustacean to mollusk to gizzards, as a chorus of fishmongers' wives fanned away the pesky vermin with rolled newspapers. He scrutinized the people with the same disdain as they scrutinized him. This was an unpleasant place, and he was beginning to wonder if he had made a flawed decision. Though Neville reminded him that their situation was temporary until they had earned enough money to leave; he was a caged bird in a house filled with cats.

Broadway is recognized as a "cure for the blues," Fifth Avenue for its "romance." When a gentleman takes a stroll, he is free to wander; but women without a chaperone find themselves out of luck regardless of how adventurous they wish to be. It is a male-dominated world which includes business, politics, and dining out. Admission into the Astor House Restaurant is off-limits to single women. Respectable and proper single ladies who wish to eat out are welcome in establishments that have set aside female only dining areas. These establishments set aside safe spaces for women who wished to keep their sterling reputations intact. The city offers a goodly number of suitable free-standing ladies' eateries that abstain from the selling of hard liquors. Thompson and Son's on Broadway is billed as "a Lady's Saloon" with a delectable menu sans whiskey, while housed upstairs in the same building, is the popular Brady's Daguerreotype gallery. The ice cream parlor at Taylor's accommodates unaccompanied women, but finding it quite popular, a lady often must wait for a seat.

New York City was a tease, and though Sydney had always been aware of the inequalities between the genders, a stronger trace of annoyance possessed her in this opulent land of plenty. The perceptive young woman believed she had both the intelligence and ability to be an independent business owner. However, the politics and laws prohibited her any legitimate claim to such a right. Sydney walked the divide between satisfaction and displeasure; more than ever she was determined to design a scheme that would make her a force to be reckoned with. "It's more than equality that I want," a voice in her head whispered. "I want power!" She felt herself blush as if her statement might have been overheard, as if someone in the hustle and bustle of the streets might have been a party to her private thoughts. Yet, it was obvious that her feeling remained secure and now a tingle of excitement occupied all of her. As she hastened her pace a plan had effortlessly jelled. Solidifying the main idea had become quite easy; all she needed was an accomplice and two, she decided, were only a few blocks away.

Those who entered the Saint and Dickie Studio would indeed assume it was a successful gallery. Upon admittance, the clientele entered by a lavish parlor and subsequently escorted to one of several cordoned-off rooms; each staged with furniture and props with all intentions of transporting the sitter into a distinct period in history. But despite all the smoke and mirrors this establishment offered the public; it could not disguise reality. The two owners were crushed beneath a ponderous financial weight and deeply in debt; not a debt that comes from legitimate business expenditures, but a debt that had manifested itself over months of indiscretions and self-indulgence. You see, they had a very nasty habit of gambling. And as much as they tried to make their liabilities "go away" by amending the financial records, the depth of their misappropriations only grew worse making each partner very guilty of embezzlement. As such, to secure additional revenue at a faster rate of return was most imperative.

Sydney entered the cramped stairwell and with one hand on the wrought-iron banister rounded the stairs up several flights to the top floor. She stepped lightly noting the dim light made everything appear shabby. Her heart fluttered with anticipation as she clutched the top railing and drew a deep breath. Once she made her proposition, there was no going back, but she felt confident that the two men would find her proposal financially advantageous. Her only trepidation was the bombastic male psyche and their constituted legal advantages. But the clever woman's offer of a 50/50 partnership was non-negotiable. Without her, there was no plan. She pulled the drawstring open and rummaged through her bag, pulling from the case the small photograph. She smiled cunningly, eyeing her provocative self. This was just the kind of image that could bring money, especially if a person were able to get their hands on other seductive and suggestive photographs. Sydney knew she possessed what it took to be successful, and she would use every bit of her feminine guile to become an independent businesswoman. The notion of her mother, who was relegated to a financial allowance by her husband despite the woman's own family wealth and prestige, had cemented Sydney's decision to raise a few eyebrows. Sex sells, and if this were the only way to obtain autonomy, she would have to take a risk. Slipping her picture back between the bag's silky folds, she ran her tongue over her lips before knocking.

Dickie leaned against the bar contemplating the opportunity Sydney had proposed. He puffed the cigar and a twist of smoke traveled up and out of the gnawed butt like a gray serpent. While losing money at the roulette wheel, Saint was affirming that a most fortuitous set of circumstances had come their way, despite his momentary bad luck. The woman's proposition did not seem so outlandish, finally giving a reason for optimism in what was just days ago a bleak situation. Dickie's thoughts restored him to a more agreeable mood as he swaggered through the crowd and found a place to stand along the perimeter of gamblers. He tossed his cigar on the floor and mashed it with his heel. Bella, as she frequently called herself, would take charge of the new models and he and Saint would do what they did best, photograph. Across the smoke-filled room, a new type of clientele, one with a distinctive taste for the bawdy was standing right before them like zebras at the watering hole, oblivious to the pair of lions preparing to pounce. Saint glanced over at his friend and with a nod of his head tossed a few more chips down on the table hoping his luck was changing. But what they didn't think about was the lioness, and she was ready to take on the whole of the herd.

Sydney's risqué prints were more than a success as were the erotic poses of other unsuspecting female clients. Neither man felt any shame for the violations of trust they had broken regarding the sales. As far as they were concerned, the sitters had purchased the photographic services they wanted, and a few more prints sold without their knowledge wouldn't cause anyone any harm. Anonymity was upheld by buyer and seller. After dark, any money they lost at the gambling tables could be clandestinely recovered selling pictures beneath the hazy glow of the lamppost. Whereas during the daylight, riding the uptown omnibus proved profitable. Male riders were solicited, and with just a quick glance at the small portraits, tempted buyers were convinced. A seductive pout and titillating pose were all the persuasion needed. Omnibus drivers were soon brought into the scheme, and with a bit of a financial incentive, they turned an eye when a stodgy customer complained; often setting the griping rider back into the street.

In a very short time, the selling of promiscuous portraits was appraised as handsomely lucrative; producing albumen prints was cheap, while the capability of multiple copies proved easy to replicate. Unlike the early one-of-a-kind daguerreotypes of a decade ago, Saint had the foresight to keep up with photographic developments, honing his skills with his natural artistic talent. But even with his creative abilities, as more New York studios were opening clients willing to have seductive portraits taken was limited to the more audacious and high-spirited woman. Those "femme fatales" such as Sydney were a rare breed.

It was getting on towards a month since the initial partnership of the unscrupulous threesome when a first-class carriage stopped in front of the studio. A rather delicate debutante of barely eighteen stepped down and floated into the studio for a portrait sitting. She was chaperoned by her pretentious mother, a pompous and overbearing woman with a remarkable propensity to chatter. Such a tender young thing belonging to such a harpy seemed very unnatural, but then nature does produce some rather unusual things. How the caterpillar with its plump, fleshy body can metamorphize into an elegant butterfly is a testimony to the magic of nature. Mrs. Van Clef, the woman in question, was on this day in a state of urgency being as she was late for a luncheon, and promising to be back by quarter past two, gave the child a peck on the cheek and left her in the care of Sydney.

Timid as a sparrow, Miss Van Clef accepted the advice of Sydney, who brewed her a cup of the Aboriginal tea mixed with tincture of opium to calm the dear child's nerves and then set before her a trunk filled with elegant costumes. Settling upon a Renaissance gown consisting of two velvet tunics and several layers of undergarments, by the time the young lady had slipped into the first pale silk slip, she was admittedly quite relaxed and in need of some posing assistance. Cooperative and subdued,

Miss Van Clef's demure personality, her deep blue eyes and auburn hair across her shoulders was radiant through the camera's lens. All three partners gloated over their success; and as for the assistant, Albert, he was as tipsy as a drunk, professing that he had fallen in love with an angel. When the well-fed woman returned, the delicate debutante was waiting in the parlor in hand with a leather-bound carte-de-visite, posing as a stately Medieval maiden. And remembering nothing of her seductive alter-ego she left behind, mother and daughter departed quite happy.

However, if only the disclosure of information were all the truth. Had the photographer imparted more, then most certainly the innocent model would not sleep nearly as well tonight. So, it seems, unbeknownst to the lovely Van Clef, she had in hand a single portrait, only to have left behind with Saint and Dickie several identical prints.

Chapter 17

Not all insane asylums are equal. Those who can afford care in chartered hospitals are treated with compassion, and those who are poor are sentenced to misery.

Dr. Bushnell looked down and over his spectacles at the visitor from London, a boorish physician who was relegated to the task of visiting both state and community-run institutions for the insane in America. Now that he had carried out his job with the utmost proficiency, cataloging the day-to-day management and treatment of the asylum's patients, Dr. Langmuir was more than ready to sail back to Europe and give an oral account to the Regional Assembly of the Royal College of Physicians. He had completed his "unbiased report" and set a copy on Bushnell's desk on top of his stack of papers. Though no mention of the findings was made, for it mattered little to the Englishman, he settled in his chair and sipped the port that had been expressly set aside for just such an occasion.

"A good year," he said smacking his thick chapped lips. Acknowledging the protrusion hiding beneath his girdle, the comfortable man patted his stomach with contentment. Bushnell wondered if he had been too honorable; perhaps he should have wined and dined this ninny of a doctor in hopes that he would have extended more leniency in the report. He stared down at the papers sheathed in a brown leather cover and shuddered. Not at what lay beneath, but at the thought of his wife chastising him for being so "utterly honest." If only he had her cunning. The American sighed and brought his thoughts back to the glutton sitting before him. "What did he know about caring for idiots," charged the doctor. "The war created more than the displacement of body and home, it stole the mind and ravaged the spirit." Dr. Bushnell was ready for the Englishman to leave; he had been a courteous host, gave him full reign of the place, of course with Vole by his side, and it was time for the oaf to be gone. To his dismay the pompous English doctor prattled on, never once discussing anything of importance, only giving his accounts of the insufferable roads he had to endure while traipsing up and down the east coast. The mud, the rain, the sun, the heat; he had nothing positive to say, complaining that he found it rather dismal, and all those limbless men! As for the treatment of the insane, well it was a "mixed bag." "A mixed bag!" shouted Bushnell to himself as he nodded his head like a marionette attached to a set of strings. He followed each word as the stocky doctor sipped his second glass of port and then spouted his remarks as though he were spitting peanut shells and talking at the same time.

Bushnell smiled at Vole who slithered in and stood behind Dr. Langmuir until he was acknowledged. "The doctor's coach is here to take him to his hotel," said the assistant. "Your coat?" he asked and stood with the enormous garment that sheltered the slight fellow just as if he were holding a tent. He raised it and waited. It took a moment for the off-ish man to get his too thin legs to lift the rest of him up and out of the chair, and another moment to find the sleeves and wriggle in. "There," he remarked looking about the room in such a way as though he had forgotten something.

"Your umbrella, Doctor," remarked Vole.

"Yes, never know when you need it!" grinned the Englishman.

"Must be like tea," said Bushnell. The doctor looked perplexed. "You know, rain, England, tea...?" But the joke went over the stuffy man's head, and with a grunt, he waddled out.

"I got it, Sir," remarked Vole and winked at his boss before closing the door behind him.

———·———

Mrs. Bushnell had no intentions of working with the suffragettes although the cause was certainly one that she could rally behind, she was far too busy to get involved. She had been liberated even before the first convention was held at Seneca Falls back in '48 and with men thinking she was a helpless woman; this notion only gave her more power over them. From the time the "Declaration of Sentiments and Grievances," a treatise by women for women was read on the convention floor, Sydney's past clandestine life had profitted her well, both financially and socially. It provided her pleasures that she might not have been able to enjoy had she waited for women to get their rights equal in status to men. As it was, there were still many political and social injustices to break through.

She mulled over her conversation with her husband, confident that she would be able to gain access back into the hospital. Having dropped a crumb of an idea for her husband to choke on was semantically the same as a hairball to a cat. He would cough up the suggestion of her entering the political arena and reconsider her request; a far better outcome for him was for her to be at the hospital, yes, much safer than her going off in New York advocating for women's rights.

Having helped during the war, she was quite familiar with hospital protocol, especially how to administer both mental and medicinal comforts. The understaffed nurses liked her; she had been a regular Florence Nightingale. Sydney had read about this courageous British nurse who cared for the wounded soldiers during the Crimean War. Her reputation extended all the way to the United States, and at the same time the war between the states was going on, Miss Nightingale continued her charitable efforts establishing a nursing school in England. However, Mrs. Bushnell knew the staff liked her not only because she took away some of their burdens, but because she brought them sweets and trinkets.

Sydney finished all but a few sips of her tea, swirling the cup around and around as it made a small whirlpool in the cup. "Rosalie!" she called. "They're ready!" She tipped the last drop out and set the cup upside-down on the saucer. Then she lifted it up and peered in; as always, the leaves adhered to the sides creating a new pattern. "Rosalie, hurry!" Her voice lifted and trailed down the hallway to the housekeeper. "Look!" the woman exclaimed and pointed to the streaky pattern. "What do you make of it?" Her inquiry accompanied a curious grin.

The elder woman wore her plaited gray hair under a silk headscarf which twisted around her head into a pink band. She lifted the cup and peered in, holding it firmly in place.

"Well?" asked the agitated tea drinker.

The housemaid said nothing but returned a stern glare in her mistress's way. Rosalie was the only person that could get away with such behavior. She was the only woman, aside from Sydney's mother, who had earned her respect. After several long moments, the cup was set upright on the tray.

"It looks like a bird, a fat bird, don't you think, so?" Sydney asked picking up the cup again. "See, here are the wings and the legs, and a beak.

"Oh, yes, a bird, but not just any bird," remarked the seer. She squinted while turning the cup in several rotations until concluding with, "It's a hen."

"A hen?" Sydney lips puckered with disappointment. A peacock or even a pigeon would be so much more glamorous, but a hen. "I don't see a hen. Looks more like…" she paused and then looked up. "An owl."

The elder shook her head with disapproval. "The leaves don't lie. It is a hen."

"And, what does it mean?" Sydney was growing impatient. The fact that it resembled a hen was useless without the woman's interpretation. Rosalie had been brought up in the spiritual folkways of the Chinese herbalist and Suan Ming fortune-tellers. So saying, she professed to have the knowledge to determine a person's fate. Having worked for years to rid her speech of the Cantonese accent, she studied with an elocution teacher in exchange for domestic services, who trained her tongue to resist the forbidden language, and acquired a refined and metered infliction that fit her pale and powdered countenance. Escaping civil war in South China, she emigrated to the United States from the Guangdong Province. When asked about her Western name, she relates the following story. *Upon boarding the ship to America, she was offered a rose by a haggard and weary refugee resting slightly atilt against the deck railing. She welcomed the compassionate gesture and bid him a safe voyage too, but her sentiments were no match for what had been forecast for the old man. It seems that he unwittingly contracted "ship fever" and several weeks into the rough voyage confined in close quarters, he died. Illness and death were a frequent occurrence on overcrowded ships, and the only provisions set aside for the deceased was to be lowered overboard and set free with a prayer. The entire length of the plank was covered in sailcloth, and after two seamen slid the body off the board, she tossed flower petals into the sea after him. In only a few moments, he disappeared, however, the crimson petals clung to the pulpy kelp long after the scene was out of view.* Hence, she adopted a name to better fit her new identity, Rosalie.

"What it means is riches, more riches. Might be money or might be another person. The hen doesn't tell what kind of riches. What do you want Miss Sydney, money or another somebody?" The question dangled and then crept its way into the thoughts of the mistress.

The seated woman smiled. "Can never have too much money, now can we, Rosalie?" She picked up the cup again and examined the inside.

The older woman shrugged her shoulders, "I wouldn't know," she exclaimed and then scooped up the cup and set it on the tray, whisking it away.

It had been almost a month since Sydney had enjoyed the serenity induced by her "honorable" tea-blend. She knew that Richard disapproved of her habits, but being the sensitive man that he was, he did not keep her from yielding to her desires. He had witnessed too much suffering during the war, and if his wife enjoyed her opiates, then the least he could do was to not lecture her on the subject. He enjoyed the entitlements received in his position as a surgeon and asylum administrator, although admitting to himself that stealing from the battlefield medical supplies had been more than deceitful. With wartime supplies of morphine practically depleted, pilfering for his wife's personal needs was not only criminal but morally indecent. And so, his conscience got the better of him, and he no longer took what she demanded. Another means of feeding her habits had to be found, and as luck would have it, she struck gold with Rosalie.

Sydney leaned back and pulled the small bottle from her pocket. "Rosalie!" she cried, "Can you bring me a little more tea?" She waited only a few moments, and the elder woman tottered in, a muslin cloth slung over her shoulder for she had been interrupted in her chores.

"Bush tea?" she asked.

"That would be fine. Yes, just a half cup, though." Her eyes fluttered and then she added, "Richard won't be home for dinner, he has some report to go over."

"I sure hope not," the woman remarked. Sensitive to Sydney's habits, she did not wish to explain to Dr. Bushnell why his wife was not coming down to dinner. His absence would make the housekeeper's life much easier.

The pungent aroma of the brewed tea wafted into the room even before the housekeeper entered. She placed the rose laced cup and saucer on the table and then uncorked the small glass bottle and poured several drops into the tea. Then she added two lumps of sugar and stirred it with a silver teaspoon. "Do you want me to turn down the lamp?" she asked.

"That would be nice." Sydney lifted the cup and this time did not delay by sipping, but rather swallowed all the liquid at once. It burned a little going down her throat; a sensation that would last only for a few minutes. She placed the cup back on the saucer, leaned back and rested her legs on the ottoman. She closed her eyes and sighed. The patter of feet exiting and a door closing was just the beginning of sweet dreams. A hen was the first image that came into her mind.

———•———

Time, the carefree freeloader, drifting lazily on the back of the afternoon had suddenly grown miserly as it neared the end of the day. The sun began to set and was leaving behind a sheer orange blanket over kneaded flour-domes. Italian crockery had been lined up along the window sill; its contents doubling in size during the few hours that had passed while waiting to be baked. Rosalie enjoyed the quiet, grateful that she lived in a household that respected her privacy. Every home had its secrets, and this one was far from being free from skeletons. But isn't that what makes life interesting? Rosalie poured her elixir into the glass. The amber liquid was her own brew, a recipe that had been passed down to each generation. Occasionally someone along the Jin family line may have deviated from the recipe, trying their own incantations, but this was her Po Po's way and the only one she attested to. "Take a short cup of elixir every day, and you'll never need the doctor." There was a strong flavor of orange blossoms that she savored, but it was the addition of snake wine that gave Po Po's tonic its medicinal powers.

———•———

Richard Bushnell shifted the document towards him and lowered his spectacles, balancing them on the bridge of his nose. He had the unfortunate dilemma of having to decipher the British man's scribbled handwriting; a sure sign that the latter was generally in the company of a secretary. The doctor scowled as he reflected. It was bad enough that he had spent most of the day reinterpreting the English language as he had listened to the pretentious man drivel. "I can only assume that you and your institution are familiar with the work by Dr. Conolly's published volume *The Treatment of the Insane without Mechanical Restraint*. As in agreement, I have examined your wards, true to his recommendations. You will find everything right here." The corpulent observer had too much fun at the expense of the American tapping his pudgy finger against the papers he had set down. His eyes almost twinkled when he passed the information over.

Dr. Bushnell tipped his head forward and while using his index finger as a guide, studied the first few pages. Then he smiled and readjusted his spectacles as he reread the paragraph. *With every disposition to advocate the disuse of restraint to the utmost extent, I am compelled to admit that the result of my observations, as far as the present, has led me to the conclusion that cases may occur in which temporary employment of restraints are both necessary and justifiable. Besides the occasional practice of confining the patient's hands, when employing a stomach-pump to feed the most uncooperative, a more prolonged use of restraint was necessary and effective as seen fit by staff…".* Dr. Languire's footnotes regarding the paraphrasing from Dr. Conolly's book reaffirmed what Bushnell already surmised; the observer hadn't any personal experience caring for lunatics. The man was a doctor only in title likely having spent no time as a practitioner.

The American continued to read, stopping every now and again to redirect his attention back to the report. He obeyed his higher-ups by agreeing to have the Englishman traipse about and like in the military; he complied dutifully. "I wish this prig would have learned to write legibly," he silently complained. *All correspondence in the form of letters, written or received, pass through the doctor's hands, whether opened or not, I do not know.* Bushnell found this as not any revelation that needed to be noted, but he shrugged it off and continued to read. *Reports of the condition and the changes of it depend upon the warders who take their first cue from the aforementioned doctors. However, during their work shifts several groups of ward keepers were observed holding personal conversations; some raffish in context about gambling houses and horse racing, a few were taking wagers from the idiots, while, varying these activities with hospital gossip and foul language. Rough horse-play with patients by staff appeared at times almost sadistic and especially evidenced during water therapy and patient recreational time in the courtyard.*

Richard pulled a monogrammed handkerchief from his pocket, wiped his spectacles, and methodically put them back on, slipping the curved earpieces carefully behind his ears. He had on occasion informally reprimanded a few of the younger wards about being too rough. He ran his hand over a clean sheet of parchment, dipped his pen into the inkwell, and scribbled a note to remind Vole about this. He compared his neat and well-formed cursive against that of the sloppy visitor's as he rolled the blotter over his parchment several times before setting it aside. "Now, where was I?" he muttered searching for the place where he had left off. So far the report contained nothing scathing, nothing that would be considered unethical or even out of the ordinary. Though it didn't matter to him, things in writing have a nasty habit of reappearing later.

Administering the asylum was so much less stressful than his life during the war. Now all he had to do was keep the veteran soldiers from killing themselves. On the other hand, a lost mind was harder to heal than a wounded arm. He often wondered if his job was to heal or to incarcerate since most of these poor souls were all but forgotten even by their families. They had witnessed death, dismemberment, loss of friends and family. They killed the enemy while unable to prevent the fatality of a comrade, and barely able to ward off their own reminder of imminent death. But what was most curious was how many soldiers developed nervous disorders years after the war had ended. There were those obsessed with talking about combat, aroused by violent spells combined with nighttime wanderings; nightmares of the viciousness and brutality of battle, and the constant fear of being killed. But even though family members tried to keep a watchful eye, the frequency of violence became a burden. This was something that would not be in the report.

Mechanical restraints such as straps and mittens, chemical restraints to control behavior, manual restraints provided by attendants, locked doors, and seclusion were reserved for the most wretched of patients. According to staff, patient overpopulation has been on a steady incline. War veterans and widows "suffering from chronic mania," those seen as devoid of mental faculties, were more common. A large number exhibit acute mania described as paranoia, hallucinations, insomnia, confusion, hysteria, memory problems, and violent behavior. The mechanism by which rapid pulse, anxiety, and shortness of breath evoke or accelerates in veteran soldier-patients without physical trauma is diagnosed as "soldiers' heart." Over-stimulation of the heart's nervous system, "Da Costa's Syndrome" has similar symptoms; shortness of breath, palpitation on exertion, and giddiness. (If my memory serves me correctly, it is named for Dr. Jacob Da Costa's and his observations during the American war.) A transcribed account of newly admitted Patient #304 shows symptoms of "irritable heart." "A shell exploded. Everywhere there were the blasts of cannonades; I remember I fell and could feel what I thought was rain, but it was falling dirt and body parts. I wanted to get up, but my legs wouldn't work. When I woke, there was ringin' in my ears that wouldn't stop. That's when my sleeplessness and headaches started." Many similar cases were admitted by family members that can no longer control or cope with the patient. Alcohol has been diagnosed as the root cause of many of their neurosis.

Bushnell smirked at the last note. "I should be a lunatic too if that's all it takes to throw a man into the category of the insane," he grunted, affirming his lack of confidence in this sort of medical conclusion. Yet those who advocated temperance claimed that the evils of mankind were a direct link to whiskey and the like. Tossing aside the already perused pages, he leaned his head back and yawned. It was not a small inconsequential yawn that one does if in the company of another, but rather a big mouthed cat-like yawn, typically displayed when fatigued or bored. Dr. Bushnell was feeling both symptoms of the day. He set himself squarely in his leather chair, a snuff-colored George II design with handsomely carved walnut legs to compliment his desk. He leaned forward to read and found himself skimming the paragraphs. The next two pages were filled with discussions of the lack of clean linens and towels, food rations, and other mundane parcels of information. However, it was his turning to the sixth page which caught his interest.

Patient number 129, a woman of average height and comely appearance, calling herself Margaret, was being escorted back from the courtyard to the women's ward. As we approached through the same corridor, upon seeing me, she called out as if in despair. At first, her rants were difficult to discern because of the use of colloquial expressions and southern regional accent. The female ward tried to restrain her, but the woman was slippery as an eel and before she was restrained, lunged towards myself and Mr. Vole. Nearly falling, for she was wearing only cotton slippers on her feet, grabbed on to me, holding dearly as if we were father and daughter. It was here that she cried pitifully, sobbing how she wanted her picture taken again so she could get her "good feelings" back. The distraught woman was trembling from head to toe, but thankfully in only a matter of moments, she was bound in a straitjacket. As she was taken away, she cried out, summoning me to 'look for the room where they take the pictures.' It would not have seemed odd in most accounts, being as she was quite out of her head. But not more than an hour had passed when our tour took us past an open door which had a sign that read "Laundry" posted on the wall. Able to see inside, I noted that the small room could not be used for such purposes considering no wash basins or clotheslines were anywhere in view. In the place of laundering facilities, backed up to the adjacent wall there appeared to be a standing tripod with a box attached, a box that I can assume to be a camera. Dr. Bushnell opened his mouth again, but this time not in response to a yawn. He sat there agape at what he had just read and then slowly folded the page into several halves until it no longer would allow him to crease it anymore. Keeping the crumpled parchment in his fist, he pulled open the bottom desk drawer and tossed it to the back where he secured entry with a key. He needed more time to think.

There was an anemic rap on the door, followed by, "The Englishman has gone, Sir."

Dr. Bushnell smiled. "Come in Vole." The door admitted the wiry man. By most accounts, he appeared older than his age, perhaps because of his graying sideburns, or perhaps by his tottering gait. "We have some maintenance to do, Vole. A bit of maintenance." The doctor folded his hands and rested them on the pages he had completed. The compliant assistant nod. "You're a good man, Vole," portioned the doctor.

"Thank you, Sir." He stood patiently, wondering if he should leave or to remain standing. The pendulum twittered like a lone cicada, much louder than he ever remembered. His eyes roamed to the face of the clock. Vole shifty restlessly. Time was scant, and there was much to be done. "Is there anything else you need, Dr. Bushnell?"

The physician looked up as though he had just been awakened. "Here," he said, reaching for his scribbled note. "Seems to be a bit of rough-housing." Vole accepted the parchment and grinned.

"Anything else?" He slid his bony fingers along the edge of the paper. There was something on the doctor's mind; he knew that expression, a face clouded in uncertainty.

"Not right now," the doctor replied. Vole turned and started for the door when he heard his name. "Vole, I can count on you." Was this a question or demand? Vole was accustomed to erratic behavior, after all, he worked in an asylum. But the tone projected could have crushed him with its weight of ambiguity.

Facing the seated man, he felt suddenly as an equal. "Always, Dr. Bushnell."

"Good man, Vole." The voice now resonated with a tenor of ease as it followed the secretary out. Silence spread like vapor charging the air with anticipation. Bushnell stared across the room at the closed door and with an unexpected compulsion he started to laugh.

———•———

Sydney's youthful personality was fortified with candor, ambition, and individuality; traits not becoming of a lady of her standing. However, these characteristics had been passed down the family line and therefore rather than fighting their existence, she accepted her behavioral inheritance even though society proclaimed them as faults. How she had fallen in love with another at the same time she was engaged was simple to understand if the observer were filled with the same passion and independence as she, the betrothed. For although Richard Bushnell was a conglomerate of all the positive makings commanded of a successful and upstanding husband, he lacked a certain quality that made Sydney's heart flutter. He was sexually unappealing.

She had not set out to fall for another man, and unlike the storybook rendition of love, it was not at first sight. Rather, she loathed him, found him in all accounts uncouth, even curious. He looked like no one she had ever met, and he spoke in an odd deliberate manner, but it was his eyes that set him in a league apart from other men. When he looked at her, it was as if he read her soul. How she hated him, the mere thought made her cringe, even shudder; so was that feeling hatred or was it desire?

He was secretive, and perhaps that was part of the allure; a man who did not have a need to prove to others that he was his own person, and for Sydney, she saw herself in this same way. They were polar opposites, she was talkative, he was silent, she was demure, he was rugged, she was white, he was black, she was sophisticated, and he was savage. And the more she thought about him, the more she found him to be like the forbidden fruit; it was sinful on so many accounts, and she lusted for him in a way that made even her blush. She had never told anyone about her desires; secrecy was her specialty, and something as delicate as taking on a lover would have ruined not only herself but the family. For her sake, she was spared public disclosure, but for Mallabal, it was his ruin.

The accumulation of time kept her secret safe, and like a bird that does not return to an old nest, she needed to keep her distance from returning to old memories. Sydney opened her eyes. The drawn curtains kept the soft haze of her dreams intact. She liked that feeling, as if she were floating, free from the burden of her body, only her mind kept her tethered to her physical form, and if she was not careful, it could be released and never find its way back. There was a sigh; she felt the words come out of her mouth and then the sound as a slow din wandered around the room. It remained invisible until she felt a light breath. Someone had stolen a kiss from her slightly parted lips. She smiled. "I knew you would return," she whispered. She strained with famished eyes to see her lover, but all she conjured up was an illusion of a time coming back. She felt sleepy and restless at the same time. If she fell asleep, she might lose him again. She watched herself take a lap around the room and then hover above her body as if aligning to her form. She laughed hoping she would not crush herself and closed her eyes with renewed relaxation.

She was as light as dust. Ruffled layers of air entombed her in a locked memory that she could not lift away from, so she became the audience at a show she had seen before. *The dog was not in view, in fact, there was very little reason for anyone to have noticed its cunning presence since it was lying in the shade beneath the peddler's cart. It did not belong to the sooty-faced man; although the cur kept one eye on the vendor since it must have taken lickings from the likes of him before. Like other mongrels, it was distrustful, and though it was not a large animal, its nasty temperament resembled that of the dingo found on the Pacific islands. And perhaps for that very reason, the dog took an immediate dislike to Mallabal. Now had this stray been the least bit smart, it would not have provoked this customer, however, being as it was feeling brave, as soon as Mallabal stepped up to examine the wares, the dog leaped out from its hiding place. There was a shrill cry from the group of carping women who were on the far side of the cart. But their shrieks did not deter the wild dog, for its barking and growling deafened their cries. The vicious animal lunged, latching onto the man's leg, however, in an instant, the dreadful animal was silenced and lay like a limp pelt of fur on the ground. Blood gushed from the slit throat, while Mallabal wiped his sanguine-stained knife on the peddler's rag. Then, tossing a coin in the old man's cup, he paid for the cloth and walked away. Commotion after the incident took the form of a meddlesome crowd labeling the Aborigine as a coward, a killer, a good-for-nothing. But Sydney, like a few others, believed his action was exonerated and this added to her belief that he was someone she understood. But, it was more than sympathetic understanding . . . she wanted to know this man intimately.*

On the edge of another universe, Mallabal's uncertain world unraveled at an unparalleled speed. Upon stepping off the ship with Neville, he was an explorer in an already discovered world. There was no mercy for the inexperienced, and so he quickly learned to adapt because time does not soothe, nor does it wait. He was the rabbit, fast, alert, and ever so vulnerable. But he knew how to survive, and so he kept to himself and accompanied Neville, for he trusted the man; having no other choice.

"Sydney!" Dr. Bushnell rapped lightly at her door and waited in the hallway for what seemed like several minutes. Then, he put his ear against the panel and rapped a bit more loudly. "Are you awake, Dear?" He stood erect, and like a dog waiting to be let inside, he was patient.

"Ah, Dr. Bushnell, you're home early. Would you like your dinner now?" Rosalie came up behind him as quietly as an apparition. He turned with a bit of a start. There was something about this woman the doctor didn't like.

"Is my wife sleeping?" he asked; his tone did not reconcile the hour of the evening with the question.

"She was feeling a bit tired, so I put her to bed," the dutiful woman said, choosing her words carefully. "But, I can wake her if you wish." She was standing before him with a pot of tea.

"No, no, let her sleep." His voice, a bit aggravated for having to dine alone, was quickly masked by, "I'll eat in my room, Rosalie. I have some work to go over, so I'll take a tray upstairs." He sniffed and then made a face. "Never could stand the smell of that tea," he exclaimed.

However, his dislike of the hot beverage was ignored. "Of course, Dr. Bushnell. Will you take your port upstairs too?" She smiled like a cat.

"That will be fine," he muttered, and with a bit of a good-natured grin he thanked the woman and set out to his room.

Rosalie watched and listened as he entered and closed the adjacent room's door. The teacup rattled on the saucer as the maid managed both the knob and the tray and slipped into Sydney's room. "I've brought you a bit more tea," she whispered, setting the tray on the night table.

The woman opened her eyes. "I've had the most enchanting dream," Sydney said wriggling into a sitting position. She took the cup from Rosalie, sniffed the tea, and then smiled. "I love the smell of this," she said. "I really do."

 half-dozen sticks of pitch pine were enough tinder for Lucas to get a small fire started. Having steeped a ration of parched chicory and yesterday's coffee grounds, he would have to make do with the watery concoction that was stained more like tea than the strong brew he craved. The events of the morning coiled around his thoughts like a hedgehog. Despair and revenge had worn grooves in his head, an ill-fitted consequence for a man who had participated in the wartime suturing of a divided nation. Years had gone by, and while both North and South were holding together, there remained gaps in the seams. The survivor squatted beside the dwindling flame. A few flimsy sticks continued to burn as he held the cup above the heat. He dipped his finger below the rim and swished it around the liquid, testing the temperature. It would have to do. He packed one of his only remaining sugar cubes into his cheek and lifted the cup to his lips. The liquid, though weak, tasted good as he swished it around his mouth, allowing the coffee to break apart the sugar. "This was the way Dennet liked his coffee," he thought as he swallowed. Then he gulped the rest in one slug, wiping his mouth on his sleeve.

"Damn." There was no time to dawdle or reminisce about the past. Whoever was wearing Dennet's boots knew too much. He scooped up some dirt and tossed it into the pit smothering the miserable fire. The sun lay heavily against the vacant sky adding to his misery. All future plans the brothers had schemed were extinguished in one erratic decision. "Shit!" The disgusted brother picked up the two haversacks and slung them over his shoulder. The bedrolls had been tied together with a leather strap, and he repositioned the awkward bundle over his other arm and across his back. He pondered for a moment, exhausting all possible hunches as to which direction he should head; so he flipped a coin. Heads meant left, tails meant right. It landed heads. He glanced about, displeased with the unforged landscape before him in contrast to the tamer path in the opposite direction he was not destined to travel. "The hell with heads," he decided and started down the grassy path to the right.

———·———

Lucas wasn't sure what he was going to do to the man in his brother's boots, but like the first time he'd "seen the elephant", he would know when he found him. He wanted to loosen the grip of past transgressions, but as disciplined and fit as he was, there was no peace. The war always found its way out from the recesses of his brain. *Unstrained passion for victory consumed all desires as he and his regiment fixed their sights upon the approaching cloud of dust kicked up by ten thousand enemy boots. As the column neared the front ranks, a ricochet of artillery and clamorous howling were delivered first by the wind. Any reckless feeling of despair was cast aside by a unified craving to win.* Like a mountain lion, Lucas was an opportunist, and like the big cat, he needed to maintain law in his solitary kingdom. But the emotion of vengeance was more potent than any rational and being a renegade; he cared even less for meaningless rules.

Briers and thistle weeds peppered the hillside, and though they clawed at his pant legs, he preferred this scrubland over mud. The descent was gradual, and with his gear light, he could keep a quick pace. Wild-roses were in bloom and opened their petals up towards the sunlight, which claimed most all their energy. But while they were enjoying the sunlight, Lucas cursed his thirst, a reminder that he would have to find water; his canteen barely holding a morning's worth. Soaked in sweat the heat licked his body, but he knew better than to take off his wet shirt. The sun rendered objects unrecognizable, and as he tramped, he bowed his head aligning his hat brim with his brows. He tucked his pants into his boots, hoping to keep the ticks and chiggers from crawling up to his bare skin. The retreat downward was turning steep, and like a rocking chair set too close to the edge, Lucas shortened his stride. The sky was white and held no promise of rain. *"Lemonade?" His mother had a secret recipe when he was a boy. "Just add a loaf of sugar and a whole lotta love!" she'd whisper.* He wondered if Dennet knew the secret recipe. His trek downward was finally rewarded as he found himself on level ground once again. Reminded of a sailor returning from sea, his legs wobbled as he took several steps onto the barren ground. Cleared of scrubs and brush it stretched for at least a mile in both directions. If his observation was correct a clearing so well defined had been planned for the main purpose of leading into town. The challenge set before him was in which direction to walk. But unlike his earlier decision-making method, he would not rely on luck. He crouched down and tilted his head parallel with the ground. But none of his trapper instincts or skills could find any human tracks heading in either direction. "Not worth a pinch of shit," he muttered at his worthless efforts. Lucas stood up and dusted himself off with his hands and spit into the dry, windblown roadbed. Wishing that he had come across mud, he kicked a stone and watched as it wobbled across the road and stopped just shy of a split cross-tie. The wood had been stripped free of its bark and appeared out of place in this rustic setting. "Railroad ties!" Lucas shut his eyes and let the wind settle as he longed for the whistle of a locomotive. But the only sound made was the annoying hum of gnats. He slapped his neck and

cursed his situation, but not before draining his canteen empty. His indecision to go in one direction or the other was approached with the concern
only to find water. The heat of the day was melting any desire to remain
where he was, and without hesitation, Lucas headed in the opposite direction the sun had chosen to throw itself upon.

———— • ————

There are four reasons that people ended up in a shanty camp; some were
born there, some were destined, some enticed, and some just happened
upon it. Many look upon its inhabitants as a useless group of vagrants,
yet they are a class of folks when left to themselves assume the same roles
as those in the cities. Some read old newspapers, some the Bible, some
smoke pipes or rolled tobacco, but all carry with them an air which defines
them not as castaways, but rather the forgotten. Set on the outskirts of
town near the railroad tracks, the camp's inhabitants pilfer from the trash
of residents or nearby fields, taking the castoffs for themselves. When the
nights are cold, they sit around open firepits, crack jokes, spin yarns, get
drunk, argue, and fight. They are by ordinary rights not a thieving bunch,
though it would be foolhardy not to keep one's meager belongings on
your person.

It was the middle of the afternoon when Lucas appeared at the
camp. Having tramped all morning, he was tired, hungry, and ready to
rest. Several of the lodgers were leaning against the large oak rolling cig-
arettes, while the remainder of the camp appeared uninhabited save scattered piles of blankets and straw matting. It was the responsibility of each
man to bring his share of firewood to the pit, so one can only assume
many were in search of kindling. There was a looming stench not unlike
the smell of decaying meat that brought Lucas to wondering if he should
turn around and leave. Only the commanding eye of a burly fellow cast
upon him made him proceed towards the heavyset smoker. "Don't suppose there's room for one more?' Lucas asked, slowly walking towards

several men as if he were approaching a pair of dogs. "Maybe you could spare some food?"

The man dressed in black snarled, "This ain't a rooming house." He looked up and winked. The other, a small churlish fellow with a neglected beard and mustache laughed.

"Probably better than one. No rent." Lucas smiled and went on. "What'll it take to camp here; maybe a night or two?"

The grizzly man spat out a piece of tobacco that had stuck on his lower lip and elbowed the smaller companion. "What'd ya got to offer up?" he asked with more interest. "Looks to me like you got as much as the rest of us, nothin' but a bunch of shitty war stories!" He pointed to the army issued blanket and nodded. "Yankee."

Lucas shifted uneasily. The last thing he wanted was to get into it with a grayback. After all these years he was sick of having to defend his honor. He stood with his hands in his pockets contemplating his options. Both men were seated giving him the advantage. He could easily unsheathe his knife and in a matter of seconds slit their throats. He decided to let the conversation play out; he much rather friend them than kill them. "Yep, that I am. And I guess you're not."

"Sure as shit I'm not. But it don't matter now 'cause it looks like they got everything they wanted out of the both us." The disgust for the two armies was expressed in his voice. "Set up where you want," the burly man said. "You can pay your way in cards." Now it was the smaller man that elbowed the brute.

But as soon as the word 'cards' was uttered, the crass voice snapped in Lucas's ears. Could this be the same Rebel he and Dennet met in the boxcar? Was he the same man the cripple had called Bodie? He tried to reconstruct the event; the sky had the look of sandpaper, the train's wheels creaked as they revolved around and around over the pitted tracks. The colors of each passing hours were changing until suddenly the trees and hills were covered in a filmy gray with the unraveling of dusk. He couldn't be sure if it was him. No, he could not be sure, not after they entered the jaws of nighttime. A cold shiver ran down his back deploying a sensation of regret that when he had the chance just moments ago, he had not confronted him. Lucas settled on the far side of the fire away from the others and tossed his belongings on the ground. He sat down and pulled his hat below his brim with his head resting on his knees. Why did he want to kill this worthless man? He had done him no harm. Yet, there was something terribly insidious about this fellow that brought the worst out in him. There was something vulgar and despicable that made him loath such a creature, so much so that his immediate reaction was to gather up his things and leave. Leaving would do him no good. He had to rest first, and then when renewed could he set out to find the man with Dennet's boots.

The afternoon was spent following scrubby trails worn down by those walking back and forth from the creek that runs along the east end of the camp. Buckets of water were carried from a small stream several meters away and poured into the communal barrel. Lucas liked this spot and its tranquility, but the ground near the stream was soft like a stew, too wet to sleep on, too wet to bury a man in. He wondered about the owner of the land; maybe he had been carried off a battlefield or listed among the quota of lost veterans. It was fine land, but trespassers who tried to tame it always wandered back into the campsite to build his shebang or set up his canvas among the others. Drifters who were ready to move on often left behind some of their belongings; some because they were charitable, others because it was too heavy to carry, and a few to be remembered by. Pots and pans, salt and pepper shakers, salted beef, and even a wooden bench were among the contributed items that were quickly confiscated by way of a pecking order. But they were as poor as Job's turkey, and the majority had little more with them than a capbox filled with wax and a wick with which to light his way.

At the hour when most of the inhabitants had returned before dark, the new arrival made his acquaintance with an old-timer they called "Frisco," who took it upon himself to fry some salt pork. Here the designated cook mixed the yellow grease, fat, and fried cracklings into a pot of boiled red beans, hence serving supper for twelve. The pot and tin cups were lined up on the benches along with a few harsh words and vulgarity. But the warm meal softened these hardened men, and for the most part, they conducted themselves as gentlemen of a shanty camp should. By trade these "yesterday soldiers" were counterfeiters, sellers of trinkets, junkmen, and drifters; but it was the brute dressed in black who profited the most from his sought-after enterprise. Although his sultry pictures should have been the subject of the evening's entertainment, it was rather the arrival of the stranger that kept some half-awake.

There were no armed guards to watch the camp; only the evening stars shined brilliantly over the good and evil, the wretched and the unfortunate, the winners and losers. When morning broke, Frisco was tending to the campfire. Those sleeping or too hungover to crawl out from under their blankets missed out on cornpone and barley water, which meant that the good-natured cook had most mornings to himself. Reports had drifted back about the hiring of day laborers encouraging a few industrious men to set out early. But those who decided it was too hot a day to work were satisfied to offer a song and dance to any sympathetic ear in return for a handout. Yet despite all their wrongdoings and philandering, within the confines of the camp, the vocation of vagrant united them into the fraternity of brotherhood. Theirs followed an unwritten code of moral standards that would have stood up in any society; "Though shalt not squeal."

Only Bodie shared the company of the cook this day; where directly after breakfast he took it upon himself to examine the belongings of the most recent arrival. However, to his chagrin there were only two bedrolls neatly tied up, nothing more was behind. "It's getting to a point," remarked the cook to the empty-handed man, "that it's harder and harder to steal for a living successfully. Take this sock," he exclaimed wiggling his big toe, "who hangs hole-riddled socks on the clothesline! Next thing you know, we'll be the victims."

———————•———————

Julio Tamayo and his good-hearted wife did all they could for the child, except for taking her back to the burned down house. Flora stood on the hill and tiptoed, trying to see over the tall grasses. With hopes that she might catch a glimpse of her home, maybe her mother or Colonel coming up the grassy knoll to fetch her, this practice had become a morning ritual. But life does not work that way, even for a parentless child, and all the finger-crossing and nighttime prayers did nothing except give her hope that if she tried a little harder and waited a little longer then her wishes would be granted. But there was one absolute she knew she could count on; Asa would come and take her away from these nice but simple farmers. "It's not that I'm not grateful," she reminded her doll, Caridad, "but it is time for me to go home." The dark-eyed doll looked back blankly. "I know; you're wondering where we will go." Flora leaned the doll back on the pillow and then lifted the blanket, so it settled just under the neck. It was a gift from Señora Tamayo, and although it looked as though it may have been owned by another little girl before, being as the lace on the dress was re-stitched, it was indeed a very nice doll. "I have to tell you that I'm not always a good mother, sometimes I have to leave you alone, even at night." She re-tucked the blanket pressing her fingers along the doll's stiff figure, creating a neat crease. Flora stared at the doll and smiled cunningly. Her mind drifted for a moment as she wandered out the window and down the hillside to her real home. The charred building disappeared and became the neat house with the open porch. She lingered into the garden and along the fence line. Her eyes brightened, and she looked at Caridad. "There was a witness," she whispered. "The tattie-bogle saw everything," she added. "He knows." Then she twisted her mouth downward. "But he's too much like you, just a listener." She flashed to Asa, "Another listener," she reminded herself. "Maybe I'm not such a good listener," she decided. "Even quiet things have something to say, they just do it differently."

She put her head down next to the doll and lay still for several moments, a task that was difficult for the child...lying still. A tranquility lingered over the two of them; the morning light rising and then tipping over the sill, spilling into the room as if it first dipped in yellow ink. Flora turned to the doll and placed a kiss on its rose-painted cheek. "Thank you, Caridad," she said, "I love you too."

——·——

Asa unraveled the scrap of paper from out of his pocket and read the name. "Bushnell." He set the photo in his palm and raised it towards the thin veil of sunlight. There was no mistaking the woman's image he was in possession of; the face and name matched. But the woman he remembered was an older version; this one made him grin. He could understand the appeal; her powers of seduction rivaled that of Homer's Sirens, and even the more matronly Mrs. Bushnell could turn heads. *I think you should give him back his paper and charcoals; let him be free to express himself.* She liked his drawings, and when she liked something, it became an obsession. She saw beyond the charcoal and ink; there was more to his work than a soldier's recollections. Her voice echoed in his head when she spoke, resonating down the vacant hallways, and as she walked away, her words slowly diminished like her suggestions. *"He's not just your average lunatic; this one's got talent."*

"This one," he shrugged at the phrase. "Number 191." His identity was full of irony; the same number matched General Lee's infamous missing orders, 191. He shoved the paper and photo back into his pocket and leaned against the timbered wall. The barn was sufficiently sealed preventing rain and vermin means to an easy entry. That is not to say with a little ingenuity a field mouse could not find refuge. Rather, the filled cracks simply made the rodent's work a little harder. The barn was a dusky and solemn place where the swallows alighted on the rafters when the large double-doors remained opened. Those birds that were occasionally shut in may have been rather disappointed by the accommodations which are shared by the owls.

Asa liked the quiet, and he liked his new boots. These were the finest pair he had ever worn. He leaned forward and brushed the tips with his hand. He glanced over to the corner of the grain storage at the light dusting of hay he had placed over the hole that now hid some of Colonel's dug-up stash. Señor Tamayo was an attentive farmer, but even he and his field-hands would be too busy to notice something as insignificant as a handful of hay sprinkled here and there. The shovel had been put back right between the hoe and rake. Everything was in its place.

The shorthorns were grazing on the hillside while the pigs, turkeys, geese, pigeons, and chickens kept to their own kind in the barnyard; only the cat had decided to see what the man inside the barn was up to. It was a scraggly looking feline that had mothered one litter too many, so its stomach hung low and swayed as she walked. Speckled brown, white, and orange, she was anything but pretty. Asa held his hand out, and it warily slinked over. A slow, elongated meow broke from its mouth, showing a set of very sharp canines. It sniffed, looked up; but when the man had nothing to offer except a pat on the head, it strolled indignantly away. He watched as it sashayed out into the dusty barnyard creeping about with an air of superiority as if it knew it was freer than the other farm animals. Asa didn't trust cats; they were too sneaky. "All cats are the same," he had decided long ago, "they keep to themselves until they want something." The cat strolled about the barnyard, keeping its distance from the turkey until it came to the shade of the pigsty. Tiptoeing around the muck where the largest druid hog was enjoying a mud bath, it found a puddle, lapped up some water, and then strolled away. Ravaged coops might be blamed on the huntress, but the burden of fault ought to be placed on the nighttime's invasion of rats. The farm was the catalyst for a vicious cycle of blame, much like the army.

The observer retreated inward, his contemplation singling out the rabbit released into the wild. Led only by its ancestral guidance, it had scampered away into the night to foot-print the hills. Liberation of this kind is presumed both exhilarating and frightening; a deadly combination experienced by deserters and cowards. But the rabbit is not a coward nor a deserter when it scurries across the field dodging the silver moonbeams.

Asa stretched, shedding his memory and leaving the rabbit behind. His complaining stomach and the whereabouts of Flora redefined his morning plans. It was time that he made his presence known. The sunlight was blinding, and he tugged on his hat, lowering the brim across his forehead as he stepped out from the cool shade of the barn. The cat was no longer in his sight. A pair of buff leghorns that had been scratching for grubs strutted towards him, raising their pointy beaks and issuing a series of complaints, but seeing that the man did not throw them any millet, they continued their protests by-way of the watering trough. Asa followed the birds as they perched on the rim. The thirsty man cupped his hands together and plunged them into the trough. His throat was caked with dust, and he slurped the captured water, dipping his hands in and out until he had quenched his thirst. He tossed his hat aside, bent over, and dunked his head into the water until it was completely submerged. The water was cold, having been recently filled from the well. He kept his eyes tightly shut allowing a familiar darkness to smother his senses while he hummed to drown out the churlish chattering in his head. When he could no longer hold his breath, he snapped his neck back and sucked in the air as if it were his first breath. He leaned over the trough and pressed his hands hard against the sides. There was a ringing in his ears that sounded strange and out of place until, like the tide, it came roaring in and he could hear with such clarity. It was the same baleful voice who had taken his name away.

"You'll get used to this," the man sputtered. A half-dozen coffin-shaped bathtubs were filled with cold water. "It's like taking a bath outside in the winter!" The attendant's sadistic taunt was imitated, and like ripples in a lake, the cackle of ten barefooted men followed one after the other until the entire line of lunatics ignited into a chorus of hysterics. The twisted fool with the keen eyes of a sniper called from the back of the queue. "By outside, you mean over there!" All heads turned towards the man's poor sense of humor, the site of the asylum's graveyard.

The voice chattering in his head went quiet. Asa clapped the dust free from his hat slapping it against his knee. He combed his fingers through his hair, pulling the wet strands off his forehead before placing his hat back on, crushing the brim forward. There were no tombstones or walls or cold baths where he stood. There was no human stench or indiscriminate cries; only the odors of a farm: manure, animals, and feed. Asa inhaled deeply, exhaled, and then drew in another breath. The smells he missed were those of the seaside; a sensation he had not been in touch with since before the war now suddenly wanted to climb out of his skin. He had a mental list of things he had to accomplish and retrieving the notebook he had asked Colonel to keep, was now out of order in his mind. It needed to be placed back where it belonged, towards the bottom of his thoughts. One by one they would be taken care of, all of them.

———•———

"I am going to keep this rainbow as a pet," Flora announced. Señora Tamayo turned to her husband with a dull expression of misunderstanding. The stout man shrugged.

"I do not understand," said the dear woman. "This rainbow?" she asked poking her finger at the sky, "you want to keep it?"

Flora nodded and smiled. "Yes, that's right."

The kindly farm couple looked upward as a thin veil of colors arched overhead. Its brightness was rapidly fading. "A pet, like a dog?" Señor Tamayo questioned. Then he grinned, "Oh I see, this is a game, no?"

"No," said the child. "I'm going to keep it." She paused for a moment and then exclaimed, "and I'm going to call it Toni."

"Toni?" The woman seemed now even more confused as she tried reason once more. "But you can see that it is not going to be with us for very long? Mira; the colors are going away."

All three turned upward, but it was Julio who spoke first with great realization. "Oh yes, you are correct, they are very light." He nodded good-naturedly but when he turned to his wife he could see by her expression that he was not helping her cause. It was not he that needed convincing. Smiling meekly at her scowling face, he turned to Flora. "How you are going to keep this rainbow?"

"Oh, it won't give us any trouble; you will hardly know it's here. It doesn't need to be fed and likes to sleep outside. I've had them before."

The two adults were now even more baffled by this matter-of-fact explanation; Flora, quite content with her reasoning hopped on one foot and then the other calling, "Toni, Toni!"

"Well, if you want a pet as easy as that, why don't you add a few stars, too. I am sure the rainbow might want some company," Señor Tamayo chuckled.

Flora stopped dancing and taking notice of the man's honest desire to be helpful whispered, "I am afraid they wouldn't be very easy to care for, they like to go out very late at night." The man nodded, his wife frowned, and with an exasperated sigh wondered who the child really was.

"What will you do when you can't see Toni anymore?" Señora asked. This was a question Señor Tamayo wanted the answer to but decided to leave the remainder of the interrogations to his wife.

Flora flitted about, weaving in and out between the couple as if they were a pair of maypoles. "Toni is sitting right here in my head!" she said, "I can see him perfectly." She laughed, smiling cunningly while the farmers turned once again to the sky where the final trail of what was once a rainbow was all but gone. "I know what you're thinking, how can it be a pet if it's gone off? It's got a bit of a wild streak and doesn't like to be tied up in one place for very long. I let it roam around and go where ever it wants. But it always comes back. You wait and see; it will come back."

Señor Tamayo plugged his pipe with tobacco from his favorite leather pouch and fumbled with the match as his wife took her protest out on the vegetables. The more she complained, the tinier the carrots were diced. "Flora is the most unusual child; no wonder the other children do not want to play with her." The carping cook tossed the diced carrots into the pot and began to decapitate the celery. "She does not act like the other little girls! Not at all, not at all!" Six peeled potatoes and the celery leaves were dropped into the water altogether, causing the cooking water to splash out and onto the pipe smoker. Such a commotion hadn't been made in the kitchen since the New Year's goose had managed to escape from the cage and was chased around the room by Señor Tamayo with his fishnet. Fortunately, he succeeded in catching the goose before it got into the flour barrel; unfortunately, the cat that had come inside to see what all the noise was about was accidentally captured too, leading to a very stressful extrication from the net.

"Is it the rainbow?" the patient husband asked as he mopped his forehead with the dishcloth. "I am sure it means nothing."

Señora Tamayo scooped a fistful of salt into her palm and then splattered it into the pot. The cut celery followed and plunged to the bottom as if each piece was shot from a rifle. "I don't know if we should keep her for much longer," she whispered, "I don't think…" But before she could complete her sentence, she was interrupted by a squeal of delight.

"Asa! I knew you'd come back!"

"Oh, Dios mío!" mumbled the elder woman and hastily crossed herself with the reverence of a nun. "Flora, bring Asa to the table," she called. "You see, Julio," warned the woman. "No good, no good at all!" she muttered under her breath as Asa was led into the kitchen by Flora who was pulling him like a reluctant dog.

"I'm so happy!" the child cried. "I knew it, I knew he'd come back!" Her enthusiasm filled the space in the gloomy room that had been occupied by the owner's pessimism. "I bet he's hungry!" Flora declared with the disposition of a hostess. "Señora, can we give him some breakfast?" And without regard for a response, she escorted the dusty man to the table and pulled out a seat. However, Asa had little intention of sitting, retreating behind the chair as if it were a fence and he was looking for an escape. "Come on Asa, it's okay for you to sit," the child explained and patted the seat. "Can't he, can't he sit here?" she petitioned. The stunned cook had all the while been contemplating her next move, and though she did not think the man was undeserving of a meal, she was just too consumed with her former concerns. A slight tug on her apron by Flora brought back her good-natured disposition. "He can sit here, right?" she asked again and placed her hand on the back of the chair giving it a little rattle.

"Of course, he can. Siéntate, Asa! Sit down," she insisted, "we have plenty." She looked him over and smiled. "I see you have brought your appetite and clean hands, too."

"Asa has very good manners, he's a gentleman," Flora announced.

"Yes, a gentleman with very fancy boots," the woman said admiring his footwear.

Her husband puffed happily, glad that there was someone else in the house to soak up the attention. Twisting around in his easy chair, he examined the boots and raised an eyebrow in agreement. "Sí, very nice," the stout man muttered between puffs.

Flora pounced on these words as she turned her glance to the floor, and with the manner of a schoolgirl holding a secret she lifted her eyes towards Asa. He stood unfettered by the chatter following the cook to the table as she served a hearty portion of bread, smoked meats, and cheese. "Provecho!" her voice rang happily, for she was always happy when she could feed someone. The over-filled platter was an invitation to sit, so he obliged the hostess by folding the napkin into his unbuttoned shirt collar.

"Milk?" the woman asked and poured him a full cup. He nodded and began to eat heartily, never looking up from his plate. With elbows squarely positioned on the table and his head bowed, Asa protected his food as he ate. The woman enjoyed seeing him relish his meal and served him several more slices of ham and cheese. When he finished, he pushed his plate away, drank two more cups of milk, balled the napkin up, and set it back on the table.

But all the while, Flora had one eye on his feet, and the small voice in her head reminded her of the incident she had seen. "I'll tell him later," she thought. "I'll tell him I saw who owned those fine boots first."

———— • ————

The converted laundry room door had not been tampered with, an unfortunate mishap the grim-faced doctor could only surmise occurred when it had been inadvertently left unlocked. However, the fact that the visiting physician happened to glance inside was inexcusable. He had always been so discrete, so careful when arranging the photography sessions. It was a playful pastime for many of the female patients, a way for them to express their inhibitions. At first, it was just a hobby, but without much effort, it snowballed into a lucrative business. And to think that it all began with an innocent interception; his own fiancée concocting such a brilliant scheme on her own. If it hadn't been for his chance finding of her photo, so provocative, so steamy... The Doctor felt himself flinch with disgust. Rather than recalling her secret photos as pleasing, he scorned her youthful lust. Would he have married her had he known before their nuptials that she had carried on in such a manner unsuited for her position? This was a question he decided did not need to be answered. He had discreetly dealt with her affaire and settled the score; even if he were the only one that knew.

Richard Bushnell dug into his pocket and pulling the door shut, he pushed the key into the lock and twisted until the tumblers rattled and finally clicked. He wriggled the handle for good measure, satisfied that it remained secure. Vowing there would be no more mishaps, he glanced about like a common thief and stole away back to his office.

But as quiet as the man thought that he had padded away, unbeknownst to him there was one pair of eyes that happened to see him. Perhaps it was the muted color of her hospital gown and her light-footedness that made her almost invisible in the gray hallway. With only a few flickering lights, for it was not out of the ordinary that there were always a few not lit, the passageways were morbidly grim. "How did you get in here?" a belligerent voice demanded, and then without waiting for a reply, the gruff custodian took swift action and grabbed number 456 by the arm, yanking her towards him. The startled patient squealed like a frightened chipmunk, and without any forethought to her reaction, reached up and scratched the aggressor's face. The orderly put his hands up to his bleeding cheeks and howled. "Bitch, bitch!"

This momentary release of the woman's arm gave her just enough freedom to escape; and that she did. With no slippers to impede her flight, the scantily dressed woman took the only route she could and wildly ran in the opposite direction from whom she perceived as the enemy. Her primal cries of despair partnered with those others who also heard her, and as if they were jungle animals sensing approaching danger, so did the inmates of the asylum instinctively band together and become unified in their hysteria. From adjacent rooms, those who were able crushed together in the open portals to see, clapping and shouting as the woman ran by; all of which was immediately followed by booing and jeering at the trailing attendant. "Run, run, run, run!" a frenzied chorus sounded from every nook. Patients unaware of the source cared little for a reason for the shouts and readily joined the commotion by way of stomps and jeers. And as the fleeing woman ran by, they threw out their hands in hopes of giving her a good-luck slap on the back.

But like all labyrinths this corridor came to a finish, except this one was by way of a dead-end; and as the fitful woman anticipated no escape from the approaching attendant, Mr. Vole just happened to be exiting the very door at the end of the hallway. "Stop her!" growled the bleeding man, as he saw her push the unsuspecting secretary aside. But just as the startled Mr. Vole began to lose his footing, he grabbed hold of the open door, only to be pushed aside again; but this time with the brute force of the enraged ward. "When I get a hold of you, you'll never see daylight again!" he threatened, and as he bounded through the portal, his eyes groped all corners of the room until he spotted what he had come for.

Huddled behind a wingback chair the frantic woman crouched and like an over-sized child, she hid, peering out cautiously from her place of refuge. Her fingers grasped the sides, and her fingernails dug deep into the brocade fabric fearful of the repercussions. But this was a small room, and as much as she tried to believe she might be safe, the attendant pulled the chair forward to expose her hiding place. She shrieked, and then she cursed, tossing profanities that would have rivaled any sailor. The attendant reached forward, grabbing hold of her hair and mercilessly tugged until a tuft was pulled out from the roots!

"What is going on, what is going on!" Doctor Bushnell cried, bounding into the office. Sighing audibly, he examined the situation deciding how best to retrieve the hysterical woman that had evidently crawled beneath his desk but was too plump to fit completely.

"She needs to be locked up, Doctor Bushnell!" the attendant cried and pointed to his face. However, with the torn lock of hair still grasped in his hand, the physician had little sympathy.

"I believe she is locked up," said Mr. Vole in his usual straightforward manner. "After all, she is living at our institution." But his sense of humor did not lighten the situation, and so, he stepped forward to see what was under the desk. "Oh, I think it's the backend of a woman, Doctor Bushnell."

"Of course, it's a woman," the exasperated Doctor complained, "only I would like her to get her posterior out from under my workplace!" Mr. Vole smiled at the off-color comment, however, based on the look on the Doctor's face, put back his serious expression. "Who is she Crawley?" asked the physician.

"Number 456," the ward sneered. "A bitch!"

"Not her number, her name!"

Vole slid open the filing cabinet and plucked her records as easily as a gardener identifies the name of one of his roses. It was his filing system, and therefore he was the master at finding information quickly. "It's a Miss Margaret, Sir. She's been with us since …" he efficiently calculated the years and said, "Since right after the surrender, the war's surrender. It appears that she has a problem with telling stories, some very wild stories too." The man looked up from the documents. "It was you who had her committed." He had caught the attention of the Director who now seemed to ruminate on the patient with a glint of recollection. Vole left the file open and handed the papers forward when both men were startled by a piercing denial from beneath the desk.

"Lies! Lies!" The woman screamed and crawled backward out from her hiding place. "You keep me here against my will; you're all liars! You're the enemy, not me! Especially you, Doc, you're nothin' but old puke!" Then, with an ungainly effort, she attempted to stand, at which time she was intercepted by the ward who wrenched her arm behind her back and held her fast against the desk. Margaret screamed from both pain and fright and then began to sob.

"Not too hard Crawley, don't want to hurt her," said the Doctor in a more sympathetic tone. "Sit her down, gently." Then turning to the secretary, he demanded, "Vole, a jacket!" The woman looked tearfully from man to man, and as if she were a rabbit trapped in a snare, she stopped her sobbing and began to shake. "Now there, Miss Margaret, we're not going to harm you. But, it wasn't nice to hurt Mr. Crawley. See what you have done?" The ward grimaced as the Doctor turned the patient's face up towards the scratched cheek. Over the short amount of time, the scratches had become markedly red and inflamed, giving the man a sinister appearance. The woman looked wide-eyed and then spit at the distrustful face of the attendant.

"Why you, you!" Enraged by the disgusting act, the ward wiped his face with his hand and cleaned it on the back of the woman's head sticking to the tangled hair. "See, Doctor Bushnell, she's not fit, no sir, not fit to be with the other patients. If I were you, why I'd ..."

"But you are not me!" scolded the Doctor. "Vole," he yelled, turning towards the open door. "Vole, where is that jacket!"

The pattering of a quickened pace racing across the floor made its way into the office. "Here, Sir," he said, a bit out-of-breath. But as soon as the straightjacket was in clear view of Margaret, she opened her mouth and howled like a cat. "Shut up, woman!" the Doctor cried. "Shut the hell up!" All his years of trained composure had finally given way, and if there were any sympathy in his heart, it too had been eradicated. "Crawley, get her into this thing immediately," he instructed handing over the jacket. "And after she is secured, take her to the lady's ward, a nice cold bath should do wonders for her temperament!"

A glimmer in the attendant's eye sensed that he was winning this battle. "Of course, Doctor Bushnell, whatever you prescribe!"

"And Vole, don't just stand there, help him!" snapped the Doctor. The wiry secretary stared at the erratic woman as if she were indeed a trapped beast.

"I hate this part of the job," he thought, and without any more hesitation, began to assist the orderly by tightening the unstrapped belts around the torso. "Shhh, shhh," he petitioned, but the more he begged, the more the desperate woman yowled and wailed. "She is a tiger, isn't she?" Vole declared when they finished. He dabbed his brow with a handkerchief, wet from determination.

But neither of the other men responded since each was preoccupied with private thoughts; Crawley scheming retribution for her attack, and Doctor Bushnell in contemplation of a secret. As for Margaret, the only part of her upper body she could move was her mouth, and that she did freely and vehemently, without respect for any man or woman.

"What do you suppose got into her?" Vole asked after Crawley and another attendant carried the uncooperative patient away.

"That my good man is a question doctors have been trying to solve for all of time. Why do any of these idiots go on the way they do; clearly it is part of their illness. What you witnessed was a classic case of what we in the field call "a delusional complex.""

Vole nodded his head as if he understood. "Yes, I imagine so. But it is rather disheartening to believe that for all the years Miss Margaret has been a patient, her progress is not very far along. Why even her appearance gives an ordinary person a fright. Of course, the drab uniform doesn't help," the observant secretary noted. "It is a shame, though. Having lived through the war was hell itself, and to end up here, it certainly gives one reason to wonder if she will ever get out."

"Well, Vole, we will continue trying to help these poor souls, but sometimes there are some that need to live out their lives under our lock and key. Tell you what, I will personally attend to the woman myself and see if I can get to the bottom of today's outburst." The Doctor glanced over and reading the secretary's expression, the mouth making only a glimmer of a half-smile, he continued with his good-will; "check my schedule and set aside some time tomorrow morning for ...what did you say her name was, Maggie?"

"I believe it is Margaret, Sir. Miss Margaret."

"Margaret," repeated the Doctor, and then without realizing it, he licked his lips.

———·———

But Margaret was no stranger to Dr. Bushnell, and though he had been on the board of admissions for over a decade, often forgetting one patient as if they were as unimportant as what he had for supper on a particular day, Margaret was different. Not only did he have her committed, but he had made sure she could never leave.

Richard Bushnell caught himself watching a spider angle its web into the corner of the room. It was a small black creature with quite a bit of ingenuity and as he watched he found himself thinking about the war; a subject that he often told his patients not to dwell upon. And here he was bridging the past and present into a daydream, such is the hypocrisy of life.

After the battle, it was time to carry off the dead. It was time to lay the wounded upon stretchers. It was the time when weary soldiers plod through the crimson mud and search for comrades. It was the time when ambulance wagons and funeral trains are one and the same. A few injured soldiers hobbled out from the underbrush. Those with enough life in them dragged the fallen. All the while, affliction moved silently, some wearing pained regrets and others with blank expressions watching for their lost childhoods. The dead waiting to be consigned to the earth while trenches are dug. Their faces covered with handkerchiefs, kepis, or battle-worn coats; their limbs, visibly mangled and severed give pain to the living. This is where legends are made.

The camp was a hive of activity as the injured were brought to the field-tent, a temporary hospital that accommodates twenty-five soldiers. Its flooring was constructed by stretching rubber blankets atop of the bare earth. Straw-tick cots kept the wounded off the ground. It was a full-time job to keep the hospital dry and drain the water that flooded into the tent even after digging an eight-inch-deep trench around the base. Field hospitals that escaped the barrage of grape and canisters were supplied with bare necessities; quinine and blue pills, adhesive plaster and bandages, chloroform and saws. Federal surgeons suffered from fewer shortages in comparison to their Confederate counterparts who relied on smugglers and blockade-runners to replenish their often-meager supplies. Poppies grown abroad and compounded into morphine and opium were accessible to the Union by way of world trade. By the end of the war, they had dispensed over 80 tons of opium powder and tinctures. In contrast, attempts by the South to grow and harvest poppies resulted in an inferior crop that provided very little morphine content. Despite their challenges, morphine was liberally administered to the South's wounded. Ladies on both sides of the battlefields readily took tinctures to calm their shattered lives, but its numbing relief did not end with the final battle. Broken lives remained shattered long afterward, and the favored remedy, laudanum, a tincture of opium mixed with alcohol and water helped one cope with death, injury, and lingering pain. Survivors turned to opiates and morphine at a most alarming rate.

Trees were felled and branches chopped into logs for great fires that burned and heated the air when it grew cold. Hot bricks were brought to the tents for warmth. The smoldering logs crumpled, splitting, splintering, dying embers dwindling like the lives of those whose faces were lit by its fabulous glow. A log is tossed into the ring, and the hot embers ignite the gray bark. "If only it could be so easy to reignite the life of these heroes," says the attendant. A procession of soldiers forms a queue during "Morning Sick Call" for a dose of ipecac. The more infirmed and cadaverous are pushed to the front for a measure of whiskey-mixed with quinine. The Doctor does not reply; he blinks away the soot left behind from the smoke the fire has tossed upward. Confusion, terror, the sick and wounded, all are tired and hungry; these are bloody days. Many are handed over to the "Lost Souls Inn," where everyone is welcome; some who have misplaced a day, a week, a month, a lifetime, they lie among the groans of the wounded while the pleads of those nearer to death are left unanswered. It is a most unfortunate place to be born.

———— • ————

Richard Bushnell was not interested in someone else's bastard; for that reason, he offered the infant to the only reasonable person, the Uncle. The war made strange alliances between men; those that would not have been acquaintances during peacetime ultimately became comrades in war. So it was at the field hospital that the woman's meager belongings were rummaged through. Among the contents of her bag were floral-scented soap chards, an iodine bottle, a pair of darned stockings, a portrait ambrotype, and several undelivered letters. Being consciously indifferent and at the same time militarily efficient, Dr. Bushnell read the private correspondence, whereupon he determined the identity of the intended recipient; the woman's older brother, Lt. Colonel Jameson.

But what the surgeon did not know was that the words in the letters were carefully constructed codes, and the sister and brother were co-conspirators; smuggling within the pockets of dead soldiers' counterfeit bills. The foiling of such a lucrative enterprise was not the exposure of their underground plot, but rather the capture of the woman during the raid on the Confederate outpost that brought her in from the confines of the enemy. Only her mad ravings and the fact that she was pregnant kept her from being hung for treason.

So, this is how it came about that the Union's surgeon, Richard Bushnell, would deliver his first baby and how he was able to unite brother and sister in the boundaries of nature's cheerless place. The countryside laid waste with a landscape barren and treeless; it was a hellish place for a reunion. But on the other hand, perhaps it was a most appropriate location seeing as Lilac's scandalous behavior would have tarnished her brother's fine military record and unblemished reputation. Bushnell might have been a scoundrel, but he was also reasonable, and having taken the Hippocratic Oath he was obliged to uphold ethical standards and to do no harm. (The latter was something he felt was a matter of interpretation.) Additionally, the burgeoning surgeon had more in common with the soldier than he was going to divulge, being as his fiancée could have brought disgrace upon him. He was more than happy to rid his friend of his sister and her burden, and when she would awaken, she would be told that there never had been a baby. It would all be explained away as a figment of a troubled woman's imagination. Colonel would be in his debt, and there just might be a time that he would be able to return the favor. But such was not the case. Richard Bushnell would not have to perform this heinous act of deception for the woman conveniently died after having been administered a bit too much chloroform to ease her pain.

Chapter 19

Chance is something you're dealt at a poker game. Some hands are good, some bad, some promising. Whereas Asa being deemed insane may not be a chance coincidence, but rather, the unforeseeable collateral damages of war. He was once a free spirit, but while under the charge of the asylum, it was necessary that he be bridled. Only Mrs. Bushnell seemed to recognize he was different than the others and felt an immediate affinity for Asa's creativity. But Sydney was a woman that flitted about like a bird, and as her interests varied, she never seemed to be able to keep herself invested in one mission for very long. As for Dr. Bushnell, he had a knack for longevity and allegiance to duty. But amid the anguish of the day, there was parceled some tranquility in sleep; where the taunts of the asylum could not touch Asa's soul and the spirit of the artist remained unto himself.

"Close your eyes and promise; promise no harm will come to her, promise!" Asa nodded "yes," like he had done when the wild-eyed woman first whispered her appeal in his dream. "Good," Her eyes smiled at his response but quickly reignited as she confided in him again. "I know her brother is raisin' the child as his own, but I got a bad feelin'." She drew towards him with a hushed voice. "No one can ever know; no one. Not even the child." Asa understood. "No child of Lilac's is gonna be a bastard. There's too much sin, too much." He could feel his hand

being pulled through the fence. She opened his palm and placed a gold charm in the shape of half-a-heart in his palm and kissed it. She raised her chin up, and her eyes fell upon his face. He folded his fingers securing the object as if it were sacred and then she grasped his fist with her two hands. This time her clasp was gentle. It had been quite a long while since he felt gentleness. "When you see her, give this to her." He opened his eyes just as the angel turned away from the garden fence and back up the hill. Asa looked down at his hand, and recalling the dream, he smiled.

Flora was safe, and Asa was secure in knowing that the elderly couple would treat her like their own. He rose from the table and then carried his plate over and handed it to the woman. "See what a gentleman he is!" Señora Tamayo goaded her husband with praises for Asa. "Why can't you carry your plate from the table?" she whined. The husband did not reply but sighed as if he had been provoked. "Such a gentleman," she rattled.

"Come along, Asa, come with me!" Flora whispered. Then she turned to the woman, "May I take him to see the chickens? Oh Asa, you cannot believe how many baby chicks we have, at least twenty!"

"Pollitos!"

"Yes, pollitos!" echoed the child.

"Go, go, take him with you. Just be careful of the boar. He does not like to be disturbed when he is taking a nap. Reminds me of someone else." She pointed her finger in the direction of the resting man.

Flora skipped ahead of Asa who followed dutifully behind. But it wasn't until they had reached the barnyard that the little girl grabbed Asa by the hand. "I know where you got those boots!" She bent down and pushed down on the toecap. "They fit just like they were made for your feet!" she exclaimed. "That was lucky the man had the same foot as you!" Asa continued to look at his feet and then back at the child. "I'm glad you took them, he was evil. I'm glad he ended up in the ditch. He belongs where the worms can eat his brains." Asa no longer seemed uninterested in the child defiling the memory of the dead man, but it was what she said afterward that held his interest. "I saw him, Asa. I saw who dragged the bad man to the ditch and bury him. I can tell you what he looks like if you want. But you must be careful wearing these fancy boots; he wants them back! I heard him say, he would get them back and give them to the man in the ditch!"

He evaluated her words with new energy, *"I'm glad he ended up in the ditch."* Asa smiled to himself. There were two, and he had rid the world of one, now he had to find the other. But Asa didn't need any help, his memory of the Timpson Brothers could not be forgotten. There was little doubt that the two men would meet again.

———•———

Sydney's risqué behaviors were not a secret to her husband. His first encounter with her promiscuity was early in their engagement before the war. Richard knew little of her escapades in New York, so naturally, when he happened upon a clue while looking in her purse for coins to tip the coachman, he was stunned. Tucked within the silk lining was her seductive portrait along with a handwritten note.

> *"My Dear Mallabal,*
>
> *You are a stranger here and find so little comfort. Far from your homeland, I wish to bring you a bit of joy. You have made me rich in so many ways, more than any other man has been able. If only I could sing out and let the world know the happiness I have discovered. But I will take heed, if our relationship were to become common knowledge, there would be dangerous consequences. How I wish to sit in the park beneath the trees if only to have you close to me. I feel full of words yet languish in empty spaces only you can fill. Love is best as the world to me is full of you.*
>
> *Goodnight, it will be a lovely sleep because I will dream of you."*

Richard read the terse proclamation several times over. His hands trembled with anger, but he was a controlled man and rather than mincing the note into confetti, he refolded it along the creases and slipped it back into the bag. An engagement retraction would only lead to scandal, and strangely he now found her even more attractive. He would find this bastard Mallabal and do what was necessary. And as he mentally plotted against her lover, what the letter did not reveal was that it began as a one-sided affair. The Aborigine had no desires for a relationship; but Sydney was a convincing woman, and though her advances did not initially tempt him; her invitation to leave behind the busy streets and picnic at a nearby park gave the foreigner enough of an incentive to follow her. As much as the day had given over some of its hours, the division of time was unequal. The woman split hers into "shopping time," "teatime," and "dress fitting time," while the etiquette of Mallabal's time never was permitted to be idled away; until she manipulated the clock.

The pair did not seem too out of the ordinary when they set out for a stroll; Mallabal could easily have been mistaken as her servant. Nevertheless, had their seemingly innocent walk been unraveled and their romantic interlude been revealed, each participant would have paid dearly. But this thought was not on either of their minds. The cloudless sky was the color of a robin's egg and the air uncharacteristically cool; the day was too lovely to bring any disharmony into their afternoon. Sydney twirled her parasol as if she ruled the world, while Mallabal walked beside her finding for the first time in this strange country a sense of tranquility. Mother Nature has a generosity so plentiful, so abundant, that her recipients' impediments only curtail it. And so, nature was secluded behind the city, only to be dispatched to the forefront by intense concentration or a trained eye. It was not until they found a secluded spot in the shade, did Mallabal's new perspective unroll like a panorama. He sat on the ground while Sydney spread a blanket before him, and though he was invited to sit beside her on the plaid tablecloth, he chose to remain in the grass. He stroked the blades with a nostalgic tenderness. The canopy of interlacing leaves and branches offered him a cool and comfortable shade. Nature, the silent weaver; embroiderer of the landscape, positioning greens and browns against a pale blue background. Mallabal understood innocent pleasures, the element of life he dearly missed. Still, he was no saint, for he too had committed what one would believe were sins. But on the other hand, if he were singularly pious, then he would not see the failings of man, the decaying leaves in dense forests or the jagged teeth-like rocks biting the angry water.

To survive, he would have to adapt and shed his outer-self without damaging what was in his heart. The Aborigine wanted to understand his new surroundings, but to his chagrin, even Mother Nature was being controlled. She was cut, razed, toppled, and domesticated in exchange for buildings, roads, bridges, and dams. He could defend himself but was defenseless to protect the exploited. Mallabal felt more isolated among the throngs of people filling the city streets than when he lived a solitary existence. Day after day the warnings from Neville poured over him. He was to remain invisible and not make any unusual overtures or advances. If anyone questioned him, he was to say he was with Neville Young, and they were earning money to continue North. He agreed and offered no resistance, identifying his friend as trustworthy. And while life was going on around him, he was a piece of driftwood: homeless, shapeless, leaving no imprint. The path to which Mallabal had been instructed to follow was intended to secure his safety, however, what it did not anticipate was the power of one who has been betrayed. Honor was shaking Richard Bushnell by the shoulders, and although he had never met his rival, it would not be difficult for the jealous fiancée to locate the recipient of Sydney's 'billet-doux.' For as big and crowded as New York City was, to find a man who went only by Mallabal would not be a challenge.

"Mallabal?" sneered the fruit vendor. "What's it to ya?" The stranger reached into his pocket, removed a bill and waved it before the bitty. She snatched it away before he could change his mind. "I heard his name around; I think he's Neville Young's man." She nodded. "They sell dreams." She grinned, displaying her missing teeth like a badge of honor.

"Dreams?"

"That's right, dreams. They got all kinds of herbs and teas and pieces of bark. A real odd pair, but this Mallabal, he's the curious one. A dark fellah, but not from around these parts."

The thickset man listened with interest. "So, where can I find them?" his gloomy shadow fell over her like a cloak.

She surveyed him squarely from his polished boots to his too snug bowler. She held out her flattened palm. The man reluctantly pulled out another bill. This had been the eighth vendor, and he was running low on funds and patience. "Try Broadway; it's a big street so keep walkin'." She clasped her fist closed and then held the money up to the light and snapped it a few times. "Anything else?" she asked greedily. He shook his head, but before he stepped away she called out, "What business have ya got with Mallabal?"

The man turned and smiled, "I'm a hunter," he explained.

"Hunter, in New York City? If you're lookin' for squirrels, there's plenty in the trees!" she added with a laugh.

"No, runaways," he said, "runaway slaves."

———·———

Mrs. Magill's boarding house was more respectable than many. Perhaps its ability to maintain such a reputation was really owed to the Sergeant who was taken care of in return for his looking the other way at the comings and goings. And then there was protection from The Sons of St.

Tammany in exchange for her keeping her eyes and ears open. It was a three-way relationship that worked in congruence, each one doing his or her part. As for John Boyle, a man that was attracted to talk, he profited by swapping information with the widow in exchange for his cheap room.

So it was that one evening; John Boyle dangled information between bites of potatoes as if he were waving a mackerel at a hungry cat. "It was a most curious day, that it was," he started to explain, getting the attention of the landlady as she rounded the supper table. "I was minding my own business when I feel this hand taking hold of my shoulder." Mrs. Magill leaned over and dropped another potato on his plate. The gossiper could feel her impatience and decided to keep her waiting while he stabbed the spud and rolled it around his greasy plate. There was an especially unusual strangeness lurking in the dining hall; an uneasy stillness that guided the mood. With a great shake of his head, the speaker continued. "So, I turned to see who it was that had taken hold when I found myself lookin' squarely into the eyes of evil."

"Yer talkin' crap, John Boyle! If you're tryin' to scare us, it ain't workin'!" the woman frowned.

"May the Lord strike me down dead if it ain't true. I tell you, it was the eyes of the Devil!"

"Well, what did the Devil want with you?" she smirked.

"It wasn't with me that he wanted," he mocked. "He was lookin' for a runaway. He says the man was travelin' with a companion, pretendin' they were friends." The gossiper smiled crookedly at the landlady who intruded into the man's story, her eyes silently curious. She trolled for some truth and waited for the other to speak. "I said nothing to the Devil, mind you. Told him I didn't know anything." He looked from the woman to his plate of stew and began to eat.

"Aww, gw'on," she sneered. "You don't mean, the two in room 4?" The landlady placed the serving bowl on the table and slumped down into the empty chair. The air had grown hot and heavy, and she pulled her apron up and wiped her upper lip. "Why the pale face?" she asked, pulling herself close to his ear. His sudden change of temperament gave her reason to pause. She knew that she was sitting among a very large secret and the arrival of such a lucrative inheritance made her heart jump.

Exhausted by the few words, she wondered if he understood the ramifications of what he heard. "Seems like a man could get a handsome reward for turnin' in a runaway," remarked the storyteller. "I don't suppose you could help me?" He lifted his head and waved his hand before the two empty chairs.

But before anything else was uttered Janie Magill jumped up from her seat and pulled the knife from off the table. "It's my roomin' house," squealed the woman. "I ain't havin' you or no one turnin' in my boarders. If there's turnin' in to do, we do it my way!" There was a fierceness in the woman that made the gossiper recoil. "Now, just what did you really say, John Boyle. Speak, or I'll cut your throat!"

Only the woman moved as she roamed closer to the meddler demanding an answer. "I told 'em I would ask around the shipyard, ya know, find out anything." His voice quivered as he spoke, recognizing the woman was not shy to use tableware as a weapon.

"And?"

"And, I told him where he could find me." Knowing that this acknowledgment would not go without punishment, he hid his head down as the woman lunged and slapped him behind the head.

"Fool, damned fool!" she exclaimed. "Whats' iz' name?"

"Whose name," remarked the frightened man, too scared to show his face.

"Idiot, the slave hunter's."

"Slave hunter?" With one eye peering out from between his bowed head and the table, he lifted his chin. "Who said anything about a slave hunter?"

"You fool, the man is a slave hunter, and he just might be lookin' for our man upstairs." Her eyes gleamed.

The other nodded with understanding. He was once a moral man, a churchgoer, abiding by the rules of his faith, and so he was torn between piety and greed. "What do we do?" he asked sheepishly.

"The only thing we can do. We're law-abiding citizens, ain't we? I'm gonna call in my favors and find this hunter." she remarked. The man shook his head reluctantly in agreement. "We side with the law."

"The law, side with the law." The ambiguity in his voice needed to be reconciled. He would have to go to confession.

"What's his name?" She interrupted.

He rummaged through his thoughts. It hurt his brain, and he was sorry that he had roused the incident. "He didn't say, but you'll know 'em. He'll be the Devil dressed all in black."

The conspiracy moved like an undertaker; so deathlike was the arrival of Bodie. He slipped into the hallway through the unlocked door, and if Mrs. Magill was still awake, she did not make her presence known nor bother to latch the door until morning. There was no struggle or resistance when Bodie held the knife to Neville's throat. The cold blade rested against his skin and any movement would have drawn blood. "I'm not a Confidence Man," he snarled, "was just sent here to get the contraband, obeying orders like any good patient." The only defense for his companion was for Mallabal to give himself to the assailant and leave without incident. The arm of the brute untangled from around Neville's neck as he was met with threats of ultimate death for the victim if they were followed. However, as soon as Neville heard the men retreat down the stairs, he quickly followed, only to be foiled by a pair of wooden drays heading in opposite directions. One, intended as a decoy, and the other, engaged in the seizure and detention of an innocent man. The porcelain moon eclipsed between the clouds just as Neville attempted to throw open the door and call for help, unaware that standing against the wall someone was waiting to intercept his actions. Grey eyes glared up from deep sockets in the skull, and a square jaw pinched the cheeks of the ragged figure shuffling forward. A chord with a weight tied to it was looped around Neville's neck and in a low soft tone a voice jeered, "Guess that's fait accompli."

But in his haste, Bodie was unsuccessful in finding another accomplice, so he had to rely on the hired-driver to take his captive to the dock while he drove the decoy. Opportunity for Mallabal to escape would not wait, it had to be now. But his hands were bound finding it was nearly, though not impossible, to wriggle free. He had just a few moments. He listened and waited as the wagon rolled sheepishly for a time until the reins pulled back and the wagon rumbled to a stop. He heard the driver mutter a complaint. In the near distance, the clatter of another wagon sounded, its wheels rolled and turned as if being pulled by horses in a great hurry. "Bodie, over here!" instructed the driver. The two men were drawn together by their ruthless task. The contemptuous smile of his capture formed in his mind. He was drenched in sweat in spite of the cool night air. Tipping over the side-rails, Mallabal relied on this moment of distraction. The only means of escape was to sneak out of the wagon. He froze for several seconds between life and death when fate unlocked his knees. With an awakened fury he jumped into the blackness and ran away, leaving behind the untied slip of rope.

———•———

White canvas flattened against the mackerel sky while the ship rolled over the breakers like a drunkard. The sun played the antagonist and shined mercilessly upon the deck. No effort or man had been spared to draw him out into the open, and while the sailor on the poop deck leaned over

the railing searching for an overboard body, the locker had been carelessly overlooked. "Find the devil, find him!" Mallabal pulled the sail over
his head and wrapped himself between the folds so tightly that he could
barely breathe. The narrow confine of the sail-locker was not a clever place
to hide, although its unlatched door had invited him to enter. He held his
hand over his mouth, and for a few breathless moments, he waited. The
hinges snapped like the sudden release of a rat trap as the door flung open.
At once the smell of prejudice entered. A blunt object prodded the sail,
and with a single thrust, the club dislodged the cloth, slowly tearing into
his freedom. A figure came into view as the cloth was pulled and drawn
aside. The shadow of a boy lowered over the hidden man, and he felt the
eyes of the youth set upon his. Mallabal had heard stories of such eyes,
tales of demons possessing each pupil of a different color. He trembled
as the boy peered closely and then the intruder immediately reared back.
It was apparent that the young sailor was equally startled by his discovery beneath the sail-cloth. "Shhh, don't move." The boy covered the man
again and shut the small door.

Beneath the shelter of the cloth, Mallabal waged war against his
instinct to flee from his hiding place. There was scarcely a breath of air
stirring though he could smell the ocean and hear the water lapping
against the hull. Nearly an hour had passed, and within this time muffled
voices and feet running on deck acknowledged that he was still in danger.
His effort to remain under the sail was stifling his ability to hear, and as
much as he wanted to put his ear to the door, he knew better than to move.
A steady crusade of feet finally surrendered as the crew was called off from
the hunt and the boatswain piped the orders. "Cheerly boys, cheerly, hoist
er' up. You, lend a hand." The command of the first mate roared, and the
spirit of the crew was set into motion. From where Mallabal lay he understood that he had been spared, yet his destiny fell on the leniency of the
boy. There was a fine wind, and the ship was making a good run out of the
harbor and into the open sea. He didn't know if he had been deceived, but

he waited with hopes that the boy would return with some food. The ship raised and lowered upon the swells, and while he tried to keep one eye open, all attempts failed as he succumbed to fatigue. His was the sleep of physical and mental exhaustion, his was a dreamless sleep.

The sharp tongue of the first mate was the first sound Mallabal heard in the morning. The turning of the latch was the second. The boy brought pilfered provisions and water, enough to keep Mallabal in hiding for several days. During the night, he deserted his voluntary imprisonment to catch a glimpse of the stars, until the sounds of a human voice sent him retreating to his refuge. He was afraid, not like a coward, but like a man who fears the loss of freedom. The element of ruthlessness over another human being was brutality all too familiar. And so, he was the rabbit in waiting, listening, and planning for his chance to escape. As for Jo, he had poked the hornet's nest, and his discovery released more than he had bargained for. If he revealed the stowaway to the Captain, he might be implicated as conspiring with the fugitive since he was the only crew member to know of the hiding place. Then again, the man hiding might be a slave, and if he turned the runaway in, there would be a handsome reward for his capture. But it didn't take the boy long to come up with his decision to abandon what most men would do and to follow his gut.

His father looked into the strange eyes, and the boy's face turned slightly away masking a breaking heart. "Damn it, Captain, want him or not?" Jo swallowed hard and wiped his nose on the back of his hand, but he didn't hear what came next, having been given orders to follow the sailor and when he turned around his father was gone. The rejection was as potent a curse as his defect, and though he learned to live with abandonment, he never forgot his father's looks of distrust. He drank and swore like a man, but still felt like a lad. As fast as he had grown, kindness had been stunted. His only recent remembrance of compassion was when he was secretly set adrift evading the murderous plot. The tiny vessel struggled against the seas. Two nights had passed when he was discovered drifting in the fog and had the Captain been a believer of incantations, he would have been set adrift again. Frightened, hungry, and dehydrated, he was brought aboard. If any of the crew happened to notice his eyes, they didn't say. For the superstitious, they would struggle with what they perceived as bad luck, while the others would rejoice in having another scapegoat.

How long could he keep this clandestine hiding place a secret? How long would a man survive hidden away like a hibernating animal? Jo had narrowly escaped the perils of irrational thinking, but if this slave were set adrift, as he was, he would only be met with a fate worse than the one he now owned. There was only one thing to do; he would have to keep this man hidden until they anchored at the next port. He would help him escape. Jo smiled for the second time since he was saved. Years of acrimony had toughened the boy. "Oh, sweet revenge," he grinned, "this will be sweet revenge indeed."

Guided by sea charts dividing the shallow from the deep, they prowled the mouth of the harbor until it was well-established that it was safe to cast anchor. Though not as long a voyage as many, the shoreline was a welcome sight. The port of Savannah was always greeted with revelry, and the Captain feeling generous, had decided to give the crew shore leave. The fog, gray and thick, was lifting slowly when Jo awoke. The skipper's and first mate's cabins had to be cleaned, and their beds made before he stoked and tended the fire-hearth for the cook. The Captain demanded his coffee black and strong, and to be set before him with plenty of sugar. So, when a dense plume of smoke began to engulf the galley, it did not take long for it to wind through the cabins and choke the still air. Confusion broke out rousing the men into an uproar. No one could be sure what part of the ship the fire was devouring, and the goodly crew set to work. They floundered in the darkness, some wearing only their long-johns being as the first bells had not sounded. Meanwhile, Jo crept stealthily through the morning fog and made his way through the slate-colored smoke, and as though nothing more than a boyish prank, he set the Aborigine free as easily as one would open the wire-hinged door of a birdcage.

And without attracting any attention to himself, the grateful man slid down the waterlogged rope and into the jolly boat towing astern. The dinghy rocked impatiently as the solemn-faced Aborigine looked up at Jo for a second or so, and then, being a man of little words, handed him a gray pearl. "Can you swim?" Jo whispered, but the reply could not be heard for Mallabal had wasted not a moment and plunged the oars beneath the surface. They sliced through the black water, and every now and again he would settle them upon the surface as if for a breath of air. His immediate future was unknown, with the exception that all hope of survival was waiting for him on the nearing shore. His destiny was chosen, not by himself, but by an unlikely acquaintance, the boy with the blue and violet eyes.

The breeze scrapped against the haze, parting a way for Mallabal. He was the only object between the ship and the dim blue outline of the land ahead. The pulling of the oars against the water had remained undetected, sending him further away from the voices of his captives. The turbulence that ruled the morning soon faded along with the immediate sense of danger. A retinue of porpoise pursued the jolly boat, and as he neared the somber shades of the shore, a soft mantle of fog shielded him from any onlookers. A flock of terns flapped their wings like scissors, as a few came close to inspect the oars dipping in and out of the water. His arms had grown tired, but all thoughts of respite were ignored as the rocky strips of shoreline were marked by the thundering sound of the breakers. Mallabal steered the dinghy away from the seething white foam and round to the southern point into calmer waters. Here the swift current guided the small boat to a sandy inlet that lay nestled along the scarp.

Bodie's indifference to his employer accompanied his decision to keep his incompetence a secret; for as good a tracker as he was, his attempt to recapture the escaped man only proved the abducted man's ability to elude him was that much better. Such an acknowledgment that he was outwitted overtaxed his brain and the lout's only recourse was to pocket a shiny gray "bead" he found in the rear of the wagon and forget the whole incident in a bottle of whiskey.

On a clear night, a man at sea could walk out on the deck and align the stars and horizon. Archipelagoes of stars set the frame of the ship, familiar nautical stars; Polaris, Capella, the Big Dipper, all chart a course the helmsman would steer. Admittedly this was the same kind of clear night, except such a soul-satisfying feeling did not settle over Neville. Rather, unlike the stargazer, Orion and the Seven Sisters did not offer him any comfort. The constellations did not pilot a steady path, for on the same night Mallabal was abducted, Neville was accused of harboring a runaway slave and conniving his escape. The Sheriff, having been keeping company with the landlady, did not betray who had tipped him off. However, the landlady's frozen smirk implicated herself as the informant. As such, the outside world was at liberty to administer its penalty, and the dumbstruck suspect was charged. Arrested and handcuffed, Neville was escorted by rifle muzzle and greeted by the prison's Captain Macey. Two prisoners, each with eyes jumping from the Captain to the gun, were being let out as he was led in. "You two shits are free to go, but don't come back unless you want to stay for good." A scurrying of feet faded away as the cage door was locked behind.

The severity of Neville's situation was crystal-clear. He rubbed his side, it hurt. A young officer with sunburned cheeks had prodded him with a billy club. He hoped he hadn't broken a rib. A smoke would settle his nerves, but that was impossible, he didn't have a pipe. Everything looked brown and smelled brown. He speculated the walls were at least three feet thick, constructed of double hewed lumber with masonry stones placed between the timbers. The rubble floor was packed solid and reasonably dry where a layer of straw beneath a blanket served as a bed. Except for a water-can and tin night-bucket, it was furnished with nothing but a three-legged stool. Three open-grates fastened against the back-wall admitted the only source of light in this otherwise dank and bleak cell devoid of any fresh air or sunshine.

Jossey Browne was eighteen when a call went up for volunteer guards. It was but two years later that he found himself fully employed as the jailkeeper. He didn't believe in ghosts, but on occasion, after a few drinks, confided to others that he could hear and smell the sounds and scents of men who had been sent to the gallows. For that reason, he slept with a knife under his pillow. He stood five-feet-ten and a-half, thick-necked, and broad-shouldered. His good-humored laugh rang freely, and though some would call him slow, he was perhaps more measured than simple. His red mustache drooped just below his chin, and when he spoke, which was often, he smoothed the whiskers away from his lips. From the onset of his prattling, it was discovered that he and Neville had much in common, for the guard's father was a commercial whaler. When he was just a small boy, Jossey and his mother accompanied the mariner aboard ship rather than being without him for months at a time. "With her makin' the long journeys the crew called our bark a *hen frigate*, only the Captain didn't mind 'cause she did his washing and darning.'"

Neville felt bitter and cynical as he paced the floor of his cubical. His time was split between silent worries and listening to the guard's small talk, which serendipitously proved lucrative. Unforeseen respect between the two men earned a timely introduction to the guard's Uncle Abner Swift, a criminal lawyer. The industrious relation was summoned by his nephew and the arrival of late afternoon brought the distinguished visitor to the cell. Opposing his colleagues in the courthouses by morning and enjoying their company in the taverns by night, most would say the lawyer was fair, and those that disagreed would say nothing. The visitor exhibited little expression, and as he listened to Neville's account, he scribbled notes with a fine tipped graphite pencil. His round shoulders folded into his chest as his list grew long and when the defendant was finished Abner Swift closed the binder to begin his counseling. He explained that if Neville had forcibly taken Mallabal, such an act would be considered *lucri causa* and fall under the intentional taking of property in the case of larceny. But, if his motive were to harbor a fugitive and help him escape to a free state, then the case would come under a different statute.

The night of Mallabal's abduction revealed a painful affirmation about humanity. For Neville, he could try to prove his innocence, it was Mallabal's freedom that would be unjustly deprived. The accused lowered his head and looked down at the floor. He had to convince the lawyer sitting before him that he was telling the truth and hope the man was as fair-minded as the nephew claimed. "Mr. Swift," exclaimed Neville clearing his throat, "I haven't committed any crime nor is my friend a slave. A victim, yes, this is true, but a slave, he's not." ... *Is he hearing me, I can't tell. At least he looks like he's listening.* "I have evidence that will prove my innocence, but the papers are back at my rooming house. If I could show them to you, they'll confirm everything I have said as the truth. Mallabal served with me aboard ship where we first set sail from Van Damien's Land, that's where he's from... *Damn, does he even know where that it? Why would he care about that?* "His capture as a runaway is nothing but a well-orchestrated lie. You must believe this has all been a trap." With a sinking heart, Neville pulled his hands behind head and interlaced his fingers behind his neck. He knew the lawyer was accustomed to felons and thieves each claiming their innocence. He feared that the man might have become indifferent after so many years in court.

"Continue," said the Esquire, his manner gravely serious. He pulled out a handkerchief and blew his long nose and then stuffed the monogrammed linen into his pocket. ...*The man looks like he could use a good smoke. He's a smoker, can see it on his teeth.*

"You see, I'm certain that even while we speak, Mallabal's life is in serious jeopardy; not because of his actions, but because the law permits him to be hunted and enslaved. For all we know he's chained somewhere waiting to be sold. Mr. Swift, you've got to get me out of here right away, or I'll never find him in time." The prisoner stood up confounded by his predicament; he was at this man's mercy, and this notion frightened him. "There's no other translation I can give you except what I say is the truth." ...*Lord, let him believe me.* Swift, fidgeting uneasily on the ungainly stool, began to pull on his chin and for a moment appeared to be deep in contemplation before he spoke. "If it's your fee you're worried about, I can get money," Neville said, squelching any hesitation on the part of the solicitor. ...*Bless my wife for being so frugal.*

"I am a servant of justice ...," replied the lawyer and putting out his hand in a gesture of a handshake exclaimed, "and justice will be served." ...*Now that I know you can pay me.* Knowing nothing of how the next few days would serve out, the shrewd lawyer set out to explain to Neville the time frame he should expect. "I will get the habeas corpus before the Judge and prove your identity and that of your friend Mallabal. A hearing in a day or two will prove your story, and then we'll have you released." He then grinned and dug his fingers into his vest pocket. "In the meantime, here's a peppermint candy until I get you a pipe."

————————•————————

It could be said that the hungover Judge, having received the writ after a night of debauchery, may have been influenced by his foggy brain, or it may have been the excellent work of the astute lawyer; regardless of the reason, this case's truth prevailed. The main purport of Abner Swift's proceedings, that of proving the innocence of Neville and the illegal abduction of Mallabal was quickly resolved. Nevertheless, the released man having been liberated was not in possession of much time, a commodity he desperately needed.

Lost in his drink, Neville set the glass on the dining table. "There's an angel out there with a broken wing," he said.

The lawyer looked at him with an obscure eye. "I'm not quite sure what you're getting at, friend."

"There are so many things to reconcile that this is the only explanation I can give to make sense of it all. The earth is a beautiful place, but its inhabitants can make darkness even in the presence of daylight."

"My, aren't you the philosophical one," taunted the lawyer.

"Can't help it," he sighed. "Fate has flirted with Mallabal all his life. He saved mine, you know."

The host poured off the rest of the bottle into each glass and nodded. "And he did it without regard for himself," the client remarked turning his thoughts back to his reverie. "But if the wing wasn't broken then maybe..." He was visibly distressed and drummed the table with his fingers.

"Maybe he'd be with you?" Swift added.

Neville stood up from his chair and leaned in towards the hearth as if the fire could warm his empty soul. "See how the flames lift so effortlessly up to the heavens. But even they leave behind impurities like soot and ash we have to clean up." The lawyer, having once believed himself too pragmatic to become caught up in sentimentalities, was now feeling a softening towards Neville's convictions. "Exploration parties hired Mallabal as a guide; they told him they were there as 'peacemakers,' so he agreed, but only with intentions of covertly helping other Aboriginal bands." Neville's face was chalked white with disgust as he raised his voice. "He didn't give a damn for the colonists. He loathed every one of them but had to keep up a façade of loyalty; if not they would have exiled or worse, killed him." Neville combed his fingers through his hair stopping short to pick out a bug. "Filthy prison." He crushed the vermin between his fingers and flicked it to the floor. A popping of damp kindling broke the stillness urging Neville back to the present. Both men sipped their drinks, and though the whiskey burned the throat, such a sensation was not of discomfort, but rather of invigoration.

"Perhaps," thought Swift aloud, "you are underestimating your friend. The Colonial victory can be added to the Crown along with their brutality; yet, you must not discount the resolve of the native population of Van Diemen's Land. Mallabal's hardship is a testament to his resilience and a testament to the strength of his people. If he's alive, he won't be idle. If what you say is the truth, then acknowledge his honor is rooted in the values passed down to him." The man finished his drink and brought the decanter up to the light. "The only problem I see is that there is no more in this bottle!"

Neville grinned. "So, this is what lawyers do," he said, "you present a most convincing case I can't dispute. Your oration may have changed my attitude from remorse to encouragement, but unfortunately, the grim facts remain the same." He lifted his glass to his lips and let the remaining whiskey run down the back of his throat. When he had drained all its contents, he pushed the glass to the middle of the table.

"Facts are facts, and they are not meant to be changed," Swift contended. "The only sane measure is not to dwell on the why, but rather the how. I'm sure that is what Mallabal is doing. As for you, how to go about finding him is the task at hand. As for me, how to get another bottle of whiskey is my present dilemma."

Asa and his mother received the letter and though it took less than a minute to read from beginning to end; its contents would become so firmly rooted in the boy's mind that years later, its message was never left behind. As for his mother, even before she opened it she complained that it had the stink of bad news. She wouldn't open it right away, so Asa had to wait patiently before she finally picked it up from the mantle where it rested with the other letters of bad news.

She weeded through the sweet sentiments until she came to the heart of the letter and followed with her finger, reading the sentences aloud so the boy could hear it too. "Death is not hiding but waiting at the door among the living." The child's eyes wandered away from the parchment and searched his mother's face for clarity. He knew that his father had a fanciful way with words, a reader of poetry and literature many others ignored. Still, this was a riddle, one that needed interpretation which his mother's furrowed brow and pursed lips began to simplify. "Your father is very upset, Asa." She folded the letter in half and slipped it into the apron pocket. "Mallabal has been taken away." There was a long sigh of concern. "Your father was arrested and charged with unlawfully hiding Mallabal. But it's all a big misunderstanding. He's free now." Her declaration affirmed a tone deserving of good triumphing over evil. "Neville is going after him. Then, he will bring him back home. He says that 'friendship is a risky acquisition.'" She smiled and went about her chores in her usual businesslike manner. But Asa's curiosity could not wait for her to finish dusting.

"Who took him?" he asked. It was a reasonable question; its answer would certainly govern the timing of his father's return.

She turned away from the boy, and he could tell she was frightened. The feather duster feverishly fluttered as she skirted across the ragged-edged Bible. "Slave hunters." She moved, and her shadow claimed the book like a gray ghost. He didn't want to believe her, but the immense silence between them abducted his doubt. He would have to forgive her for telling him.

The room reeked of uncertainty. "Oh," he simply said, and as the boy absorbed the consequences of his father's letter, Asa realized what he was capable of.

———•———

The temporary lull of not knowing is akin to an ostrich that hides its head in the sand to avoid danger. Eventually, the head will re-emerge to confront its fears. For several months there was no word home from Neville. Asa apprenticed with a ship's carpenter while Mrs. Young continued to work at the salt flat. A letter finally arrived; however, it revealed little more assurance of Neville's returning home than the first post. *"I wish you had met Mallabal so you can understand my commitment to finding him. My only reliable clue to his abduction is a woman who had clandestine meetings with him. She has since married a doctor and speaking with either of them has proven a dead-end; both are of prominent means and unapproachable. Yet, I sense that there is a connection between Mallabal's capture and those two. But even if my instincts are correct, the local authorities are unwilling to help, and so I have sought assistance from an emissary of the abolitionists. I have copied their response to you in case something happens to me. My correspondence with them must remain in complete secrecy.*

'Dear Mr. Young,

There is news that may give you a reason to be positive. On good authority, I can acknowledge that agents have been notified to keep a look-out for the fugitive you have petitioned us to locate. A report of an escaped stowaway who jumped ship was reported to have possibly reached the shores of Portsmouth, Virginia. If we can make contact, he has a chance of reaching Canada or a free northern city. Tributaries that flow into the Ohio River from Virginia furnish convenient channels of escape. Vessels near the mouth of the rivers are used by members of the Vigilance Committee to provide safe passages north. If however, the claimant of the escaped man, Mr.

N. Bodie, confronts him before we do, the law will not provide us the assurance of his safety.

Our conductors have recently passed forty-three runaways through safe passage to other underground operators, and while the earnestness of your appeal is such, we sincerely hope that your friend is among the sheltered. Abby K. Forster's farm in Worchester is used as a feeder of the "through line." I have personally sent word to her. She is an elderly woman, but her cunning and experience make up for her delicate health.

Since Mallabal is not of African descent but arrived with you from Van Diemen's Land, his predicament brings a most unprecedented situation. Unless he can prove his British citizenship, I fear that it will be his word against the slave hunters. The abduction of your friend, even in a free state, will mean extradition. It is imperative that you keep the contents of this letter private for the sake of all involved.'

Most sincerely,
J.N.P.'

My dearest, whether this news will bring rain or sunshine is unknown to me. Whatever comes next, we will weather this tempest. Tell Asa justice will prevail. Thank you for the payments to Mr. Switft. Until my next letter.

Yours,
Neville

A single star was the only pinprick of light in the dense fog. And then, one by one, more stars began to appear. The salt-air and ragged seaweed smelled pleasantly familiar as Mallabal emerged, one-hand braced on the bow, wading through the rocky shallows. The waves broke against the shore as he stumbled, his gait swayed like a drunkard while he guided his legs through the water wedging the boat into the narrows. Had anyone been on shore to see his arrival he would have been a frightful sight, a large and imposing figure of a mysterious dark stranger. Mallabal was aware of his miserable plight, and he cursed himself for having come to America. He had only his wits to rely upon, and though his knowledge of the natural land surpassed most, he was the outsider in this unfamiliar country. Dawn was approaching, and he needed to use what was left of the wee hours to his advantage. Once the hunter, he was now the prey; it challenged him to become an even more formidable opponent. Wet, cold, hungry, but fearless; he would never be confined again. His thoughts trailed to the boy with the strange eyes and then to the armed men that had chased him from the wagon. *He could smell their anger smoldering in the underbrush. Savage hatred as theirs' could not be far behind. He had run, follow-ing his instincts, so he thought, and suddenly found himself at the foot of a wooden gangplank. The jeers once in the distance were gaining momentum. "Catch him! Catch the bastard!" The sinister threats unleashed his instinct for survival; hesi-tation was not an option. Mallabal raced up the gangplank and rounded the ship's deck where he happened upon a narrow and unsecured door. Without avail, he had crept inside, and though too long for the compartment, he slid onto the shelf, flattening himself between the sails like a slice of beef between two pieces of bread.* He wadded back from his thoughts of the day, intoxicated with the notion that he was free.

If it weren't for the morning mist, only Mother Earth would know she was breathing. Cloaked in a patchwork of haze, Mallabal followed the shoreline until the ocean's briny smells gradually mingled with a scent concocted from a coarse landscape that rose silently beyond the remote shore, wresting free from the craggy rocks that protected its cove. The exhausted man reached forward and climbed, following a natural path upward, one that snaked around and around the hill until it opened into what appeared to be a stand of trees. Too tired to walk, he fell upon his knees and crawled hand-over-hand to the nearest trunk where he lay upon the earth and rested his head on the gnarled roots. Gathering fallen leaves, he tried to cover himself, but he was a big man, and the tree had shed few leaves. The canopy rustled lightly, and his mind drifted. He didn't know what kind of tree he was under, but he did understand its place in the world. He thought of a woman, young, strong-willed, smart, and beautiful. He loved his wife; she had been a good woman. "Should I die here today," he thought as he rolled his hand over the ground beneath him, "my body will join with this old tree."

———•———

Cliffside, among the scars of time, a long-forgotten hollow of earth was discovered the following day. Its cavity was dank and cool and quite secluded. Mallabal was not inconvenienced by its broken rocks and silent hours; instead, he welcomed the cave's cell, its solitude and refuge from pursuers. Within the recesses of the cave he could sleep wrapped in his own valiance, and by the first light of day, he could venture out to find whatever the earth and sea might surrender. Mallabal occupied the next few days foraging for food and becoming acquainted with the immediate surroundings. His mental excursions into the past gave way to hours of planning the future, turning to the sky, the land, and the ocean. No written language could give him any more hope than the signs he read. A flock of swallows sweeps across the sky like a smoke cloud, and for several moments their gray shadow darkened the ground spanning north. He crouched down, taking in the details of this lovely spectacle when he was interrupted by a too-peaceful-feeling which gave him reason to be mindful. And though he wished to remain where he was, he decided it prudent to retire from the hill. Having gained only a few meters, whatever tranquility he may have enjoyed was suddenly challenged. "Not sure what you're doin' in these parts, but you better have a damn good reason fer bein' here!" Mallabal moved only his eyes as he swept the ground for a rock or stick. He glanced to the left and then to the far-right side of the trampled path. It yielded nothing that could be used as a weapon, only a small hillock of green and brown scrubs and bushes that grew unabashed.

"I asked ya a question?" The voice, more raspy than angry, compelled him for an answer. However, as soon as he turned around any provocation against the speaker was deflated.

"You're a woman," he said.

"And you're a trespasser," she confirmed. "Now that we got formalities out of the way, you and I had better get our asses out of here."

"Asses?" Mallabal repeated, questioning the word.

"Yeah, yer ass!" And she pointed to her posterior and laughed.

Mallabal shrugged, and though confused by the colloquial expression, he followed. She may have been a small woman, but she was the one with the rifle giving him enough reason to comply.

———·———

"I don't s'pose you even know where you be," the old woman said and leaned the rifle-butt against the doorframe. She sat down in a rickety cane chair, pulled a corncob pipe from her pocket and began to gnaw on the stem. "You smoke?" Mallabal stood straight and tall as a ram-rod, at least a foot taller than the woman. He looked down at the step leading to a worm-holed, planked floor and then sat down. The small cabin before him was shut tight with a sturdy door securing the entry. A small paned window was its only source of light. The man shook his head "no." She nodded and then puffed vigorously, sucking hard. A bit of smoke was expelled as she started to speak. "Hearty as a buck." She leaned forward, grabbed his arm, and squeezed. "Somebody must be sorry you got away." She nodded again. "Good lookin' man, mighty good lookin." This time she smiled, exposing her missing teeth. Her gray hair was bobbed softly around her dark face, and she wore her age-lines with sage-like dignity. "They're lookin fer ya, ain't they?" Her question stung and for the first time since his escape from the ship Mallabal felt compromised. "I can see it in yer eyes. Yer lookin' this way and that like an old hare on the run." She tapped the bowl of the pipe and let the residue fall to the floor. "They're always lookin' fer one of us, always huntin, trappin', hangin', but they can't git all of us." In the withdrawing sunlight, he saw she was composed of grandmotherly features, and he recognized this as a good omen. The elder lifted her face to the sun and then took hold of the chair arms and rose. "Come along," she commanded.

A gnarled pignut hickory shaded one side of the cabin and on the other side, the sun shined upon the ramblers that had inched their way to the top of the roof. Around the back grew a vegetable garden of greens, onions, sweet potatoes, and beans; while a rickety fence penned a small but rather portly pig. Several grouchy hens rooted about taking care not to disturb the sleeping sow, who appeared to be quite content and settled beneath the lean-to. But it was the herb garden that interested Mallabal the most. "Goldenseal," she said and pointed to the new sprigs. Cherokees mix it with bear grease to keep the vermin from biting." Unfamiliar with whom she was speaking, he simply nodded. "I chew it, good for what ails." She was pleased with his interest and continued to point out the contents of her garden. "Lemon balm for indigestion, blue hyssop for coughs, and then yarrow if it's a wound that needs healin'. These pretty flowers are belladonna," she turned and wagged her finger at him. "Stay clear, 'cause it can kill ya!" Mallabal nodded with understanding. "Used to have more hogs, but two got out," she grumbled and smacked her lips in disgust. She leaned over, lifted her petticoat and pulled a large key from her boot. Her small frame wavered like a willow branch as she regained her posture. "Well, come on, can't stay out in the open," she commanded, and as she led him out of the garden she barked, "careful not to trounce over my boneset, it makes a tea that will sweat the fever right out of ya!" She guided him around the plants to the front of the dwelling where they stepped onto the stoop. He waited beneath the overhang while she rattled the key around the lock and with two hands pushed the door open. A scent of corn and hay was emitted, along with a hint of mint and sage. "Come on now, don't stand out there and let the buzzards in!" And so, without hesitation, he ducked his head under the threshold and followed.

"I can see what yer thinkin'," she said. "How'd an old Grannie git a cabin? Well, we don't all belong to somebody. Bin here for a long time," she mused, "and I'm not all what you think." However, Mallabal wasn't really thinking anything contrary, even so, his stony, expressionless face was interpreted as curiosity surrounding the woman's good fortune. "My mother was Creek, and my daddy was a runaway." This revelation meant nothing to the man who had again entered a menagerie of words and meanings that were foreign to him. She looked at him with a hint of disgust as a mother does to a child that does not understand and shook her head. "You don't know what I'm talkin' bout, do you?" She shuffled over to a slat back chair and settled into it. She lowered the rifle and slid it between the legs of the chair. A small orange cat appeared from out of an open cupboard and jumped onto the elder's lap and curled up in the folds of her dress, ignoring the intruder standing by the hearth. The old hand stroked the cat for several minutes. It was obvious the feline was quite content, and then both began to drift off to sleep.

The dwelling was a double-pen-cabin constructed of roughly hewn logs pegged together and supported on a foundation of rocks. The interstices between the rails were caulked with moss and daubed with mud. The chimney was originally built with stone, wattle, and a mortar-mixture of clay, sand, and straw; but after years of use, it needed attention. Tucked inside the flue a slab of butchered salt-pork hung from an iron hook. The fat was trimmed so it wouldn't turn rancid, while the persistent smoke helped to cure and preserve it.

A center ridgepole supported the interior rooms, and the thatched-roof was braced with pine beams. The floor was made of planking, and the walls, once whitewashed, were stained with soot. Grannie's most favorite possession, a three-legged Dutch oven stood by the hearth. She could boil, stew, fry, steam, roast, simmer and by placing the lid upside down on the stove, she could use it as a griddle. A narrow threshold opened into a smaller and narrower room furnished with a cot, washstand, and chest of drawers. A cane-chair pushed against the wall was stacked with a few belongings and helped hold down the corners of a corn shuck floor-covering beside the cot. Outside the window, a rocky trail led to the outhouse and forked left leading to the pigeon loft. And so, here he stood, a large grown-man at the mercy of a tiny old woman. He almost smiled at the irony of the situation, but his perplexing dilemma warranted more than humor.

The scrappy cat and woman remained motionless for a short time. The warmth of the cabin was remarkably comfortable until a cool wind stole inside and the cat, now feeling the intrusion, woke up and promptly jumped from the old lap. Mallabal was still standing by the hearth when the elder lifted her lids and came alive as if having been awoken from what must have been a restful dream. The old woman tapped her finger against her temple knowingly. "I know what ya need, but it ain't so easy to come by." She raised herself up and moseyed over to the bureau and pulled open the top drawer. She fumbled around for a few moments and then removed a wooden box cut in the shape of a treasure chest. The hinged lid was pried open; sluggishly, it squeaked as if its contents hadn't been inspected for quite some time. A concealed parchment was unfolded. "This here is my freedom paper. It's a government certificate; says on account that I was born a free-woman, I can stay here in this Commonwealth. There's nobody that's got the right to take me away." She nodded her head affirmatively. "We need to git you one of these." She refolded the sheet and returned it to its safe place. "If somebody comes around, all I gotta do is show 'em that piece of paper." She settled back in the chair and stared at the visitor. "What's yer name?"

"Mallabal."

"I never heard that name before," she said. "Well, Mallabal, we got to move a mountain, but we can do it. The Lord said that If you have faith and do not doubt, you'll not only do what's bin done to the fig tree but even if you say to this mountain, 'Be taken up and thrown into the sea,' it'll happen." She eyed him agreeably. "I got a feelin' you've seen more of the world than anybody I ever met. Why yer a regular explorer. Seems to me that you might find a better place to go than up north." Her comment was hoarse with anticipation, however, when he offered no response, she went on. "There's a place better-suited fer a man like you. You'd go stir crazy in Canada; ain't nothin' there! Yes indeed, I think I know just the place." The old woman relit her pipe and sucked hard. Her taut lips puckered around the stem, and the wrinkles on her upper lip grew deep as did the furrows on her brow. She was deep in thought. Mallabal crouched down and poked the embers with the poker. A flurry of ash scattered about the hearth, and with a bit more negotiation he was able to get the fire started again with the help of some dry straw. "Californya," she said. "We gotta git you to Califoryna." Mallabal swiveled round. The weight of his body rested on his toes as he tipped forward to listen. "Ever hear of it?" He nodded "yes." "Good," she said. "No one's gonna bother you there. Know why?" She didn't wait for his reply. "'Cause they don't care for slavers in Californya. An African by the name of Raffey, Mr. Alvin Raffey, left St. Louis with a wagon train, crossed over the Missouri River at Savannah Landing, made it to Fort ...," she paused for a moment and smacked her lips. "Now what was the name of that...Oh yes, Fort Laramie. Why folks were dyin' left and right!" She chuckled, "But not our, Alvin. No, sir, he got to Black Rock by crossin' the desert! Even the beast of burden died, but not Alvin Raffey. Finally got to Sacramento. He was a digger. A digger!" Her eyes gleamed with the words. "He was a digger of gold." She crooked her finger at Mallabal to come closer. "And as long as you got gold, you can buy yer way to freedom."

Mallabal returned a curious gaze and then stood up and walked over to the window. In the hills around Lefroy, at Nine Mile Springs, gold was rumored to exist, but exploration had been discouraged by the

Colonial government fearing the convicts in Van Diemen's Land would find out and rebel. Alluvial nuggets lay in the creek gullies and under the basalt rock, while most lay scattered waiting to be recovered by reefing the quartz rock which formed in the Savage River and at the base of the hills. As such, Mallabal and his people had discovered gold independently and traded it among themselves. The Aborigine knew all about gold, and he understood what it was capable of. It has the power to overrule the natural order of fate.

Mallabal pulled the curtain aside and passed through an invisible wall of indecisions. The insightful Grannie recognized that the man before her thought twice before he spoke, so she was patient. However, she did not know how long she was going to have to be patient. Like other men, women, and children, most had learned to be wary, not to trust anybody even when they said they would do no harm. "This Mallabal, he just might need more time, too," she decided. The old woman felt that she was right, so she started to hum, and though she may have appeared to be in a state of indifference, she was scheming, for to let a mind be idle was like allowing the land going fallow. As for Mallabal, he too was in contemplation. Only the orange cat was animated and scampered about chasing its invisible playmates.

———•———

The newly wedded Sydney Bushnell lies amid sheets of white linen in her four-poster bed. Besides her slept her husband. She listened as he took in a gulp of air and then exhaled through his mouth with an annoying guttural sound. Over and over, he sputtered in his sleep. She tried to ignore the noises, but it was nearly impossible. She tugged the pillow closely around her ears and tried to smother his snores. She should be happy, but she felt little for this man. She reached across with her left arm, daring not to wake him; pulled gently at the nightstand drawer and traced the spot where a pistol once lay. A set of lace handkerchiefs were stacked neatly in its place. Richard shifted, grunting an inaudible word. It sounded like a name, but he muttered nothing more. She feverishly shut the drawer and turning over feigned sleep. Her only ambition was the arrival of the first morning light, and though rest was what she desperately needed, nighttime resurrected her clandestine interludes with Mallabal.

A hopeless teeming of sadness fell. She lusted after the man, and though feminine charm orchestrated her powers, she found that he could not be seduced in the manner she yearned. "Undeclared is not loveless," she decided. This was a notion she stated as a déclassé in an unfair and unequal society. She being a woman and Mallabal an Aborigine, their destiny could not be righted. Could Richard have possibly known about their relationship? The young surgeon was so shrewd, so cunning that she almost felt as though he had been watching her from afar. If so, then it all made sense. Mallabal's disappearance; no, even Richard could not have been that cruel.

She recalled her last days with the Aborigine. She had taken his worn-out jacket home to patch. He was a proud man, and no matter that she wished to buy him a new one, he would not accept it. More than grateful for her sewing job, he gifted to her a gray pearl. "The new bride turned to her husband and frowned. "I hope you didn't do anything to him," she warned. But his only response was a loud snore.

Chapter 20

r. Bushnell, you have a visitor."

"Visitor?" The Doctor had just finished his port when he heard the rap on the bedroom door.

"Yes, Sir," remarked a slightly irritated voice on the other side of the portal. "A man, quite disheveled and dusty."

"Disheveled?" Again, the Doctor had no other response except with the repetition of the maid.

"Yes, and gruff."

"Gruff?" But this he said under his breath while trying to decipher who it could be, and at this hour of the evening. "You can come in," he griped, taking his frustration out on the messenger.

The housemaid turned the latch and stepped in, but only as far as the threshold. "He wouldn't give his name, only said that he had information for you and that you'd want it."

"Information?"

The woman nodded, but she was beginning to become irritated with his indecision. Either send the brute away or find out what the man desired.

"He's a burly one, so I think you should attend to him," she remarked as she sized up her employer against the bovine waiting downstairs.

Still rummaging through his inventory of likely candidates, for it was a highly unorthodox circumstance before him, Bushnell tapped his fingers on the arms of his wingback. "Burly you say?"

"Well, perhaps more brutish than burly," she decided.

The Doctor contemplated for a moment until finally, as though the last drop of juice had been squeezed from a lemon, he managed to pinch from his memory a name he hadn't thought of in quite some time. "Tell him I will be right down," the Doctor said sourly and smoothed his palm over his graying hair.

The maid shrugged and stepped back into the hall when she heard him say "and whatever you do, do not give him whiskey."

Her hand cradled the latch, but she poked her head back in before securing it from intruders. "Sounds like you know him," needled the maid.

"In my line of work, we run into all kinds, only it appears this one had been set free." Then he waved her off and with a disgruntled disposition, for he was already in a bad mood, unlocked his desk drawer and retrieved the revolver. He picked up the gun and sighed, "Damn fool."

He was indeed brutish, gruff, and disheveled. Dusty too, but the maid had not mentioned that he was wearing all black. Black boots, black vest, black pants, black belt, black hat, even a black bolo. "Got this in Mexico," he announced, fingering the onyx laced between the string ties. "But she hadn't asked nor did she care. "You Chinese?" he pointed at the woman.

"Excellent observation." She smiled sweetly as her sarcasm remained unnoticed by his ignorance.

He grunted and eyed the sofa.

"Sit down, Mr....?" her voice lingered in anticipation of a name tagged to the end of her sentence.

"Bodie," he said, "just Bodie," and then with an exhausted set of humphs, he plopped down into the cushion, taking up almost all of the settee. "I don't suppose you could offer this old soldier a whiskey?"

There was a part of the woman that wanted to oblige, to remove the decanter from the den and fill a glass to the brim; just to see what would happen. Would it be like waving a red cloth before a bull? She laughed silently; however, being the dutiful employee, she replied, "No."

The man twisted around and scanned the room hoping to foil the woman's stinginess, whereupon he was suddenly interrupted by the sound of Richard Bushnell making his entrance behind the scruffy man. The greasy hair he remembered as being black was now streaked gray, but what the Doctor could see of the thick neck was still bronzed and weathered. Bushnell's eyes met the housemaid, and his look dismissed her from the room. "If you need me, Dr. Bushnell, you know where to find me." She scowled at the self-imposed guest and softly padded out the parlor door.

"You done well in your civilian life," grumbled the brutish fellow. He reached over and picked up the silver lighter from off the mahogany table. Fingering the filigreed metal, he pushed down on the top, and it came to life, emitting a blue flame. Bushnell reclined into the opposing chair, an ornate caned high-back with carved arms that stretched forward like a pair of banisters. The man flicked the lighter for several more times and then becoming bored set it back on the table. This was his wife's sitting room, and the two men looked awkwardly out-of-place as they faced one another between the floral backdrop of rose wallpaper. He mentally chastised the maid for setting the lout here, but on the other hand, he did say no whiskey and prohibition was strictly enforced in this feminine setting. The other didn't appear to mind the decorum and seemed to be settling into the brocade like a mastiff that jumped up on the furniture when no one was looking. He stretched his feet before him and as he did Bushnell wondered how he would be able to get the large man out of the house if he did have to kill him. The housemaid would be of little help, and so he decided that such an act would be more trouble than it would be worth.

"So, Bodie, what is it that brings you to my home?" Bushnell spoke in the same deliberate and calm voice that he used with his more volatile patients. Only now he did not have the luxury of having him in a straight-jacket. He examined the man as he spoke and noted that he was dirty as well as wearing a gross amount of black, he did not find the acquaintance to appear agitated.

"You did good by me Doc. During the war you kept me safe, and after the war you kept your word."

"As did you, Mr. Bodie, as did you." He was pleased that the fool still felt indebted. However, the last thing he needed was for him to be seen in the house. Such a slovenly man making himself at home had never taken place in his wife's parlor, and as he looked him over, the disgusted doctor was beginning to detest this oaf with his filthy clothes and muddy soles. "Still in black, I see."

The man lifted his brown eyes, and their grief-stricken stare was that of one who had seen too much death. "Only color I know of when you're in mourning," he chided.

"It's been over a decade since the war ended."

"That so? Well, to tell ya the truth, it's never been over. Never gonna be over as far as I'm concerned." There was no regret in his voice, only disdain coated his tongue.

The doctor looked up at the old clock and wished to hurry this along. "Tell me, why are you here? Money, I suppose. Isn't it always money?"

But as if he hadn't heard the latter statement the brute tipped forward. "I'm not here to talk a bunch of shit about the war," he sputtered. "I came to warn you."

"You, Mr. Bodie, have a warning for me?" the arrogant physician leaned in.

"Remember that picture of yer wife, the one the ornery cripple was peddling? Well, he lost it in a game of cards. And what's more, it's got your name on it."

The doctor felt his mouth grow dry and he had an urge for something to drink. "What picture, Bodie?" he demanded, dispensing with formalities.

"You know, the one." The grizzly man was searching for a sign of recognition from the listener but could interpret none in Bushnell's blank expression. He tried again. "The one that show'd more than usual," and as he spoke, he made a suggestive gesture as if holding up a pair of large breasts. "The one she gave away to…"

But with the utterance of those words, the jealous husband grabbed the vulgar man by the throat and slowly added pressure to the fleshy neck. "Don't even try to mention that name again, do you hear!" he cautioned; and although this warning was not loud or imposing, it likened to the devil delivering a threat directly into the man's ear.

"He's gone, Doc!" insisted the victim as he reached up to pull the hands away from around his throat. "What's got into you? Wasn't it me that you called when you needed a slave hunter. I don't give a shit about him. Didn't I get rid of him for you?" The doctor released his grip from the animal sitting before him. He was right. This bastard was a part of his life: before, during, and now, even years after the war had ended. Bodie was a stooge, but the fact was that everyone needed a man like Bodie. Bushnell leaned back in his chair as the oaf massaged his neck. "Shit, you're one strong old man!" The doctor ignored the statement, stood up, and beckoned the moocher to follow; they both needed a drink.

When Bodie left the home of Dr. Richard Bushnell, he was "don't care" drunk. He staggered down the street singing the chorus of *The Bonnie Blue Flag*. He was smart enough not to be too boisterous, not to attract attention. Like the fox in the barnyard, he was an opportunist. He felt no obligation to time, destination, or morals. His new assignment gave him enough money for a room and drink; all that he needed to feel content. It was now up to him to find the sultry portrait, but he would worry about that in the morning when he was sober.

———— •·—— ————

In the course of the evening's intrusion, Richard had not forgotten that his unfinished glass of port was waiting upstairs. Unlike the brute, he was as sober as a judge and upon returning to his private quarters, sat down to finish his drink. Resuming with his evening rituals, he removed his shoes and stretched his stocking-feet out before him. He was a man that did not like his dominion or his business untidy. The character of the uninvited visitor came to mind; he was confident that Bodie would be successful in finding and retrieving the photograph. Though he passionately worshipped his wife, her inability to return those feelings was a blow to his manhood. He resented her independence, her relationship with Rosalie, and her ability to squander away time. As for himself, money was easy to let go of, but time was altogether precious. He stared moodily in the direction of the window. The brocade drapery appeared to be drawn shut, if not for a stream of moonlight breaching the divide into the bedchamber; and though he was too tired to read, he picked up the folded newspaper next to the port and feigned interest. But within only a matter of moments, he lowered the paper to his lap fearing that perhaps he had woken his wife. It was possible that the verbal altercation may have inadvertently divulged too much information regarding the disappearance of her.... Disdain immediately overpowered any tranquility he was feeling. Oh, the word "lover"; it audaciously intruded into his thoughts, and with its violation, he once again loathed the man.

Harassed by his imagination, Bushnell tried to restore matters by detaching himself from the past and allowing the future to unfold. He picked up the paper and began to read. But in the babel which had transpired, it was not Sydney that had been listening. At the bottom of the stairwell, standing in the shadowy confines of the cubby hole, Rosalie had been in earshot of the two men. Their banter had displaced all normal conversations trading polite talk with guile and deception. Her ear was directed to the speakers, and she pilfered the words as if stealing fruit from the grocer. It was a most memorable scene contrived of lies and deception where the housemaid's allegiance to her mistress was poetically reaffirmed.

———— • ————

"Look, Asa!" Flora pointed to a bridge of colors arching from the earth to the sky. "Which color do you like the best?" she asked, and as if on cue the rainbow began to materialize like a peacock unfolding its feathers.

The unresponsive man glanced up with indifference. The rainbow was a familiar sight offering little promise. He didn't believe in wishes, falling stars, or four-leaf clovers either. The child inspected the sky and then as if forgetting her question changed her attention to a more pressing matter. "So, what should we do today?" she asked. However, the "we" in her inquiry would be met with disappointment since Asa had no intention of submitting to a "we." "Maybe we should go home and see the tattie-bogle; he seems to be the only thing around here with any sense." Flora was referring to the elderly couple. She was too young to admit that she needed their help and now their old-fashioned worries were stifling her freedom. No longer was she able to wander outside without supervision and though she didn't much like schooling, she feared that Señora's "tolerable" lessons would sooner or later be replaced with a strict schoolmarm and a room filled with dirty, unruly children. "He must be lonesome, swinging up on the pole all by himself. The garden will need tending and the rabbit," she remarked, "maybe it came back!" There was a slight lilt in her voice as she darted from thought to thought. "Yes, that brown bunny just might be eating all the carrots and lettuce." A moment of pondering cultivated a wrinkle in her small brow. "But it can have the radishes," she explained hoping to draw Asa out of his apparent ill mood. "I think I need a pet," she said and picking up a twig, scratched beneath the dirt. "What do you think of this?" she delighted and maneuvering the stick, goaded a six-legged creature onto the twig. "Oh, such shiny black wings."

Her voice claimed Asa's ears, but not his attention. *Out of sight from the attendants, the old soldier directed his troops. His musket, a carefully selected stick, was positioned by his knees. He sat beneath the shade of the toolshed where a small brown bird had made a ragged nest in the lattice. The crusty patient scratched his head and picked out a louse. "Want it?" he asked holding out his pinched fingers. "I don't have teeth to chew it with." He gummed his lips together and then sucked the insect into his mouth."*

Two unyielding minutes passed without any challenge put to the beetle. Flora carried the stick around the yard until the beetle opened its wings and flew away. She traced the black bug for a few moments until it was swallowed up in the morning mist. "Well, that's the end of him! Not sure where it's headed. Probably home. Lucky bug!" and tossed the stick to the ground.

Señora Tamayo was hanging starched linen and coarse bath towels on the line to dry. The day was warm, yet the woman shivered as she bent up and down over the wicker basket. Flora was one of the thousands of displaced and damaged children. Some orphans ended up with relatives or adopted by families, while others often became wards of the state. Señor Tamayo had delivered the great truth, her parents were gone, and when she saw the expression on Señora's face, the pained look of both pity and dismay, Flora did not really understand. This was a void that could not be patched; it was severed too quickly to be stitched with platitudes. Memories are immortal. For the child, her parents' images were being safeguarded by her brain, their words still echoed in her ears, the lilacs still smelled sweet, and the buttercups still stained her fingers. Her parents could not truly be dead. "They were misplaced," she had decided. "Silly, Señora, why does she always look so sad?" Flora gazed at the elder hanging the clothes. The starched linen hung limply, and she felt a bit of remorse for the woman. Señora's plump arms and legs were tired as she pulled the heavy wash from the basket. Sweat had formed on her brow but daring not let go lest her clean tablecloth would fall on to the ground, she leaned her forehead against her upper-arm and wiped it dry. Preoccupied with house-work, the woman did not notice a pair of ravens that had decided to settle upon the clothesline; only the eyes of the child fell upon the resting birds. Under most circumstances, this would not have been out of the ordinary since birds often liked to perch upon the clothesline. It was the reaction that took place and set in motion a most curious situation.

"I saw them, I saw them in my dream! They've come back, you see them, don't you?" Flora cried and lifted her hand towards the blackbirds. Upon hearing her voice, the startled birds twisted their ebony necks and in a single gesture swooped up and then flitted around and over the child's head. "See, they know me, they know me!" she laughed.

However, the woman, not convinced that this was a friendly ges-ture, proceeded to flail the damp cloth at the marauders. "Away, away!" she cried and snapped the wet linen like a whip.

"No, no, please, don't scare them away!" But the pity in the child's voice did not deter the matron from standing her ground and with all her energy continued to shoo the birds away until they alighted on the most out-of-the-way branch.

"Flora are you hurt?" asked the woman. Her hands trembled, and while she encouraged the child to follow her, she peered up into the tree, shielding the little girl with her broad bent figure. "Come, let us go into the house," she suggested and gave Flora a nudge.

"Señora, you shouldn't have chased them away!" exclaimed the insightful child. "They'll only return. There's no reason to hide in the house."

The uneasy woman sighed, muttering a bit of opposition, "Al jacal viejo no le faltan goteras." (the old house does not lack for leaks); and surrendering to her charge, she proceeded in shaking out the cloth she had used to frighten away the birds. When she had stretched out most of the creases, she pinned the dishcloth across the line. "Si, I suppose it is alright to be outside since I need to finish," she acquiesced but kept one eye to the treetop. Flora dipped into the basket to help. "You go with Asa," she said and tried to smile, however, her crooked mouth only seemed to add more worry to her face.

Asa had seen the pair too; feathered in black like funeral directors; the birds that summoned the arrival of death. He looked beyond where the woman was hanging the clothes, and a cold spasm of memory separated him from the moment. *A soldier hiding behind a screen of grape and canister-battered trees surrendered a desperate plea. "Git them, git them! I could have a good meal if I could git them!" The ravens flew over acres of carnage, and though the birds never did anything of merit, their cries summoned survivors to amass. Caws, three at a time, as earnest as bugles sounding taps were a postlude not just for a Yankee or Rebel, not for the victor or the defeated, but for the slain. It was for the women who ventured down to search among the fallen, the women that picked up scattered feathers to adorn their funeral bonnets. Hands in bloody hands shared fates and fragmented lives. What do the ravens know? "No one would have chosen this place to stop and rest," Asa decided, "but the ravens; they do." Among the intertwined, the torn, the broken, they would caw one to the other; a cry of rejoice or a melodious tenor, it was difficult to discern their intent.*

But among uncertainty, it mattered not, and Asa had seen the birds once again in a way unlike the child.

Death was something that could just happen. It happened to animals, to plants, to the flowers in winter. But mastery over her fate made the death of her parents an objectionable notion just as inadmissible evidence was viewed in a court case. "Colonel and Mother are not dead, they're only invisible," she explained to Asa. "You see, invisible," she explained and blew air between her fingers as she formed a small circle. "I can feel them around, like the wind. But last night they come back to me. Not in the usual way, like invisible people. You see, they can fly like, I guess like angels. Only," she whispered, "they were birds; black and shiny and very nice. And that's why I need to talk to the tattie-bogle. I need to tell him not to scare the blackbirds away." Asa listened as the child pleaded her case. "You just gotta take me home Asa, you just gotta."

Flora's voice was punctuated with sorrow. Señor Tamayo had taken the wagon into town, and the stout woman standing between blankets and sheets was busy pinning them on the line. Asa had wanted to go to town with the old man. Flora raised her face and looked at him. Her eyes and mouth were formed just like her mother's. He turned away and looked towards the hilltop. *"Got a secret to tell you, Asa. She really isn't our child."* The image in the locket; the one that he dug up in the back, behind the house; he looked at Flora and recalled the woman's eyes, the smile, it was the same as the child's. He turned and started towards the barn. "Asa, please take me home!" she cried. *"Please, take me home! I want to be buried at home." Wasn't the woeful soldier entitled to such a preacher-made funeral? The voice in his head was faint; he could barely hear the Sergeant; there was too much noise, too much gunfire. What home? He didn't know where to take him. He had tried to pull him out from under the dead horse, but it was useless. The animal was so heavy. "Please take me home!" The words were slow and labored in his head, despite the intensity of the fighting.* "Asa, did you hear what I said. Can you please walk me home?" *The soldier quieted down. Asa bent over the horse with an awkward sigh of relief, "You'll be lashed no more." Then with a flick of his hand, he shooed away the raven wishing to quench itself in the muddy water and saluted the man and steed lying prostrate on the bloody earth.* "Asa, did you hear what I said. Can you please walk me home? I don't want to be left here."

They crossed over the lowly hills, and the wildflowers tipped their petals as the child drew closer. They came upon a familiar sight; the mound rose slowly as it always had, only now it was peddling anticipation. The view touched her heart. From their vantage point, the curving horizon was drenched in sunlight hiding the shameless plunder committed by the fire. Below them was where she was called daughter and where she rejected her new position as an orphan. "I can't wait to see him!" Flora announced. "I wonder if he needs a new eye? Mother could patch anything that got torn." She skipped without trampling a single flowering weed. "Careful there, Asa, you almost crushed a daisy!" Sounding marginally disappointed in what she had reckoned as the man's clumsiness, she pointed out the crown of yellow. But he was careful. He had marched with thirteen-thousand men over rivers, through towns, and in mud. He had marched around the entire length of the Rebel lines, and never once stepped on a daisy. He would have known if he had; finding a daisy would have been the only bright spot in the day.

The wind was extinguishing the clouds, and as it blew, it cooled the two travelers approaching the overgrown garden. "Wooley!" cried Flora. Her enthusiasm heralded the delight offered when greeting a long-awaited friend, and she ran up to the stuffed man and shook his foot. "Hello, Wooley, did you miss me?" The tattie-bogle had outlasted everyone. As keeper of the garden, his dead-button eyes and painted expression remained unchanged; even now he remained steadfast in protecting the sun-ravaged garden. The carrots, the beans, the tomatoes, all transcended recognition, rotting on their vines and decaying back into the earth. The tattie-bogle cared little for what vermin or worms decided to eat the blackened flesh of the vegetables. He was here to keep away the birds. "He looks a little thin," she exclaimed to Asa. "See how the pant legs need more stuffing?" She held up the cuff. "I better gather up some hay."

The man followed the child as she wandered about the overgrown garden gathering dried straw. Her hands clasped the loose pieces as carefully as one holds a bouquet. But just as Aurora brings the light of day, a sudden slip of darkness filled all crevices of brightness. The small bundle of straw dropped from her hands, scattering over her feet. Dropping to her knees, Flora leaned over her find. "Wake up," she whispered. But the birds did not stir. She twisted her head and cupped her hands over her brow as she searched for an answer in Asa's face. "Maybe they're asleep. Ravens need to rest, too," she explained. But the blue-black wings would not move nor would the tail feathers. Asa lifted the pair in his hands and blew gently. Flora watched, but only the soft feathers stirred. "I guess they can't be put back to life," Flora murmured. "It wasn't the tattie-bogle's fault." Asa gently held the pair of ravens and then placed them before the little girl. Her eyes met his, and with her finger, she stroked them. The wind blew across the garden and with it arrived agony. It cared not for the child or the man or the dead birds. Agony brought with it pain, distress, and reality; and finding a juncture, it tore into the child and found its way to her heart. "Asa, does it hurt, does it hurt not to talk?" Her eyes welled up, and the tears began to fall down her cheeks slowly. She held out her hands, and he placed the dead birds before her. "I saw you, I saw you both," she whimpered.

They were laid underneath the tattie-bogle where the rain will fall like teardrops. Asa sprinkled earth over the burial mounds and Flora placed two stones at the head. He watched and wondered if in her dreams the birds would return or if they would all finally rest. "I think we need to say something," Flora whimpered. "Don't you?" Asa bent over the little gravesite and removed his hat. "I wish you could talk," the child said. The wind rustled, and the scarecrow's leg swung against the pole. "Oh, did you hear that?" she asked and tapped the man's shoulder. "Wooley told me not to be sad. He said that he saw who did it." The child shook the strawman's arm and waited. Her eyes opened wide as if she had had a revelation. "He said the man who did it is dead, and another bigger man pulled him into the field." She leaned over and tipped Asa's hat away from his brow. "He told me, you believe me, don't you?" She squeezed his hand, and he squeezed it back. "Wooley is gonna watch over Mother and Colonel; he won't let anything disturb them. They'll rest here." Her shadow fell upon the mound as she brushed the dirt and patted it down with her hand. "I don't know what will happen to you now, Asa. I think I should take care of you. Mother would like that. She would like it if I did that." Her small voice quivered with sadness. Then she meandered around the garden and after a few minutes returned. "It's a beauty," she exclaimed and set the small object before him. "Mother liked shiny things," she remarked. "It's better than a flower; it will never die. You put it on them," she requested and opening her fist, dropped the find into his palm. Asa slowly turned the object over and pushed it into the mound. Flora nodded approvingly and with her hands folded she knelt and closed her eyes for a moment and then opened one eye in anticipation of something happening. However, like all who expect the unexpected, all remained the same. The only out of the ordinary occurrence was the finding of a smooth gray pearl.

Chapter 21

man haunted by an obsession is dangerous, in essence, he cannot be tamed. Richard Bushnell's indiscretions came at the expense of his trusting patients. He was treated with loyalty by his staff and humored by his dispassionate wife. While Sydney remained aloof outside the pretense of wifely duties, the doctor self-prescribed other means of distraction. What began as an infatuation over her bawdy photograph grew into a fixation and then a profitable enterprise. The nature of this business may have appeared sordid to a layman, but by inviting female patients to "let go of their inhibitions" allowed Dr. Bushnell to absolve himself of what others would see as "wrongdoings."

The sullen woman spoke to Rosalie peering back at her through the looking glass. "Are you absolutely sure this is what you heard? Is there any remote possibility that perhaps you are mistaken?" However, the annoyed look of the housemaid was proof enough. "No, I suppose not; it's just that I was looking for an excuse." Sydney turned back to her reflection and started to comb her hair. "What you have told me has strangulated any hope of trusting him. Richard was bitten by jealousy years ago, and now he's as mad as a rabid dog!" Her voice trembled with anger and then despair. "Am I to blame? Tell me, is it my fault?" She wanted to reevaluate her grief but not through the exploitation of her uninhibited side. She would take no blame for what others saw nor would she chastise herself for seeing herself through the lens of those people. After all, that was the job of Mr. Saint when he captured her image. She was sure her husband had done something heinous to Mallabal and… she could barely come to terms with whatever crime may have been committed against the innocent man. What self-defense could Robert claim? It was years ago, and the past was just that, the past.

Sydney's mind was in turmoil, and her heart already broken was severed again. She looked at Rosalie. The woman's lips moved and then the words floated into her ears where the voice of reason registered. "Of course you aren't at fault. Is it your fault when he's seized with indigestion after a spicy meal or hungover after too much whiskey? I would weep for a dead dog before I would weep for your husband. You are without fault, my dear." Sydney smiled and handed her confidant the comb. With a slow pass through her curls, she continued to comb her mistress's hair.

"Revenge is a necessary outcome regardless of its imperfect justice. Mallabal, how sorry I am, how sorry." The seated woman turned her eyes downward and sighed.

Rosalie stared into the mirror and then placed the comb on the dressing table. "I will be back in a minute." She had been given the run of the household, a privilege rarely dispensed to servants, and consequently, she took her work both seriously and secretively, all for the benefit of her mistress. "I found this while I was straightening the shelves in his armoire," she whispered after returning to the bedroom.

"Do I want to see inside?" asked the gloom-ridden woman.

"I would if I were you," and handed-over a cigar box as if it were an offering made to the altar.

"He's not a cigar smoker, but then, he has other habits I wasn't aware of either," she joked cunningly. She lifted the box to her nose and then wrinkled it with disdain. "Yuck. I suppose all his handkerchiefs smell of this," and as she raised the lid, it unleashed a scent, not unlike a men's smoking room. Sydney lifted out a neatly folded silk ascot setting it aside and then removed a handful of images, counting out twelve in all. They were all of women lewdly posed and clothed in not much more than a sheer tunic. "Oh," she said and handed the set to Rosalie. "When did you discover the box?" she asked.

"When you were resting," she said alluding to the "teatime" nap. "Odd that there are duplicates." She shuffled through the pictures hastily. "Where do you think he got them?"

However, to Sydney this question was obvious, in fact, it was all becoming quite clear. "How very stupid of me," she thought. "But perhaps, he has given me enough rope to hang him with!" She reshuffled through the lot until pausing at one picture. "Where have I seen this woman?" She tried to remember the face as her recollections flitted back to years ago, in New York, at the gallery of Dickie and Saint, but quickly dismissed that idea. *No, it was not there.* The woman in the picture was hardened, something or someone had altered her life. Her countenance revealed that the world had taken too much, taken all she had to offer and now, all care for the living was lost. Sydney closed her eyes and drifted like a wind-wafted dandelion. Her thoughts scattered until she called them up and remembered. "I know where I have seen her!" she announced.

"You know this woman? From where?" opposed the maid. Her voice echoed disapproval despite her acquaintance with Sydney's sorted background.

"In the sketches, the ones drawn by that patient. Oh, what was his name? The talented soldier. Yes, this must be the same woman!" she exclaimed tapping lightly on the photograph. "Richard had his drawings, pencils, paper, all of it taken away; but his pictures were too interesting to be disposed of. You can defend my memory, can't you?" she said soliciting the listener. "I distinctly remember asking if I could keep them." And, as Sydney scrambled about like a winter squirrel hunting for an acorn, Rosalie opened the linen-chest and pulled from it a roll of papers. "You are the best!" squealed the woman and like a child opening a birthday present, she sat on the floor and untied the ribbon. The drawings were unruly, wishing to curl back into themselves, however, after placing an atomizer on each of the four corners, they complied in keeping flat. After a quick examination, she lifted one from the pile and placed it on the bed. "Hold the corners at the top," she told Rosalie, while with her fingers she held fast the bottom edge. Reluctantly, it flattened.

The solitude within the drawing could be felt by the two onlookers. A trio of women, all dressed in identical hospital gowns cinched at the waist with a braided cord, had been resurrected on paper by the artist. And had they not been within a stone enclosure, one would have imagined a solarium; for outside the walls, it was many shades brighter. Yet, the shadows cast over the women gave credence to their grim existence. "It's her!" confirmed Sydney and compared the same faint ghost of a smile in both the tintype and drawing.

"He drew her sadness," said the maid, treating the picture now as if it were silk.

"Then you see it too!" Sydney lifted her fingers away from the drawing allowing Rosalie to set it aside.

"I tell you I'm right, it was a Rebel's bullet, and he killed Abe Lincoln in 1861. I know I'm right because it was the year the bank came and stole my farm."

"No, stupid! Abe wasn't shot til' '65; I know 'cause that was the same year Lilac had the baby and died."

"And I said it was, Margaret!"

"And I'm tell'en you, it wasn't!"

Sydney reassembled the general tenor of this conversation. *She was exiting Richard's office when several asylum orderlies intervened and tried* to distract the squabblers with a cautionary warning. But the discourse was renewed after the orderlies' backs were turned and the two women yowled like a pair of war widows. The Matron, whom the patients both knew well, wielded a calm voice, approaching like a wolf. "I'll get her," she pointed, and as the startled patient shrank back a hand reached around and grabbed the frightened lunatic by the scruff of the neck. "You know fighting isn't allowed," the Matron reprimanded; but ignoring the reminder, the whimpering patient suddenly came alive and levying her weight she lunged forward with an open jaw. "Trying to bite me?" laughed the Matron. "You're feisty, Margaret!" she snarled and clamping down harder, tightened her grip around the neck. "Come along now and quit your devilry!" the Matron snapped, and without any pity on the miserable woman, the attendant standing watch was summoned to take her away. The Herculean ward, affectionately known as the "Puppy" by some because of his big brown eyes, and unaffectionately called "The Cur" by those he crossed, already had his simpering charge air-borne and was briskly hauling her away like a squealing piglet. Hidden within the portal, Sydney choked down the feeling of dread accompanied by a remote impression that she heard muffled shrieks of anguish; but the ungreased hinges of the great doors locking behind them made her think that perhaps she had been mistaken.

Sydney weighed the incident again in her mind. "Margaret," she recollected, "the woman's name is Margaret."

Being afflicted with homesickness is like no other malady. A longing for the familiar succumbs to substitutes and token reminders, and all one can do is channel pleasures through protracted memories. But what if this wistful melancholy steals noiselessly into the heart of one that has no place to call home, no safe anchorage, nowhere to moor the weary body or feed the hungry soul? What then do we ascribe as homesickness? Perhaps this is simply called loneliness, and the only bright antidote is the inheritance of the sun.

Grannie's contacts stretched well-beyond her community while her aged appearance and intentionally exaggerated mannerisms, indicative of her years, provided the anonymity she needed. Gaming the enemy was the art of survival, and those whom she conned were the fools. The elder was shrewd, and everything she did was with the intention and diligence of the "ambassador of freedom," a nickname given to her by those who had escaped by way of her "passage." It was money that Mallabal would need right away. This was worrisome to the old woman, but not impossible.

"There's jist three ways to git there," she explained. The hen simmered in the cauldron. She tossed several carrots into the stew. "Like carrots?" Mallabal nodded "yes." She dropped a few more in and then settled the lid on the great pot and sat down. "Land, water, or a combination of the two. Them's the three ways. The last way means takin' a ship south and then crossin' overland in Panama, or Nicaragua, or through Mexico and then getting passage on another ship. Don't seem like a very good idea. Now, overland across the country is not only hard, but ya got to get a mule, and a wagon, and provisions, and then ya might run into slavers. Too many folks askin' questions. Overland ain't any good. Seems to me that goin' on a ship round Cape Horn is yer best bet."

Mallabal said nothing. In his usual pensive state, he was mulling over what the woman said when he realized that he didn't even know the old woman's name. He'd been sleeping in her barn for weeks, yet a formal introduction had never taken place. All he knew was that she was called Grannie. The egg farmer, Daniel Hughes, had sent his son, Iggy, with five eggs in exchange for sugar. A boy child not more than seven years of age, barefooted and shirtless, called her Grannie. "We got enough eggs, but it wouldn't be right not to take em', don't want nobody to feel like they can't pay their way," she had said after the boy scampered away. It didn't seem odd that he would know her as Grannie. John Henry Hill was a carpenter by trade. He passed beneath the shadows of night and entered the old woman's cottage masked in stillness. He had only stayed one night, and the next morning, before the sun-speckled the land, he was armed with a paper and gone. He called her Grannie too.

Mallabal looked out the window with his back turned away from the cook. The orange cat must have smelled the stew for it was parading under foot, twisting in and out between her legs. It rubbed its face against her woolen stockings, leaving behind tufts of loose fur. "I ought to spin some of this into thread," she cackled, pulling the bits of hair into the trash bin. "It would be soft as you, Spat," she said to the feline.

Mallabal bent down and stroked the cat that had now gingerly approached the man. He didn't like animals inside where he slept unless they were intended to eat. He smiled to himself thinking how eating a cat would surely raise eyebrows. Grannie cut off the rooty white bulb from the scallions and threw the greens into the stew. Immediately, it emitted a pungent odor. Mallabal turned from the window and sat down at the table. "Whaler," he said.

The woman smacked her lips and nodded. Her mind was like a beartrap. Whatever went in could always be retrieved, but only under her conditions. "I know just who can help. It might take some do'in, but nothin' is impossible." Her brow furrowed in thought. "An older lady; lives up in Maine. Cohen, Minny Cohen, and a pair of youngin', a boy and girl. They can help, yep." Her eyes widened as she spoke. "They come from a whaler town." Mallabal pursed his lips and leaned back in his chair. "You sure are a fine-lookin' man," she said. "Too bad I ain't younger." Her eyes met his and then dropped back to the stew, and as she looked away, he smiled as if he had a revelation. "Ambassador of freedom," he thought, "that's her name."

The covert plan began to congeal when Grannie returned to the table with writing materials. A crow-quill, inkwell, and parchment were set out before her as she sat down to compose her thoughts. With a steady hand, she reintroduced herself and referred to names of agents and stations. And though there were no guarantees to safeguard Mallabal from becoming captured, the expectation that the experienced seafarer could work his way to California aboard a whaler seemed more than promising. Actively seeking protection through anti-kidnapping statutes and the spread of free black vigilance committees, Grannie was sure her contact in Maine would find a way to secure passage and protective services for Mallabal. Her missive was succinct, and the exchange of coded words concealed the underlining message lest the note made its way into unscrupulous hands. With such sensitive information at risk of discovery, the cautious woman only trusted her letter to a personal friend of Jim Sturge, a prominent Quaker businessman and abolitionist, to carry it swiftly northward. Safety was more important than time. Consigning the next several weeks over to patience and hope, Mallabal kept his movements close to the cottage and wandered only as far as the slopes or the protection of the tangled undergrowth along the hillside.

Mallabal held a great appreciation for the old woman's generosity. Theirs was a friendship of trust and respect; a symbol of strength rooted in a common human element, compassion. Three others dwelled in his mind. Softly they would come before the arrival of dawn and the burning-off of fog-like dreams. Neville, a sharer of happiness and grief; alluring Sydney, as light as a bird's whistle and strangely discontent; and the third, his wife, pragmatic and faithful. Four pieces of rope, he knotted into one, suspended in his mind and like pictures in a gallery they fulfilled the anatomy of a man: physical, spiritual, sensual, and honorable. If he was only of one-man, extrication out from his armor of darkness remained unlikely. But if he were a man shared by four, this dubious singularity of his persona could be shed; where once dark patches were could now reveal light. No, he was not unlucky, he decided, for in one's lifetime he had something few can boast of. He would take them all with him on his journey.

———————•———————

The expectation of a reply was like waiting for the thaw; as each day passes the frozen lake gradually melts until the trapped vessel is finally set free. The letter arrived by way of the Quaker's son almost a month to the day from when it was sent. Grannie fumbled nervously with the seal as if the note was about her own son. She rested her spectacles on the bridge of her nose holding the letter close. After it was read, she was content. "You're sailin' on the Oranto," she said. "A Captain Davenport is settin' out from Rhode Island." She folded the letter and handed it to Mallabal. "Trust in the Lord with all your heart and lean not on your own understanding; in all your ways submit to him, and he will make your paths straight."

"Amen," replied the boy. It was the first remark he made since entering the cottage. He shuffled shyly over to the hearth to warm himself thinking hard of something useful to say.

Mallabal read the letter, and while he tried to imagine California, his only reference was to its mild climate. He had no reason to reject this arrangement and having no other choice, he was visibly satisfied.

"Tell Jim we'll be ready," she said to the boy. "You got that, right?" The woman's tone commanded an answer.

"Yes, Ma'm, I'm to tell my father that you'll be ready."

"That's right, now git on home and keep sharp." Then, she rewarded the boy with a sweet bun for his trouble; which he promptly gobbled up even before he had mounted his pony.

That was the last they heard from the Quaker's son for several days. Grannie stayed busy, provisioning Mallabal with dried herbs, tonics, nuts,

and a small leather book. On its blank pages, she transcribed the prepara-
tions of herbal remedies for medicinal use. With an air of subdued authority, she found it satisfying to pass along her ancestral knowledge to be
added with Mallabal's trove of Aboriginal medicines and treatments. In
gratitude, Mallabal gave the elder three gray pearls; one was payment for
the Quaker, another for the widow Cohen in Maine, and the largest for
Grannie. "The kingdom of heaven is like a merchant seeking fine pearls,"
she exclaimed upon receipt, and at once wadded up her gift in a scrap of
cloth and stuffed it into a crack in the chimney wall.

Grannie's scheme of life was unselfish. However, there was now a
part of her that felt differently. She knew it was wrong, but she had grown
quite fond of the stranger that wandered on her land up from the sea. She
had taken great pains and sacrifices to be independent, but this outlander
from so far away carried with him a gentleness she would miss. So, before
the Quaker's boy arrived with the buckboard and the chestnut mare, she
thought she had time to prepare. Perhaps it was the lonely time of the
afternoon, or maybe it was the solitude of the moment.

———— • ————

"There is always a hole in the map for wanderers," Mallabal said. Trusting
himself entirely to the guidance of destiny, he would navigate by way
of instinct.

Grannie closed the shutters as if it would shut out the whole world.
Morning would arrive soon enough fanning pale, yellow waves of sunlight just before breaking into the cottage. The Quaker's boy would arrive
before dawn bringing with him a promise and a cart. Except for the owl
mocking her sentiment with its hoots, the cottage was so quiet that the
stillness seemed to be melting down the walls from the roof. There was a
heaviness that the old woman felt, and it tired her. She slowly settled into
the chair and bent over wearily to readjust her woolen stocking that had

slipped down to her bony ankle. The orange cat stole into the room and waited as the elder renegotiated her position in the chair. She tapped her hand, and the feline obeyed, perching itself on her lap. "I won't be here when you leave," she said. "I got to tend to the Reyes baby. It's colicky. I'll leave some corn-pone and coffee out for ya. Be sure to save one for the boy." Mallabal nodded approvingly. It was growing dark, but neither of them stirred to light the oil lamp. She mulled over her statement and sighed heavily. The fact was, she didn't want to feel like a quivering beggar waiting for a handout. The eventuality of saying goodbye was imminent. She averted her eyes away and sat stroking the cat. There was much on her tongue, but she chose to remain silent.

Mallabal sat facing the hearth and closed his eyes. His mind swooned with memories sprouting from a wakeful dream. *In the first of the century, when he was a young boy, Van Diemen's Land was a wilderness walled in by trees and flamed by sunsets against a gallery of high clouds. Once swarming with life; almost everything Mallabal had loved was torn away. The "sage trees" where the elders would gather were felled, canals dug, rivers re-routed, and all simple life eradicated. The land had been captured and enclosed; he was no longer welcome. There was no word for a trespasser in his native vernacular, but this is what the natives were called. Expelled from the land once freely roamed, where generations held ceremonies; Van Diemen's Land was depopulated.* He opened his eyes and tossed a corncob into the hearth. The cat was purring keeping tempo with the light breathing of the old woman. Mallabal closed his eyes again. *He longed for the old days when he was young, before the paving of flat streets unsuited for his bare feet. But getting, like receiving, is a beggar's wish. He would have to settle his identity in a new place even though his heart was housed in a life of remembrance.*

———•———

It was a perfect morning to stay beneath the blanket; cold and damp. Only the orange cat was wise; it remained asleep beneath the folds long after the Quaker's boy had jiggled the reins and long after Grannie had slipped away with her medicine bag. And when the sun split the gray fog to warm the damp earth and seduce the buds to open, Mallabal stomped-out the flickering embers before shutting the door behind him. He climbed onto the buckboard next to the boy, offered the sweet roll, and looked straight ahead. He felt no lingering grudge or hostility against the world, rather, he thought about the woman who had taken him into her home. The track was coarse, but the boy was skilled and maneuvered the wheels along the grooved dirt road, and as they rode he chatted idly about what he perceived as the world. But when all the responses he could muster out of the man were a few perfunctory nods, the younger decided to hum instead; and that he did the whole way they traveled.

The parchment lay open on the table. The handwriting was finely scribed, well-defined and thick with ink. *"We are all visitors to this time, this place. We are just passing through, and then we return home. If you get there before I do, I will not be far behind."* Mallabal

Grannie held the paper in her hand and reread the words. She folded the letter and slipped it between the pages of her Bible. Her eyes widened, and then the old woman smiled contently.

———————•———————

She had all the makings of a fine ship; her masts stood as straight as tapers, and the bowsprit expanded beyond the prow carrying the remnants of a sea-washed nymph that once lead the way. Like all whalers, she wore the distinguishing marking needed to fulfill its mission; a pair of fitted whaleboats hung from davits and an up-side-down-spare boat wedged in between a railed-frame. A brickwork furnace sat in the middle of the deck taking up a considerable amount of space for it was a well-constructed square of ten feet in length along each side.

At the top of the gangplank stood the boatswain, a large, round-shouldered man with an unwhiskered face. A too small cap shading him from the sun rested on his yellow eyebrows. The newcomer was given a slap on the back as he made his way past the sailor. "I can see yer a strong man, that's good, we need strong men." Then he grinned exposing tobacco-stained teeth and pointed the Aborigine to the bow. There he was directed by the pitiless voice of the first-mate whose command gave Mallabal reason to be cautious. "Naow then, git below an' stow yer dunnage, 'n look lively up to the deck!" The steps leading to the forecastle led to a shadowy, triangular-shaped den already occupied by a variegated crew. Men representing all nationalities were claiming their births; though crowded together, they reacted like needles on a compass and found their own private directions. Hanging from the wall-post was a crude bulkhead lamp offering a sufficient amount of light and too much smoke. Without ado, Mallabal claimed an empty hammock, stowed his meager belongs and climbed back up into the sunshine to join the crew hauling up the great anchor.

He had nothing against the whales nor against these men who sought to hunt them. He, like the whale and the crew, would ultimately confront danger, only the whale was predictable. Mallabal recognized his vulnerability and the inescapable fragility of life, and while he was moving forward, he could not speak for the others. "Maybe," he thought, "this making of a new beginning is freedom." He looked at the others, a motley group of curious and hardened faces, and wondered who among him was also free. However, his circumstances were unique; he would not be able to leave the next generation of Van Diemen's Land the chronicles of his experiences; inflicted by the last penalty which can befall a race, few native people were remaining. Such a revelation may have been considered or justly obscured. His memory would safeguard the past and lead him to the future.

Chapter 22

A half-dozen wadded up pieces of paper lay in the bottom of the tin bucket. But finally, after several days of rewriting, Flora felt her poem was finished.

> MY HOUSE IT WAS A REAL HOME
> WITH MOTHER'S DEAR SWEET FACE
> AND COLONEL'S KINDLY WORDS
> IT WAS OUR SACRED PLACE.
> BUT LIKE A SHOOTING STAR
> THEY'VE FLOWN SO FAR AWAY
> AND NOW MY SOUL IS WAITING
> TO JOIN THEM BOTH ONE DAY.
> SO WHEN MY LIFE HAS ENDED
> WHEN PEACE HAS COME TO DWELL
> LAY ME BY THE BLACKBIRDS
> AND THEN THEY'LL KNOW I'M WELL.

The young poet gently blew across the words, and when the ink was dry, she stood up and stretched. The make-shift desk, a wooden plank placed across a pair of sawhorses, and stool occupied a cubby next to the window where sunlight would stream in during the morning and extinguish itself by late afternoon. Señora promised that if she completed her assignments each day, she would not have to attend the Minister's school. This was an arrangement that was agreeable both to Flora and especially to Julio Tamayo. He did not relish the idea that he would have been the one to take her each morning. So, lobbying for the latter, he set aside a special little space in the barn for her studies. Books and paper had been collected by the charitable-side of the Minister's wife's, although the pious woman displayed little sympathy for the child since neither Colonel nor Agnes ever found their way to the Minister's Sunday sermons.

The arithmetic book and speller were in the same spot Flora had stacked them two days ago. In just a matter of a few hours, a new weekly assignment would be delivered. Flora frowned, wriggled her nose, and sighed as if a heavy load needed to be lifted. She slipped the poem into the portfolio and opened the speller. The schoolwork was too easy, too boring, and "Absolutely, unimaginative!" she had declared. Yet all Señora could do was nod in agreement. Flora mulled over the "dull" children that attended school and smiled that she did not have to be party to their insipid games or boorish manners. Besides, they were mean. Why the one time she and Señora Tamayo went to visit the schoolhouse she over-heard the children making fun of the way Señora talked. They gathered in small groups, whispering, pointing, and some even called Flora a waif. The teacher scolded them for their ill behavior, but during playtime, they returned to their cruel ways. "No," Flora had told herself, "can't think of any reason to go to school when there's the whole world to teach me." Nature doesn't care about bells, or books, or mistakes. Flora prescribed to no formal rules or schedules; she simply acted appropriately, which was beyond the expectations of most other children. She liked to uncover acorns in the snow, read to the cows, and hide carrots for the rabbits. She would search for the green toad that had a scar on its back from a garden hoe. Snails that had lost their way were returned to the dandelion greens. She occupied her days outside, while the nights she shared with the stars and her doll. Even in the absence of Colonel and Agnes, she would take apart and put back together their words in her head.

Flora sat staring at the books, her chin on her fists immersed in thought. She pulled the arithmetic book from the pile and reluctantly opened it to the addition. *"How much do you love me?"* Colonel asked.

"A bushel full!"

"Just one?"

"No, a million bushels!"

"Oh, that's much better!"

How much do you love me?" she asked.

"To infinity!" he said.

"How much is that, Colonel?"

"That, dear Flora, is endless!"

———•———

Asa followed the telegraph poles lining the road. Only the remnants of a smoldering campfire lingering in the air gave him proof that he was not alone. He rounded the bend and tracked the scent into an encampment. There were no grand features, just a subdued clearing of solid ground made years ago from the felling of trees. The face of the camp is brown as is the base of its hillsides until you wander away from the furrowed ridge into the surrounding green wood. Who had slept under these same stars? Comrades, enemies, generals? Where are the cigar-box houses, its people, its farms? The face of the land had been forced to change, and so have the soldiers that returned. Seated on the ground by a campfire were two tramps roasting a handful of corncobs pillaged from a neighboring field and drinking barley water from tin cups. The grayer looking of the two was nursing a 3-day old toothache. His fitful groans were only slightly muffled by the dirty hand cupping his whiskered chin; he poked the fire with a stick. The other vagrant, a scruffy, bearded-fellow resting his elbow on his ragged gunnysack, sat up when Asa approached. "Know where a fella kin git a job around here?" the tramp asked.

"Why you askin' him?" said the companion. "If he knew he wouldn't tell ya." A pathetic moan emanated from the man with a toothache along with a sour smelling breath of rotting teeth.

"Want some corn, only cost ya a nickel. Picked it fresh just about an hour ago."

Asa tipped his hat and turned to survey the campsite.

The man with the abscessed tooth leaned over. "Think he's dumb," he whispered to the friend with an air of superiority.

"Dumb?"

"Ya know, he can't talk or nothin."

"Don't say," replied the older tramp and then turning to Asa he decided to test the charge with a question.

"My friend here says ya can't talk. That so?"

Asa knelt down and picked a corncob from off the embers and tossed a nickel between the two men. Like dogs fighting over scraps they lunged for the coin and within a matter of seconds were rolling over one another, each claiming they were the rightful owner of the money.

"Hey you, Yank, where ya from?" A miserable example of a man was bending over a large kettle he had "borrowed." He was stirring the vat of water that was feverously bubbling over a fire. "Shirts!" grinned the man and displayed a ragged garment draped over his stirring stick. "Only way to kill lice. Don't suppose ya got some tobacco to spare?" Asa nodded "no" as he watched the disappointed man drop the shirt back into the vat.

"He can't talk!" yelled the winner of the coin. "Got his tongue cut out. Can't say a damn thing, poor fellah."

"Not a word, not even a whistle," the other vagrant claimed, adding his part to the story. There was an indescribable bleak and barren silence as each man was caught up in his own interpretation of the statement transforming this modest stranger into a war hero.

"Damn bad luck," exclaimed the washer. "Damn bad," and shuttered with the idea of such an inhuman act.

Scrutinizing the drifter was the gimlet-eyed Bodie resting against the tree whittling a stick with his knife. The enormous blade was a hyperbole next to the piece of wood he was cutting. And though he may have appeared engaged in his work, he was as keen as the sly wolf he resembled and eavesdropped into every detail of the conversations. "I don't like Yanks," Bodie sneered. "But seems like you fought-off a formidable enemy! That takes more than guts. Too bad ya can't tell me about it, I always like to hear a good story." For a man that rarely smiled he appeared unusually animated. And with considerable clumsy effort, he pulled himself up to a standing position, wiped the blade clean on his pant leg, and slid it back into the sheath. It hung from his belt in plain view as a deterrent and warning to others. The man before him did not appear to be a vagrant, and the rogue wondered what had lured the visitor into the campsite. But it didn't take much convincing to ignore his suspicions since it was the fancy boots that dominated the immediate attention of the greedy pariah.

Asa looked above the brute's head where the clearing lifted into the rising landscape. *"Only three roads lead over the mountain. Take your men to the left flank. The enemy is formidable, but if you secure the position and keep your powder dry, you'll cover yourself in glory when you take their colors. Deprive the enemy of their trophy, men! Don't let them plant their flag unless it's the flag to surrender."* Six color-bearers had been shot down, a heavy loss for a bullet-riddled flag. Asa wondered what happened to the flag after it was handsomely won.

"Can't talk?" prodded Bodie. The question brought Asa back in from the war. "Suppose it ain't so bad, nobody's gonna ask ya any questions," he added, as he turned his intentions to the finely stitched boots. "You can camp here if you want." He pointed to the bedroll strapped to Asa's back. It was apparent that the mute might be looking for a "safe" place to sleep. We take contributions of all kinds, money is the best, but we'll take food, dry kindling, anything ya can spare." The disclaimer signified that moochers were not welcome. Asa reached into his pocket and indifferently handed the wretch a silver coin. "If ya play poker, we always like to get up a game after dark," leered Bodie and pocketed the silver." If you want, you can leave your belongings here, just be back by nightfall 'cause things have a way of disappearing." He winked. "That piece of information was free, the next won't be," he warned.

By the withering light of day, Asa ambled back to the clearing. An assemblage of men scattered about the campsite; some huddled in small groups, a few sat by themselves while the remaining waited like dogs for Frisco to serve up seconds. It was a slum of scavenged vegetables, a charity potato, and dandelion greens boiled in water. Asa looked in the pot and then dropped a burlap sack at the cook's feet. As soon as it touched the ground, the creature inside squawked and pecked, frantic to escape, but to no avail for it was abruptly grabbed up by Bodie who shook it furiously before the clambering men. Immediately a roar of gratitude resounded as loudly as if celebrating a hunter returning to an African campfire with an antelope. "Well, well, the unspoken hero has returned," chimed Bodie, "and not too soon. Frisco, what do you say to this?" he asked and reaching into the sack pulled out a guinea hen.

"Well," he said giving the bird a once-over, she's strange lookin', but got enough meat for our mulligan!" A hearty roar of approval resounded again. However, Asa paid no attention and had already drifted away, blending in with dusk. Unrolling his bedroll, he smoothed and stretched it out, sat down, and pulled off his boots. He listened to their celebration grow more exuberant, and as each man added his voice to the revelry, it drowned out the earthly appeals from the bird.

To the disappointment of all, the sun rose with the bird missing and the only meal they could look forward to eating was over-boiled vegetables and beans. Only Bodie was not feeling any displeasure for the new morning and was in an out-of-the-ordinary good mood. A most fortuitous trade had taken place sometime during the velvet hours of night. It was reasonable to assume that the mute was a good Samaritan. "Maybe," thought Bodie, "he was making up for his bad luck." All he remembered was when he woke up his boots were gone, and another pair stood in their place. With much pushing and cursing, the fat-footed man jammed his feet into the fine leather boots. He stretched his legs out, admired the ornate eagles, the pointed tips, the hammered soles; brushed the leather with his sleeve and howled with delight. He stood up, walked, and then winced. "They just need a little breaking in."

"Like a good saddle," Frisco added grinning like a sage, but Bodie did not smile back. He was too busy imagining his new life in these finely stitched boots. "Wonder if we can find that bird," brooded the cook as he scowled at the idea of beans again. But if he wanted to cook the fowl for dinner, he would have to look long and hard. Asa had gotten an early start and was well on his way to returning the guinea hen back into the wild.

Chapter 23

The North River piers are dedicated to the great ocean steamships while the East River's anchorage is dominated by both sailing vessels and steamboats. Vast in number are the ships bound for domestic and foreign ports. With so many seaworthy enterprises in one location, it would not be unreasonable to assume that lodgings near the waterways would cater to sailors and crew. And because they are adjacent to the wharves, it too would not be unreasonable to assume these establishments are in the lowliest and most squalid part of the city. Luring these seamen are weather-stained signs boasting of their specialty, "Sailor Boarding Houses." Affixed to their leaky overhangs are any one of a variety of marine relics. A ship's brass bell hangs on the doorpost to summon the landlord and hardware is placed to give the potential patron a sense of maritime familiarity purporting authenticity to the welcoming nature offered. The room charge is cheap, the squalid surroundings free, and an immediate inspection of the vestibule proves proportionately inferior. The sleeping quarters are dank, small, unclean, and crowded with narrow bunks. But despite the squalor and rancid smells, there arises the landlord's selling point, a smoky tavern filled with music, dice-boxes, cards, and women. It doesn't take long for the regimented and orderly shipman to transform into a reckless and undisciplined drunk.

Not required to have a license, the boarding house is often run by unscrupulous persons who take advantage of these shore-hungry seamen by getting them drunk and then robbing them of their money and property. The following morning the swindled sailor awakens with a hangover and empty pockets. Some were conned by the bawdy women, some cheated by gamblers, and others tricked by the innkeepers. Without any money, the only way to pay for their boarding is to sign over any future wages to the landlord, which will be handily collected by the ship's captain. The unscrupulous Captain now is guaranteed a crew, and this pitiless cycle of poverty continues.

Yet, go to any saloon, tavern, or dance hall, and the stranger will sense a feeling of camaraderie. Between mugs of ale and rum are jokes and exaggerations, recollections and arguments; there are no shortages of braggarts and boasters, and each one has a better story to tell.

The drunk seaman lifts his arms as he twirls. With one hand, he tries to steady his grog, and with the other, he leads his imaginary partner around the tavern. And while constant traffic of regulars assembles around the tables, a pair of newcomers, two crusty sailors fresh from the sea, were taking in the pleasures. Each claimed to be enjoying their rum with competing gusto. "Did ya know," said the mariner with a grizzly beard and thick eyebrows to match, "a mule is a horse and a donkey." The other eyed him with skepticism, for being a sailor, he had never been acquainted with the matters of animal husbandry nor had the thought ever crossed his mind. As to be expected, he's occupied with doubt. "Tis true," remarked the self-assured friend, "that's how come it's got such long ears, from its father, the ass!"

A chuckle followed a clinking of drinks together and the unloading of pewter. "Well," says the listener with a swagger of his tongue, "Used to be that the best ship design was 'a cod's head and a mackerel's tale,' but not sure anymore."

The interested old-salt raised his bushy eyebrow, and it shifted like a black caterpillar. "Gwa'on," he says, knowing he was taking the bait.

"Well, when it comes to a steamer I'm thinkin' it's more like a mule; a seafaring mule, that is!" Now it was the turn of the old-salt to be befuddled. "'Tis true," winked the man falling in closer. "That's why it's got sails, its mother was a Clipper, and its father was a Steamboat."

My Dear wife and son,

I have managed to keep out of trouble, and there is much trouble to be found in New York City. Drunkenness, ruffianism, and squandering shake the walls. Thanks to Mr. Swift he has kept me out of harm's way. However, my next piece of news may not give you a reason to believe this. I have been persuaded by my conscience to sail west, to California. Swift received information on what he says is on "good authority" that Mallabal is heading in that direction. We thought of plan after plan, but they all came back to me setting sail. I know this scheme is crowded with insurmountable difficulties, but it must prove successful. The trammels of slavery offer me no options. Mallabal must be found.

Forever yours,
Neville

The Pacific Mail Steamship Company was contracted to carry mail to California by way of the Isthmus of Panama. But when gold was discovered only days after the newly annexed-territory became a state, the company wagered that its services would be in greater demand and took on the route with their newly purchased steamer, the SS Carolina. At the time, other shipping companies were making the voyage, so putting money into a mail transport seemed like an uncertain but tractable gamble. Yet despite the odds of "a long shot," may it be horse racing or stocks, there is always someone willing to take a risk. In anticipation of the trip, a scheme was concocted by a wealthy English gentleman, who, while in New York on business, solicited the advice of Abner Swift. Hearing about the recent purchase by the steamship company, he was most interested in the adventure. Tickets to travel were up for sale at such a competitive price, being as competition from other lines were great, the Englishman was going to scoop them up on speculation, hoping to turn a hefty profit at resale. Not having a local solicitor, and in a hurry to further his ambitions, the agent retained the services of the lawyer. Once engaged in negotiations, Abner Swift was confident he had hooked a winner. Not only was he able to settle for a handsome fee, but he was also able to arrange passage for the determined Mr. Young to San Francisco.

With moral senses and a blind chance of success, he had secured a steamship ticket to Panama. It would take him to the Chagres River, where by way of a dugout wind his way to Las Cruces, and then across to Panama City by mule. Once there he could re-embark aboard the SS Polly headed to San Francisco. It was deemed a demanding 60-mile slog by river and trails from the Chagres to Panama City. The narrow river was winding and dangerous, taking up the first part of the journey. There were no comforts along the trip, and each passenger relied on his own belongings to use as bedding and rain cover. Swarms of mosquitoes, flies, and gnats invaded the journey, while torrential rain and intolerable heat tried to dampen the spirit. Yet, the exotic beauty of the river kept Neville from feeling let down. "You appear ill, Mr. Young. You might have a touch of fever." Miss March, a pint-sized woman with a chronic sniffle, offered her observation as her donkey walked alongside his. She was one of four missionaries that had taken the same ocean voyage and was presently heading into the jungle with several sacks filled with Bibles. "I believe you should abandon any more ideas of traveling much further and go home. A few of us have witnessed men more robust than you carried with fever to the wards at daybreak and then carried to their graves at dusk." His misery was preying on his vitals, but he would not submit to her words and so, supported by sheer will, he managed to look over with a smile and thank the woman for her advice. It wasn't until he finally reached Las Cruces where he was afflicted with joint swelling, acute fatigue, and ultimately a raging fever. Without a doctor or nurse, the native guides offered their only source of remedy; to chew fenugreek seeds. The situation for the sick man could not have been worse. Clinging to the back of his mule, he was forced to turn back or be stranded in this raw country to die. The journey across Panama had proved too arduous even for the will of this noble friendship. It was not until he was on his way back home that the diagnosis of jungle-fever proved more devastating than the illness.

Neville was sure that he saw his friend standing over the bed, but it was only the fever's wild imagination. He settled the damp cloth over his swollen eyelids. His body and soul ached while disgust constricted his temples like a cord tightening. His greatest malady was not yellow fever, rather it was his failure to find Mallabal. Neville removed the cloth and dropped it into the bowl of water. The voice in his head bleated, "Unless a man was dying, there was no excuse not to perform his duty."

"Did this mean he was dying?" His temples pulsed, his skin jaundiced, and his legs had turned thin like a pair of knitting needles. "How do you pack someone's forefather in a trunk?" his delirium stirred such questions. All of Mallabal's personal belonging, along with some of his own, had been shipped home by the good lawyer. When the trunk arrived, it delivered some hope that Neville would be returning safely with his friend. However, all optimism was dampened when a letter arrived a month later. The words were sparse, but the scrawled handwriting forewarned much more, "On my way home, alone."

Asa's heart fluttered with anticipation as he watched his mother apply a poultice to his father's chest made with the herb, yellow dock, which she also steeped in boiling water for tea. The physician wanted to leech the sick man, a remedy that was prescribed as far back as the yellow fever outbreaks in Philadelphia and Atlanta. But there was no epidemic, and as far as she knew, that same "cure" had killed George Washington. No one was going to leech her husband.

Neville was half-asleep when he was roused by someone stealing past on tiptoe. He raised steadily, sitting up in his bed. He slid nearer to the edge and smiled at the boy. Time had wedged a distance between him and his son. "What the hell happened here?" he asked. Asa searched his conscience but finding no reasonable answer he stood silent and puzzled. The father's smile altered the boy's fears. "I was just wondering what the hell happened that got you so tall?"

"You've been gone," Asa reminded him.

"So I have." He observed the youth as if he were admiring a portrait. "And handsome, did you know you were handsome?" Asa blushed and reached for the twig-like hand resting on the linen. He held it gently as if made of porcelain. It didn't feel like it belonged to the same man he remembered when he was much younger. However, as much as Neville appeared frail, his voice lifted firmly in strength from his convictions. "Asa, you know that I adhere to old-fashioned ideas," he began. "And if we want to live in a civilized society, it is necessary to respect authority." The boy nodded with affirmation. "But," said the father with a voice softer than silk, "when the authorities are wrong, then must we turn inward and follow our moral and intellectual compass." A respite of silence followed as Asa weighed the meaning of these words. "For a thinking man, there is no room for wastelands, briar patches, or wilderness; one must see clearly all sides and then proceed in fairness, even if it means breaking a few rules." Neville desired that his son be principled; he loathed supporters of blind allegiance. Rigidity in thinking was like a dry branch that would snap under even the slightest bit of pressure. He was perhaps religious, just not holy.

Day followed day; time was a Ferris wheel circling around and around, stopping to let others aboard, and then circling again. But then suddenly, when you're sitting on top of the wheel you realize how much of the world has changed. For the child, his life was without incident, as if hidden in the shadows. Asa sat staring at his father, his chin resting on the back of the chair. He had listened to the letters brought by far away ships and watched his mother tie them together with ribbon. Summer rain and winter's winds had thrashed the window. And while he was settled snugly in his bed, he would wonder where and how his father was. Finally, the man was home, and the boy was pleased. Determined as a hearse, malady is the knot that keeps a family together.

Asa remained bedside, sitting in a chair usually kept in the kitchen. His eyes darted around the room. This was his parent's bedroom, a space where he always felt safe. The dressing table and mirror were placed next to the window so his mother would have the morning light when she braided her hair. On the opposite wall was his father's armoire, an imposing piece of furniture which seemed to have a character of its own. A framed picture Asa drew of his father's whaler hung on the wall over the bureau. Everything in the room had its place, until now. The curious things his father was saying had begun to forge a breach in his harmony. But before he could ask a question a hand gently brushed across his shoulder. "It's time for your quinine, Neville." The man acknowledged his wife with a groan and stuck out his tongue. "Now behave," she laughed and turned to the dresser where she retrieved a bottle of tonic and poured out a healthy teaspoonful.

Reluctantly, the patient opened his mouth and swallowed the bitter medicine. "Yuck!"

It was moments like these that gave Asa reason to be happy and sad at the same time. He was happy they were all together but fearful that this happiness would end too soon. "So, what are you two men talking about?" she asked. "If I didn't know better I'd think you were scheming to take over the world."

"Nothing quite so sinister," Neville laughed. "Just trying to make sense of it all."

Lucie set the extra blanket by his feet, "In case you get cold, Asa will help cover you," she said. "I'll bring you some tea in a little while."

"I'd rather have some rum," he suggested. "Just a thimble full to wet my whistle?'"

However, her dog-eyed response poked a hole in his suggestion as she turned away muttering, "Men!"

Neville had traveled around the world and back and as a result had become intimate with the workings of mankind. What he saw and what he reconciled was not reassuring. There was a repetitious pattern of immoral and inhuman acts committed in all the ports he had journeyed to, all legal. Acutely aware of events in the political sphere, he was compelled to speak earnestly.

"How do you see a wilderness, as beautiful or threatening?"

Asa knew this was one of those trick questions his father liked to ask to trip him up. "I suppose it depends on how I got there. If I got there on my own free will, then I 's'pose it's beautiful."

"And if not?"

"Then I would look at it in a different way."

"How come?"

Asa bit his lip and thought. "Because if I wandered in and couldn't find my way out, I'd be lost and even if I moved ahead carefully there would be no certainty to my safety."

"What if you could escape, if you happened to find your way out, would you then be free?"

Another trap was set. Asa smiled knowingly at his father who did not show any movement, other than a slight grin. Slow and steady, the boy needed to think. "Escape, Papa doesn't mean free."

"That's quite right, Asa." His eyes glinted with approval.

"Just like Mallabal?" whispered the boy.

"Just like Mallabal."

Lucie escorted her son into the kitchen where his drawing paper and charcoal were taking up all the space on the table. A partial sketch of the neighbor's collie was laying face-up. "I like it so far," she said. It was rare that his mother did not like one of his drawings. Asa brought the picture to the window and pulled back the curtain.

"It's for money," he said.

"Money?" the woman sallied over to the window to share the last bit of daylight. "It's a good likeness, except I never did like that dog. What's its name?"

"Harry."

"Harry? I thought that was Mr. Doherty's name."

"Oh, then I'm not sure 'cause Mrs. Doherty said that the head dog's name was Harry, so I just assumed…" The boy's eyes grew wide and at once let out a loud, "oh!" He rolled-up the drawing and leaned it against several other drawings in the wicker basket.

"So, how did you come to get her to pay you?"

"I was outside sketching Harry, the dog that is, and Mrs. Doherty was hanging clothes. She must have been bored because she came over and watched me for a few minutes. She asked that when I was finished if she could buy it."

"Seems to me, you could have yourself a good little business on the side. Everybody wants a portrait of themselves," suggested his mother. "Could always use a little more money. Your father settled with the ship's company, now that they know he'd been stranded on that awful island and not dead! Seems like they owe him more than severance pay. He's just too good for his own good. All he needs is lots of rest, lots of rest." She had begun to mutter to herself, not paying attention to Asa, who was contemplating her words. "To find new is to keep moving forward," she sighed. Outside the window, the evening was approaching. Patches of blue and not very much sun were making a somber canvas called dusk.

It pained Lucie to concede that her husband was a sick man. He carried with him thoughts that crawled around in his brain but were not shared. The pinched expressions and distant eyes shifted to selected targets unknown to her. How fundamentally naïve it is to believe that he or she knows everything about another individual. But, his confinement to the house now offered the couple time to reconnect.

Neville sat in the rocker beneath the porch canopy. At times his thoughts journeyed through the past drifting from place to place; a porpoise rolling with the waves or the sound of bare feet walking the deck. Some mornings he was content to simply sit and listen to the rain or watch the cumbersome piling of clouds one over the other. In the evenings, he and Lucie would plan the future, but both knew this was merely wishful chatter. The same doubts occupied their private thoughts. The country was in great turmoil, and the future was as unpredictable as a summer storm. Much of their time was spent talking about Asa, money, and regrets.

Asa was working as much as a youth his age was expected. He was an apprentice to a shipwright and earning a fair wage. But unlike his father, he only enjoyed the building of a ship, not the sailing. He had an excellent eye for marksmanship, although he had no use for hunting. Rather, he liked to draw what he saw, not kill it. He added his wages to the family coffer, however, after finding him sketching on any available surface, his mother insisted he take some of the earnings to buy paper. The walls of his bedroom, the posts supporting the porch roof, and even the floor timbers, all were etched with charcoal.

"The boy's got the heart of an artist and the hand of a master, just not sure what good it'll do?" She reached over and tapped her husband on his hand. A corpulent robin dipped its beak into a puddle of muddy water. There was a joyful clearing in the evening sky as the sun and moon were both going their individual ways. The shrubbery surrounding the house appeared impenetrable in a citified sort of way. A low brick fence confined it away from the road, keeping the shadowy shapes sitting beneath the canopy of an old oak out of direct view.

Neville gave Lucie's hand a slight squeeze. It had been a long time since he watched a bird. "Well," he mused, "Asa sees things most of us miss. It just might come in handy one day."

"How do you draw a rainbow when the only color you have is gray?" asked the man.

"It's not the color in the paint box," replied the artist. "Rather, it's the expression of the painter."

A gentle hand pressed the charcoal over the paper as a light breath scattered the loose pieces. The sharp penciling of a face changed from a sketchy gray cloud into a detailed image. "Does he look like this?" He turned the paper in the direction of his father, pronouncing that it was nearly complete.

"Yes, why yes, I think you've captured his likeness!" exclaimed Neville.

"Well, it was your description that guided my hand. I only followed what you told me." Asa blew gently over the face and the residue scattered like a confused cloud of fog.

"So, this is your friend, Mallabal," Lucie said. She twisted her head to the side and smiled. "He has a very sincere expression. I am sure we would have liked him."

Neville smiled meekly. "I'm sure you would. Having an artist in the family certainly is our fair wind. Except for the charcoal dust on my bedsheet!"

"Oh, sorry, Papa. Here, let me finish it tomorrow when the light is better," he said and quickly rolled it up.

"Good idea, Asa; your father needs his rest. You can go get ready for supper, but first bring some firewood in and then wash your hands."

At once the suggestion was respected as Asa charged down the narrow flight of stairs tapping the rolled-up drawing along the banister rails.

For six months Neville had been home, but he was not getting better. Everything that could be done had been, and now the woman believed that the diagnosis was incorrect. Perhaps what was thought to be yellow fever was something else. A sickening perception of this thought brought forward more than fear; it brought anxiety. An aching sense of loneliness paralyzed her. Lucie looked at her husband and silently prayed.

The uncertainty of his father's health denied the boy the advantages of youth. Locality had become his universe. He was committed to his father and now to the man's convictions. It may have been a foolish act, or it may have been his resolve that drove him to hold up a banner at an anti-slavery rally. A pair of fox hounds sniffed and snorted weaving between the walkers with little respect for order. The marchers had advanced only a block when the attack on truth began in earnest. Just as the last group of protesters had joined the procession, a bystander flicked a lit cigar butt into the line. Another followed. Provoked by shouts and whistles, profanity was exchanged, a shove, threatening jeers, and then a rock heaved from the opposing side. Asa dropped his banner and instinctively grabbed behind his head. The skin was broken. Blood matted his hair while anger salted his words. He retaliated with profanity, and before he knew what he was doing, a mass of arms and fists grappled like bears, growling curses. Half-crazed babbling demanded justice and was answered with punches. A line of agitators stormed the protesters, and when the fight was over, Asa started back home a little bit taller. A man on crutches saluted him with his good arm. "It's just the beginning," the lame veteran cried. "Just wait, in a few years, you'll be fightin' for real. None of this chicken shit protesting." Asa nodded as he walked by. Like wolves take to mauling, his banner had been shredded by the mob. The only piece that survived was a scrap sticking to the bottom of his boot. His head throbbed, and he was angry; angry to have been accosted from behind. Next time, he would be ready.

His mother had a different idea. "Why you're just a child," she griped while cleaning his wound. "You're lucky you have a hard head like your father. No more protesting, no more fighting. Understand?"

"But we didn't start it. It was peaceful."

"Not that peaceful," she said and showed him the bloody rag. "Peace doesn't look like this!"

"But it can take bleeding," he muttered. A disgusted sigh exchanged his mother's degree of tolerance with impatience. "I understand," he promised.

But as much as she didn't want to admit it, she was feeling a little bit of pride. Her frustration about his fighting had mollified, and she now managed to find understanding for his conviction. But this was not a fight for a child. "Well, there's only one thing more I can do for you to make it better," she said with a bit more sympathy for his efforts and gently kissed his head. "Now, I need to tend to the tonic. See if you can distract your

father from his melancholy. He's always happy when you sit with him."
Although, she was afraid that even the boy could not abate the depression
that was brewing like wind advancing from the north. She could only
hope it would survive.

Neville was listening to the ebb and flow of the kitchen's tide. The
iron pot that was put up to boil was bubbling with a fury. Lucie moved
the crockery, set-aside the skillet, and arranged half-dozen small bottles
side-by-side. Corks were tossed into a basket for later. It was her opinion
that a decoction of minced cherry bark, loaf-sugar, and half-a-pint of gin,
administered at a quarter of-a-gill six times a day, would kill his cough
and soothe the patient. She hummed sweetly as if her voice was basted in
butter, but it was the kitchen that he heard singing.

———·———

Not a blade of grass appeared when the fog lifted revealing the dry
California mountain range. Mats of tangled kelp drifted on the water's
surface, a brown layer so thick that the progress of the ship had all but
halted. Despite its hindrance, the kelps' utility was not ignored for rocking on this mass of seaweed were nesting gulls and pelicans. In 1847, Yarba
Buena was a village of shanties, a few dozen residents, and half-dozen
trading vessels. But during the first half of 1849 with the discovery of gold,
it acquired over ten-thousand people and a new name, San Francisco. This
drowsy city meant for only eight-hundred was grossly unprepared for its
tumultuous growth. Its current state offered few accommodations: crude
wooden buildings, canvas tents, saloons, gambling houses, and muddy
streets. Abandoned by their crew and captains in search of gold, hundreds
of vessels remained anchored in the harbor like ghost-ships, lonely and
barnacled. The town laying at the foot of the mountains resembled Babel,
and like Babel, the disembarked scattered across the region to find their
dreams. Throughout the last half of the year, one thousand immigrants
a week were arriving. The first foreign and Indian gold seekers came

from lands to the north, south, and west of California. Native Hawaiians, Chileans, a smaller number of Peruvians, and Mexicans arrived either overland or a combination of land and sea. News of the California strike arrived in New Zealand by way of American whaling ships, while at the same time newspapers from Hawaii notified the Australians. Word of the gold strike reached Canton aboard American and British trading vessels, adding a new wave of Chinese immigrants seeking their fortunes. By 1850, thirty-thousand people had arrived, though most did not remain in the harbor city and hastened their way to the mines and rivers.

A wall of foreign voices amassed, and although these first arrivals may have worked side-by-side with little derision, seeing as there was plenty of California to go around, as more new-comers tried to stake their claims, hostility and prejudice became the great divide. The first foreign miners' license tax, aimed at Latin Americans, was adopted while the Act for the Government and Protection of Indians, contrary to the name, denied native Californians the right to testify in court and allowed white Americans and Californians to keep native people as indentured servants. Mallabal may not have been out-of-place in this mismatch of cultures; however, he wanted no part of the ill-fated promises that were luring the greedy prospector to dig and pan for gold. He found this world troubling. A familiar sense of distrust summoned him to be wary of San Francisco and its inhabitants. On the other hand, he was a man that was not afraid of being pricked by thorns, and upon his arrival opened his eyes to the opportunities he could take advantage of. Entrepreneurs had set up bar-ber tents, sold bulk canvas, and weighed out soap. There was money to be made in shovels and picks, grog-shops and cigars, water-barrels, dried beef, salt, and prostitution. The influx of so many and the scarcity of provisions enabled supply and demand to govern what the vendor could charge. It did not take very long for poor diets, fleas, coldwater streams, and tainted water to contribute to the ill health of the prospector. While many knew of taking cream of tartar and vinegar in combating scurvy, there were no doctors to guide these unprepared "Argonauts" for their future ailments of dysentery, fever, dyspepsia, and ague. For the few who had reached the port with advice as to what salves and tonics to pack among their shovels and picks, such an afterthought was often too late for the others. Where to find these palliatives was difficult and often impossible.

A vast number of flimsy canvas tents and fire-trap shanties littered the landscape. Overcrowded boarding houses tied cots together and hung muslin partitions to accommodate as many lodgers as possible. But if a person were clever, he might arrange a more amicable place to sleep. Such a decision of where to find shelter was going through Mallabal's mind when a thick-set man leading a woefully sad mule came walking up the street. The dusty animal limped, and the dusty man cussed, both were observably quite miserable. Mallabal, with regard to the Mexican's dilemma, approached them with compassion, showing an immediate interest in the animal. Such a mule was more than a companion, it was more than likely his livelihood. "It is his hoof," an irritable sigh followed as the owner bent over and lifted the foot. "I thought it was a stone, but no, it is not a stone." He dropped the leg, and the mule shifted uncomfortably. "Don't pull your ears back at me," glared the Mexican, but he could not be angry for very long; theirs had been a long friendship. Mallabal knelt and lifted the sore hoof and for a long minute he pondered.

"I can help," he said and rose.

"Si?" asked the man.

The Aborigine nodded "yes," and a brisk trade sprang up between him and the mule-dealer. Herbal medicine for the mule's hoof in exchange for a bed of hay to sleep on in the barn; such a reasonable transaction of services was bartered and agreed upon.

There was nothing more than a hint of daylight when Mallabal waited on line for a loaf of Isidore Boudin's sourdough bread. Born in Burgundy, the Frenchman was the son of a master baker, who originally emigrated to Yabar Buena in 1835. "Ever read the inscription on a grave-stone?" he asked, wrapping up a crusty loaf. "You can thank a stone-carver." The baker grinned, and as he handed Mallabal the bread, he leaned over the counter pulling the buyer in with a clandestine look. "Take my advice," he said in a low voice, "a man can profit not by competing, but by support-ing." And then he winked. Mallabal turned over in his head what the baker had said and nodded at the man.

The next morning Mallabal rose with the sun. The empty day needed to be filled, and here in the early hours, he knew what to do. He had never thought of himself as a healer nor a salesman, only a survivor. Mallabal opened his haversack and saw his future: elixirs, teas, and herbs. He reached inside and felt the small leather pouch of gray pearls, the booklet from Grannie, and his freedom paper. Everything he needed was secure. "Perhaps this San Francisco," he decided, "wouldn't be so bad after all."

Chapter 24

The Doctor was well-liked and trusted, especially among the elite whose social graces were tirelessly honed. It would be a far-stretch for anyone to consider that Richard Bushnell was capable of illicit behavior or salacious improprieties. He was an honorable man that had served his country during the war and continued years after to commit himself to those who had also served. Yet, despite all the distinctions placed upon his character, his untarnished reputation was about to be tested. His secret had inadvertently been discovered and placed in the possession of his wife. Sydney sat at the dinner table across from her husband with proof of Richard's ruthlessness. And though she had unintentionally lost her heart to another, at no time during their matrimony did she yield to her desires. The couple had reached a mature stage in their relationship where the comforts of the home and their place in society remained intact. Only memory had fallen heavily upon them both.

The conversation between the two was cordial, animated, and as usual trite. She recounted her day with little more alacrity than, "it was good," and "Samantha Chandler's granddaughter was on the society page," while Richard nodded his head affirming that he was listening. Sydney's eyes were fixed upon her husband, weighing his every move with newfound scrutiny.

"What are you staring at, you're looking at me as though I have picked up your white scarf with ink on my fingers!" he said and then wiping his mouth on the dinner napkin placed it on the table. "Have I done something wrong?" he asked. Sydney smiled tenderly, patted her lips and then set the napkin back on her lap. Again, the man drove his question forward in a manner that required a response. "What is it? You've been acting strangely all through dinner." It was a long table, and suddenly it seemed so much bigger. Sydney felt paralyzed by the question; she wished that they were seated closer together so she would not have to speak loud enough for Lucretia to hear. The swinging door into the kitchen was shut, yet she wasn't convinced that the matronly cook could not overhear. Richard looked at his wife with amusement; she was still beautiful. He ran his thoughts up and around her ruffled dress, following her long hair pulled up in a French twist, and then slowly down the bare skin on her neck. She was wearing a single pearl necklace, and he wondered why he had never noticed it before. She reached forward as if wanting to grasp his hand but fell upon the wine glass instead. She lifted it up by the stem and tipped it to her lips. "Well," he asked.

"Well, what?"

"What's going on?"

"I found some of your pictures," she said with a tone thick with ridicule while the irony in her contempt almost made her laugh.

"What pictures?" he questioned. But before she could answer, his dubious expression turned to acknowledgment. "Now my love, you're not jealous of a few pictures?"

"I don't give a damn for your pictures," she snapped. "I only care that you lied."

"Lied? There can be no lie for something that you knew nothing about."

She stared at him with indignation. She knew that he was correct; it was only because of her snooping that the cigar box was revealed. The lewd images were not her concern; only his involvement with Mallabal's disappearance gave her reason to loathe him. "I didn't think you were capable of such a heinous act," she whispered. "But now, I know it was you. You were the one that…"

"That what!" he snarled. "What heinous crime are you accusing me of? If you have something to say, woman, say it or keep your damn mouth shut!"

Sydney placed her hands on her lap; she didn't want him to see that she was trembling, not with fright but with anger. He had made it impossible for her to keep her accusations to herself; her mask of composure was cracking, and she was getting lost in disgust. "When I get through with you, Richard Bushnell, you will be sorry!"

"Sorry, sorry for what?"

"For what you did to Mallabal!" The explosive nature of her accusation brought the immediate entry of the cook's curious head peering through a partial opening of the door.

"Is there anything I can get for you, Mrs. Bushnell? Some more asparagus, perhaps?"

Too angry to speak, Sydney shook her head and waved her hand for the maid to leave. The door eased shut, and the pair of feet on the other side shuffled away.

"I suppose the entire staff now thinks I'm a monster," remarked the Doctor. "The least you could have done was ask her to take our plates away and bring dessert. I could do with some of that apple cobbler we had yesterday, what about you?"

Sydney looked up at the mantle clock where time had ticked away the years. It was the same one that had resided in her family home, and as such, she felt a strong attachment to this object. It always kept very reliable time unless someone neglected to wind it. There remained only the slow tick of the clock between unspoken thoughts as the storm of words was lifting. "Yes, apple cobbler would be nice," she agreed.

"I hear they are going to start up the bandstand again. We were thinking of taking some of the patients; as a reward for good behavior. What do you think?"

"Charming idea," she said. "Music always seems to be able to tame the wild beast."

"Yes," he mused adding a sigh of complacency. "That is one way to tame the wild beast."

Doctor Bushnell removed the photographs from his armoire and counted them out. Just as he suspected, a set of duplicates was removed. He frowned as he put them back into the box. He refused to let Sydney ruin his evening. He drew from his breast-pocket a leather booklet and in small neat-letters wrote a note to himself. "Delusive on subjects." He placed the book on the night table alongside the cigar box. He wondered how long his wife had been harboring suspicions about him. A wife of a public figure was placed in a unique position, and it would be a shame for reputations to become soiled. He sat down on the edge of his bed and pulled off his shoes. But removing one's stockings at the end of the day was the ultimate surrender to night; which he was not quite ready for. He enjoyed spending time in the privacy of his bedchamber, it was the one room of the house where he had overseen the decorum; and even though Sydney did not like the framed-drawing above the bureau, it remained a favorite. Hunting dogs represented what all men wanted, loyalty. "You must get rid of those dogs," she had said. He wasn't sure why she had such an aversion to the picture. But now her displeasure resonated with new meaning. "It's time to get rid of some of these old things and start fresh. Store it in the attic if you won't dare to part with it!" She could be so convincing. Yet, when it came to this picture it had become a sticking point, her will against his. "On the other hand," he thought, "getting rid of useless objects can be a sort of catharsis. I imagine the attic would have been a compromise we both could have lived with."

It was times like this that she felt a need to have her tea and tonic; it helped calm her nerves. Her mind was not in possession of its natural poise and clarity. She did not feel any disappointments or gloom, just a slight sense of euphoria. Sydney's desire for revenge slipped away like a dream. There was a light knock on the door, and she wasn't at first sure if it was a figment of her imagination. But when it came again, she smiled. "Mallabal, is that you?"

The door opened and then quickly closed behind the figure. "It's me," whispered a woman's voice. She floated to the bedside and gently shook her foot. The semi-conscious woman slowly aroused, but the half-lids did not wish to open. Her private world did not wish to be disturbed while she was in a sentimental dream. Rosalie set the teacup she was holding on the table. "I will leave this with you, it's hot, just the way you like it."

Sydney opened her eyes and turned her head. She reached for the teacup, but her hand seemed too heavy to lift. "Let me," said the voice. She felt someone help her tip her head forward and gently place the rim to her lips. After several sips, she rested her head back on the pillow again and fell into a deep and very lovely slumber.

———— • ————

Sydney poured over the correspondence with indifference, although the recipients would not recognize the ambivalence she had for the task at hand. Each note executed with precise and diminutive handwriting was written on linen stationery and signed with her scrolling initials, *SB*. There was an undercurrent of annoyance that she felt, having to remain indoors when it was so beautiful outside seemed more like a punishment than a choice. Even the staff had gone out; Lucretia to the market and Rosalie was running an errand for Richard. He sent her away directly after breakfast with money to buy his favorite mustache wax and chocolate for herself. The last time the reluctant maid went shopping at the gentleman's shop, she returned smitten with the clerk, a tall, gray-haired man with a salt and pepper beard, and a pencil stuck behind his ear. "Andre," she laughed when she repeated his name as if she were a girl of twenty. "It was his accent that attracted me to him; he is French," she said. Sydney dipped the pen into the inkwell, held the nub over the parchment, and signed her initials with an extra-long tail after the *B*.

"I never thought a French accent was very attractive," she thought, wondering if this 'Andre' would have been impressed with her. "He's most likely married," she had told Rosalie. "Most of the good ones are." However, the mention of another woman did not deter the maid from keeping her hopes high, and when Dr. Bushnell suggested she run the errand, there was not the usual eye-roll that she saved for him.

By eleven o'clock Mrs. Bushnell had completed all her correspondence and placed the envelopes on the Wedgewood plate in the foyer. The conversation from a few evenings ago still lingered in her mouth like a bad taste. "What a jackass," she thought. She moved slowly through the foyer and back into her sitting room when she heard a light knock on the door. Her first thought was that perhaps Lucretia had forgotten her key, the woman was forever becoming more and more frivolous. However, the idea of replacing the woman came along with a parade of interviews and reference checks; all of which seemed to be more bother than it was worth. Her dress rustled as she briskly walked to attend to the door. "Have you forgotten your key?" she asked, and with a good notion to chastise the woman, she hesitated, for rather than being greeted by the saintly cook, a man with a serious cold expression was relighting his cigar. "May I help you?" she asked, assuming the homely man was looking for her husband.

"Are you Mrs. Richard Bushnell?" he asked.

The space between her and the stranger appeared to shrink as he stepped into the frame of the portal. "Who wants to know?" A feeling of uncertainty was looming.

The man smiled and then turning to the street waved his hand at the fellow waiting in the carriage. "Be a minute," he called. The other looked up and tipped his hat. "Don't be afraid, Mrs. Bushnell. We are here to help you." Again the man advanced, and within a few moments, Sydney found herself standing in her foyer and the front door closed.

"If it is money that you want, I have none!" she trembled. Slowly she backed away with all intentions of escaping up the stairs.

"I am not here for your money, Sydney. I may call you Sydney if it is alright."

The startled woman laughed with a nervous pleasure, hoping to deflect away from her appearing afraid. "I don't believe you have told me your name."

"Sergeant Dennehy," he said removing the unlit butt from the corner of his mouth. Glancing about for an ashtray, he shoved the cigar in his pocket.

"A police officer, why didn't you say that before." A sudden sigh of relief was expelled, and at once the woman became reanimated. "Please, would you like to come in. My husband is at work, but if you would like, you are welcome to leave your calling card." He followed as she directed him to the parlor. "Would you like a drink?" she asked noting his eyes scanning the whiskey bottles. He nodded "no," although he was lying. What he really wanted was to sit down in one of the plushy chairs and have this bitch serve him up a nice big glass of whiskey from one of the fancy bottles. His eyes roamed, and his mind began to go to places that would get him into trouble. "Well, if you didn't intend to call on my husband, then I hope you can tell me the reason for your visit." This time it was Sydney's eyes that roamed over the officer. He was a ruddy fellow with an orange beard and scuffed shoes. He could have been a peasant if they were living in another time. "Yes," she thought, examining his every move; she almost felt sorry for him. "Dennehy, the only Dennehy I know is from the hospital. My husband has mentioned...." She paused and looked up at him wide-eyed. "I don't suppose you are that Dennehy?"

"Patrick Dennehy," he added giving her more of a clue.

"Patrick Dennehy," she rolled the name over several times but shrugged. "Are you the same man?" she asked.

"That I am, Missus. Now, to the nature of my business. "I," he said and then corrected himself, "we are here to help you." A long shadow had stealthy entered the room. Standing directly behind him was his counter-part, the other half of the "we."

"Come on Pat; we don't have all day!" The impatient man wore a rumpled pair of trousers under an oilskin raincoat. How he came in without being detected could only be attributed to his wiry build. He was hatless, having left his bowler in the carriage. Although he was in the room for only a few moments, his presence made a frightful impression upon the woman.

Sydney walked behind the sofa, placing the sturdy furniture between herself and the men. "I think you both had better leave," she requested and held her hand out towards the door, gesturing for them to go.

"You look flushed, Mrs. Bushnell. Here, let me take your pulse," but as the rumpled man, who called himself Doctor Newall approached, she ran to the opposite end of the room. "There, there, no need to be worried," he said slowly trailing her until she unwittingly pinned herself into the corner. "We want to help you," he whispered talking to her as if she were a frightened animal. Lifting her trembling hand, he pressed it to his cheek.

Astounded by his advances, she pulled her hand away and hissed, "What is this all about! When my husband finds out about this intrusion, he will have you arrested. He is a very important man, you know!" The sound of her indignation instilled a newfound boldness. "I want you to leave, both of you!"

Doctor Newall had something in his face she recognized. She glanced around the room and noticed the policeman had sat down. His buttocks rolled over the seat like an overstuffed bread pan. He was a sloppy fellow, and it disgusted her. "Your husband has sent us here," the Doctor said. "You are not well." She watched his lips move and as he spoke there was an echo in her head that repeated each word. "If you do not go with us voluntarily, we will have to carry you out."

"Carry you out." She wondered if he was finished. The parlor was growing incredibly warm. *"Why won't he take off his raincoat? He must be very hot wearing that sticky thing."*

"Do you understand what I have said?"

Sydney barely had time to digest his words when Dennehy stood up and waved a piece of paper before her. "This is a legal document obtained by your husband, Richard Bushnell."

The mention of his name invited suspicion. "Let me see that," she snapped. But her request was ignored, and he intentionally pocketed the paper.

"Mrs. Bushnell, your husband has deemed you insane." Such a statement should have provoked a gasp, yet it was smothered by stillness, and as such, no sound was immediately uttered. Dennehy hesitated as if awaiting her cue, but the woman remained silent. The explanation was easily carried out as if he had repeated it many times before. "The legal system empowers men, husbands, in particular, to institutionalize women." He reached back into his pocket, unfolded the paper, and after a clearing of his throat read aloud. "The statute expressly states that the judgment of the Medical Superintendent, to whom the husband's request is made, is all that is required for him to incarcerate his wife for an indefinite period of time." He looked up and into Mrs. Bushnell's stunned face. The paper appeared to shake in what was once a steadfast hand. "Therefore, Sydney, your husband has made all the arrangements, and we are to deliver you to the asylum."

"Insane, me, insane!" she shrieked. "On what grounds?" she demanded.

"On the grounds that you're delusional," said Dr. Newall. "Do you know what that means?"

"Of course I know what that means. I may be accused of being insane, but I am not stupid!"

"Good, then since you know why, we have no other reason to remain here," Dennehy said, and with one hand placed upon her shoulder, he gave her a slight nudge towards the door. Immediately her mind began to reassemble the past few days. The two men before her ignited a fear that rose as quickly as a brush fire. With most men, she could charm her way out, but they were different. They were not men; they were monsters. "Don't touch me," she warned, and like a sly cat, she slid out the door and slammed it shut. Without looking back, she ran into the foyer, only to be welcomed by the rattling of the front door's lock. "Lucretia," she shouted, "is that you!" Her heart panted wildly as Dr. Newall was turning over the armchair in his way. Sydney reached for the knob just at the same time the door was pushed open. "Help me!" she screamed, "Help me!" But the world that expanded outside the open door drew her back into herself. "You've come home," she whimpered, "you've come home."

The wind blew lightly, coming in from the east. Dr. Bushnell stood beneath the overhang, took off his hat, and kissed her cheek. "Yes," he affirmed "Now, come along, we don't want the neighbors to talk," he explained.

There are a few alternatives that a dream could devise, but this was not a dream. Sydney looked frantically about. The neighbors, they would help her; but as soon as the idea alighted the clammy skin of the raincoat was draped around her so tightly that she could not move her arms. The sweet smell of mustache wax rubbed off onto her cheek as the kidnapper tried to console her. His fingers pressed hard into her arm, as he guided her down the steps. A small dog traipsing through the garden stopped and wagged its tail. "Rex!" she shouted, but if it recognized her it mattered not; it was only a dog. She thought she saw the neighbor's door opening, but the sun was too bright, and its brilliance blinded her. "Help, help," she screamed.

"Yell all you wish, but no one will help you. I am your protectorate," Bushnell reminded his wife as he herded the woman into the small cab. The policeman lifted the reins and with a single snap of the whip they were trotting down the cobblestone street.

Like watercolors splashed on wet paper, everything was a blur. The bright yellow of the morning was running into the black interior of the cab. There was no distinction between happiness and tragedy; in a single hour, the lines were crossed. "When I get out of this filthy coach, I will kill you!" she screamed, wriggling like a moth trying to release itself from a cocoon.

"Mrs. Bushnell, when we get to the hospital I am afraid that I will need my coat back," mocked the disheveled doctor. He breathed heavily and wiped his brow with his handkerchief. The confined space grew warmer, and his ruddy face now flushed a blotchy crimson.

Sydney studied him with contempt having learned the truth about her captives in a most underhanded way. "Are you making a joke?" she asked.

"No, my dear, this is no joke. When you get to the asylum, we will exchange my coat for something lighter in fabric and color, a white dressing gown." But it was not what he had just said; rather it was what he did after this statement which provoked Sydney to lean forward. It was not a laugh, but rather, a single short scoff articulated under his breath.

"You stinking dunghill," she snarled, and with all the might and saliva she could muster, she spat directly into his face! And what a glorious execution it was, for what was not caught up in his beard and eyebrows was trickling down his cheeks and neck. "There, we're even," she laughed, squirming back into the crotch of her seat. "I took your shit, and now you've got my spit!"

The stunned man removed his handkerchief again and wiped his humility off of his face. He balled up the sticky cloth fumbling with it like a chastised schoolboy until it was stuffed back into his pocket.

"You see, Newall," the husband remarked to the miserable man sitting across from him. "It is like I told you, she's mad."

———— ·—— ————

Lucie Young was a plain, to-herself woman. She was devoted to her husband, assured her son was well-educated and maintained a respectable and clean home. When Asa grew from boyhood into manhood, he enlisted in the army, earning her boasting rights about him as an honorable young man. And when he went off to war, she urged him to take care of himself, advised him to keep a supply of cayenne pepper on hand (for indigestion), and to only write if he had good news to share. As such, very few letters were exchanged. She ignored the flowerbeds having determined the blossoms were destined for funeral wreaths yet dusted his room as if he would return at any hour. During all his years growing up he never remembered his mother being sick, so it arrived as a complete surprise when a telegram from the Military War Office was delivered. It was a slim letter that he read over very slowly, then he folded it up and placed it in his pocket. "Anything wrong, Young?" asked the Sergeant.

Except for the time he had witnessed an amputation, he had never felt so nauseous. "Seems that my mother has died," he said. "And with my father in his grave, guess I'm an orphan." He stared at the words; such a letter was astonishingly nonchalant for its content.

"Sorry, Private." His sincerity sounded genuine, but after a while death was so frequent that the soldiers' senses become dull. "Want a minute?" the Sergeant asked.

Asa looked up. "Sir?"

"Just wanted to know if you need a minute; ya know." But Asa didn't know what good a minute would do. When he had gone into battle for the first time, there was a mixture of impatience and fear and wonderment. But today, he was dangerously close to understanding. It is the experience of astonishment which constitutes the meaning of war; it is the moment of returning not as partaker but as a witness. Then, after the violence of battle, there is an unfettering from everyday life, and the soldier turns to stone. Asa had become a vessel so bare that it seemed like he could never have been filled with life. War is alive through the organisms that assume its character, and it was sucking the life blood out of each man and woman in its way. Asa held no grudges against the enemy that had set him in their rifle sites. He was a thief that had stolen lives too. But war is sternly predictable, ending up always the same, and he no longer wondered how it could be summed up in a single telegram.

"No Sir, I don't need a minute."

———•———

The gardener entered the courtyard with his hoe resting against his shoulder. He was a coarse man with gnarled fingers twice the size of most others. He wore a new coat of mud on his shoes which left behind a wake of dirt as he walked. But the fact that he was the caretaker of the flowers pardoned him for leaving behind a path of black clay. The sight of the gardener made the woman call out his name. "Spud!" But he was trained not to talk to the patients, so he ignored her. "Spud!" she yelled, this time louder. She thought he looked her way. "Come over here and meet my new friend!" The gardener reached for the latch but was stopped by a hand grasping his. "Spud, come on over and say hello!" He gave a grudging turn of the head.

"Shit!" he said pulling his hand away and let the gate swing closed again.

"Come on and say 'hello'!" she cackled and walked back to the bench. "That's Spud," explained the woman to Sydney. "Know why they call him that, cause he's from Ireland. Get it?" But the forlorn patient was not in the mood to talk. "Cute, isn't he? What I could do with a man like that!"

Sydney fingered her gown, pressing her hands to the sides.

"They're scratchy, but you'll get used to that. After a while, you won't even care that you look like a sack of potatoes! Nobody around here gives a damn what you look like. You wouldn't believe that I was once rosy-cheeked and fair, quite desirable." She leaned over and whispered, "I did things no one would dare." There was a smile that ran across Sydney's mind when she heard this, and she wanted to laugh. So, this poor wretch held a secret too. Did all women have the same kind of forbidden desires? A man can be hungry and satiate his lustful appetite, but when a woman does the same, she's committed as delusional. Three days ago, she was a free woman enjoying the pleasures of a comfortable life. Three days later, she was under lock and key of a lunatic asylum. She looked down at her feet and frowned. It was the taking away of her clothes that were most demeaning. She wanted her shoes back. She ran her hand across her head. "Don't worry dearie, if you play your cards right you won't have to have your head shaved! It's all a matter of not annoying the vermin."

Hatred welled up inside and then tears. "I'm not crazy!" she cried. "I'm not crazy!"

A small gathering of three approached the mournful woman until there was a gathering of seven surrounding the bench. "What did you do to her?" asked a pockmarked woman.

"Nothing, she just started to cry."

"Well, you must have said something."

"Do you want to hold my doll?" invited the gray-haired woman. Sydney pulled her hands away from her eyes and through her teary lens saw the outstretched gift of a bald-headed doll with a pink dress. "Here take it, her name is Bella."

"Bella?" repeated Sydney. The yellow-toothed woman grinned. Such was the strange world of coincidences found even within the confines of these impenetrable walls. "Bella," Sydney laughed, and with a cry of hilarity, she said again, "Bella!" The gray woman wriggled the doll and then cradled it in her arms. The others, finding this all amusing suddenly echoed the cry, "Bella, Bella, Bella!" The name grew louder and louder until what was once an amusing chant had turned grotesque.

"Stop this now," demanded the attendant, "unless you all stop shouting I will have you transferred to the Fifth Ward."

The threat of the Fifth Ward sent the women scattering like a flock of frightened sparrows. All except the gray lady that was still standing over Sydney. "Even Bella?" she asked the attendant.

Incensed by the question, the aggravated attendant snatched the doll away. "How many times have I told you that you're too old for this?"

"No, no, give it back, it's my baby, give it back!" cried the frantic woman and reaching into the cradled arms, the heartless woman yanked away the doll and threw it over the fence. "My baby, you killed my baby!" Too horrified to move, the old woman stood in place and moaned, still rocking her arms back and forth. "My baby, oh my poor baby."

For Sydney, the presence of such a callous act brought her to her knees, and with a blood-curdling cry she burst into uncontrollable sobs of despair and wept.

———•———

A half-rotted corpse appeared in the melting snow. The dead man would not have been of much interest to anyone, except that he was the photographer at the Saint and Dickie Portrait Studio. The flamboyant partner, Mr. Dickie, had drowned years ago during a battle retreat across the Tennessee River. The lucky one, Mr. Saint, had made no mark while serving in the war. He was honorably discharged and went back home to New York to resume his business. But when the war ended it triggered the gathering of similar businesses. There was hardly a block in the city that did not have a portrait studio; the spirit of competition brought prosperity and fame for some and an indifferent decline for others. No one remembered seeing Mr. Saint leave his room above the studio and no one remembered if he returned. "Apparently, not," confirmed the newspaper reporter. Sydney grew pale when she read the half-buried article in the newspaper. "There are presently no leads or motives for the murder," reported Detective Chandler of the Broadway Precinct. "The only clue is that his studio was ransacked, presenting speculation that the killer was looking for something."

Sydney leaned into the newspaper becoming one with the article when her eyes took a nonlinear path. The word before her scorched the paper. "Murder?" Her mouth went dry as she tried to catch her breath. She felt as if she too had been violated and wondered if any pictures of herself were among the looted items. The walls of the recreation room had grayed like the ceiling and floors. Three barred windows metered light into the room and through the slats and over the garden wall there was a clear view of the world as she knew it. Sydney sat in one of the chairs, and though she wanted to pull it closer to the table, it had been secured to the floor. The attendant had loaned Sydney her newspaper, with the promise that she would not fold or tear any of the pages.

"Murder, what's that about murder?"

Sydney glanced up and in the first flash of recollection, a woman that had possessed her memory just a few weeks earlier was the very same person speaking. Her heart suddenly was filled with such loneliness that she almost wept with happiness to see a familiar face. "Margaret?"

"You know me?" questioned the wretch. "You look too fancy to be in here. But even crazy can be fancy," she cackled.

"I'm not crazy," warned Sydney, "my husband says I am, but I'm not."

"They all do," laughed Margaret. "But you'll survive, women are like cats, we've got many lives." She dropped her knitting into the basket by her feet and shoved it back under the table. "What makes us different from them is our cunning." She tipped forward and knocked on the table for good luck. "Play poker?" she asked.

"Not well," Sydney admitted.

"Just remember, don't let 'em think you're winning. That's how you got to play this game, don't let 'em think you're winning. No one can live on hope. Hope is bullshit in here. You'll stay sane if you remember who you are." Margaret rubbed the back of her neck and stretched. "What's that murder, shit?"

Sydney pointed to the newspaper. "Just someone I once knew a long time ago. He may have been murdered."

"Don't say," she said and grinned having gotten pleasure from Sydney's remark. Her thoughts drifted loose, slipping between the bars on the windows. "If I could get out, ya know where I'd go?" Sydney nodded "no." "I'd go find my friend's baby." She tapped her finger against her temple while conjuring up her next remark. "Just remembered, it couldn't be a baby anymore; by now the squeaker is a little missy. I'm only in here on account of my friend. She's like a marker you choose when you walk in the woods. The way out is to follow the markers back. You can't follow your footsteps 'cause they get washed away. But the marker, like a tree or a bush, they'll still be there when you return." She yawned and displayed her broken tooth. "What's your marker?"

A flurry of images flashed, but only one settled to the forefront. "Revenge," Sydney said.

"That's pretty good," remarked the woman. "Not sure where it'll take you, but if it suits your purpose, I can respect that."

"How do you plan on finding your friend's child?"

"I got a marker out there," Margaret said pointing to the bars. She glanced about, her eyes darting from the window to the door, and then back to Sydney. She put her fingers to her lips and spoke. "He used to be in here, and I made him promise. He'll help me," she whispered. "The artist kind are all heart."

"Artist?"

"Well, he was a soldier and an artist."

"Asa, was his name is Asa?" Sydney petitioned an answer with her gloomy mood.

"Shit, why is it that you know everyone's name?" the suspicious woman asked and grabbed Sydney by the hair, jerking her head backward. "You a spy, cause if you are I'll stab you right here and now with this." Pulling a knitting needle out from the basket, she ran the pointed end across the nap of the pearly neck.

"Go ahead, do it," cried Sydney. "Do it!" she dared. "Do it!"

"Crazy bitch!" laughed Margaret. "You're the craziest bitch in here!"

A darkness fell over Sydney at the same time she felt her whole-body stiffening. A man silently sidled up behind Margaret and without making a stir tossed a rubber blanket over her. The concealed woman screamed in horror as she frantically attempted to challenge Carl, a large and unsympathetic attendant who handily proceeded to restrain the overwrought patient. She cursed and struggled to set herself free, trying to claw her way out from beneath the tent, but the oversized ward was not the least bit moved by the profanity and found her expletives more amusing than alarming. "Time for a nice cold bath and then bedtime restraints!" mocked Carl as he dragged her away. "Maybe even a pair of mittens, but not before we clip these nails."

"No, no!" cried Sydney, and unable to accept this load of misery, she lifted her arms above her head as if to repent. "Please, don't! She didn't mean any harm."

"Shut your trap!" scolded Mary and pulled the lamenting woman to her feet. "If you weren't Dr. Bushnell's wife you'd be off to the baths too."

An immediate crackle of thin whispers ignited as if across a telegraph wire, and in a matter of moments the entire room was abuzz with, "Hear that, why she's Dr. Bushnell's wife." The pale women in matching yellow smocks leaned against the walls like spiders delighted in the gossip.

"Let's go, ladies!" A voice rumbled like thunder and howled with such force that the room grew quiet and shivered. Mary waited by the door, her arms akimbo until the stragglers had all lined-up single-file. Like bizarre shadows swaying, rocking, toddling, some on tip-toe, they followed her down the corridor; all except Sydney who walked ladylike, appearing the most out-of-place one of them all.

———•———

Rosalie stood outside Dr. Bushnell's office, the picnic basket dangled by her legs. The doctor had been quite emphatic that coming down to the hospital would only be a waste of time. *Sydney was in too fragile a state for visitors; what she needs is a safe environment where she can get the professional help she needs.* "In here?" thought the maid. Her glances fell over the ten-ebrous hallway. "In here among the wretched, the imbeciles, the slow, the abandoned?" She rapped on the door and waited. Rosalie hated the build-ing already, with its barred windows and gloom.

An old man dressed in a worn-out garment and smelling of spoiled milk was being led by an attendant. He stopped in front of the office, readjusted his dirty eyeglasses, and craned his neck forward to get a better look at the curious woman. "Come along, it isn't nice to stare," scolded the attendant. The patient shuffled a few steps, turned and smiled; Rosalie was nauseated, but smiled back, ashamed of her disgust. She knocked impatiently on the door and wondering if she should turn away when it opened. A lanky man stood between her and the entrance. A few seconds of awkwardness settled over the open doorway before the visitor spoke up. "I'm Rosalie, Mrs. Bushnell's companion. Please let Dr. Bushnell know that I have brought some of her things from home." She lifted the basket up and waited for the secretary to take it from her.

"A picnic?" said Vole. "How very thoughtful," and at once, intrigued by the directness of this Chinese woman, he stepped aside and let her enter. "I am afraid Dr. Bushnell has been called away. Perhaps I can take it to her." He placed the basket on his desk and fingered the handle. "Who shall I tell her it is from."

"Rosalie." For a few awkward seconds, they stood silently. "That smell?" she asked wrinkling her nose, "sandalwood?"

"Your quite right, although I prefer patchouli. Sometimes it's necessary to rid the smell of..." His words suddenly had gotten lost in his throat.

"Death?" she suggested.

"I was thinking more along the lines of despair."

It was not difficult for Rosalie to put this fastidious and delicate man in the company of lighting incense. "So, how is she?"

"Mrs. Bushnell, I am sure she's well." He smiled meekly, shifting the basket away from the edge of the table. "I will be sure to let Mrs. Bushnell know someone was asking for her."

"Yes," she said, but doubt was dampening her trust in the man. "You will tell her it was me, won't you?"

"Of course, Madame. Rosalie has brought you something from home and wished you well," he repeated. "Now, if that is all, I really must be getting back to work." He walked over to the door and pulled it open.

"She's not crazy; you do know that." He was a bony man with a sunken face. He looked more like a gentleman's gentleman than a secretary. "Dr. Bushnell, he's the crazy one," she said brimming with irritation, and not feeling that she needed to justify her opinion, she turned and hurried out.

Vole sat down behind his desk, but not before peeking into the basket. However, if he wished to see the contents, he would have to be disappointed because each article had been neatly wrapped in brown paper and secured with twine. He liked Mrs. Bushnell even though she could be rather audacious, perhaps even pushy, but crazy; he couldn't help but agree that it did seem rather unlikely.

———•———

On Sundays, there was the customary herding together of ward B and C into the common room before lunch and after chapel. The attendants gathered at one end of the table chatting feverishly, placing bets over a confiscated deck of cards. A pair of silver-haired biddies walked round and round the room picking imaginary flowers while one nervous young woman wearing an eyepatch took refuge under the table. For amusement, she would crawl over and with a blue jay feather tickle any pair of feet resting on the chairs' rungs; whereupon there was a frequency of yelps sounded whenever she was kicked. It was not possible to tell what joy this kind of recreation brought the patients, but it was visibly enjoyed by those in charge.

"Turn your head, Missy! You don't need to hear what I'm saying!"

Sydney did as instructed. "Don't mind her," whispered Margaret, "she thinks she's Mrs. Longstreet."

"Longstreet, the General's wife?"

Margaret nodded and then grinned. "That's nothin'," she said pointing to the corner. "Over there's Verna Davis." A sad and disheveled woman wrapped in a black mourning cloak rocked. "She thinks Jefferson Davis is comin' back to get her. But I don't think so." Sydney passed a glance across to the woman and then lifted her eyes nervously at Margaret. "He's not coming back, don't worry," she promised Sydney and leaned forward. "Hey, want to see Mrs. Longstreet get excited?" Her voice once lowered to a whisper rang out, "On to Richmond! On to Richmond!"

However, the enthusiasm that fell from her lips was nothing in comparison to the assertive response shouted back. "No, no, go back!" retaliated the Confederate widow, which was immediately followed by a defiant defense of her countrymen. "We're not only fighting to protect our land and families, but also to defend our fine whiskey. Now, I never touch liquor myself," she explained, "but it's the principal. The principal of the matter." Mrs. Longstreet stood up and walked in the direction of Verna. "Mrs. Davis, it is an honor to be in the presence of the President's wife. May I sit a spell with you?" The woman wrapped in black never broke her stride and continued to rock, although she did turn her head and smile. "You remember, Mrs. Davis, you remember when the dead-wagons turned their wheels from the battlefield to our Capital? There wasn't a house that didn't have a black streamer hanging on its door. It was the most horrendous sight to see; all those stiffened soldiers piled one-on-top-of the other. But you remember, Mrs. Davis, it was the only way to keep the birds from defiling our boys."

Mrs. Davis stopped rocking and then turned her head away. She closed her eyes and started to rock again, this time a little bit faster.

"The children were terrified when the wind and flames swept through our city; the trampling of feet, and the buildings, they all came tumbling down. They didn't leave a thing, not even the whiskey. It caught fire, you remember, don't you Mrs. Davis, when the Yankees rolled out the barrels and smashed them open? Even the molasses caught fire, one long river of fire. And then, dear Brigadier General Shepley, the very Governor of our great Capital, Richmond; why he turned to me while we were standing under the linden tree. And he said, '"The war is over, Madam."'"

"Can't you stop her!" cried Sydney. Her voice stretched thin and nervous from a quivering throat.

"Mrs. Davis doesn't mind," Margaret remarked and patted the fretful woman's hand.

"It's not her; it's me! Why are you doing this?"

"Doing what?"

"Getting that woman all upset?"

"Cause it's funny, isn't it? She's ridiculous. It's funny. What do you think is funny? Don't you think anything is funny?"

Sydney paused, she looked around the room and then at all the others. She looked at her dress and passed her hand over her hair. It didn't feel soft anymore, but rather coarse from the lye in the soap. She flipped her hands over on her lap, they were chapped. She then looked at the curious woman sitting beside her, waiting for a response. "I suppose you're right."

"You see," exclaimed Margaret, "It's funny! It's all too damn funny!"

Chapter 25

Bodie was a brute of a fifteen-year-old when he helped carry his father's casket to the gravesite, but it never occurred to him how heavy a coffin could be. He wasn't always a bad man; he was once a little boy with a bad father. But, true to the expression, "the apple doesn't fall far from the tree," he too grew to become a very rotten apple.

The sound of laziness permeated the vagrants' camp. The decision to play cards was never turned down; however, Bodie was not in the mood. He was restless and longed for a change. He had lost interest in the men around him; the fancy boots had elevated him into a different category. He sat with his legs stretched out and leaned back on his elbows. The three men under the tree were bickering, each claiming that the other was cheating. Bodie smiled, pleased with himself and his guile. He was a vain man and enjoyed attention almost as much as he enjoyed his whiskey. Together they were a winning combination. He pulled his blanket up over his shoulders wrapping himself like a stuffed sausage. The mid-morning sun was doing all it could to warm the earth, yet the cold was possibly the only thing keeping the quarreling men from extracting themselves out from under their shrouds of wool and getting into a scuffle.

"Well, look who's back!" cried Frisco as Lucas appeared from behind a stand of trees carrying an ungainly load of kindling. He had eaten nothing since last night, and the exertion of his task gave him all the more incentive to drop his pile of wood into the Cook's fire. The miserly bunch of twigs snapped with gratitude as the flames latched onto the fresh supply of branches. "Grab one of those tins and let me dish out some beans!" Frisco suggested and handed him a spoon.

"Where ya been?" roared Bodie. Too curious to be left out of the story; he stood up and lumbered over to the where Lucas was devouring a tin of beans.

Lucas detected Bodie's interest but didn't look up until he had scraped the sides of the cup and licked the spoon clean. He wiped his finger along the inside of the tin until he was convinced there was nothing more to eat. Although not provoked to answer, he felt compelled to offer Bodie an explanation. "Nowhere special," he said, "just scouting around. Wanted to see how far it was to town. Now I know, too far. It was too late to get back here before dark."

"Could have told you that," Frisco piped in. "You wear out your shoes before you git there!" He laughed with a "told you so" attitude. He submerged the tin into a bucket of filmy water and began to stir the lot of dirty cups and spoons with his hand.

The sun was shining with all its might, but its intentions were not enough to keep a man warm. Lucas tipped forward on his toes with his palms open before the dwindling campfire. "Damn cold," he complained, "goes right through my boots."

Bodie grinned and sniffed the air like a dog. "Not mine," he boasted. "Don't go through my boots." The three companions under the tree had stopped bickering and stopped to listen. The winning hand of poker had been revealed with each deciding the other was man was a liar; something they could all agree upon. In full view, several birds circled as if they anticipated trouble.

Lucas surveyed the sky. "Hunger never rests, and birds never sleep."

"Good leather boots are hard to come by," Bodie goaded. Lucas nodded in agreement but was more interested in keeping the fire hot and turned his attention to the single light. "Yep, no cold going to my toes in these good-lookin' boots." The beast-like face leaned over and with the hem of his blanket began to dust the toebox. But as he did so, he also accidentally flung his blanket so that it disturbed the man prodding the fire. Lucas's eyes meet Bodie's and then followed his line of vision down over the vamp of the braggart's boot.

"Shit!"

"You're damn straight, shit!" mocked the louse. The startled expression on Lucas's face gave Bodie reason to believe the drifter was jealous of his prize possession; all of which made him quite happy.

The quick examination of the boots demanded an answer to only one question. "Where did you get those?" His voice flat and monotonous, while his eyes wild with the discovery flitted with agitation. "You stole them!" he accused. "You killed my brother and stole his boots!"

Scarce was there a time when such an accusation would have been false. But under present circumstances there loomed a distortion to Bodie's good fortune. His eyes pounded the accuser, his breath hot and short. "I'll just pretend I didn't hear what you said."

The three men huddled around the Cook's fire, afraid of falling out among the favored in the eyes of the brute. They dared not speak; all except Frisco who felt obliged to offer his advice. "That's some shit you're throwing around, Timpson. Don't push your luck."

A chorus of support echoed the Cook as the three frightened tramps found their courage as one voice. "He's right, Timpson, clear out!"

The weathered faces behind their liquor-soaked brains were a grim reminder to Lucas that he had spent most of his life taking bad advice. He had been selfish and insensitive to his brother but never unloving.

"Injustice has no odor," he used to tell Dennett. But now, Lucas could smell it. Surely, they must smell it too? There was the stench of rotten wood, a lewd remark was thrown, someone blew their nose, and then the parroting of heckles began. The area around him reeked with malice and in an instant, he felt himself responding while the others remained rooted in their places. With teeth-clenched, he edged towards Bodie until the two stood face to face. "Confess you coward, confess or I'll rip your heart out!"

"My money's on Bodie!" shouted the churlish vagrant. But they were all surprised when the man with his usual ill temper did not immediately reply with profanity. Instead, he simply bent down, removed his bowie knife from his boot, and brandished the weapon."

"Cut him!" squealed the Cook.

Lucas saw the flickering blade, and then he saw the tips of the boots. In a frenzied fit, he reasserted himself, reached behind his back and pulled out the pistol tucked into his belt. In less than a second, he aimed and shot point-blank. The blade wavered for an instant, and before it could find its mark, Lucas fired again. This time the large man tipped forward, and as if a branch was severed from its limb, he fell face forward onto the ground.

"Holy shit, you murdered him! You murdered him!" cried the Cook. But none of the men dared come forward to challenge the shooter. The pistol that felled Bodie still had three bullets left.

"It's not murder," Lucas explained. "This is brotherly love." He stood over the body as the blood oozed free from the bullet holes and the gash on the forehead caused by the fall. The groan expelled sounded more like a wounded animal than human.

"He's not dead!" proclaimed the silver-bearded tramp. Lucas kicked the knife from the outstretched arm, and then bent over the body. There was no compassion for the dying man; he was the enemy. The duty of a soldier is to kill the enemy. Lucas shook the limp arm and then the leg.

Bodie was immobile. He looked over at the others; they stared wide-eyed like frightened boys. "No need to worry anymore, this bastard's dead," the killer said. A slow, gradual pain in his temples was becoming uncomfortable. He rubbed his forehead and realizing he was still holding the gun, jammed it back into his belt. Stepping over the prostrate body, he pulled off his brother's boots. "You can bury him if you want or just leave him here for them." He pointed up towards the circling buzzards. He had entered this covenant of revenge with the purpose of finding his brother's killer; now, all he needed to do to fulfill his promise was to return the boots to their rightful owner.

The joker was still affixed to his mind. Its effigy, mute and misshapen, would slip into the middle of a dream; sometimes it was floating and other times just a head impaled on a stick. He wasn't sure what it meant, only that it woke him up wondering. He shuffled through the deck until he came to the joker; an impish fellow that sneered instead of smiled. He would finally rid himself of these cards, the boots, and all the memories attached.

"Mister wake up!" Lucas heard the voice and opened one eye. He wasn't sure how long he had been asleep. Maybe just a few minutes? "Your station," barked the conductor. Lucas turned and looked with groggy eyes through the window as the train was slowing down. A succession of travelers was waiting like crows on a wire, each with a valise in hand or set alongside their feet. The engineer pulled the brake, and the train came to an abrupt halt. A billow of smoke spewed and settled over the tracks with a sooty brown haze. Lucas stood up, grabbed his haversack, and followed the passengers out.

In several minutes, the train chugged away. In the seat once occupied by Lucas now sat a moon-faced woman and her ten-year-old son. The pudgy little boy was busy fiddling with a playing card he had found lying on the seat. "What is this, Mother?" he asked pointing to the picture. The woman looked and then shrugged, for having never seen a joker before she simply called it "the fool."

———•———

The fallen tree was a mass of rotting timber throwing attention to the destructive splendor of the fire. The property, though condemned, had been re-inhabited by field mice, beetles, spiders, and an occasional raccoon. It was eerily quiet during the day, however, by twilight, the world came alive. It was during this gray time of the evening when Asa would come over the hill; sometimes he would venture as far as the garden, but most of the time he would dig in the back field behind the desolated property. *"We got to stay in the works till nightfall on account of enemy sharpshooters.* Sometimes all he could see was his own shadow cast over the very spot he was unearthing. It was the same shadow that came and went with him every day. *"With the help of the infirmary corps, we can retrieve the wounded and bury the dead at sunrise. Dig a trench six-feet-wide and two feet deep. Lay them on their backs side-by-side and then cover those gallant men with blankets… Only then, can we return to our posi*tion." He hated the snow battles; they could never dig deep enough.

The air was sharp and cold and dry. The foliage was waiting for the rain; it had learned to be patient; even so, many would wither into stems of dry threads. Patience never withered in Asa. The brother would make good on his promise; he would return the boots and place them on the shallow grave. This Asa was confident of; he understood the meaning of a promise. He used to wait by the pier; the clouds would bank at the horizon, and the same tide that pulled back would roll forward. He was not alone, others were waiting for ships, but he seemed to be the most patient.

Like hair untended by a barber's scissors, so did the garden become unruly without the management of hoe and trowel. By midsummer what was left on the vines had rotted or been devoured by the multi-legged inhabitants. Weeds strangled the once domesticated garden while the thistles confiscated the beds. But to the eyes of the tattie-bogle nothing had been rendered so irreversible that it could not be scratched out of the earth again, and he continued to reign over the patch of garden. Asa leaned over the fence and looked out towards the hills. No longer subjugated to remain behind the fence line, he was free to come and go as he pleased. He pulled his flat-brimmed hat up above his forehead, his eyes channeling the land behind the milky haze. He knew every scrubby hiding place, every trail, and all the rabbit burrows. This land belonged to Flora. Asa climbed over the railing and started to walk. His list was getting smaller; this was a good feeling, accomplishments.

———— •————

"My heart breaks when I think about the motherless little stranger born into the world. You know, I feel like she's my niece." Margaret's reproach entered silently into the conversation. "I don't understand how Lilac died; she was healthy as a horse, and then, just like that, something as normal as giving birth did her in." She sighed dramatically, and then as if the candy would revive her remorse, she took another piece of chocolate from the picnic basket. "I like the ones with nuts," she said licking her fingers greedily. "What else you got in there?"

Sydney dipped her hand in and pulled out two books, a wrapped bar of soap, a comb and brush, silver mirror, and a tied bundle of twigs. The neat parcel of clothes was confiscated. "I gave the peppermint sticks to Mary," she remarked.

"Shit, next time don't give that bitch anything!" warned Margaret. "What else can you get?"

"What would you like?"

The offer lifted the woman to her feet, and she began to pace. After musing for a moment, she leaned over the cot and pointed to the woody stems. "What the hell is that?"

"Just a kind of tea."

Margaret snorted with discontent. "Well, I don't want whatever kind of tea that is. It stinks!" she sneered. "Maybe some whiskey!" her eyes glinted. "Can you get that?"

"I can try," replied Sydney, feigning optimism into their dismal existence. Tired of this woman, she began to put the gifts back into the basket. Margaret watched as she replaced them one-by-one and then pushed the basket beneath the bedframe.

"Want to know a secret?" Margaret whispered. "You can get out of laundry detail if you know which laundry room to go into." She peered around, snarled at a pock-marked patient pacing too close to the bed, and then slid closer to the occupant of the cot. At first, the statement must have sounded more than confusing, but as the speaker's muffled voice poured out her secret, Sydney was receiving evidence to what she already knew. "So, you see, all you have to do is get your picture taken. It's easy to keep these soft hands away from lye," she claimed and lifted the slender hand off its lap. You don't want your smooth skin to get like hers," she said coolly and tossed her chin in the direction of the neighboring cot. "Hey, Mel, get out of bed and show us your scaly hands."

"Mind your own business," cried the woman and pulled the blanket over her head.

Sydney slipped her hand away from Margaret. "Shh, I hear Mary," she whispered. "You better go to your own side."

A strange silence fell over the room as the matron's heels made a click, click, click like horseshoes across a planked floor. "Time, ladies." Despite the grumbles of a few patients, all followed the routine and returned to their cots. There was an audible round of profanity, but soon, like the drizzle of rain, there sounded only an undercurrent of indiscernible noise. Some women whimpered, others argued with themselves, and then, there were those who prayed. If anyone was listening to another, it was not apparent for after an hour only the rats revealed themselves to those still awake, scurrying across the splintered rafters.

Another day passed into night, and Sydney had cleared the difficulties of wakefulness. No suffering had been incurred except her own personal need to separate herself from the others. The entire population living within the asylum walls seemed to be composed of hibernating animals, complacent to be asleep until provoked. She was growing drowsy, moving from the real to the unreal, and into a looking-glass image of her wretched accommodations with its stained walls and moldy plaster. She saw herself floating, her mind was clear, and she could hear herself think but could not wake up. *"I am free,"* she told her sleeping self, *"free from obligations, affairs of the house, and domestic commitments. I am free to read, to pray, to think independently. But it is savage freedom I want, not this controlled existence."* She saw herself as a barefoot peasant, scantily dressed and bitterly cold. *"Maybe I'm dead."* A light wind guided her along as she drifted over the sleeping patients, and like the sleeping Sydney, they too had been granted freedoms that couldn't be asserted. The snow was melting; it would soon be spring. Sydney pulled the blanket up to her chin. The matron had brewed the tea just as she directed, with a tincture of laudanum. "Thank you, Richard, you remembered." She thought she saw herself smile.

A farmer does not place all the animals together in one pen; so too does the asylum segregate their patients. There is a ward for those who follow the rules, a room for patients who wish harm to themselves, another for those that are violent, and still another for the incurables. What keeps them as an entity, aside from the physical building, is their lack of privacy and a shared identity. There are no lockers, no storage places, nowhere to keep personal items or possessions. Clothes issued to each are without guarantees that a patient will wear the same one over and over. Personal items are often pilfered for use or sale by the staff, and though it is against hospital rules, it does not inhibit any number of attendants from confiscating and wearing a patient's personal clothing. In order to limit conflict over individual possessions and different social status, the hospital justifies its practices, and as much as Sydney petitioned to wear her own clothes, she was relegated to hospital gowns and slippers.

So much as the farmer does not tether all his animals; seeing as the goats and pigs are free to roam, the bulls and oxen may need to be yoked. So too does the asylum give some patients freedom to roam the grounds, while there are others restrained by straitjackets and fingerless gloves, and the more "excited" patients are tied to their beds.

Every morning Sydney received a flower from the garden, and every day she plucked the petals free from the stem. She wanted no part of her husband's gifts, and yet, he continued the ritual as he did when she was living at home. "Mrs. Bushnell," said Vole, as he entered the recreation room with a violet-colored pansy, "Dr. Bushnell told me to give this to you." Her blue eyes, once bright and cheerful, had grown tired, yet she was still a lovely looking woman despite her situation. She finished her stitch and then peered up from her knitting. Vole stood before her, his hand outstretched as if it were he that was offering her the sentiment.

"Thank you," she replied, but before she took it and proceeded as usual, ripping the petals from the stem, she paused. "Tell me, Vole, why do you come day in and day out when you know I will take this flower from you and tear it into pieces. Don't you tire of my ingratitude?"

"I would do the same thing if I were you, Madame," he said sounding like a dejected lover.

She looked at him curiously, "Why is that?"

"Because, with every flower, there is a bee."

Sydney smiled, "Then, one must be careful not to get stung."

"Or maybe, you get more bees with honey," replied Vole and handed her the pansy. "You're looking better, Mrs. Bushnell."

She placed the flower to her nose. It was sweet. "And one more thing; would you give this to the woman who lost her baby." Sydney reached beneath her cot and pulled out a doll and handed it over. "Tell her it is Bella."

Vole picked up the bald doll and smiled. "May I ask where you got this from."

"The gardener."

"Very astute of him, I must say. I always thought of him as an old Billy goat."

"I can see why, he does have that pointy little beard," Sydney agreed.

Vole placed the doll under his arm and stood for a moment. "Of course, Mrs. Bushnell," he said. "Bella."

"Thank you, Vole, see you tomorrow."

"Yes, Madame, tomorrow."

———•———

Robert Bushnell brooded as he sipped his glass of whiskey. He had taken to drinking bourbon after dinner, but this evening he felt like something different. The authorities had sent over a Detective Wright with word about a large man fitting the description of Bodie. The dead man was shot at an abandoned vagrant camp. The detective described the matter as if he were either dissatisfied or annoyed. The reason for his visit was to inquire about a silver lighter found with the belongings of the dead man; engraved with the name, Robert Bushnell. Such a valuable item was assumed to have been stolen.

Richard Bushnell's face lit up with pleasure after hearing the account. "Well, this is a sight for sore eyes! It went missing a couple of days after a carriage ride. I just assumed I had carelessly lost it." The Doctor turned the lighter over in his palm and smiled, handing it back to the officer. "You say you found it on a dead man?" He shook his head incredulously.

The Detective nodded in agreement with the logical order of the incident recounted. "How this low-life had possession of it can only be assumed it was by chance." He fingered the lighter with a bit of envy, mentally deciding that he was indeed in the company of a very prominent man. The Department recognized the Doctor's reputation as an upscale citizen.

"I don't suppose I can have it back, it was a gift from my wife," Bushnell remarked more like a demand than a request.

The Detective, now having been plied with a glass of whiskey, had grown a liking for the Doctor and in exchange for the hospitality did not see any reason to retain the owner's lost possession. For just a few short minutes he was one of the fashionable people; the splendor of the room and the opulence of time was most agreeable. He sat for a while feasting his eyes over the expensive liquor. "I admire your taste, Dr. Bushnell. Can't remember when police business was so pleasurable." Bushnell smiled and ran his fingers across his mustache smoothing it like a cat. The simpering fellow sitting across from him was getting on his nerves. The Doctor glanced up at the clock and then quickly finished his drink. He hoped that the Detective had been groomed in the manly etiquette of taking a hint when to leave. Fortunately, he had. "Well, I've taken up too much of your time," he said, and with his hat in his hand, he stood for an awkward moment until Rosalie came into the room. The Doctor remained seated.

"Dr. Bushnell, it's been found?" she exclaimed.

"Seems that our Detective Wright has located my lighter." The man beamed like a child upon hearing his name while the Doctor looked vacantly at him. "Rosalie, please see the Detective out, that is unless there is something else?" he asked turning his question to the man.

"Oh, no nothing more. Sorry to trouble you, Dr. Bushnell." He positioned his bowler on his shrubless knoll of a head, tapped the brim, and sauntered on his way, a trifle happier than when he arrived.

The disgusted doctor snapped the lighter open and shut as he damned the dead man for stealing it right under his nose. He wondered if anything else was found and cursed his bad luck.

Rosalie reentered the room with a silver tea service and cookies. "Thought you might like something to help you sleep, especially now that Mrs. Bushnell is away." She set the tray on the table and stood over the man like a nursemaid.

"I hope it's not that bush tea my wife liked," he grumbled lifting his eyes from his newspaper.

"Oh, no, I know what you might like. This is a natural herb, one of my personal favorites." She leaned over the sugar bowl and lifting the tongs asked, "Two lumps or three, Dr. Bushnell? I remember that you like your hot liquids sweet."

"Three," he said and from the corner of his eye watched her perform the ritual of pouring the tea through a silver strainer into the empty cup. Then she stirred it slowly until satisfied the sugar had dissolved.

"Don't wait too long; it's best drunk when hot. The cookies are your favorite, right out of the oven." Turning away, she padded out the door.

The tired man's expression was a wrinkling scowl. "Her nicety was rather odd," he thought as he blew across the steaming cup. "Perhaps she had gotten wind that she wasn't going to be needed anymore."

The Cook sighed as she cleaned the kitchen. Ever since Sydney's departure, the woman went about her work with moans and groans. She wiped the counter and swept up the stems and leaves that had dropped onto the floor. The glass jar sat open on the counter. She put her nose to the lid and then spooned the spilled residue back in. "Belladonna?" she read and then closed the lid. "That Rosalie and her Chinese remedies," she muttered and picking up the empty cup and saucer took it over to the sink to wash.

A gathering of ten outcasts congregated around the bucket of community stew. They were "blanket-stiffs," rovers that begged from town to town with only a rolled-up blanket and a hard-luck story. The tramp with an iron-gray beard had taken charge, ordering the rest to line-up with their tins. He was mean as a dog and just as greedy. Only those who had contributed to the watery stew were entitled to eat. However, no one seemed to mind the transient who walked into camp with something more inviting than a potato or onion. For no matter how stingy a man might be, he can always be persuaded to be generous under the right circumstance. "Too bad for Bodie," the tattered man thought as he licked the tin clean. "Pickpocketing a dead man was easy, but to come away with a blonde like this was damn good luck."

Chapter 26

"It was the war," explained Margaret, "it did strange things to a person. Take me for example, I was only one out of hundreds making a blind pilgrimage behind Mr. Lincoln's army. I was never so fortunate as to have met the great man, all I got to remember is a few tales." She glanced up at Sydney and then smirked at her own words. "Shit, I don't have any regrets and I sure as hell ain't goin' to give any apologies." Sydney did not stir, rather, she had become intrigued and knowing the few moments separating the other's thoughts may lapse into forgetfulness, she decided to prompt the speaker by patting her on the knee. "What's that for!" squawked Margaret and jumped up. Sydney, equally startled grew wide-eyed, begin to explain that her intentions were not to affront and only to be understanding.

"I'm not used to that kind of attention," Margaret said, sitting back down. There was a stillness between the two women now which began to console the misunderstanding. "I can tell you about that time if you want." She pointed up at the sun and then looked down at the shadows creeping towards her from the elm tree. "We don't have to go in yet, lazy Mary is sittin' on the bench like an indolent shepherd too content to bring in her flock." Disdain for the head Matron slipped off the tongue easily.

"Not all those who were brave were the soldiers," Sydney said. For the first time, Margaret sensed the freedom to relax. She cocked her head back and let the sunshine flow over her as a feeling of listlessness emancipated her own war story. If Sydney heard or not, she didn't really care. She rarely relied on others to listen.

The sun lay against the sky like a pale-yellow disc. "How can it be flat; it's always so round!" exclaimed the older of the two women. She placed her hands on her hips and leaned back as though she were charting the heavens. Her eyes darted from one cloud to another.

Her friend to whom she was speaking, a round bosomy woman, did not feel it necessary to oblige. "Look for yourself, there," complained the first tugging at her companion. She pointed up and to the left of their shadows. Her gray eyes squinted as she shaded her head, steadying her hand over her thin brows as if it were enough to keep the bright light of daybreak from distorting her vision. She was quite right; it was a flat sun, fastened like a piece of yellowing paper onto the hazy white sky as though someone had taken mucilage and pasted it up after the morning had begun. Such a sun was an afterthought.

The two women were not the first ones to rise for the day; several others were already bustling about; two were bowing over the washtub, half-naked, soaping their bodies with what meager bits of soap shards remained from bars made from pig fat. A line of women formed behind, each waiting their turn. They shared small talk, exchanged chatter of little importance, mostly how one or the other slept and what they would be eating for breakfast. The earliest risers were assured the cleanest water, and those at the end of the queue would have to be content with a filmy tub of milky white liquid.

The first woman fished into her apron pocket and released a few splinters of soap. Her hands smelled of lavender; she always smelled of lavender; hence her nickname Lilac. It wasn't her true name, but like many of the others, she chose not to use her birth name, not that anyone would care. Most had several aliases anyway and were as expendable as their stories. An unaccompanied woman was often considered unrespectable and losing virtue in the eyes of a sanctimonious gossip could be ruinous. Two years had passed since the magnolias and blueberries were offered at tea, two years had passed and now all the able-bodied men had either enlisted or were drafted. Was choosing to be a camp follower a poor decision? On the contrary, in the deadly defense of the injured parties, it proved to be decisively advantageous and quite profitable.

Lilac never regretted her decision to abandon her miserable life. Her brother was married and had been drafted into the military. And though they had been close, time had a way of separating families. She may not have been well-educated, but she was certainly not stupid. She detested the Rebels, but to remain behind would have been bravado. A spinster with a dog and three pigs were no match for even a small string of Sunday soldiers. She didn't run from the Confederate army, she had heard they were gentlemen, but rather it was the threat of deserters that frightened her. When the Yankee brigade came along hungry, she gave them her pigs and what food she had saved, but when she was left with nothing more to eat, she surrendered her life. "I got a feelin'," she mumbled with a touch of mysticism in her voice. "There's somethin' in the air."

Margaret was used to Lilac's rambling and found it comforting. "What's in the air?" she snapped back. She waited briefly for an answer as her friend seemed to be contemplating her own premonition. "Those are not nice woods," Margaret remarked breaking the silence and tossed her head about as though she had just arrived. "See over there; I bet if you went behind that hill there'd be a thousand Confederate dogs just waitin' to slit your throat."

"My pearly throat?" grinned the fine smelling woman. She craned her neck upward as though she was a water-bird sunning itself. She ran her hand lightly down her neck and then back up to her chin mocking the other woman's statement with gestures of seduction. "Do ya think they would slice this fine neck?"

Margaret soured with her friend's poor attempt at humor. "Ain't funny, they're all killers! Just because our own kind still finds us a comfort at night don't mean you'd win your way into the bed of some enemy."

"You know," Lilac announced, "what you say has a bit of excitement!" Then with exaggerated movements, she wiggled her rear end and nonchalantly bent over and picked up her bedroll. She began to fondle it, fingering the loose thread between her fingers.

"No Confederate would find you desirable!" squawked her irritated friend. "Besides, what about that Captain that's sweet on you?" She raised the woman's skirt and pointed to a mud-stained petticoat. "Ya don't get one of these for bein' purty! Just be thankful you got one of the officers askin' for a bit of sugar!"

Lilac frowned with disapproval and dusted her skirt as though it had been contaminated. "I only thought that, well..." she paused as if in a moral dilemma.

"Whatever you're thinkin' get that nasty notion out of your head!" demanded her listener. "Any woman in this camp would die to be bedded by your Captain. I'm tellin ya right now, don't mess with fate." Margaret's unfavorable verdict echoed in Lilac's ears. She had been traipsing behind the Yankee army for over six months; the air was thick with musket fire and the hellish cries of misery. Everything she owned fit in a moth-eaten carpetbag and now even her store-bought shoes were beginning to grow holes. She was tired of moving without an end in sight. She had begun to feel rather sorry for herself and longed for a morsel of sympathy. Lilac sighed as she tried to reconcile her indifference to the Captain. He was considerably older, however, if he was so smart why hadn't he been promoted. And even though it was flattering that he picked her out from all the other women, there was something in her soul that needed to be rekindled; but why now? Like flipping leaves in a book, she turned her mind out of the camp and into enemy territory. She tingled with a secret desire to be wicked, very wicked.

A mud colored dog with a black tongue stole a glance in her direction. He rolled out of a shallow hole he had dug to cool his underbelly in the wet soil, stood up, and shook his matted fur; then scampered in their direction. "Wher' ya been Scout?" Lilac asked with the same tone one addresses a spouse who has been out all night. The dog sat before the two women and wildly thumped its thin tail at the sound of his name.

"If your Captain sees this dog wearing the scarf he gave you...," Margaret shook her head disapprovingly.

"I don't like yellow," she replied hastily. "Besides, Scout doesn't have a collar, all dogs need a collar," she retorted and stroked the animal on its head. Again, its tail pounded the earth.

"Perhaps," Margaret snorted. "But a silk collar?" she exclaimed and threw the dog a look of disgust and jealousy. Lilac did have to agree that the gift may be ridiculous for the dog, which actually looked rather silly wearing a yellow bow under its chin. She may just as well have put the animal in a bonnet. The dog had now gotten up and was scouring the ground for food. A woman several yards away called out, "Here puppy!" and tossed in his direction a piece of stale bread. Delighted by the invitation to breakfast, he quickly scampered off.

The flat sun grew hot, and the two women lay their bedrolls aside and sat under the makeshift lean-to. The canvas roof provided shade and shelter from the rain and with a bit of ingenuity, they were able to fold over the extra length for privacy. Some women decorated their lean-tos by putting out personal belongings such as photographs in gilded frames; others picked wildflowers and placed them in tin cups. But most found this practice an unnecessary waste of time for no one really knew when the army would be on the move. Margaret and Lilac took the latter approach.

The dispirited woman surrendered herself to a wooden crate and waited impatiently for her friend to notice her restlessness. However, she had earned no sympathy, and Margaret busied herself by darning her stockings. Lilac closed her eyes confining her thoughts to her immediate situation. Sharing her ideas seemed fruitless where Margaret was concerned; it would only be a waste of time. However, only a few minutes passed when the seemingly bored woman sat forward and whispered with a strange almost savage energy. "Do you hear that?"

Margaret looked away from her sewing though her hands never stopped as she spoke. "Hear what?"

"Shhh, shhh!" barked the other, her voice even more hushed and grave. "Not so loud...just listen!" Margaret heeded the warning and put her stockings on her lap. She cocked her head like a dog where Lilac was more like a hunter. "That, that!" she announced and raised her finger in the air.

Margaret pursed her lips together and scowled. "That's a guinea hen," she whispered. "Same one we've been tryin' to catch for days."

"No, really, come here!" and with an immediate urgency, she jumped up and grabbed her friend, pulling the stout woman out of her chair as if retrieving her from a fire.

"Now what is all this about!" grumbled the larger woman and followed as if her own safety was at risk.

"Listen!" demanded Lilac and pointed towards the mountains. "It's a song, yes, a song!" For a moment Lilac felt an oppressive sense of dizziness, and her heart began to pound. "I do believe I feel faint!" she cried and began to fan herself with her hand. Quickly she unbuttoned her blouse and blotted her bare skin with a handkerchief she had stuffed in her pocket.

Margaret made no challenge, for now she too heard the melodious notes. There was no other option for her reluctant mind but to admit someone out there was playing music.

"It's a sign!" cried Lilac with the enthusiasm of a Christmas morning, her face lit up, and she dashed round towards her friend. "I must go!"

"What, are you out of your mind!" exclaimed her companion grabbing the other by the arm. "Now just git a hold of yourself, Missy!" and she held her fast as if she were to let go the spellbound woman would vanish from the very spot where she stood. "What's goin' on with you?"

"I'm telling you that this is the best time for me to go. No one will suspect me missing, and besides, what harm could it do? Just think of it Margaret, wouldn't a little excitement do us both good?" Then as though she was possessed, her eyes twinkled with specks of light, the likes of which she had never revealed.

"That's it, come with me! Right now, the two of us! Oh Margaret, imagine our fun!" Her voice became breathless as she spoke. "It would be so, so...romantic!"

"Romantic?" the other cried and laughed aloud. "It would be treason, yes, treason if anyone but me ever heard your foolish talk. No, stop it, now!" she contested, and with the frightened look of a wounded animal, she pulled Lilac back under the shelter of the lean-to. "Promise me you'll stop this talk. Why just thinking of leaving for the enemy..." the mere words made the larger woman shudder. "They will hang you. Do you hear me? The Yankee army will hang you! And even your lover Captain would agree; in fact, he'd probably erect the gallows himself." Margaret could barely get the words out, and she trembled as she whispered her prediction.

However, Lilac only scoffed at her friend's simple notion. "I won't be gone but a few hours. After all," she pronounced running her hands along her hips, "I got my urges too!"

Margaret's temple throbbed as if an alarm was raised; she shook her head decisively leading with an authoritative "no"; all she could foresee was trouble as she once again unleashed her tongue. "Urges, you speak of urges; why you foolish woman, you've got the whole Yankee army to gratify your so-called urges!" It occurred to Margaret that Lilac liked to add a pepper of excitement when there didn't need to be. "You've got young men, old men, married men; bearded, tan, black, white, tall, short, fat, and thin to choose from...what's wrong with you?" cried the confused woman; her voice bleating like a hungry ewe.

By now Lilac had stopped listening. She squatted before her meager belongings, fumbling about until she pulled from her cache a scarlet choker laced with black velvet. She smoothed her hair aside and fastened the two ends of the ribbon into a tiny bow behind her neck. Then she stood up and turned to her friend who had remained steadfast. "Now, you keep your trap shut, ya hear me?" she announced with a degree of intimidation tied to her voice.

Margaret knew that she was defeated. She made a sign with her hand as though she was locking her lips shut and tossed the imaginary key over her shoulder.

"Looky here," Lilac said, speaking in a more consolatory tone. "I promise nothing can go wrong. If it wasn't for that music luring me… I tell you everything will be fine. I'll be back before dark!" she exclaimed and squealed with anticipated delight. "Now go on, scoot, and when you get back no one can make you say nothing, 'cause you saw and heard nothing!" And before her friend could begin to protest, Lilac pushed the favorite companion out from beneath the shelter and hid out-of-sight as the large woman reluctantly lumbered away. Lilac folded her arms tightly around herself and held her breath. She closed her eyes and listened to the music, however by this time of the morning the cackling of the other women was too loud, too close; the camp was alive with conversation and gossip like tentative forays before a battle.

Margaret passed several anxious hours. She tried to keep her mind occupied with the doldrums of chores. There was always plenty to mend, and her appearance of being committed to her work did not seem out of the ordinary. A few women came by to chatter, asked where Lilac was; and seemed content with Margaret's gesture of a casual shrug. It was not uncommon for a woman to go off in search of firewood, to fetch water, or simply wander away with a soldier for a few hours. But as the hours passed and the flat yellow sun bowed like a drooping daisy in need of water, the stout woman wrestled with her concentration. The click, click, click of the needles was followed by the sucking of her teeth while she unraveled the poorly knit stitches. Margaret tilted back in her makeshift chaise; a loosely wound ball of wool lay in the folds of her dress and the scarf she was knitting dripped down onto the ground like a striped snake. She had hoarded balls of wool during the early threat of war, and now this scarf had eaten up the last of her supply. Restless, she got up, set the needles on the seat, and lifted the canvas aside peering up into the hills and listened. Beyond the camp the hills stood dark, wet, lush, and green in contrast to the dry, oatmeal colored earth that dusted her feet. She imagined the younger woman rolling about in the shadows of the hickory elms in the presence of an enemy soldier, maybe more than one, her skirt stained by the damp moss, while her soiled petticoat smelling like raw earth. There was a tinge of curiosity, a pang of jealousy as she slipped her hand into her pocket and *drew a laced handkerchief to dry her face. It was wet with nervous perspiration, and she ran the cloth over her forehead, drew it along the side of her face and then down her neck and slowly dabbed as though blotting parchment, within her deep cleavage. "Fool," she thought and stuffed the damp handkerchief back into her pocket. She wasn't sure how long she had been standing, but it must have been quite a while for the hills had grown almost black, and there was a scurrying of activity as women and children began to prepare the campfires.*

She dropped the tent's canvas and found herself picking through her carpet bag until she came upon a pale gingham skirt, the one that she had been saving for a special occasion she had conjured up in her mind, for it was clean and crisp, and only worn twice. It still smelled like freshly starched laundry. She removed her apron, her muslin skirt, and pantaloons, and slipped carefully into the skirt. Wishing she had a mirror, she looked down and pulled the skirt aside as though it was a rose-colored sail. She felt pretty, very pretty, and she knew that her large womanly shape was desirable, and she felt such.

It had grown gray, and everything was bathed in a languid haze. Margaret lit the small lantern, lifted the canvas flap and stepped out. She stood casually next to the lean-to and ran her fingers through her un-tethered hair. She waited for several minutes and wondered if anyone would notice her change of clothes, but no one did. The crackling of fire spit embers into the air and the moths circled the many lanterns that were dotting the campground. Small children cried, a few women cackled with idle gossip. The mud-colored dog sauntered past, and she called its name affectionately as if it had taken on the character of an old friend. The free stepping canine scampered eagerly up to the woman with the wanton approach of getting something to eat. Margaret lowered her eyes and noticed the scoundrel of a dog was no longer wearing the bright yellow sash around its scrawny neck, but instead donned the velvet choker. She bent forward and tugged him towards her. He brushed up against her skirt, his fur freckled with briars, and his paws discolored from the damp earth. The woman let go and looked up into the dark hills, and then back at the dog that had grown tired of waiting for a hand-out and turned away. The entire camp lay before her. The golden disc of sun had shriveled away, and a white glow stole its place above the tawny landscape.

Without the slightest provocation, she went back in to retrieve the lantern and held it before her. She lifted her eyes and cocked her head to the side. A gentle rhythm rolled and ebbed in the breeze; a light whisper tossed about from a flute. The Confederates were playing music, and they were calling, beckoning, seducing, and awakening her. "It'll just be for a few hours," she thought. Then, with a seductive smile, she too sallied towards the hills, leaving the army behind.

Margaret rested in the sun as placid as a child and presumed asleep when Sydney leaned over to gently stir the woman out from her dreamy escape. But her tepid shake of the arm did not get an immediate response, which had caught the eye of the impatient attendant. "Come along Margaret, and you too fancy lady!" Mary snapped. "We got enough fresh air for one day!" Turning her back to the bench she bellowed with more energy. "That goes for the rest of you idiots too. Time to go in. Hurry up and get in line!" A groan of disappointment was volleyed back as the women reluctantly traipsed slowly towards the Matron. Amusing one another with coarse language and odd laughter, they lined up single file to be herded back to their wards.

"Here I go again," whispered Margaret.

"Go again?" Sydney repeated with misunderstanding.

"Yep," she said, "seems like I'm always bringing up the rear."

Chapter 27

The frozen crust melts and a new persona, spring, inherits the land once again. Patches of new growth displace the blackened and scorched property. What little remained of the house has surrendered to the elements; its timbers weak and rotten falter like the feeble whisper of a dying man. Still, there prevail two opposing paths that have endured the scourge; one leads to the field and the other to the garden. Knotty vines with taut buds lay heavy upon the dirt, while the sheaths-of-grass part themselves in the early morning sunlight. On the surface, the sun evaporates the dew and all the memories. Beneath the soil hides another world; it's cool and damp and easy to pierce.

And then it rains.

Asa waited beneath the lean-to. The rain fell, and he watched the drops slip between the slats in the roof and get caught in an abandoned spider web. The wind tried to shake the orb free from the corner, but the silky threads held fast. It must have been tested many times for it looked so gray and dusty without the eight-legged weaver. The ground lapped the muddy puddles like a thirsty dog while the drops splattered the brown muck and rinsed the web. Asa stuck his hand outside, and the water filled his palm and ran down between his fingers. He wondered if he pulled on the web how far he could get the thread to stretch. It reminded him of a crochet doily his mother kept in a box. "Why was it in a box?"

At last the rain surrendered. The web no longer looked weary. Water droplets of tiny balloons had filled with sunlight crisscrossing across the spokes of the spider's netting. Asa brushed his wet hand across his shirt and dug into his pocket. Several gray pearls and a gold half-heart pendant were jammed in the corner. There was not much that he wanted from his past, but he needed to keep these close as a reminder of the final items to cross off his list. He couldn't wait for everything to right itself, so he walked back out to the garden.

The soft earth hugged the plants, splattering the green tufts which stood upright like new growths of hair. *It's everywhere, hear it gurgling?* Asa crouched down and cocked his head to the side. *They're drowning in it! Damn mud!* He flicked the crinkled leaves, but the mud stayed firm. *A trickle of mud fell from his kepi onto his letter.* "Private! Get your butt out here and help pull the mare.!" *The soldier bounded from the trench sending clods of dirt over the letter.* He held the leaf carefully and picked away the brown stain. Beneath the watchful eye of the tattie-bogle, the garden was safe. The hay stuffed man was duty bound, silent and breathless, guardian of all that grew and died. Only the winged creatures were not welcome.

An angelic humming announced the arrival of the child and when she made herself present Asa was struck by the contrast in her expression. Her lip quivered as she approached the charred remains, but as soon as she saw him her veiled smile reanimated. His hands were clenched behind his back, and he was staring straight forward as though he were on a secluded beach watching the tide. He had seen too much ugliness; his eyes shifted downward. Was the mud still his enemy? He twisted his neck and roamed the field where the rain erased each footprint with the same ferocity the ocean erases sand-tracks at the shore.

The garden soothed the child and though she was very sad the fear of being forgotten was ever more painful. She needed to return to the pure and spotless mounds of the blackbirds. "Hello, Asa!" she exclaimed, skipping as if there was not a care in the world. "Señora and I have come to an understanding since she knows you tend to the vegetables. She liked the tomatoes, except for the one with the worm!" Asa bent down and searched for weeds as he listened. The same sun that once baked the trenches of war lay upon the garden like a gentle blanket. Flora's impish curiosity sought the tattie-bogle that was hanging center stage. She was like a terrier nipping at its heels, as she pranced around his stake. "Well hello, Wooley! How are you today?" She stopped and with wide-eyes examined his footwear. "My, don't you look especially fancy! I see you're wearing a new pair of boots!" Flora smiled cunningly and ran her hand over the finely stitched leather attached to the over-stuffed trousers. Asa tipped back on his heels, crouching forward. He gently pushed the bushy tufts of green apart where a rabbit, a tiny doe, shivered as the shadow of the scarecrow fell over the timid creature.

"Look, look, the brown bunny, oh I knew it would come back," Flora exclaimed. Delighted in the discovery, she knelt next to Asa. The frightened rabbit tried to remain motionless, but its pink nose twitched feverously, defying all its efforts. Flora shrank back, and she grew teary-eyed as the anxious animal hedged forward and escaped. "Promise me," Flora wished. "Promise me you won't ever leave me." She squeezed her lids shut and crossed her fingers.

An exchange of peaceful silence sweetened the moment before she heard the words uttered, "I promise." Asa stood up and wiped his brow against his shirtsleeve. The cloudless sky was infinitely blue. The tattie-bogle swayed gently; its clunky boot rapped the pole waking the morning out of a dream. Asa dipped his hand into his pocket. He felt a gray pearl, the half of a heart pendant, and a locket. Flora turned her face upward, her hand shading the sun from her eyes. She looked at Asa and then at the tattie-bogle. "I knew it!" she whispered. "I knew you could talk."

Beyond the fence-line the rabbit scampered away... away from the hutch, the garden, and the scorched earth. Into the open field it kept running... running towards freedom.

EPILOGUE

"DEATH OF THE LAST MALE ABORIGINAL OF TASMANIA. The last male of the Aboriginal natives of Tasmania, William Lannè, better known a "King Billy," died on March 3rd at the Dog and Partridge Hotel, Hobart Town. The remains were interred in St. David's cemetery on Saturday afternoon, March 6th. The coffin was covered with a black opossum skin rug, fit emblem: of the now all but extinct race to which the deceased belonged; and on this singular pall were laid a couple of native spears and waddies, round which were twined the ample folds of a Union Jack, specially provided by the shipmates of the deceased. It was then mounted upon the shoulders of four white native lads, part of the crew of the Runnymede who volunteered to carry their Aboriginal countryman to his grave. At the cemetery, the Rev. Mr. Cox read the second portion of the impressive burial service of the English Church, and the grave closed over "King Billy" the breast-plate on whose coffin bore the simple inscription '*William Lannè died March 3rd, 1869. Aged 34 years.*' "

March 27, 1869, Launceston Examiner